Andrea de la
MOTTE
DEEDS of
AUTUMN

Anders de la Motte is the bestselling author of the Seasons Quartet; the first three books of which – *End of Summer*, *Deeds of Autumn* and *Dead of Winter* – have all been number one bestsellers in Sweden and have been shortlisted for the Swedish Academy of Crime Writers' Award for Best Crime Novel of the Year. Anders, a former police officer, also won a Swedish Academy Crime Award for his debut, *Game*, in 2010 and for his second standalone novel, *The Silenced*, in 2015.

To date, the first three books in the Seasons Quartet have published over half a million copies. Set in southern Sweden, all four books can be read independently.

Also by Anders de la Motte

Rites of Spring
End of Summer
Dead of Winter

Anders de la MOTTE

DEEDS of AUTUMN

Translated by Marlaine Delargy

ZAFFRE

Originally published in Sweden by Bokförlaget Forum in 2017
First published in Great Britain in 2022 by
ZAFFRE
An imprint of Bonnier Books UK
4th Floor, Victoria House, Bloomsbury Square
London WC1B 4DA
Owned by Bonnier Books
Sveavägen 56, Stockholm, Sweden

Translation by Marlaine Delargy

This is a work of fiction. Names, places, events and
incidents are either the products of the author's
imagination or used fictitiously. Any resemblance to
actual persons, living or dead, or actual
events is purely coincidental.

A CIP catalogue record for this book is
available from the British Library.

ISBN: 978-1-83877-616-9

Also available as an ebook and an audiobook

1 3 5 7 9 10 8 6 4 2

Typeset by IDSUK (Data Connection) Ltd
Printed and bound in Great Britain by Clays Ltd, Elcograf S.p.A.

Zaffre is an imprint of Bonnier Books UK
www.bonnierbooks.co.uk

To my boys, who will one day conquer the world

'Come little leaves,' said the wind one day.
'Come over the meadows with me and play.
Put on your dresses of red and gold.
For summer is gone and the days grow cold.'

George Cooper

Prologue

29 August 1990

The water began its journey in the darkness somewhere deep inside the ridge. It flowed from an underground spring with such force that it was pushed upwards, driving metre after metre through rock, mud and sediment. The ridge was over two hundred metres high, and without human assistance the water would have eventually lost its momentum, turned downwards, found its way out between the roots of the deciduous trees that covered the slopes and ended up as a stream in one of the steep ravines that sliced through the sides of the ridge. However, at the beginning of the twentieth century, a quarry was opened up high on the ridge. Diabase and amphibolite – hard, black varieties of rock well suited for gravestones.

The workers blasted and excavated eagerly, deeper and deeper, until the day the shaft crossed the path of the water, providing it with an easier route to the surface. And the water thanked them by gushing forth with a power no one could have imagined. Only six months later the pumps were shut down, the machinery was taken away and the quarry was abandoned.

As time went by, the place was all but forgotten. The water transformed the quarry into a small, deep pool, surrounded on three sides by steep, dark cliffs, and on the fourth by a sloping bank. The forest swallowed up the access road and the undergrowth reclaimed the area until all that remained were a few overgrown ruins of former workmen's huts, and a glade right next to the bank where the shards of rock were packed so tightly that no living thing could fight its way through.

The quarry wasn't rediscovered until the '60s, when the logging machines required new routes. In spite of the fact that no one was allowed on site, the beautiful, hidden pool became a favourite place for the young people in the area to swim and sunbathe. It was a perfect spot to meet and do whatever they wanted, without the feeling of constantly being monitored. By that stage no one had any idea how deep the quarry was. Some claimed that the water must be at least twenty metres deep, others forty. Some even said the quarry was bottomless, although how that was possible was a complete mystery.

There were lots of rumours about what was hiding down there. Old cars, the proceeds of robberies, the remains of people who had disappeared long ago. Rumours that couldn't be verified, and therefore grew even more fantastical with each retelling. However, all those who had ever visited the quarry were agreed on two things: that the black water was so deep that even high summer in Skåne couldn't raise its temperature above twenty degrees, and that one of the young men who chose to scramble up the steep rock face on the far side in order to dive from the highest point was going to kill himself – sooner or later.

It took four firefighters to get the body out of the water. The bank was slippery and covered in sharp stones that made it difficult to get traction. On a couple of occasions one of the men stumbled and lost his footing, almost as if the water was putting up a fight, trying to retain the body for as long as possible.

Seen from a short distance away, the young man looked as if he was sleeping. He was lying on his back with his eyes closed, the pale features so peaceful that it was possible to believe that he would wake up at any moment.

But when the body landed on the stretcher with a horrible, heavy thud, the illusion was shattered. Cold water poured from his clothes and his long, fair hair, carrying with it blood from the back of his head, which had been crushed. It formed pink, shimmering puddles on the stretcher before it gathered enough weight to make its way down among the stones on the hard ground and disappear into the darkness.

Water always finds the lowest point, thought the police officer who was standing just a metre or so away. He wondered whether he ought to jot down that observation. Turn to the last page of his notebook where he collected such thoughts, small reflections that didn't really have anything to do with police work, but ought to be recorded anyway, possibly to balance out everything else he wrote. Instead, he stayed on the page he'd just started.

He had written the place, time and date only a minute or so after getting out of the police car.

Mörkaby quarry, 05.54, 29 August 1990.

Underneath he'd left space for the names of the four young people in front of him, one on each line. Their faces had taken on a greyish tinge and they were trying in vain to avoid looking at the body. He knew who they were, how old they were, where they lived; he even knew who their parents were and where they worked. Under normal circumstances, this was something he liked about his job out here in such a rural area – familiarity with the locals, the sense of community. But on this particular morning, he wished for the first time that he worked in a city.

Alexander Morell
Carina Pedersen
Bruno Sordi
Marie Andersson

They were all nineteen years old, as was the young man on the stretcher. As recently as June he'd seen all five of them careering through the village as they celebrated their graduation from high school – drinking cans of beer, blowing whistles, waving their white, peaked student caps and screaming with joy at the future that awaited them.

Simon Vidje, he wrote at the bottom of the list and underlined both words in black. He had known the identity of the victim for quite some time now, and yet there was something about seeing the name on paper that made the situation even more unpleasant.

Everyone in Nedanås knew who Simon Vidje was. A child prodigy. One in a million. Someone who was destined to conquer the world, visit amazing places and take his home village and everyone in it along for the ride. Instead, his story had ended here, in cold black water in the middle of nowhere, not too far from the place where he'd grown up.

The police officer's radio crackled into life, then he heard a rough, familiar voice conveying instructions which he immediately carried out.

'Your father is on his way, Alex,' he said to the muscular boy with protruding wrestler's ears and broad shoulders. He received a brief nod in response.

The officer gazed at the four of them for a moment, then frowned and made a note below their names.

Marie Andersson's clothes are wet. Alexander Morell's, Carina Pedersen's and Bruno Sordi's clothes are dry.

Maybe it was a pointless observation, a fact with no value whatsoever. At least that was what he would claim later on, when it had somehow found its way into the official police report and people started asking him what those fifteen words actually meant.

However, he was currently unaware of the difficulties ahead. All he knew was that he had a job to do. Questions to ask, answers to write down in his notebook.

He began as gently as he could. 'So, what actually happened?' No one answered. The four of them had given up the struggle and were staring at the stretcher, where pale red water still dripped from Simon Vidje's crushed head and continued on its way to the lowest point, deep down in the darkness.

1

Autumn 2017

The long, winding route up the ridge is steep, edged with streams flowing through ravines, and with tall deciduous trees, their glowing colours reflected in the car's paintwork as they reach up into the sky.

'The Swedish summer chooses exactly the right way to die,' Håkan always used to say. 'A massive explosion of colour before eternal darkness, that's the way to go. Don't you agree, Anna?'

Then he'd start humming the riff from 'Out of the Blue', playing air guitar until she and Agnes were helpless with laughter. Håkan loved the autumn, loved being outdoors. Camping, climbing, walking in the mountains. They were young then, the two of them, without a care in the world. Agnes was still little, bobbing along as light as a feather in the carrier on his back. Fifteen years had passed, yet Anna can still conjure up the memory with ease. And the song.

According to Neil Young, it's better to burn out than to fade away.

But that's exactly what Håkan did. He slowly faded away, out of the blue and into the black, until all that remained of him were the whispers inside her head.

Please help me, Anna!

She turns up the volume on the radio station that Agnes chose before switching her full attention to her phone, as usual. They've been travelling together for almost seven hours, yet their mother-daughter

5

conversation has filled no more than ten minutes. Anna tightens her grip on the wheel, keeps her eyes fixed on the road. Avoids looking at the trees, the sky, the colours that slice right through her. Razor blades in red, gold and blue.

She hates the autumn. Hates it.

Three keys dangle alongside the one in the ignition. The first is for the house in Äppelviken which is no longer their home. The second is the spare key to Håkan's rented apartment, and should have been returned last winter when the auctioneers emptied the depressing little rooms. Number three is the key to her office at police HQ in Stockholm. She knows she should have handed it in the day before yesterday along with her official pass, but she didn't.

Because if you open the ring and start removing keys, then you have to go all the way, Håkan whispers. *You have to remove everything. Not just the keys, but the locks, the doors, the rooms – the memories.*

She mumbles to him to shut up.

Nature up on the ridge is completely different from down below. The open landscape has been replaced by deciduous forest and small meadows surrounded by sturdy stone walls. White cows gaze at them as they pass by; it's almost as if they realise that Anna and Agnes are outsiders. There is a white line in the middle of the road across the top of the ridge, but it is still so narrow and winding that Anna automatically slows down when they meet other cars. As they approach the crossroads, the satnav on her phone seems to hesitate. She can understand why. The vegetation along the sides of the dirt track has recently been cleared, and the gravel is dark brown and fresh. In contrast, the metal sign bearing the word TABOR is old; it almost looks creased, as if someone screwed up a piece of paper then tried to smooth it out again.

Milo is on Agnes's knee, and as the main road disappears in the rear-view mirror, the white terrier places his paws on the door and presses his nose to the window. His tail is wagging eagerly as if he knows where he is, which of course is impossible as he's never set foot in Skåne before. Agnes doesn't even look up as her thumbs continue to move across the screen of her phone.

Anna glances at the clock. The removal truck is just over an hour behind them. She reminds herself yet again that they are simply moving house, nothing else.

Sure, Håkan grins inside her head. *Who do you think you're fooling?*

She turns the radio up even louder in order to drown him out. She recognises the song, one of the few new ones she actually likes.

'This is good! Zara Lah-hrsson,' she says, mainly in an attempt to break the silence, and immediately falls into the trap. The name tangles itself up into a little gasp, and Agnes responds with one of those sounds that is somewhere between a sigh and a snort. She still doesn't look up. Anna's sixteen-year-old daughter has plenty of ways to punish her. Colouring her beautiful hair pink, the ring in her nose, the five in her right ear. The ripped jeans, the dark makeup, the military-style jacket, the worn-down Converse trainers, the full rebel uniform that has erased virtually any trace of the Agnes she once was. Not to mention the left-wing tendencies, the ultra-feminism, or the badge on her jacket informing everyone that ALL COPS ARE BASTARDS, or all the other hidden landmines that Anna has to pick her way around so that not every conversation ends in an explosion. And yet none of these methods are anywhere near as effective as the one her daughter is deploying right now: silence.

People usually open up to Anna. Håkan always said that there was something about her that made this happen, but in fact it's all down to her stammer. She knows it's barely noticeable, a minor stumble over certain sounds that she can sometimes pre-empt, sometimes not. She never even thought of it as a problem until her parents sent her to a speech therapist at some point during her years in primary school. As a result she began to avoid speaking and focused on listening instead. Most people listen with only half an ear; they're mostly thinking about what they're going to say next, and so they miss what is really being said – not only the words themselves and the nuances of tone, but also the involuntary micro-clues that human beings constantly give. The head movements, the gestures, the grimaces, the pauses. Signs that sometimes directly contradict the content of the conversation. That was how she realised at an early stage that her parents were going to split up. And that Håkan was cheating on her.

Agnes's silence, on the other hand, makes Anna hyper-conscious of every word, every syllable that crosses her lips, and somehow that feeling transfers to her speech centre. It becomes an electrical fault in the communication between her brain and her mouth, makes her appear uncertain. She hates this, because stammering has nothing whatsoever to do with uncertainty.

Breathe, breathe . . .

She glances at herself in the rear-view mirror, sees that she is clenching her jaw in the way she really doesn't like. She has inherited her dark hair and eyes from her father, along with her slightly angular nose, but that particular bitter expression is definitely a legacy from her mother. She shakes her head, tells herself that she is doing the right thing in following the school counsellor's advice to be patient and avoid confrontation. Which of course is easy for him to say, because he only sees Agnes for an hour a week. He doesn't have to live with her.

Breathe . . .

The trees are closing in around the track, and Milo is still pressing his nose to the side window and making excited little noises. The dog was one of Håkan's bright ideas. He simply appeared on the doorstep on Agnes's fourteenth birthday with the puppy in his arms. They'd promised each other that they wouldn't turn into a stereotype. They would stick to a mutually agreed line, they would never play the divorced parents' equivalent of good cop, bad cop. And yet that's exactly what they did.

Håkan took on the leading role as the fun, much-loved daddy, while Anna, without quite knowing how it had happened, had been allocated the clichéd supporting role as the miserable, mean-spirited mother who was always going on about rules and responsibilities.

Who disliked animals so much that she wouldn't even let her own daughter have a puppy. And so she'd given in. Let the wretched animal into the house to prove that she too could be cool and spontaneous. It hadn't helped at all.

Milo whimpers again, louder this time, as if he can see something in the shadows among the trees that only a dog can detect. Rabbits, probably. The stupid creature is crazy for rabbits and can chase them for hours if he manages to escape, which he does with depressing regularity. He is both hyperactive and spoiled, and he treats Anna with the same thinly veiled contempt as Agnes does. But there is no denying that Milo loves Agnes more than anything else in the world, and she feels the same about him. Sometimes Anna realises that she envies their relationship, which of course is ridiculous.

The track winds deeper and deeper into the forest, the burnished leaves close in above them, and even though she was pretty sure they'd reached the top of the ridge a while ago, they are still climbing.

'Are your ears popping too?' she ventures in the most neutral tone she can summon.

'Mm.' Agnes continues to stare at her phone.

After about five minutes they round a bend and reach a rectangular courtyard. The trees loom in from both the longer sides, the tops so close together that there are only a few metres of sky between them. A long shed leans against the trunks on the left, and at the far end there is a lovely old brick building, with a dark-coloured car parked outside. As they draw closer Anna can see that a section of the reddish-brown brick between the ground floor and the first floor has been painted white. It bears the year, 1896, followed by the words BEHOLD THE MOUNTAIN OF THE LORD in ornate lettering.

The setting and the house are even more beautiful than in the pictures, yet Anna suddenly feels nervous. A vague sense of disquiet that she can't – or daren't – define is making her stomach churn.

As they pull up Milo's whimpering turns into an agitated outburst of barking. He scrabbles wildly at the car door, hurls himself at the window as if he's trying to break the glass.

'What's wrong, sweetheart?' Agnes attempts to pull him away, but the terrier is having none of it. He launches himself at the window once again, this time with an audible thud, leaving behind a big patch of saliva.

'Stop it, Milo!' Agnes grabs his collar, but the dog whirls around, lets out a low growl and shows his teeth. Agnes drops her phone between the seats.

'Milo!'

Her shocked tone seems to bring the dog up short. He slides onto the floor and hides behind Agnes's camera bag.

'He's never growled at me before,' Agnes says, on the verge of tears. 'Never!'

'I expect he needs a wee,' Anna says reassuringly. 'You can see how ashamed he is. Let him out.' The second the car door opens the little dog shoots past Agnes and disappears among the trees.

'Milo! Milo, come here!' Agnes grabs the camera bag and runs after him, gravel spraying up around her worn-down Converse. Anna gets out of the car and waits. Right now she has no desire to chase after Milo. Plus, as Agnes has icily pointed out on many occasions, he's not her dog.

She can hear him barking excitedly in the forest, followed by Agnes yelling at him. She can't help smirking. Stupid dog.

She looks at the other car – a newish, spotlessly clean Passat. No child seats, no McDonald's packaging on the floor, no Winnie-the-Pooh sun-screens on the side windows. A bottle of Ramlösa mineral water in the holder between the seats is the only indication that the car has an owner.

She stretches, takes a few deep breaths. The autumn air is cold and clear; it smells of earth and damp leaves, sweeping away her unease and replacing it with excitement and anticipation. They've arrived. Arrived at their new home. Once again it strikes her that Tabor is at least as beautiful as in the pictures, and in spite of Agnes's bad mood and Milo's escape attempt, this is a good start to their new . . . *flight*, Håkan whispers before she can stop him.

The shingle in the courtyard is neatly raked and looks fresh. The doors, windows and bargeboards are freshly painted. Some of the roof tiles are paler in colour, which means they've been replaced. The house has two doors – a large one by the corner of the shorter, right-hand side, although a steel bar with a heavy padlock suggests that it is no longer in use. The other door is just to the left of the centre of the building, only a few metres from where she is standing. It is green, with a wide step polished by thousands of footsteps over the years. As she is about to move closer, the door opens and a man of about her own age emerges. He is about six feet tall and is wearing black-rimmed glasses. Jacket and tie, jeans.

'Hi, there – you must be Anna Vesper,' he says, holding out his hand. 'Lars-Åke Gunnarsson, Gunnarsson Law. Call me Lasse, everyone does.'

She recognises his deep voice from their telephone conversation yesterday evening, and yet there's something about him that doesn't quite fit. Call-me-Lasse seems to have picked up on her hesitation.

'I guess you were expecting someone older? You're not the first. People around here started mixing me up with my father before I turned thirty. It didn't help that we ran the practice together for years, and used the same phone number.'

He smiles, showing his teeth. If his office had been in Stockholm they would doubtless have been perfectly symmetrical and unnaturally white, but instead they are perfectly normal for a man in his late forties.

'These days Dad spends his time playing golf in Majorca while I keep the ship afloat.' He laughs, and she can't help smiling back.

To be honest she isn't particularly fond of solicitors or lawyers – she has trouble putting up with her own. But there's something about Call-me that makes it hard to dislike him. The blond side fringe – which probably isn't natural – makes him look a bit like the Milky Bar Kid.

She glances at his left hand. No wedding ring, no indentation, not even a narrow strip of white skin. She involuntarily runs her thumb over the inside of her own ring finger. Two years have passed, yet she thinks she can still feel the little furrow where once her wedding band sat.

'I'm so pleased you've decided to live here rather than in the village. Tabor is something very special.'

Call-me smiles again, gestures towards the building behind him as if he were an estate agent rather than a family solicitor.

'I don't know if I've already told you, but the house was built as a mission church in 1896. The old story is that the missionary priest cured a sick child belonging to the man who owned the land, and was given the plot and the building materials as a thank you. It's probably just a myth. The revivalist movement was making great progress everywhere towards the end of the nineteenth century, and mission houses popped up in every little backwater. There were three more in the area, but Tabor is the only one that's still standing. Shall we go inside?'

'I have to wait for my daughter. Her dog ran off.' Anna realises that the barking and shouting have continued while she and Call-me have been talking. She probably ought to go and see what's happening, offer to help, but the fact is that she's enjoying the brief respite from Agnes and her passive-aggressive behaviour.

'We could go into the kitchen – I'll leave the front door open so she can come and find us,' Call-me suggests, as if he'd read her mind. She hesitates briefly, then says, 'Sure,' and returns his smile.

They enter a hallway with several doors leading off it, and turn left into the kitchen. Tabor is beautiful on the inside too. Thick brick walls, beams on the ceiling, old wooden floors and mullioned windows. A wood-burning stove is crackling away in the middle of the kitchen. Call-me must have been here for a while, because the room is pleasantly warm and smells somehow cosy, adding to the calming energy the old building radiates.

'The house and the land were bought by the Vidje family just after the Second World War. By that time the revivalist movement had faded away, and the place was more or less abandoned. Coffee?'

He points to a brand-new machine on the worktop; the coffee is steadily dripping from the filter.

'Please.'

He takes out two blue earthenware cups, and it occurs to Anna that the kitchen must have been renovated very recently, just like the outside. The cupboard doors and worktops look antique, but beneath the aroma of coffee and burning wood, she can also smell sawdust, paint and glue.

'Tabor was used as labourers' accommodation for many years. The Vidje family were involved in both forestry and fruit growing – as they are today – so they employed a lot of seasonal workers who needed a temporary base.'

Anna takes a sip of her coffee and glances out of one of the windows. Nothing is moving on the edge of the forest. She is beginning to feel both guilty and worried. Why didn't she help Agnes look for that stupid dog? This is supposed to be their new home, their fresh start.

'. . . as I said, it was used as an artist's studio for over twenty-five years,' Call-me continues. Anna realises that she has missed part of his explanation.

'Didn't you say you had a Karl-Johan Vidje at home, Anna?'

She nods. 'My parents had one of his prints in the parlour. Sometimes I'd sneak in, sit down and just gaze at the picture, because I thought it was so lovely.' She pauses, takes a deep breath. She hears her father telling her that Karl-Jo had a stammer too. *So, you see, Anna, you can succeed anyway.*

'What happened to it?' Call-me asks. 'It could be worth quite a bit today.'

She shrugs. 'My parents split up when I was ten. My father took it with him, and I never saw it again.'

I didn't see much of him either, she adds mentally.

'That's a shame.' Call-me sucks in air through his teeth. 'As I'm sure you're aware, Karl-Jo has come to be regarded as one of the leading artists of his generation, and his work has shot up in value. One of his larger oil paintings sold at Bukowskis auction house for almost four million a couple of years ago.'

Anna hears an engine and looks out of the window again. A pickup truck drives slowly into the yard. It must be between ten and fifteen years old. It stops by the trees where Milo and Agnes disappeared; the barking and shouting is still going on. The driver jumps out, but he moves so quickly that she only catches a glimpse of him before he heads off into the forest. A man in an oilskin jacket, Wellington boots and a flat cap.

'As you've already seen from the plan I sent you, there are two bedrooms, a laundry room, a study and a living room on the ground floor, but I thought we'd start upstairs in what used to be the chapel.'

Call-me doesn't seem to have noticed the arrival of the pickup. He has opened one of the doors in the hallway, revealing a steep staircase brightly lit from above; the top steps are barely visible because of the glare. He gestures invitingly, but Anna hesitates. Milo has been missing for almost ten minutes. She really ought to go out and see how Agnes is getting on, particularly since the stranger turned up. She hears the sound of barking again.

'Hang on a minute,' she says, going outside. She shades her eyes with her hand, peers into the gloom among the trees. Sees some kind of movement.

Agnes emerges, accompanied by the man in the oilskin jacket. He is carrying Milo under one arm, but instead of wriggling as the terrier usually does when someone tries to hold on to him, the dog is perfectly still. They stop next to the pickup and chat. The conversation seems lively, and after a little while Agnes opens the camera bag looped over her shoulder and begins to photograph the man with her dog.

'Agnes!' She doesn't really know why she called out, regrets it before she's even closed her mouth. To her surprise, Agnes raises a hand and waves. Takes a few more pictures before she and the man set off towards the house.

About halfway across the yard, he puts Milo down. Instead of immediately shooting off back to the forest, the dog trots along happily next to the man's left leg. His coat is muddy, his mouth is

open, his tongue hanging out. His eyes are firmly fixed on his companion. Agnes continues to take photographs. As they get closer,
Anna understands why. The man has a rugged, weather-beaten
appearance which, combined with the cap, the jacket and the
checked flannel shirt he is wearing underneath it, makes him look
like an older Swedish version of the Marlboro Man. He's probably
about sixty, his body is lean and he moves with ease, as if he's used
to being outdoors. Something in his eyes tells her that he's considerably older than he appears to be.

'Klein,' he says as they reach the house. His handshake is firm and
dry, his hands rough. He is clean-shaven in the same meticulous way
as her maternal grandfather always was, without a hint of a shadow.

'Look at Milo, Mum.' Agnes points to the terrier who has sat
down next to Klein's left leg, gaze still fixed on his new friend. 'I've
never seen him like this.' The tone surprises Anna. Her daughter
sounds almost . . . happy.

'You seem to have a way with dogs,' she manages to say. Klein
nods. His face is unnaturally stiff, like a mask.

'So you're the one who's taking over from Henry Morell.' A
statement rather than a question. He looks as if he has more to say,
but Call-me gets in first.

'Klein, good to see you! I was about to go up to the chapel.' He
turns to Anna. 'Klein here is Elisabet Vidje's administrator. Any
problems with the house, anything you need, just give him a call.
Änglaberga is only a mile or so away along the main road, so he can
be here in no time. Isn't that right, Klein?'

The man grunts something that is presumably meant to be an
affirmative response, then gazes over at the trees while Call-me
introduces himself to Agnes. Anna hears him say that he has a son
her age, then he leads the way back indoors.

'Careful, the stairs are steep.' The bannister on one side has
acquired such a shine that it looks lacquered. Over the last metre
or so there are oval patches in a multitude of different shades, and
it takes a few seconds before she realises they are the impressions
left by fingers.

The light from above grows more intense, and when they reach the top it is so strong that all four of them pause for a moment to let their eyes acclimatise. The chapel is roof-height and occupies the entire upper storey. Three of the walls, the floor, the ceiling, the chimney breasts and the old beams are painted white, and over on the far side there is a gigantic arched window that reinforces the sacred atmosphere. Admittedly it isn't stained glass, but it makes no difference.

'Behold the mountain of the Lord,' Call-me says with a smile, spreading his hands wide.

The house must be perched right on the edge of a cliff, because there is no garden beyond the window. There is nothing but tree-tops and sky, with forests, fields and villages in the distance, a glowing, autumn-coloured patchwork quilt stretching all the way to the mist on the horizon.

Anna has seen this view in the pictures he's sent, but the real thing is overwhelming. It is almost thirty-five years since the last time she crept into the parlour to admire the Karl-Johan Vidje print, but she recognises the motif immediately. The colours, the depth, the sense of calm. Of safety and security.

'Wow,' Agnes says, fiddling with her camera. Anna doesn't know whether it's her daughter's tone of voice, the light or the explosion of different hues spread before them, but suddenly she has a lump in her throat.

Coming here was the right thing to do, she thinks as Agnes starts clicking away eagerly. *Everything is going to be fine.* She has repeated that mantra so often over the past few weeks, but for the first time she almost believes it.

'The roof of Skåne,' Call-me goes on with great satisfaction. 'On a really clear day you can see the towers of the Öresund Bridge with a decent pair of binoculars. The bridge is over forty miles from here.'

He allows Agnes to carry on taking photographs for a minute or so before he continues his tour. He explains that the narrow staircase they've just climbed used to enable the preacher to sneak down into the house. He shows them the wheezy old organ on the right-hand side – apparently it still works. Then he moves on to the main staircase, which leads down to the barred door Anna noticed earlier. Agnes's camera records every detail, and Anna clings to the sense of security. Tries to convince herself that they are here to stay.

'As I wrote in my email, Tabor is one of the most attractive properties in Skåne,' Call-me informs them. 'Over the years Elisabet Vidje has had plenty of offers for the house; a member of Abba was particularly keen. But Elisabet has always refused, no matter how much money was involved. Isn't that right, Klein?'

The older man doesn't answer. He is still standing by the stairs.

Call-me and Agnes head over to the left-hand side of the room where the altar must once have stood. Anna is about to follow them, but Klein seems unwilling to come any further into the room. Milo is sitting on the floor beside him, gazing up at him with that submissive, admiring look she's never seen before. Klein doesn't say a word, doesn't move, and yet his behaviour arouses her instincts as a cop. It's as if he's working very hard to hide something behind that stiff mask.

'What's this painting?' she hears Agnes ask. 'Was it the altarpiece?'

'No, the mural was done later. Are you familiar with Karl-Jo?'

'Karl-Johan Vidje?' Agnes almost sounds insulted. 'Of course. We've studied all the great artists. My school specialises in aesthetics.' She lowers the camera, flashes an angry glance at her mother. 'The school I *used* to go to, that is.' Her acidic tone sweeps away the illusion of security and replaces it with the usual gnawing anxiety.

Call-me responds with his trademark smile. 'Excellent. In that case you probably already know that Tabor was Karl-Jo's studio, until he became too ill to work. You can still see his fingerprints on the bannister,' he adds, gesturing towards the stairs. 'This painting was the last piece he finished. He developed a serious eye condition that eventually left him almost blind, but he refused to leave here until the mural was completed, even though it took him almost ten years.'

Agnes clicks away again.

Anna moves closer – slowly, almost reverently. The painting is enormous, at least six metres wide and three high. It covers most of the wall. The motif is a pool surrounded by a forest. Flat rocks and steep, jagged cliffs encircled by autumn-coloured trees against a turbulent sky. The tones are muted, the surface of the water almost black. White splashes of rain can be seen here and there, disturbing the reflections of the leaves and rocks and making them change shape. As she gets closer the perspective shifts; the water almost seems alive. Anna doesn't know a great deal about art, but she realises it must take great skill to achieve this effect. She is fascinated. The nearer she gets, the stronger the illusion of movement becomes, while at the same time her own anxiety is increasing. She tries her hardest to resist; she doesn't want to hear what it has to say.

A faint noise makes her look back over her shoulder. Klein has taken a couple of steps into the chapel. He is facing the mural with his hands clasped in front of him, almost as if he is praying. His jaw is clenched, his eyes dark. The skin on his forehead and cheeks is thin, making the bones beneath protrude sharply, just like Håkan in the last weeks of his life.

Please help me, Anna!

Help me!

The anxiety breaks through her defences, passes through her mind like a gust of wind and whispers in her own voice that all of this – the move, the new job, the new life for her and Agnes – is one huge mistake.

2

28 August 1990

B runo and Alex were the first to arrive, as always. Alex parked his black Ford Escort by the barrier that closed off the dirt track, and they sat there for a few minutes with the sunroof and the side windows open, the car stereo going full blast.

Even though the nights were getting colder and beginning to turn the leaves yellow here and there, summer was having one last celebration, grabbing a few more days before it gave in to the inevitable. Which in turn meant it was time for their annual tradition – summer's last dip in their secret place, Mörkaby quarry.

They had arranged to meet Simon at two thirty by the barrier, but they knew he'd be late.

'Why is Simon always fucking late when he lives the closest?' Bruno said.

'You know what he's like,' Alex muttered.

Bruno's father always said that people who were late didn't respect other people's time, which was why Bruno was always at least five minutes early. Simon's attitude annoyed him, as did the fact that the rest of their group of friends seemed to think it was absolutely fine.

They turned the music up even louder, got out of the car, pissed against a tree trunk then lit a cigarette each. Neither Bruno nor Alex really smoked – the packet in the car belonged to Alex's girlfriend Carina, but this was all part of the ritual, something they did together on lazy days like this one. When they'd finished and stamped out the butts on the gravel, they reluctantly set off to carry all their kit the five hundred metres from the barrier to the quarry itself.

The narrow dirt track sloped steeply upwards, the kit was heavy, and Bruno was struggling by the time they reached the plateau on the left that was their usual campsite. Alex, on the other hand, had barely broken a sweat. Back in the day, Bruno had envied Alex – the body that did whatever he asked of it, the self-confidence, the way other people looked at him. But over the years Bruno had come to terms with the situation. He was Alex's best friend after all, which meant that he enjoyed some of Alex's status, making Bruno a solid second in their unofficial ranking. At least that was how he saw things.

As they finished putting up the first tent, Simon's orange Crescent bicycle appeared down below.

'Perfect timing,' Bruno murmured. Alex shrugged but didn't say anything.

'Sorry, I had to make a phone call,' Simon said breathlessly when he joined them, slipping his guitar case off his shoulder.

'Did you bring the evening paper?' Bruno said acidly. His father always made that comment even if someone was only a few minutes late. It was a stupid thing to do, but he was hot and cross, and Simon shouldn't be allowed to get away with yet another of his crap excuses. To his annoyance, Simon ignored him.

'When are the girls coming?'

Alex stuck his head out of the tent. 'Carina finishes at four. Marie's going to pick her up, so they should be here by four thirty.'

'OK, so what's happening with you two? Are you and Carina together on alternate weeks? I can't keep up . . .'

Alex grinned and gave Simon the finger. Bruno tried to join in with a witticism of his own.

'What a way to spend your days, wiping old people's fucking arses. Does Carina enjoy it?'

'At least it's a proper job.' Alex sounded irritated, which wasn't what Bruno had expected at all.

'I've worked all bloody summer,' he said in his defence.

'In your daddy's restaurant – that doesn't count,' Alex said.

'Of course it does!' Bruno was furious now. It was Simon who should be getting it in the neck, not him.

'No, it doesn't,' Simon piped up. 'Your dad's your boss, which means you can't get the sack. And there's no chance of him asking you to wipe someone's arse – unless of course it's your fantastic big brother's!'

Alex let out a guffaw and punched Simon on the shoulder. Bruno could feel his face burning.

'At least my dad's not a nutjob,' he snapped. He immediately realised he'd gone too far.

Simon glared at Bruno, but didn't say a word. A sudden gust of wind made the tent flap flutter, then there was nothing but an oppressive silence.

'Come on, girls – don't you think we're a bit old to be playing my-dad's-better-than-your-dad?' Alex said when the silence had gone on for a little too long. 'I thought we sorted that in nursery. You know I always win, because Henry's bigger and stronger than your useless daddies. Plus, he has a gun, so that's the end of that,' he added in a childish voice before handing out cold cans of beer from one of the cool bags. 'Now have a drink and play nicely!'

The cans were opened, the atmosphere lightened.

'Sorry . . .' Bruno muttered to Simon.

'It's fine – I started it. Besides, Alex is right.' Simon gestured with the beer can. 'Obviously, Henry is harder than our two daddies put together. Just look at the caveman he's raised. Neck like a bull, arms like a gorilla, one headlock away from a pair of cauliflower ears.' Simon and Bruno exchanged a grin.

'Fuck off, both of you!' Alex finished his beer and belched loudly, then stood up and crumpled the can with one hand.

'OK, let's go and grab the rest of the stuff from the car. If we put up Simon's tent quickly, we'll have time for a swim before the girls get here.'

When Carina and Marie arrived in the glade with rucksacks and plastic carrier bags, the boys were just changing into their trunks.

Alex had placed his boombox on the edge of the rock, and Def Leppard was blasting out across the quarry.

Bruno and Simon quickly got dressed again, turned the music down and hurried to meet the girls. They seemed quite happy not to have to jump in; the water was deep and the surface relatively shaded, so it never really warmed up. However, the thought of the cold didn't seem to bother Alex. He ran barefoot along the path to the far end, then began to scale the steep cliff face with ease.

By the time Bruno and Simon had helped the girls to carry their kit up to the tents, Alex was already standing on the highest outcrop, waiting. The pool seven or eight metres below him was dark and still, but the afternoon sun lit up the cliff and enveloped his tanned, muscular body in gold.

Bruno, Simon and the girls stayed where they were. None of them had ever jumped from the top, or even the next outcrop down, but they knew there was a protruding rock only a few centimetres beneath the surface directly below. Just like all the others who had ever swum in the quarry, they had heard and passed on tales of broken arms and legs thanks to jumps from the lower levels that had gone wrong. They knew that if you jumped from the very top, where Alex was standing now, the tiniest mistake carried with it the risk of death.

'Go on – jump!' Marie shouted. Alex didn't move. It was obvious that he was intending to savour the moment for as long as possible.

'Get a move on Alex – jump!' Bruno yelled.

Carina demonstratively turned away, crouched down and started rummaging in her rucksack for cigarettes. However, she couldn't help glancing up at Alex.

'Jump, jump . . .' Bruno, Simon and Marie started chanting, and eventually Carina stood up. She shaded her eyes with her hand, but said nothing.

That movement appeared to be what Alex had been waiting for. He took a deep breath and held it, stretched his arms straight out in front of him. Swayed briefly on tiptoe, then pushed off with all his strength and hurled himself into the air. At the apex of his trajectory he folded his body in half like a pocket knife. Straightened out the second before his fingers touched the water and broke the surface with hardly a splash. His entry was almost perfect; a series of rings slowly rippled all the way to the edges of the quarry.

The four friends stood motionless, their eyes fixed on the centre of those rings. There was no sign of Alex. The rings faded away. The water became still. Bruno felt a hard knot in his stomach.

'Do you think he's . . .?' Marie didn't finish the question. She exchanged an anxious glance with Simon, then Bruno. Carina took a hesitant step towards the edge of the rock, then another.

'Alex!' she called out. 'Alex . . .'

A second later the surface broke and Alex's head shot up. He took a noisy breath, then raised his arms and let out a roar of victory that ricocheted off the walls of the quarry.

Carina turned to Marie, jerking her head angrily in the direction of the water.

'What did I tell you? An immature fucking idiot!'

Bruno registered the comment. He'd heard Alex and Carina arguing hundreds of times, and knew that this was an integral part of their relationship, but during this summer he had picked up something different in Carina's tone. Something that worried him.

3

Autumn 2017

'Last one,' says the Pole who has introduced himself as Pawel and seems to be the boss. He folds up the final cardboard box and stows it in the van.

'Are you sure I can't offer you something?' Anna says. She speaks slowly, conscious that her stammer tends to be more prevalent when she is speaking a language other than Swedish.

The man holds up his hands and shakes his head. 'No, thank you. Mr Klein told us to go back when we finish.'

'OK – thank you so much!'

Pawel beckons his three colleagues and they pile into the van with the Polish registration plates. Anna remains on the step, watching until the taillights are swallowed up by the trees.

'Excellent service,' Agnes says behind her. She sounds unexpectedly upbeat, although the slightly ironic tone she adopts in self-defence is there as usual.

'Absolutely.' Anna looks at her watch. 'Furniture and rugs in place, boxes unpacked and taken away, and it's not even lunchtime. And on a Saturday too.'

Call-me had handed over the keys the previous afternoon. When the removal truck arrived, they set up the beds and unpacked a few essentials without talking more than necessary. After the men had left, Anna and Agnes had eaten a scratch meal surrounded by boxes and furniture, then Agnes had shut herself in her room with Milo and the laptop. She didn't reappear until Klein's Polish workers knocked on the door this morning, but in spite of the fact that they'd woken her, she'd helped out without moaning or sulking. She'd even seemed to welcome the contact. Almost. It might be wishful thinking, but after only one night at Tabor, Anna thinks that their relationship has improved slightly. As if the old house has a calming effect.

'Plus they built all the flat-pack furniture,' Agnes says. 'Without having a load of screws left over like when Dad . . .' She falls silent, looks away. Her smile vanishes. A hidden landmine neither of them had placed there, yet it kills the conversation.

'Are you hungry?' Anna asks, trying to maintain a cheerful tone of voice. 'I'm going to do some shopping.' She leaves the question hanging in the air. Agnes doesn't answer. She simply goes into her room and closes the door behind her.

Anna stops the car when she reaches the main road. If she turns left it will take her about twenty-five minutes to drive to the ICA supermarket down in Nedanås. If she heads to the right, according to Call-me-Lasse, it's only fifteen minutes to the significantly smaller community of Mörkaby up on the ridge, where he assured her there is a general store. The term sounds so rustic and appealing that she decides to be adventurous, and turns right.

It has rained during the night. The tarmac is dark, and a grey blanket of wet autumn fog is draped around the trees. The road winds gently through the landscape, and after approximately a mile the forest gives way to a plateau with open fields on both sides. She can just make out the edge of trees in the distance through the fog.

Over on the right she sees a long avenue of willow trees, with buildings at the far end. At the same time she notices a sign for Änglaberga. So that's where her landlady lives – and Klein. Anna can't work him out at all. He seemed sullen, almost hostile. But why?

The plain continues for a few minutes; she passes a number of smaller farms before entering a dense deciduous forest. The road zigzags and climbs sharply, and here and there narrow dirt tracks appear on either side with no warning. Most are no more than the width of a single vehicle, with a strip of grass down the middle. She drives carefully, conscious of the weather and the unfamiliar route. She is overtaken several times by locals travelling well above the speed limit, apparently unconcerned by the poor visibility. The last of them even sounds his horn angrily at her as he whizzes by.

After almost exactly fifteen minutes a white church tower peeps through the mist, followed by a sign informing her that she has arrived in Mörkaby, and that this is the highest church in Skåne.

The village itself is no more than a modest collection of buildings arranged around a T-junction. One of them has a rough patch of concrete in front of it, along with a couple of placards. It doesn't exactly fit the image of a general store that she had in mind. *What did you expect?* Håkan says with a grin. *Astrid Lindgren's Bullerbyn?*

The door is locked, but a handwritten note instructs customers to ring the bell. After a minute or so an elderly lady opens up; she is wearing a bobbly cardigan with a company logo on the pocket.

'Morning!' she says cheerfully as she lets Anna in.

The store isn't much bigger than the living room at Tabor. An old-fashioned refrigerated counter, a couple of shelves of dry goods, various tobacco products plus a newspaper stand. The air smells of vinyl flooring.

'Are you looking for anything in particular?' The woman has pushed her glasses up onto the top of her head, where they have got entangled in her hair and adjusted her wig slightly to one side. She tugs at a handful of shiny acrylic curls on the opposite side to adjust it.

'Just something for lunch, really.'

'We have fresh eggs – straight from the coop.' The woman tweaks her hair once more before she is satisfied.

'My daughter is vegan,' Anna says. For a moment she considers explaining what that means, what limitations Agnes's diet places on every mealtime. Not to mention all the arguments.

'How about some fresh beetroot? You can bake them in the oven, then serve them with cheese. Oh no, silly me – vegans don't eat cheese, do they? No animal products at all.'

'No.' Anna shakes her head in surprise.

'My grandchild is vegan.' Wig-woman winks at her. 'Don't worry, we'll sort something out.'

Ten minutes later they have amassed a pile of assorted root and green vegetables, most grown locally, along with fresh eggs and a bacon joint that smells wonderful.

'My name's Gunnel,' says wig-woman. 'You're the one who's renting Tabor, aren't you?'

Anna nods. 'How did you know?'

'We don't see many new faces up here, and we hardly ever hear a Stockholm accent.' Gunnel looks at her with curiosity. 'I believe you're a police officer?'

Anna nods again, amazed at how quickly the jungle drums have passed on the news. Her new job and the move to Nedanås were confirmed less than a month ago.

'Yes, we were all surprised when we heard that Elisabet Vidje was letting out Tabor. And to a police officer,' Gunnel says, packing away Anna's purchases. 'Tabor is sacred ground as far as Elisabet is concerned, and she's not exactly a fan of the police, if I can put it that way.'

'Why not?'

Gunnel stops in mid-movement, her smile freezes.

'I thought you knew. Has no one told you?'

Anna frowns. 'No. Told me what?'

'About Simon – Elisabet and Karl-Johan's son. The boy who died over in the old quarry. It's almost thirty years ago now – a terrible tragedy.'

'I don't know anything about that.'

Gunnel shakes her head sadly. 'Poor Simon. He was a lovely boy, and so gifted. He sang and played like an angel. Nineteen years old – taken just as he was about to step out into the world.'

'How awful,' Anna says, mirroring the older woman's expression. 'What happened?'

'There was a group of friends camping in the quarry. It must have been late summer 1990. I still remember it as if it was yesterday.' She lowers her voice. 'Åke and I were woken by someone banging on our front door just before five o'clock in the morning. It was Bruno, the restaurant owner's son. He asked if he could use our phone; he was as white as a sheet. He said there had been an accident.' Gunnel grimaces, as if the last word doesn't sit right on her lips. She leans across the counter and is about to continue when the door opens and a man in overalls and a fleece jacket walks in.

'Morning, Gunnel,' he says, heading over to the cool counter where *snus* is displayed. As he passes he gives Anna a curious look.

Gunnel straightens up and runs the palms of her hands down the front of her cardigan as if she is trying to brush off something unpleasant.

'Is there anything else I can help you with, Anna?' she asks a little too loudly.

Back at Tabor Anna prepares lunch while Agnes sulkily sets the table. They sit down to eat. Eventually the silence becomes too much, and Anna tells her about the visit to the shop. Says how surprised she was that Gunnel was well-informed about veganism, but doesn't get the reaction she was hoping for. Before she knows it she has gone through the whole thing, from the crooked wig to Simon Vidje's fatal accident.

'Do you think the painting in the chapel is of the quarry?' Agnes glances up, sounding unexpectedly interested.

'I've no idea.' Anna tries not to show how pleased she is that they're talking about something, anything that isn't linked to Håkan or the move. A safe topic of conversation, with no hidden landmines. 'We could go and look for the place if you like – Gunnel said it was nearby.'

'I'll check on Google Maps, but maybe we should wait until tomorrow when it's less foggy. I want to take some photographs, compare them with the painting.'

'Great idea!'

Agnes stands up, helps her to clear away, even washes the casserole dish without having to be asked.

Milo is confused. He sticks close to Agnes and seems as if he doesn't quite know how to behave because of the change in the atmosphere. After a while he jumps up onto the kitchen sofa and places his paws on the windowsill. He growls faintly, as if he's spotted something out there. Anna follows his gaze, but she sees only the yard, the drive and the fog wrapped around the trees.

'Stupid dog,' she mutters. Receives a filthy look in response.

Once the dishes are done, Agnes disappears up to the chapel. Anna can hear her gathering up her equipment: the tripod, the reflective umbrella with the flash, the screens, the bags containing different lenses. She knows how expensive everything is, remembers the arguments with Håkan.

You do realise you're buying her love? You're putting me in an impossible position. And how the hell can you afford it?

That all seems so unimportant now.

After a while she goes upstairs. Waits for a moment, half expecting Agnes to snap at her, say she wants to be left in peace. When that doesn't happen, she wanders slowly over to the big window. Once again it's hard to tear her eyes away from the view, even though it's completely different from the previous day. The fog rests on the trees like a lid, their tops no more than grey silhouettes. She can see a series of red lights in the distance, and eventually realises that they are the markers on the wind turbines out on the plain – prehistoric beasts made of metal, flashing in time with one another.

Agnes has rigged up her camera in front of the painting.

'Mum, could you fetch the other lamp?'

Anna tries not to show how pleased she is to be included.

Baby steps, she thinks. She tries to get Håkan mentally on board, but right now he's keeping quiet. Which is a good thing. And yet she misses his voice.

She hands Agnes the lamp, watches as her daughter fixes it in place with well-practised hands. She gazes at the mural again. The same dark sky, the rocks, the silent, brooding forest. The rain, disturbing the surface of the water and distorting the reflection.

'Isn't it beautiful?' Agnes says. 'The colours, the atmosphere, the rain – everything. I keep getting the feeling that the water is hiding a secret, that there's something below the surface. It will be exciting to see if it actually is based on the quarry – to see the place for real.'

'Mm.' Anna tilts her head on one side, studies the shifting images on the dark surface.

'I've googled Karl-Jo's work,' Agnes goes on. 'I haven't found anything like this, so it looks as if no one's ever photographed it. I might be the first, in which case I can include the pictures in my portfolio.' She starts adjusting the lamps again, small, skilful movements. The positive atmosphere from lunch is still there, making Anna feel warm inside. *We can get through this*, she thinks. *Everything's going to be OK*. Håkan still doesn't say a word.

In the afternoon they go for a walk with Milo, crossing the yard and turning right into the forest along the narrow path just before the outbuilding. The ground is covered in fallen leaves, a soft, fiery carpet that, combined with the fog, swallows the sound of their footsteps. It even muffles Milo's excited barking as he races around among the tree trunks chasing smells and impressions accessible only to dogs.

Agnes has brought her camera, of course. She snaps away at Milo, at the trees, at the red, orange and yellow leaf canopy above them. She has to stop every few minutes to wipe the lens; a light rain is falling, so fine it's almost invisible.

The path leads them to a shallow brook. Milo drinks the clear water, eagerly making his way downstream. Agnes follows him along the bank, shooting an extended series of images.

'Milo! Look at me, Milo!'

Anna stumbles, plunges one foot into a deep puddle beside the brook and frightens the life out of a frog. She shivers, decides that she needs a pair of Wellingtons.

'Where do you think the stream leads?'

Agnes's cheeks are rosy, her eyes alert. Anna would give anything to see her like this every day.

'Towards the bottom of the ridge.' She points in the direction where she thinks the slope must be. 'It'll flow into a river somewhere down below.'

'Or perhaps it's heading for the quarry.'

'Possibly – you didn't find anything on Google Maps?'

Agnes shakes her head. 'I couldn't find any quarry marked.'

'Isn't that a bit weird?'

'Maybe.' Agnes looks thoughtful. 'Shall we follow it for a bit?'

Anna glances down at her shoe. Her sock is soaked through, and the water has found its way up her trouser leg. However, Agnes is talking to her; at long last she is engaged in something other than her phone and the dog. Plus, Anna is also curious about the mysterious quarry, the site of past disaster.

'OK, why not.'

The brook winds its way through the trees, gradually getting wider and louder as it is joined by other small tributaries. Agnes and Milo are hell-bent on moving forward, while Anna stops every two hundred yards in order to orientate herself. She doesn't want them to go too close to the edge. She can't see it because of the fog, but she knows it's there. She thinks she has a pretty good handle on where they are. Nedanås itself is at the bottom of the north-western point of the ridge. It's just under ten miles from the edge of the village to their house; right now they are walking along the ridge and away from Nedanås, which means they're heading south-west. She tries to read her surroundings as Håkan taught her to do. Moss and lichen on the north side of the tree trunks, more downward-growing branches on the south side. She knows that anthills are almost always on the south side of a tree, but she can't find any. After a while she realises this isn't particularly surprising. There isn't a single conifer, only tall deciduous trees with trunks like grey-green pillars, growing close together until they disappear among the sweeping veils of fog. The impression is eerie, almost ghostly.

They're bound to find you, Håkan whispers without warning. *You're not safe, not even out here. You have to tell her. You promised me you would.*

She shudders, shakes off the feeling and the voice in her head. After a few moments she manages to recapture her joy at the fact that she and Agnes are doing something together.

They continue alongside the brook, which gradually digs its way into the soft ground, creating a steep bank. Anna checks the time. Just after five, still another hour or so until dusk begins to fall, and yet it already seems as if the light is fading. The path slopes gently downwards, yet there is no sign of any rocks or changes in the terrain that match the painting. She is about to suggest they turn back when Milo suddenly starts barking loudly and agitatedly.

He's found a big hole in the bank, and before they can stop him he is already halfway in. He carries on barking, and although the noise is slightly muffled by the earth, he sounds even more excited.

'Milo, come here!' Agnes shouts, but the dog ignores her. His back legs scrabble against the bank, and then he disappears completely into the hole. The barking is now joined by another noise, grunting followed by loud hissing that can't possibly be coming from the little dog. 'Milo!' Agnes tries to make her way down to the hole, but loses her balance and falls. The bank is so steep that she rolls over and lands on her knees in the stream. 'Shit!'

Milo is still barking; there is a new note, as if he is afraid, angry and excited at the same time. Anna slithers down the bank. She is reaching out to help Agnes to her feet when she catches a movement out of the corner of her eye, a green figure leaping across the bank and hurling itself at the hole. It is a tall, bearded man in camouflage gear. His appearance is so unexpected that both Anna and Agnes are paralysed by shock. He dives into the hole, arms outstretched, kicking his legs until almost half of his upper body is inside. Sand and pebbles rain down on his back. The noise continues for a few seconds, then suddenly the man is out again. His beard is full of soil, and he is holding a wriggling, barking Milo by the hind legs. He drops the dog on the ground and produces a black revolver from nowhere. Milo's hackles rise and he makes an attempt to attack the man's ankles. Instinctively Anna pushes Agnes behind her.

'No!' Agnes yells, but the man isn't pointing the gun either at them or the dog. Instead, he plunges into the hole once more. The hissing comes again, followed by a loud bang. Then silence.

They watch as the man braces his knees against the bank and slowly wriggles out. In one hand he is holding the revolver, in the other a large grey bundle. He slips the gun into his pocket, then raises the bundle with both hands. Claws, a black-and-white triangular head. Teeth bared in the throes of death.

'Badger,' says the man in a broad local accent as he brushes soil off his clothes. 'It can bite a dog to death if it feels threatened.'

From his belt he takes a broad-bladed hunting knife. He finds a patch of flat ground at the top of the bank, and quickly and expertly begins to gut the animal. Håkan showed Anna how to do it, he even got her to try it on a hare once, but this guy is in a different league. It takes him no more than a minute to remove the innards, and when he's finished he has hardly any blood on his hands. His fingers are surprisingly short, the nails bitten halfway down to the cuticles.

Agnes is sitting beside Milo, holding on to his collar to prevent him from investigating the remains. Both she and the dog are watching the man's movements with fascination. Anna is trying to pull herself together. For a moment she had really thought he was going to point the gun at them.

'He's brave.'

The man nods in Milo's direction as he wipes the sweat from his forehead. His hair and beard are curly, his nose flat and his eyes wide apart, which makes him look odd, a bit like a character from a Harry Potter film. The fairy-tale impression is strengthened by his almost impenetrable Skåne accent.

'Not all dogs would dare to crawl into a badger's sett. My name is Mats Andersson – I live at Änglaberga.' He carefully wipes the knife on his trousers before sliding it back into its sheath.

'Right, yes, hi, Mats. I'm Anna Vesper, and this is Agnes and Milo. We live . . .' She feels a stammer coming on, and pauses for a second.

'At Tabor,' Mats says, solving her dilemma. 'I know. You moved in yesterday. You're renting from my aunt – Elisabet Vidje at Änglaberga. My father is Bengt Andersson.'

The way he says the name suggests that Anna ought to recognise it, but she doesn't.

He turns to Agnes and Milo. 'What breed is he? Skåne terrier?'

'A cross between a Jack Russell and a fox terrier,' Agnes informs him.

'Looks like a Skåne terrier to me.'

He holds out his hand to the dog, who curls his upper lip and bares his teeth. Mats appears unconcerned, and before long Milo's curiosity takes over. He sniffs at Mats's hand, then starts to lick it.

'It's the smell of blood. A good hunting dog can't resist it.' Mats scratches Milo beneath the chin, while the terrier carries on licking his wrist.

'Can I take a photo of you?' Agnes touches the camera around her neck.

'Why?' There is a wariness in his tone, as if he thinks Agnes might be teasing him.

'I just like taking photos – I want to be a photographer. Plus, you rescued my dog.' Agnes switches on the smile that always worked on Håkan. It has the same effect on Mats.

'OK.'

The big man blushes; he suddenly looks like a shy teenager instead of a man in his forties. In spite of the camouflage gear, the bushy beard, the gun and the knife, there is something child-like about him.

He poses obediently with the badger, even obligingly pushes up the top lip to display the vicious teeth.

'They can break bones,' he says as Agnes clicks away. 'Years ago people used to say that you should have eggshells in your boots when you were hunting badgers, in case they bit you. The idea was that the badger would let go when it heard crunching. Stupid idea.' He grins, and so does Agnes.

'Can you eat badger meat?' Anna asks.

Mats turns around looking slightly surprised, as if he's forgotten she's there. Then his smile widens at what is obviously a stupid question.

'Oh no – they can carry roundworms. I usually cook the meat for my sister's dogs. Badgers are fat at this time of year. Very filling.'

He turns back to Agnes.

'I sell the skins, but this one is a fine boar, so I'll probably fix it up instead.'

'Fix it up?' Agnes sounds genuinely interested.

'Stuff it. I've got a good collection at home. Call in and have a look. You can take some pictures if you want.'

'Thank you – I'd like that.'

Anna glances at her watch. 'We'd better head home. It will be dark soon.'

Agnes rolls her eyes but doesn't complain, for once.

'By the way, do you know if there's a quarry around here?' Her tone is friendly and cheerful, but Mats's face darkens.

'Not here,' he mumbles. 'In the forest on the other side of Änglaberga. But you shouldn't go there.'

'Why not?'

He shakes his head. 'It's a terrible place. Dangerous.' He falls silent. He has no more to say on the subject.

'OK, thanks for the warning!'

They say their goodbyes and Anna, Agnes and Milo set off along the path. Mats stays where he is, feet planted on either side of the badger as he watches them go. When Agnes looks back, he raises a hand and waves.

4

28 August 1990

All five of them were lying on their towels in the last patch of afternoon sunlight. Bruno had stayed out of things when Alex reluctantly allowed Marie to change the music for a mix tape of chart hits: Alannah Myles, Madonna, Cher.

'Fucking shite,' Alex muttered to Bruno, but this time he didn't get the usual agreement. Bruno always avoided ending up in the crossfire between Alex and Marie. Alex closed his eyes. He was snoring quietly within a couple of minutes.

The girls had taken off their T-shirts and were sunbathing in their bikini tops and shorts. Carina had smothered herself in something that smelled of coconuts and made her tanned skin glisten. Marie was less curvaceous and considerably paler than Carina. She also had several birthmarks; Bruno knew she was slightly embarrassed by them, but they didn't bother him at all. In fact, he thought they gave her more character. After a while Carina turned over to let the sun get at her back. She undid her top to avoid strap marks. The curve of her breasts was clearly visible from the side, particularly when she raised her head to say something. Bruno tried to avoid looking in her direction, which wasn't easy. Carina was attractive; there wasn't a guy in the area who didn't know who she was, but she was Alex's girlfriend. They'd been together ever since they started high school – maybe even longer.

Simon, on the other hand, was nowhere near as subtle. Bruno could see him glancing repeatedly at Carina's body; he didn't seem to care if anyone noticed. For some reason this annoyed Bruno.

He'd heard some of the younger girls on the bus whispering about Simon. Not poking gentle fun as they'd done in junior school when Simon was a skinny music nerd, but in a different way, a way that Bruno didn't really like. He rolled over onto his stomach and tried to shake off his irritation, but without much success.

After a while Marie noticed what Simon was doing. She nudged Carina and nodded meaningfully in his direction. Carina lowered her sunglasses a fraction, then winked at Marie. 'Watch this,' she whispered.

She propped herself up on her elbows, raised her upper body so that her breasts were almost fully visible.

'Simon,' she said flirtatiously as she slid her sunglasses all the way down to the tip of her nose. 'Could you grab me and Marie a drink, please?'

'Of course!' Simon lumbered to his feet, but Bruno was already halfway to the cool bag.

'I'll do it!' he snapped, glaring at Simon and trying to make him understand that he needed to stay in his place – literally.

'Thank you so much.' Carina lay down again.

Bruno went over to the cool bag, which they'd put in the shade behind one of the tents. He heard a faint crunching noise from down below, and when he looked over the edge of the outcrop he saw a police car slowly turn around and stop next to Simon's bike. The window on the passenger side was lowered, and a tall man with sharp features looked out.

'Alex!' Bruno shouted as he waved to the man in the police car.

'What?' Alex muttered without lifting his head.

'Your daddy's here.'

Alex sighed and sat up.

'Of course he is. I was stupid enough to ask him if I could borrow the key to the barrier. He gave me a long lecture on why that wasn't possible. Access is forbidden, the rocks are danger-ous, blah, blah, blah. But it's OK for him to use the key to come and check up on us.'

'You should be pleased you have a father who cares about you,' Carina murmured.

'We're not kids, for God's sake – what does he think is going to happen to us up here?' Alex got to his feet and joined Bruno. He waved irritably at the police car. 'Hi, there, Henry,' he said, so that only his four friends could hear him. 'Everything's fine, you can go now.'

The man waved back.

'Are you behaving yourselves?' he shouted. His voice was hoarse and bounced off the walls of the quarry.

'Of course.' Alex didn't even bother to hide his annoyance.

'Is it the usual gang?'

'Yes!'

Henry Morell showed no sign of leaving. It took a few seconds before Alex realised what his father was waiting for.

'Jesus,' he muttered before turning to Simon and the girls.

'Stand up and wave,' he said, holding up a hand to quell their protests before anyone could speak. 'I know, I know, but it's the only way to get rid of him. Otherwise he'll just come marching up here.'

Carina, Marie and Simon obediently made their way to the edge of the rock.

'Hi, Uncle Henry!' Marie shouted with exaggerated enthusiasm, while the others gave a half-hearted wave.

Henry Morell waved back, then said something to the driver. The police car began to move along the narrow dirt track, flashing its blue lights once before disappearing among the trees.

'Sorry,' Alex said. 'You know what he's like.'

Simon patted Alex on the back. 'No problem. It's part of the tradition, Henry calling by to check on his golden boy. He'll still be doing it when you're fifty.'

Alex responded with something inaudible. He grabbed a beer and went back to his towel. Simon changed the tape in the boombox.

'Not Toto again,' Marie groaned when the music started. 'What was wrong with my tape?'

Simon rolled his eyes. 'Michael Bolton. Need I say more?'

'What's wrong with Michael Bolton?' Marie looked to Carina for support, but her friend was lying down, apparently uninterested in the discussion.

'Yes, what *is* wrong with Michael Bolton?' Simon said with a grin.

'You know, sometimes you can be a real arsehole, Simon. Just because you're a musical fucking prodigy, that doesn't make you the taste police!' Marie snapped.

Simon sat down beside her and put his arm around her. 'But you still love me, don't you, cousin?'

She pushed his arm away, he put it back. This went on until Marie burst out laughing.

'Arsehole!' she said again, but in a friendlier tone this time.

Bruno took two beers and a Coke out of the cool bag and went back to the girls. He ventured a little smile when he handed Marie the Coke, but didn't get the response he'd been hoping for as she was still bantering with Simon. Bruno sat down on the towel and opened his beer, then realised that Simon was once again ogling Carina, not caring whether anyone noticed or not.

Someone ought to teach that fucker a lesson, he thought. He took a couple of swigs of beer and smiled quietly as he toyed with the not unpleasant idea of doing so himself.

5

Autumn 2017

Anna has been up since five thirty. She spent a long time in the shower in the newly tiled bathroom before putting on her uniform. Trousers, freshly ironed shirt, the dark blue jumper with yellow insignia on the shoulders, usually worn only by office staff. She hasn't worn a uniform for many years; as a detective in Stockholm, she was always in plain clothes.

Monday morning. If she scores the weekend, it comes out with a slight plus. The weather took a turn for the worse yesterday, so she and Agnes didn't manage to continue their search for the quarry. Instead, Agnes spent the whole day shut in her room with Netflix, while Anna did a few jobs. Part of her hopes that Agnes will tire of Simon's story and realise that a tragic fatal accident involving a boy only a few years older than her is not something they should be digging into, particularly as they're living in his father's studio. Another, much stronger part is already missing the companionship they shared on Saturday. For a few short hours everything had been almost . . . normal.

When her hair is dry enough she gathers it up into a severe ponytail, puts on a minimal amount of makeup, then adjusts the knot of her tie. Examines the result in the mirror and finds a new wrinkle next to one eye. She considers trying to cover it with foundation, but decides not to bother. After all, she will be forty-six soon, and she has no desire to turn up for her first day at work plastered in makeup.

She taps on Agnes's door. 'Time to get up.' Milo is on the bed, of course, even though he's not allowed. He glares defiantly at her, curls his lip a fraction as if to warn her against coming too near his Agnes.

'Did you sleep well?' she asks as Agnes pulls on her jacket to take the dog out. The only response is a mumble. The positive mood of the weekend has clearly gone.

'What time is your train?'

'Seven thirty.'

'OK – that means we need to leave here by ten to seven at the latest.'

The front door slams shut. Anna takes a deep breath, determined not to let herself be provoked. This is Agnes's first day at school. Hers too, you could say.

She parks in front of the police station five minutes after the agreed time. The weekend's fog still lingers; it seems thicker down here in the village, and clings to her clothes. It also smells unpleasant, an acrid, burned odour that makes her nostrils prickle. She never used to bother much about smells; she's experienced the very worst in the course of her job, but over the past year they all seem to have become more powerful. She knows exactly when it started: on the morning of 2 November last year. White lilies. Håkan's funeral. She feels the nerves making her stomach churn, fills her lungs with air. *Calm down, everything's going to be fine*, he whispers. They seem to be friends again now. At least he isn't filling her head with any more dire warnings.

Henry Morell emerges from the main door of the police station before she reaches it. Presumably he has been standing inside, watching her. He is a big man, over six feet tall, and he must weigh around fifteen stone. Some of his bulk has settled around his waist, but not as much as in most of his contemporaries. He too is in uniform, which is a relief. Turning up wrongly dressed on her first day would be a bad start. Morell has a slight stoop and carries his weight on the balls of his feet; this stance, combined with the bushy eyebrows and the grey beard, makes him resemble an ageing bear.

'Henry,' he says, holding out an enormous paw. His smile is polite, but nothing more. 'Welcome to Nedanås. It's a little chilly this morning, but I thought we'd start with a tour anyway. There's coffee in the car.' He points to a Volvo; it's dark blue and unmarked, but it is unmistakably a police car.

The interior smells of aftershave. There is a cardboard cup of coffee in the holder between the seats. Anna takes a sip as Morell manoeuvres the Volvo out into the street. The coffee is lukewarm, the atmosphere strained.

'Sorry I'm a bit late.' She makes an effort to speak slowly. 'My daughter . . .' She feels the stammer coming, pauses and changes tack. 'It took longer to drive down from the ridge than I'd thought. The bends are quite sharp, and with the fog . . .'

Morell waves a dismissive hand.

'You'll soon get used to it. I believe you arrived on Friday – did the trip from Stockholm go well?'

'It did, thank you.'

'And you and your daughter have settled in at Tabor? Got everything sorted?'

'More or less.'

His tone is neutral, neither friendly nor unfriendly. He has a Skåne accent, but it is easy to understand, not thick and guttural like Mats Andersson's.

'It's a beautiful house, one of the finest on the ridge. Elisabet Vidje has held on to it fiercely for many years – refused to do anything to it, let alone sell it or rent it out.' Something in his voice suggests that there is more to say on this topic, but Morell changes the subject.

'So as I said, I thought we'd go for a little tour so that I can tell you what's what. It will also give us the chance to get to know each other before you meet the rest of the team at the ten o'clock briefing.'

'Sounds good!' Her response is too cheerful, which irritates her. Better to remain neutral like Henry Morell rather than trying too hard.

He turns onto the main road, two miles of virtually dead straight tarmac, interrupted only by the railway crossing. Anna has already driven through the village more than once and has come to the conclusion that this road is several feet too wide. Along with the straightness and the low buildings on either side, it gives a rather desolate impression, especially on a morning like this when there's hardly anyone around. The fog covers the village like a lid, but it is still possible to make out the steep ridge, looming up like a sinister silhouette along the western edge. Anna suppresses a shudder.

Hidden away from the rest of the world, Håkan whispers. *Wasn't that the plan?*

'As I'm sure you know, the police district is made up of three separate communities,' Henry says. 'We have a total of just over 25,000 residents. Nedanås is the largest with around 9,000, and this is also where most of the action happens, so to speak.'

Anna sips her coffee and makes appropriate noises as he continues his lecture, giving no indication that she has already googled the relevant information. She observes him discreetly. With the help of the police federation, he has managed to delay his retirement to the age of sixty-seven, exploiting every last clause in his contract. He has never served anywhere but Nedanås. Forty-five years – the same length of time as Anna has been alive. It is almost incomprehensible. Four and a half decades dealing with other people's problems in exactly the same place should have been more than enough, yet Morell has clung to his desk for as long as possible. He must really love his job, and now he's being forced to hand it over to her, a stranger. She tries to observe his body language, listens carefully to his tone of voice, but if Morell is feeling hostile towards her, he is hiding it well. The coffee was a nice welcoming gesture, but then it was lukewarm, so it's hard to tell exactly what the situation is. And because they're sitting side by side, it's more difficult to read his body language and facial expression. Maybe that was his intention? If so, he's a lot more cunning than she'd expected.

As they set off Morell points to the police station, a two-storey yellow-brick building that probably dates from the 1980s.

'This is where we operate from. We have twenty-six officers, plus two civilians who man the reception desk. We'll see what happens after the next round of budget cuts – but of course that won't be my problem.' Is there a hint of bitterness in that last comment? Anna isn't sure.

Morell scratches his beard.

'That's where the drunks hang out,' he informs her as they reach the small square in front of the state-owned off-licence. 'We have a group of long-term alcoholics and drug users who tend to congregate here, especially just after their benefits have been paid. But they're a dying breed – in five or ten years they'll be gone.' He almost sounds melancholy. They cross the railway line. The track curves slightly, which means the rails are at different heights.

'A bit bumpy,' Morell says, 'but that's the price we have to pay for the inter-urban trains. There are plenty of other communities that would be willing to sacrifice a few shock absorbers for a decent rail link. There's talk of long-distance trains next year, in which case they'll probably build a viaduct.'

An elderly couple on the pavement wave, and he returns their greeting. A short distance further on, a cyclist does the same. It's obvious that people recognise the chief of police.

The acrid smell is stronger now.

'Clay burning,' Morell explains, pointing to the dark outline of the ridge. 'The local gravel company, Glarea, has a big open-cast quarry on the edge of the ridge. As well as producing gravel and tarmac, they burn clay to make bricks for use in kilns.'

Anna recognises the name from the logo on Gunnel's bobbly cardigan on Saturday.

'On some days the smell is worse than others,' Morell goes on. 'To be honest, I hardly notice it anymore, but some of our newer residents have complained to the Environment Agency, and the blasting and burning will stop towards the end of next year.' He shrugs. 'Times change, and maybe that's for the best. At least it will be nice not to have to wash the car so often.'

They continue slowly through the village and Morell points out the pub, the library, the high school, the swimming pool and the supermarket. He moves on to the ironmonger's, the cobbler, the florist, and finally the fire station and the tall water tower that looks like a giant grey concrete mushroom. Tarmac, brick, dark wood and dirty grey plasterboard, the colours made even gloomier by the foul-smelling fog. Nedanås isn't exactly a picturesque little Skåne village – it's closer to a typical industrial town.

'I imagine the problems we have here are pretty standard outside the major cities. Break-ins, drink driving, the odd bit of graffiti, a vandalised bus shelter now and again,' Morell says, scratching his beard once more. 'A few notorious domestic abusers that we keep a close eye on, the occasional fight either at the refugee centre or in the park. Not particularly advanced crimes, especially for an experienced investigator like you.' The sentence remains hanging in the air as he concentrates on a left turn. Anna has a good idea where this discussion is going.

They reach an industrial estate on the outskirts of the village, pass a car wash and a series of identical corrugated metal shoeboxes. Paint workshops, car repairs, tyres.

At the far end there is a dilapidated old building that doesn't fit in with its surroundings. The place is surrounded by overgrown grass; the windows and doors are boarded up. Morell stops, pulls up the handbrake and turns to face her.

'So, Anna. To be frank, your posting here was a little . . .' He waves his hand as if he is searching for the right word. 'Unexpected. There aren't usually many external candidates for the role of local chief of police in a place like this. A few half-hearted applications from colleagues in the neighbouring district who fancy boosting their salary, or some poor burned-out sod who's tired of shift work in town. Never from anyone further afield than that, which of course is perfectly logical. If you want a career in the police you move into the city, not away from it – don't you?'

Anna nods, plays along. She can't help worrying – what is he hinting at? What does he know?

'Under normal circumstances the chief's job goes to someone who's already working at the station. Someone who's familiar with all the routines, and who already has a role as a team leader. That was how I got the job all those years ago.' He leans a little closer. 'Don't misunderstand me, Anna – of course we're delighted to have such an experienced officer joining us. Your credentials from Stockholm are impressive, to say the least. Murder investigator, team leader, sky-high clear-up figures.'

His mouth curves into something that is probably supposed to be a warm smile, but for half a second becomes a telling grimace, a brief micro-expression that contradicts what he has just said. Anna is certain now: just as she already suspected, Henry Morell doesn't want her here.

'A lot of people at the station thought the job should go to Jens Friberg, our external operations commander,' Morell says. 'The commissioner and I had already agreed on the appointment, actually – but then your application arrived, just a couple of days before the closing date. Compared with your qualifications, poor Jens didn't stand a chance. The commissioner was delighted.'

He smiles ironically, and Anna forces herself to keep quiet. She knows there is more to come.

'So, the question we're all asking ourselves is: why? Why would someone with your record and your career trajectory, without any connection to Nedanås or Skåne, apply for this kind of post? Why didn't you want to continue working as a murder investigator, or go for promotion in Stockholm? To put it briefly: what are you actually doing here?'

The polite façade is still in place, but the tone is insidious, as if he already knows the answer to his question. Henry Morell has literally been a police officer for Anna's entire life. He must have plenty of contacts all over the place. Does he know about the internal investigation? About Håkan? About her? The logical answer should be no. She isn't formally under suspicion of having committed a crime, and therefore she shouldn't be listed on the database. However, she can't shake off the feeling that Morell knows more than he's saying. Maybe that's exactly what he wants her to think? It's one of the interview techniques she likes to use. *I already know everything, so you might as well tell me.* There's only one way to find out.

'We needed a change of scenery,' she says firmly. The statement is perfectly true. 'My h-husband . . .'

She immediately corrects herself, at the same time smoothing over that annoying little stumble. 'My *ex*-husband, Håkan, passed away last year. Cancer. It hit our daughter, Agnes, very hard. She had problems in school, got in with the wrong crowd. Stockholm can be tough . . .'

She pauses, lets him fill in the gaps. A good way to avoid entangling herself in lies. Everything she's just said is accurate. She is simply missing out certain parts of the story. *Just like I used to do*, Håkan whispers in the back of her mind, with appalling timing as usual. She almost bites her lip, stops herself at the last second.

Morell nods pensively. Sits in silence for a few seconds, studying her face. Is he trying to read her, work out if she's lying, just as she tried to read him? She keeps the mask in place, doesn't allow her expression or body language to change.

He knows, Håkan insists. *It doesn't matter how far you travel. You'll never escape.*

Morell clears his throat.

'I . . . I do understand, Anna.' He takes a deep breath. 'The fact is, I myself was in a similar situation many years ago.' He scratches his beard on the left-hand side. Anna can see that the skin is inflamed and flaking.

'Eva-Britt and I were only twenty when we had Alexander. The birth was difficult, and unfortunately it turned out that we couldn't have any more children, so we focused all our attention on him.' He smiles, looking a little embarrassed, which makes her racing pulse slow down. 'I was a committed parent – school meetings, training sessions, matches. Then I was offered a really good job in Helsingborg – team leader with the narcotics patrol. Better pay, interesting and exciting work. A dream job for many officers.

But when I thought about it, I realised that it would be better for Alexander if we stayed here in Nedanås. We'll do anything for our kids, won't we?'

'Absolutely!' She nods slowly, holds his gaze. His expression softens. The atmosphere is different now, and she knows why. He has tested her, and the result seems to have come as a relief to both of them, in some strange way.

'You're probably wondering why we've stopped here.' He points towards the dilapidated building. His tone is more friendly, in keeping with a professional conversation between colleagues.

'A couple of years ago we found out that one of the big biker gangs was planning to buy this place and turn it into a clubhouse. Barbed wire, cameras, twenty-four-hour security. Definitely not the kind of set-up we want in our community. I spoke to Bengt Andersson, who was the leader of our local council, and together we came up with a solution. The environmental health inspector carried out a survey and discovered a significant amount of toxins in the ground.'

His tone remains the same, he doesn't draw speech marks in the air around the word 'discovered', but they are definitely there. Anna recognises the name Bengt Andersson – where has she heard it before?

'The property was placed on the local authority's list of environmentally hazardous sites, and the bikers dropped out.' Morell smiles with satisfaction. 'It was unfortunate for the owner, but he was compensated later on. A long-term contract with the roadworks department, if I remember correctly, so everything was fine.'

The smile broadens.

'Bengt Andersson and I have known each other for over forty years.'

Anna suddenly remembers why the name rings a bell.

'I think we met his son over the weekend – Mats Andersson, who lives at Änglaberga?'

'That's right. Mats is Bengt's youngest, and as I'm sure you noticed, he's a little ... different. But he's a nice boy, completely harmless.'

Not to badgers, Anna thinks.

'Bengt was responsible for both the state-owned off-licence and the inter-urban train coming here, and he's the one who's negotiating for the long-distance trains. He's also the chair of Glarea. Without Bengt, Nedanås would still be stuck in the crisis years of the '90s.' There is admiration in his voice, the kind that only arises when those over sixty are talking about people in the same age group.

'Bengt's daughter Marie has taken over the reins on the council. She's a smart girl, at least as ambitious as her father. She could have done anything she wanted, but she chose to stay here in Nedanås and work for the good of the community. Marie and Alexander have been friends since they were kids – she's like a daughter to me.' He becomes more serious. 'Do you understand what I'm saying, Anna?'

She nods, even though the question is rhetorical.

'In a place like this, the police are a part of society in a completely different way than in the city. Everything you do, or don't do, has consequences, sometimes on an extremely personal level.' He falls silent, weighing his words carefully before leaning so close that she can smell the coffee on his breath.

'This job is about relationships, Anna. Becoming part of the community, understanding how people think. Knowing when to follow the letter of the law, and when to . . .'

And when to do the right thing, Håkan says. *You don't think I've forgotten what you promised me, do you?*

49

6

28 August 1990

Marie put the cigarette Carina had just given her to her lips and pretended to take a long drag. Prince Red were far too strong, but all those years in the smoking corner at school meant she could be very convincing. The same applied to booze. She usually drank one glass of wine as slowly as she could, then half-filled her glass and carried it around for the rest of the evening, which meant she avoided snide comments about being boring. Carina was the only one who knew her secret, but she had never given it away.

Alex had got the fire going just as the sun began to set. The flames leaped high at first, casting shadows on the trees and rocks before dying down. Bruno had brought a grill tray from the restaurant, and the two of them had rigged it up over the heat. Meanwhile Marie, Carina and Simon unrolled the sleeping mats. The plateau was still warm from the sun, but the air would quickly become chilly and damp as darkness fell. After a while everyone except Alex changed back into their jeans and fleecy tops.

'I don't feel the cold!' he boasted with a grin as he opened another can of beer.

Marie poured herself and Carina plastic glasses of red wine.

'So how has your day been?' Bruno asked. The question sounded general, but Marie noticed that he was looking at her.

'Crap.' Carina blew cigarette smoke out of her nostrils in the cool way that Marie had never managed. 'Kalle came home pissed at about four and woke me and Mum, then it all kicked off as usual.' She rolled her eyes, not bothering to hide the contempt she felt for her father. 'I dropped the little ones off with Gran on my way to work so they wouldn't have to hear it. Then I spent all day feeding the oldies, cleaning toilets and changing nappies for a rubbish wage. Another fantastic day with the Pedersen family.' Carina pulled a face and took another drag.

Bruno looked as if he wished he hadn't asked, and Marie felt a little bit sorry for him. She was distracted by her tummy rumbling; she'd been so busy getting ready for the move next week, and had skipped lunch. Now she was starving. She sipped her wine to suppress her hunger.

'Your mum ought to report him,' Alex said, his tone of voice indicating that he didn't like this topic of conversation.

'Yeah, like that would help,' Carina muttered. 'There's no one in the whole of fucking Nedanås who doesn't know that Kalle hits my mum.'

'What about your older brothers?' Simon said.

Carina shook her head. 'They're busy with their own stuff.' She stubbed out her cigarette and looked away. Marie knew why. Everyone knew about Carina's brothers; everyone knew exactly what they were busy with. Best not to ask questions. Marie sipped her wine, discovered that the glass was almost empty.

When the wood had turned to velvety-grey charcoal, Bruno grilled pork fillets and fresh vegetables. The way he could produce a real feast in minutes was impressive, but the friends had seen him do it so often that no one reacted. Marie decided it was time that changed.

'That smells fantastic, Bruno,' she said. 'Well done!' It was probably because she was so hungry, and maybe because of the wine she'd stupidly drunk on an empty stomach. Whatever the reason, the compliment seemed to please Bruno, although he looked a little embarrassed. Marie knew why he was blushing. Simon had hinted that Bruno was interested in her, and even if she didn't feel the same way, the revelation had cheered her up. She was beginning to get very tired of the role of the pretty girl's plain friend, which she'd been playing ever since junior school. It felt good to be desired, to know that someone actually preferred her to Carina Pedersen, even if it was only reliable old Bruno Sordi.

'Friends forever,' Alex said, raising his beer can in a toast. 'Whatever happens, right?'

'Here you go!' Carina filled Marie's glass all the way to the top. Marie looked at it. If she drank the lot she would exceed her normal alcohol consumption by a considerable amount – but this was no ordinary evening. The last swim of the summer was a tradition Alex had come up with when they were thirteen, and it had continued every year since then. At least until now. Summer 1990 was behind them, just like their graduation from high school, and at any moment Marie could summon the tingle of anticipation she felt about everything that was going to happen. This was the beginning of her life – for real. She raised her glass and took a deep swig of her wine, then another. Felt the warmth spread through her body.

After they'd eaten they all lay down, enjoying the feeling of being full and slightly drunk. They gazed up at the night sky, studded with stars. It was almost completely clear above them, but a dark bank of cloud was slowly moving in from the west. Simon switched off the tape, threw a couple more logs on the fire, and picked up his guitar. He sat down with his back against a rock and began to strum a few chords. Marie noticed that Carina was resting her head on Alex's chest and sharing a cigarette with him, which meant that the earlier argument was forgotten. Marie was used to their constant bickering, but it seemed to have become worse over the past six months. Once or twice Carina had hinted that she was thinking of finishing with him. Really finishing with him, not like all the other times when it had been part of the game between her and Alex. So far Carina hadn't suggested that they should swap tents so that she and Alex could sleep together. Which was just as well, because Marie had no intention of agreeing this year. If she ended up sharing a tent with Bruno, she would be sending out all the wrong signals.

Bruno had placed his mat right next to hers. She tried to picture them together, but it was no good. She, Bruno, Carina and Alex had known one another since preschool. She'd known Simon even longer; there was an old, yellowed photograph in the family album of the two of them as babies, lying side by side in the same cot while their mothers, Elisabet and Ebba Vidje, stood proudly behind them in their best clothes. She and Simon were cousins, but it almost felt as if they were brother and sister. Marie still found it easier to imagine herself with him rather than Bruno. Nice, predictable Bruno.

'Life doesn't get much better than this,' Alex said with a sigh. He took a long drag of the cigarette, then passed it to Carina. Simon carried on playing, soft melodies mingling with the crackling of the fire. A sudden noise from the forest made Carina sit up.

'Was that a branch breaking?' She sounded worried.

Bruno got to his feet and stared towards the trees. 'Probably a deer,' he said. Carina seemed reassured, and leaned back against Alex once more. Bruno sat down on his mat, a fraction closer to Marie. Gave her an embarrassed smile when he caught her eye. Marie thought she should probably do something about his awkward advances, but the red wine had made her mellow, and right now she thought she deserved both the wine and the admiration. In only a week or so she and Simon would be sharing an apartment in the centre of Lund. She'd already got herself a part-time job at party headquarters in Malmö. Being Bengt Andersson's daughter had definitely helped, but she had no qualms about that. Her plan was crystal clear: take the minutes at meetings and make the coffee for a few years while she was studying. By the time she graduated, she would be established as a good bet for the future, with the right contacts and pedigree within the party. A couple of years serving her apprenticeship in local politics, then on to parliament just in time for the election in 2000. That sounded so appealing: the 2000 election. No more tired old 19-whatever, but 2000. The future.

Simon began to hum along to what was presumably the chorus of the song he was playing. Something happened to the atmosphere as soon as he picked up an instrument, something that had become more and more tangible as they got older.

'Do you realise,' Carina said, interrupting Marie's train of thought, 'tonight might be the last time we do this?'

'Forget "might be",' Simon said. 'I'll be keeping my clothes on inside my sleeping bag. You know how I feel about camping.'

'That's not what I meant,' Carina said.

'So, what did you mean, baby?' Alex reached for the cigarette, but Carina ignored the gesture.

'I mean this might be the last time ever.' She sounded sad. 'Alex starts his military service in two weeks. Marie and Simon are off to Lund.'

'Next Thursday,' Marie chipped in. 'By the way, Simon – you still haven't signed the lease on the apartment.'

Simon didn't answer, which annoyed Marie. He was always like that – he never arrived on time, and he put everything off until the last minute.

'It's almost impossible to find student accommodation in Lund,' she said irritably. 'And even harder to get an apartment. My dad pulled lots of strings, so you don't get to fuck it up. I'll call round tomorrow so we can sort it out, OK?'

'Mm.' Simon's attention was focused on his guitar.

Marie finished off her wine and grabbed the bottle.

'So, all three of you are out of here,' Carina went on. 'Leaving me and Bruno in boring bloody Nedanås, the worst dump in the world.'

'What are you talking about?' Bruno protested. 'I've got plans – haven't you?'

'Of course I have.'

'Plans? What plans do you have, baby?' Alex sounded amused.

'Interrailing, waitressing in Ibiza, maybe even working as an au pair if I can find a job. Anything that will get me away from this place as soon as possible.'

'But baby,' Alex said. 'We've already talked about this. You go full-time at the care home until I've finished my military service.

If everything goes well we should be able to manage a couple of weeks in Crete next summer, as long as it doesn't clash with my competition schedule.'

'Or I go without you. Right now. Away from Kalle and my mother, from your parents and everybody else who gives me funny looks. Away from this awful fucking place.' Carina flicked her cigarette stub into the fire.

'Whatever you say, baby.' Alex's tone was patronising as he patted Carina's head. She pushed his hand away, then sat up straight.

'Did you hear that?'

'What?' Marie and Bruno said at the same time. Simon stopped playing.

'What is it this time?' Alex laughed. 'Another killer deer?'

'Quiet!' Carina got up and peered down at the turning area. The beam of a single headlamp was approaching through the trees, followed by the dull roar of an engine. For some reason the sound made Marie shudder.

7

Autumn 2017

A nna's first day in uniform was 25 June 1994. She can still remember how nervous she was, the scratchy shirt collar, the gun belt sitting uncomfortably over her hips. The realisation that everyone else in the briefing room knew one another inside out, knew their colleagues' strengths and weaknesses, knew exactly what was required to do the job. Everyone except her.

Today she is not sitting quietly at the back, but standing at the front with all eyes upon her, and yet the feeling is more or less the same. Twenty-six people in total, which is virtually the entire team. She is not a natural leader like Håkan. Her strong point is listening, not talking, which is why she's been practising her speech for weeks.

'So let me introduce our new chief of police and my successor, Anna Vesper. Welcome to Skåne and Nedanås, Anna.' Henry Morell turns to her.

'Good morning, everyone,' she begins, trying to make eye contact with as many people as possible. 'As Henry said, my name is Anna Vesper, I'm forty-five years old, and as you can hear I'm from Stockholm, where I've been working as head of the Violent Crimes Unit for the past seven years.' She is deliberately speaking slowly. She pauses, takes a deep breath.

'But don't worry, I spent several summers with relatives in Österlen when I was little, so I understand the Skåne dialect even if I don't speak it.'

Her smile is returned by a couple of the younger officers, but most of her new colleagues look distinctly unimpressed.

What did I say? Håkan reminds her. *Humour isn't your thing. Stick to what you're good at, idiot!*

She clears her throat, pushes him away. *Take your time, don't stammer.*

'I take up my post next Monday. During this week Henry and I will be working on the handover. I'd also like to go out with a couple of patrol cars to get to know the area. Over the next two or three weeks I'm hoping to be able to sit down with each one of you individually to get an idea of your goals, what challenges you face during the course of your work, and how I can support you in the best way possible.'

She is particularly pleased with the last sentence, picked up from a leadership course. She has practised it over and over again until it is rock solid. She carries on in a typical Swedish way, tells them she has a sixteen-year-old daughter called Agnes who has just started at the high school and dreams of becoming a photographer. She ends – without tripping up once – by saying how much she's looking forward to working with everyone in the room. Henry Morell starts a polite ripple of applause.

'Thank you, Anna. I'm sure everyone here will do their best to ensure as smooth a transition as possible. Before I hand over to Jens, I'd just like to remind you of my retirement presentation on Friday afternoon in the council chambers. You know what I think of events like that, and it would be nice to see a few friendly faces among all the suits.'

Morell's joke falls on considerably more fertile ground than Anna's. He waits for the smiles and laughter to die away before turning to a uniformed officer sitting at the end of the front row. 'Over to you, Jens.'

Jens Friberg gets to his feet and waits until Anna and Morell have sat down before opening the black folder he had tucked under his arm. He's about the same age as Anna, toned and fit in the sinewy way she likes. His eyes are grey; they remind her of Håkan's, but without the glint that made it so difficult to be angry with him. His hair is dark and short, his close-fitting uniform shirt is perfectly pressed, and the American paratrooper boots he is wearing are polished to a high shine. She looks for more of the usual symbols. Oversized diver's watch, double sets of spare cartridges and hand-cuffs attached to his gun belt. Multi-purpose tools, low-slung fast-access holster with leg strap. She wonders if he has a military tattoo, and decides there's at least a fifty per cent chance. Raises the odds to sixty before he starts speaking. She's on the verge of bursting out laughing.

'Good morning, everyone. So, this is what went down over the weekend . . .'

Anna has met men like Friberg many times before. Village People cops, that's what Håkan used to call them. The laughter won't go away, and she can't help smiling. It's mainly relief at having got through her speech without stammering, and she pulls herself together by staring at the floor. After a few seconds she looks up, tries to work out whether Friberg has noticed any-thing, but his disciplined expression gives nothing away.

When the briefing is over, Morell gives her a guided tour of the station. The building is bigger than she'd expected, with changing rooms, an archive and an underground car park in the basement. Reception, processing and briefing rooms on the ground floor. The office on the first floor directly above the stairs has a glass wall. Inside she can see a large desk, and the other walls are covered in photographs. She assumes this is Morell's office, which will soon be hers. He shows her the staff kitchen and introduces her to colleagues along the corridor. He stops at the far end and opens a door.

'So, this will be your office, Anna.' The room is large and deso-late, and smells musty. The bookshelves are empty, apart from half a pack of photocopying paper, the armrest belonging to an office chair, and several old push-button telephones. The win-dows overlook the covered car park and the ramp to the under-ground parking; one of the blinds is broken, concertinaed into a crooked fan.

'I thought I'd be taking over your office.' She can't hide her surprise.

'Yes, well, I wanted to have a chat with you about that. The thing is, I've been asked by the police academy to update some of their teaching materials – leadership, staff management, that kind of thing.' He smiles, his voice warm and friendly. 'The commissioner has agreed that I can do the work here in the station, so I thought I'd ask you if I could stay on in my old office, just for convenience. We're only talking about a few months, six at the most.'

She is completely taken aback. Morell is looking at her expectantly, like a fond father figure. Right now he's her only ally, so she takes the easy way out.

'Of course, no problem.'

'Thank you so much, Anna. I really appreciate that. Can I buy you lunch? There's an excellent restaurant just around the corner.'

In spite of the slightly gloomy décor, the local restaurant turns out to be a very good Italian. There are none of the usual spelling mistakes on the menu, the kebab pizza is notable by its absence, and the pasta is silky and perfectly al dente. When Morell introduces her to the owner, she understands why.

'Fabrizio Sordi, but everyone around here calls me Fabbe.' The man speaks perfect Skåne Swedish, but the cadence of his sentences is typically Italian. He has dark hair and wears glasses; he looks about the same age and weight as Morell, but is considerably shorter.

'Fabbe came here in '68 to work at Glarea, like so many others, but his talents were wasted there. You tell the rest of the story!' Morell pats the other man encouragingly on the shoulder.

'Food in Sweden in the '60s was inedible – brown beans and pea soup. Tinned pineapples, tinned ham. I had to ask my family back in Italy to send over pasta and olive oil. I did a few shifts as a pot washer in the kitchen at weekends to earn some extra cash, and eventually the chef let me have a go. He was a bit too fond of the booze, so it happened more and more often. In '75 the owner decided to sell, so

I scraped together as much as I could and went for it. My boys more or less grew up here – cooking is in their blood. My older son Dante is a sous chef at Noma in Copenhagen – two Michelin stars!'

Morell pats him on the shoulder again; the little man is clearly bursting with pride.

'So, he didn't cook this?' Anna points to her plate.

'No, that was my younger son, Bruno.'

'Please pass on my compliments – it was delicious. *Ottimo!*'

Fabbe's smile grows even wider. '*Tu parli italiano – brava!*'

'Only a little – I've forgotten most of it,' she says in Italian before reverting to Swedish. 'I studied in Florence for six months in the early '90s, before I realised I wanted to join the police.'

'You speak it very well,' Fabbe assures her. 'Wait a minute – Bruno! Bruno!'

The other diners look up, and a man in chef's whites sticks his head around a door at the far end of the room. Fabbe beckons him over.

'Bruno, come and say hello to Anna Vesper, our new chief of police. She's spent time in Firenze, and speaks Italian!'

Bruno holds out his hand. He's about the same age as Anna, and is in many ways a slimmer version of his father. His hairline has begun to recede, the shape of his mouth is the same as Fabbe's, but his eyes are more serious, and he doesn't have the laughter lines. 'Bruno Sordi,' he introduces himself.

'Hi, Bruno. The pasta was delicious.'

'Thank you.' He smiles, nods in the direction of his father. 'Unfortunately, my Italian is a little rusty. Has Dad told you the story of how he acquired the restaurant by washing up?'

'He has.'

'And he's mentioned that my brother is a Michelin-starred chef?'

Anna nods.

'In that case I'm afraid I don't have much more to add,' Bruno says with a wry smile. 'I'm just a simple cook, and my kitchen is waiting – so if you'll excuse me . . .'

'How's Marie?' Morell asks a little too quickly, as if he doesn't want Bruno to go yet.

'Fine, thanks. She and Bengt are in Stockholm for a series of meetings. You know what she's like – a thousand irons in the fire. Nedanås wouldn't survive without her.' He makes a gesture which conveys both humour and resignation.

'I heard from Alex that they'd sorted out the finances,' Morell says. 'When are you thinking of making a start up there?'

Bruno glances at his father. 'We'll see. Soon, I hope.'

Morell turns to Anna. 'Bruno is married to Bengt Andersson's daughter, Marie – as I told you earlier, she's taken over the reins at the council. They also run a bed and breakfast in the house where Marie grew up, on the ridge not far from here. But they have bigger plans. A conference centre, spa and gourmet restaurant. Alex's company is laying the foundations. The complex will really put Nedanås on the map.'

'Let's hope so.' Bruno looks embarrassed. 'I must get back to my kitchen. Good to meet you, Anna, and I'm glad you enjoyed the food. I'm sure we'll see each other again.' He nods to his father and Morell, then ambles away.

'Nice guy,' Anna says to Fabbe, mainly because she feels that something is expected of her. 'You must be very proud of your children.'

He nods. 'They're good kids, all of them. Bruno, Marie, Alex.'

He and Morell exchange a glance she can't interpret, and without knowing why, she has a feeling that something is going on right in front of her. A performance of some kind, but she can't work out what its purpose might be.

8

28 August 1990

The motorbike emerged from the forest and made a leisurely circuit of the turning area before stopping next to Simon's bike. Marie could make out two people, probably a man and a woman. The engine fell silent, the headlamp went out and was replaced a few seconds later by the beam of a torch, which was directed up towards their campsite.

'Hello there!' a man's voice called out.

'Hello!' Carina, who was standing at the edge of the outcrop, waved and shaded her eyes against the bright light.

Alex joined Carina and tried to put his arm around her, but she pushed him away. Marie stayed in the background. She didn't recognise either the bike or the voice, and she didn't like the idea of strangers.

'Can we come up for a while?' the man shouted.

Alex turned to Marie and raised his eyebrows enquiringly. She shook her head. 'This is *our* party, *our* tradition. Don't you agree, Bruno?'

Bruno nodded without saying anything. Simon started strumming his guitar again.

'We've got weed,' the voice informed them. 'Me and my sister would be happy to share in return for some food.'

Alex grinned. 'Come on, Marie – it would be cool to meet some new people.'

'You just want to get stoned!' she snapped.

'So what – you only live once. Isn't that right, baby?' He made another attempt to put his arm around Carina, and met with less resistance this time.

'Sure, why not?' Carina murmured.

'What do the rest of you say? Shall we expand our horizons a little?'

'No thanks,' Marie said firmly. 'And Bruno agrees with me.'

Bruno looked away.

'Two for, two against,' Alex said. 'Simon, you have the casting vote.'

Simon glanced up; he didn't seem to have been following the discussion at all. Marie caught his eye, frowned and shook her head. To her annoyance, Simon ignored her. 'Whatever,' he said with a shrug.

'So, what's the verdict?' the man shouted. 'Is it party time?'

Alex grinned at Marie. 'Come on up – and don't forget the weed!'

Simon carried on playing, beautiful, melancholy chords heightened by the silence that had fallen among the friends. A feeling of unease came over Marie, coupled with the humiliation of being voted down. She suddenly decided to go home. She stood up and brushed down her jeans. Took a few steps towards the tent and realised she was wobbling. She stopped, thought back and realised she'd drunk too much to be able to drive. Admittedly it wasn't far to Kotorp, and the risk of being pulled over was very small, but what if something happened? People drove like lunatics up on the ridge, not to mention what her father would say if she arrived home in the car stinking of wine. A single mistake like that could cost Marie her entire career, before it had even started.

At that moment the two new arrivals appeared.

'Hi, guys!' The man holding the torch seemed to be a few years older than the rest of them. He was wearing a black leather jacket, a white T-shirt and jeans. He looked good; his hair was long and slicked back, and his face had a sharp, slightly dangerous edge.

'I'm Joe, and this is my sister, Tanya.' The beam of the torch caught the woman for only a second, but Marie noticed how Alex immediately straightened up a little. Back-combed hair, ripped jeans, high-heeled boots and a low-cut top under her leather jacket; Joe's sister reminded Marie of one of those trashy but attractive girls from a rock music video.

'Hi,' Tanya said.

Alex went over, smiling broadly, and held out his hand.

'Alex.'

Joe swept the beam of the torch slowly over Alex, from his feet to his head, then back down again.

'Hi, Alex,' he replied, without shaking hands. 'So, you're the alpha male. Introduce me to your friends.'

'Marie and Carina,' Alex said, ignoring the comment.

'Hi, girls.' For a second the torch dazzled Marie, but she didn't have time to shade her eyes before Joe moved on to Carina. He allowed it to linger on her face for quite a while before turning to Bruno.

'And you are?'

'Bruno.'

'Are you in charge of the food?' Joe gestured towards the stack of foil boxes containing leftovers. 'We've ridden a long way today and we're hungry. If you want to try your luck with her, food would be a good start.'

'What?'

Bruno was clearly trying to work out if Joe was joking, but the darkness made it impossible to read his expression.

'And here we have the troubadour.' The beam focused on Simon. 'No, don't stop playing. I mean, it's not a proper camp-fire without "Blowin' in the Wind".'

Marie was about to tell the cocky stranger and his trashy sister to go to hell, but Tanya got there first.

'Pack it in, Joe.' She grabbed the torch and shone it directly in Joe's face, just as he'd done with the others.

'Please forgive my brother – he can be a real arsehole, but deep down he's just a whining brat with low blood sugar.'

Joe held up his hands in an attempt to block the light, then gave up and lowered his arms, laughing. 'Tanya's right – I'm an idiot. A hungry idiot. Sorry if I upset anyone.'

Tanya switched off the torch and turned to Bruno, the glow of the fire illuminating her face. She was heavily made up, with thick black kohl around her eyes, and dark lipstick. The shadows created by the fire intensified the effect.

'If you can spare any food we'd really appreciate it,' she said, gently placing a hand on Bruno's arm.

Bruno cleared his throat. 'No problem.' He moved towards the containers.

'Hang on a minute, Bruno,' Alex said. He turned to their guests. 'You said something about sharing what you've got?'

Joe smiled, reached into his pocket and pulled out a half-full transparent bag. 'Plenty for everyone,' he said with a smile.

Alex slapped him on the back, then took a couple of beers out of the nearest cool bag. He handed one to Joe and one to Tanya, holding on to her can for a couple of seconds so that she had to meet his gaze. Marie glanced over at Carina, expecting her to be annoyed by the overtly flirty gesture, but to her surprise Carina looked as if she couldn't care less.

The two newcomers ate as if they hadn't seen food for days, then washed the whole lot down with several beers while Alex, Bruno, Carina and Marie watched them. Simon was the only one who showed no interest at all; he seemed to be in a world of his own, distractedly strumming away.

When the food was gone, Joe belched loudly. 'Time for dessert,' he said, digging out the bag of weed again, along with cigarette papers and a lighter. He got Alex to hold the torch while he used the lid of one of the foil boxes as a base. His long, slender fingers moved quickly and with practised ease. He rolled three joints as the excitement grew. He lit the first, took a drag, then ceremoniously handed it over to Carina.

'Have you smoked weed before?'

She shook her head.

'Take a deep drag and hold it for as long as you can. When you're satisfied, pass it on to your friend.' He nodded in Marie's direction before lighting the second joint. Once again, he took a long drag, then edged closer to Carina as they both held the smoke in their lungs.

Carina coughed, and giggled in a way Marie didn't like at all.

'My turn,' Alex said, holding out his hand. Instead of passing on the joint, Joe took another long drag and nudged Carina gently with his elbow. 'He's keen – is he always like that?'

Carina giggled again. Marie could see how annoyed Alex was. Carina turned her back on him and gave the joint to Marie, who tried her usual fake drag. She held the smoke in her mouth for a few seconds before exhaling. The weed tasted both sweet and bitter at the same time – nicer than tobacco. She tried again, inhaling more deeply this time and earning an appreciative nod from Joe. There was something about him, something about his eyes. He was clearly smart, maybe even on her level, which would be a nice change. The fact that he'd referred to Alex as the alpha male was evidence of both humour and intelligence. Plus, he was older, more mature. But there was something else too, something both attractive and slightly . . . unpleasant.

'Come on!' Alex groaned. 'Pass it over!'

'There you go – relax!'

Alex snatched the joint, inhaled much too deeply and immediately started coughing violently. Joe laughed and slapped him on the back a few times. Marie tried again, and this time a soft, warm feeling spread slowly through her entire body, washing away any trace of irritation or tension. She closed her eyes, took another drag.

Joe lit the third joint and gave it to Tanya. 'You can share with our troubadour, sis. Guitarists are your thing.'

'Fuck off,' she snapped, but went over to join Simon.

Joe edged even closer to Carina, then made a gesture to Marie that she couldn't quite interpret. After a few seconds she realised she was still holding the joint, and had smoked almost half of it.

9

Autumn 2017

A nna has done her best to settle into her new office. Her computer is sitting on her desk, and several framed diplomas cover the worst patches bleached by the sun on the walls. The penal code, various legal handbooks, her peaked cap and a photograph of Agnes adorn the bookshelf, and she has even managed to source two mismatched visitors' chairs. In spite of her efforts, the room still looks bare and inhospitable, and she can't get rid of the pervasive smell of desolation. With some difficulty she forces open one of the windows to let in the fresh autumn air, then sits down to look through the latest crime statistics and notes on current cases.

She finds it difficult to concentrate. The impressions from the past few days come crowding in. Tabor, Call-me, Klein, the badger, the encounter with Mats. Henry Morell and Jens Friberg, lunch at the Italian restaurant, meeting Fabbe and Bruno, which for some reason makes her feel as if she was being manipulated. Then there's the mural up in the chapel, and the story of Simon Vidje's death. It's hard to believe that only a few days ago, on Friday morning, she and Agnes were sitting in a traffic jam in Stockholm. Her solicitor hasn't called yet, but it's much too early to start worrying. She has followed his advice, and now it's up to him to do his job.

Morell's outline of the district's challenges was largely accurate, but he left out a number of points that interest her. Just as in most communities there is a certain amount of drug dealing and, in recent years, empty houses being used for the cultivation of marijuana have been found. There have also been a couple of noisy protests by the environmental movement, directed at Glarea. She sniffs the air, but can't smell anything today. Presumably the wind that has blown away the fog has done the same with the odour of burning clay.

After about an hour she stands up, grabs her favourite chipped mug with the NYPD emblem and goes in search of coffee. In her previous job, she and her colleagues once counted how many cups a day they drank. She ended up on six, nowhere near the top three in the team. The aroma of dark roasted beans fills the corridor, and as she approaches the kitchen she hears voices. Jens Friberg is sitting at the table with a uniformed female officer – blonde, well-built, in her early thirties. When Anna walks in they immediately stop talking.

'Hi, Jens,' Anna says, thinking it's a nice way of showing him that he's important enough for her to remember his name.

'Hi,' says the female officer, a fraction too loudly. She sounds offended.

'Sorry. Hi. We met yesterday, didn't we?'

'Frida, and no we didn't. It was my day off.' The woman's tone of voice and expression are even sourer now.

'Once again, I'm sorry. There were so many new faces and names in such a short space of time. Nice to meet you, Frida. Anna Vesper.'

Anna holds out her hand, manages not to blush, tries to ignore the looks Jens Friberg is giving her. She turns away and fills her mug. A dull roar suddenly shakes the building and the glasses in the cupboards begin to rattle. She gives a start, spills a little coffee on her trousers.

'What ... w ... w ...' She feels the blockage, the vibration between her teeth and lower lip. She swallows, puts the emphasis on the second word.

'What wa ... as that?'

Jens and Frida look at each other, then at her.

'Glarea,' Friberg says. 'They're blasting. You get used to it after a few months.'

'Right, OK.' Anna realises she has no more to add, and heads back to her office.

'D ... d ... do you th ... think she'll s ... s ... stay long?' Frida says with laughter in her voice. Anna doesn't hear Friberg's reply.

Later that morning there is a knock on her door. It's Henry Morell, and at first, she thinks he's come to invite her to lunch again, but then she sees that he has company – a man about her own age, wearing a fleece top, overalls and a tool belt. His hair has blond streaks, and he has a broad nose, a thick neck and slightly protruding ears, the kind wrestlers often have. He was probably very good-looking once upon a time. He still is, to be fair, even though his hairline has receded and his stubble is peppered with grey.

'This is my son, Alexander,' Morell says. 'His construction company does some maintenance work for us here at the station, so I've asked him to take a look at your windows.' He points to the broken blind.

'Hi, Alexander – Anna Vesper.' He smells faintly of sweat and work clothes, a not entirely unpleasant combination, at least not from a certain type of man. 'I'm taking over from your dad,' she adds, mainly because she can't think of anything else to say.

'I know. Call me Alex – everyone does, except my parents,' he says with a shy smile.

'Anna and her daughter have moved into Tabor,' Morell says in a tone which suggests that Alex probably knows this too.

'Tabor,' Alex murmurs. 'The finest house on the ridge.' He goes over to the window and starts to examine the frame. Takes a screwdriver out of his belt and separates the panes of glass without the slightest difficulty. There's something appealing about the fact that he's so reserved.

'A relative of mine owned the land next to Tabor, before old man Vidje bought it off him,' Morell says, his voice sounding more or less the same as usual – and yet she detects a hint of bitterness. 'The house has recently been done up, I believe.'

ANDERS DE LA MOTTE

Anna nods. Thinks she sees the connection, and turns to the man by the window. 'Oh, that was you, Alex – it's fantastic.'

He looks up in surprise. 'No, no, it wasn't me. Elisabet Vidje didn't want anything to do with me . . .' He glances at his father. Morell's lips have set in a thin line.

Anna has clearly made a big mistake, but doesn't understand why. 'Sorry, I just assumed . . .' She turns to Morell. 'Because you knew so much about the house, and Alex is . . . is . . .' She pauses, takes a deep breath. 'Sorry if I've trodden on someone's toes.'

Morell's expression softens. 'It's fine.' He leans closer, lowers his voice. 'Unfortunately, Elisabet Vidje has a grudge against our family.' He pauses, glances at Alex. Scratches his beard.

'It's an old story. When my relative sold Tabor to the Vidje family, he was allowed to keep the hunting rights up there. It was an agreement between him and Elisabet's father, a kind of compensation for the fact that he sold at a very low price. My cousins and I eventually inherited the rights, and Elisabet was fine with that. Änglaberga has plenty of other hunting grounds.'

He scratches his beard again. 'But one autumn towards the end of the '80s, a cousin of mine happened to shoot a deer that then found its way into the garden at Tabor and lay there injured and screaming. We dealt with it as quickly as we could, but unfortunately Karl-Johan saw the whole thing. He came running out, shouting and crying – he was completely beside himself. We had to ring Bror Klein in the end.' Morell scratches his beard for the third time. His eczema is more noticeable today, angry and red.

'Karl-Johan has always been a sensitive soul – a typical townie who loved painting nature without having the slightest idea of how it actually works. Hunting is hunting, sometimes bad shit happens.' He shakes his head.

'Anyway, for some reason Klein took Elisabet with him, although we asked him not to. By the time they got Karl-Johan into the car, he was shaking like a leaf and completely out of it. I tried to apologise, but Elisabet was having none of it. Instead, she yelled at me in front of the whole hunting team. Used words I'd rather not repeat.'

70

Morell shakes his head again. Out of the corner of her eye Anna sees that Alex has stopped working on the blind. He has his back to them, but he's obviously listening.

'Two days later I received a letter from Elisabet's solicitor. The hunting rights were withdrawn with immediate effect. Since then, Elisabet Vidje and I have never got along, and I'm afraid she's carried the feud on to the next generation.' He gestures towards Alex, who is focusing on the window once more. 'Have you met her, by the way?'

The question is couched as an afterthought, but Anna is convinced that this was the point of the whole story.

'No, only her family solicitor, and Klein.'

'Ah.' Morell nods; he seems relieved. 'There's nothing wrong with Bror Klein. It's thanks to him that Änglaberga is still standing. He took over when Karl-Johan had run the estate into the ground.'

He falls silent, seems to be thinking. He glances at Alex.

'Elisabet Vidje is bound to contact you, Anna,' he says quietly. 'She's going to want to drag up an old story. A tragedy. Her son, Simon . . .'

Before Morell can say any more, the window slams shut. Anna gives a start.

'There you go.' Alex slips the screwdriver into his belt, then closes and opens the blind to show that it's working perfectly. He turns to his father. 'So, what else needs fixing?'

Anna watches father and son as they head along the corridor. Their build and gait are almost identical, seen from behind. Just before they set off down the stairs, Alex looks back at her with a wry smile that immediately makes her feel better. *You like him*, Håkan says without sounding remotely jealous. She tells him to shut up, and goes back to her reports. However, after a while that feeling from yesterday's lunch starts niggling away at her again.

The feeling that something is going on around her, something she still doesn't understand.

10

28 August 1990

Carina took a long, deep drag on the joint just as Joe had taught her. She could feel his eyes on her, noticed that he had moved closer and closer until their bodies were touching. She tried to decide whether she had any objections. Joe was good-looking, there was no denying that. Plus, he was older and a lot more mature than Alex. Smarter too. Alex didn't have a clue that Joe was teasing him, that the 'alpha male' comment was ironic rather than a cool nickname.

To be honest, she would have preferred to skip this whole camping trip – arguing with Alex, sleeping in a damp tent, hearing about how everyone had exciting plans, except for her and poor Bruno. Alex might be openly drooling over Joe's slutty sister, but at least the two newcomers had made the evening a lot more interesting.

They were on their second round of weed by now, and the atmosphere by the fire was much livelier. Marie, who was clearly both drunk and stoned, was singing loudly and distinctly off-key, informing everybody that it was a wild world. Baby, baby.

Simon was playing with his eyes half-closed, opening them only occasionally when Tanya stuck the joint between his lips. His forehead was shiny, his fingers danced over the strings. There was something about him tonight, Carina thought. Something different, a kind of magnetism, which was not a quality she normally associated with Simon Vidje.

Alex was sitting on the other side of Tanya, making a huge effort to attract her attention. This was irritating and predictable in equal measure, yet oddly enough that wasn't what was bothering Carina the most. For some reason she hated the fact that Tanya kept transferring the joint from her own mouth to Simon's, then back again. Gently, slowly, like a kiss being passed on. Why did it bother her? Carina didn't know.

Bruno had been for a pee. He sat down beside Marie and offered her a bottle of water. She looked at him as if he was soft in the head and took a couple of swigs from a can of beer Joe had given her, even though she never usually drank beer.

Carina realised she ought to help Bruno with Marie – get her to slow down, drink some water. However, at the same time it was pretty cool to see super-efficient Marie Andersson looking like a total idiot.

The song ended and Simon decided to take a break. He leaned back against the rock behind him and closed his eyes. Tanya rested her head on his shoulder. The intimate gesture infuriated Carina, and she almost didn't notice Joe sneaking his arm around her. She didn't shrug him off.

'So, boys and girls,' Joe said, putting on an exaggeratedly adult tone of voice. 'You've graduated from high school. You have your whole lives before you. Anything is possible!'

He took a drag on the joint and passed it to Carina. 'So, what do your dream lives look like? What are you going to be when you grow up?' He pointed to Bruno. 'Let's start with you, Mr Catering Manager!'

Bruno glanced at Marie, who seemed to be having problems sitting upright.

'I want my own restaurant,' he said. 'Not my dad's, my own.'

'Ah, a chef. An honourable profession. People will always want to eat.'

Bruno nodded uncertainly, as if he still wasn't sure whether Joe was winding him up or not. Carina knew exactly what was going on, but she was enjoying the thought that she was the only one who understood.

Joe turned to Alex. 'And how about you, Mr Alpha Male? What are you aiming for?'

'An Olympic gold medal,' Alex replied confidently, trying to catch Tanya's eye. 'Wrestling. I'm number two in Sweden in my age group and weight class. Barcelona '92 – I'm planning to be in the top spot on the podium.'

He flashed his biggest smile, flexed both arms and winked at Tanya. Carina shook her head. If the same thing had happened a year or so ago, she would have made a huge scene, but she was tired of all that. Tired of the stupid game between them, constantly veering between arguments, makeup sex, everyday life, then back to arguments without ever passing 'Go'.

'Not bad,' said Joe. 'Your turn, gorgeous.'

'Anything that gets me away from here,' Carina muttered.

'Anything? Really?' Joe's voice was silky soft. He looked as if he was about to say something else, but Marie jumped in.

'Politics!' she announced loudly. 'I want to get invlov . . .' She stopped, considered the letters. 'Involved in politics. Parliament. But first I'm going to study political science at Lund. Simon and I are moving next week . . .'

'Our little troubadour. What do you think will become of him?' Joe wondered.

'A rock musician,' Simon said in a surprisingly firm voice.

'Rock musician? Wow!' Joe's tone was ironic. 'Not a bad dream. The celebrity lifestyle – sex and drugs and rock 'n' roll!'

'Something along those lines.' Simon still had his eyes closed.

'Fuckssake,' Marie slurred. 'Simon's going to the music academy in Malmö. We're going to share an apartment. My dad's helped us find this fantastic place, right in the middle of Lund . . .'

'No.' Simon opened his eyes. He looked perfectly calm.

'What do you mean, no?' Marie was confused.

'No, I'm not moving to Lund.'

'What?'

Carina straightened up, noticed that Bruno and Alex had done exactly the same.

'I'm going on tour with a band,' Simon informed them. 'Their guitarist has dropped out and they need to replace him fast. The tour starts in three weeks, so I'm going to Stockholm on Tuesday.'

There was total silence around the fire, as if everyone was waiting for Simon to burst out laughing and tell them he was only joking.

'Seriously?' Bruno said, when the silence had gone on a fraction too long.

Simon nodded.

'Which band?'

'Talisman.'

'Shit, we heard them on the radio on the way here. How the fuck did that happen?'

Simon shrugged. 'My guitar teacher knows a guy at the record company. He recommended me. I met up with a couple of the band members in Malmö last week and we jammed for a while. They obviously thought I'd fit in.'

Carina's heart was beating fast, and she could feel both joy and excitement spreading through her body. At last, something was happening! At last, someone was doing something unexpected. At the same time, she experienced a pang of jealousy, but quickly pushed it aside.

'But you can't do that, Simon. Where are you going to live?' Marie was on the verge of tears.

'The record company have sorted out a sublet apartment while we're rehearsing. The tour lasts four months – Sweden, Europe, plus a few gigs in Asia. After that, we'll see. I'd prefer to focus on my own music, but this is a good start.'

'But I've ordered furniture for our apartment . . .' Marie's voice broke.

Joe removed his hand from Carina's back and began to applaud.

'Bravo, troubadour! Your plans make everyone else look like a bunch of losers. Rock star – there, my friends, you have a real fucking dream!'

He grinned, slipped his hand behind Carina's back again, a few centimetres lower this time. She didn't object.

'And what have you done that's so damn cool?' Alex snapped. He'd finally realised what Joe was up to.

'Hey, calm down, Mr Alpha Male.' Joe held up his free hand. 'We're on the same page. I'm also insanely jealous of our troubadour.' His other hand found its way to the base of Carina's spine. She pushed him away, stood up on wobbly legs, went over to Simon and gave him a hug.

'Congratulations – that's amazing,' she said. 'Someone's getting away from here at last!'

She sat down next to him; Tanya was still on the other side.

'And when were you planning on telling us all this?' Alex still sounded furious.

'It's only just been confirmed – the record company called me this afternoon.'

'And you didn't say anything?'

'I need to digest it. Besides, I've told you now, haven't I?' Simon was getting irritated. The atmosphere had changed from relaxed to surprised to tense in less than a minute. Carina could feel Joe's eyes on her. For a moment he'd lost control of the joke, been as wrong-footed by Simon's revelation as everyone else, but now he was studying the five friends with a scornful smile on his lips.

'So,' he said. 'It's not that easy to be left on the sidelines when somebody else's dreams come true, is it? Especially when it's one of your closest friends.'

'Shut the fuck up,' Carina said. She realised immediately that she'd walked straight into the trap, been dragged into whatever psychological game Joe was playing.

'Would you play us one of your own songs, Simon?' Tanya asked.

'I'm not sure . . .'

She leaned closer, placed her hand on his arm. 'Please? For me?'

Simon blushed, glanced around then picked up his guitar.

'OK. He ran the plectrum over the strings. 'This is called "Lonely Waters".'

He played a series of melancholy chords in a beautiful descending scale, then began to sing.

'*I saw a friend today, someone I knew long ago. But I still recalled her name . . .*'

His voice drifted away from the fire, returned in a lovely echo from the surrounding rocks.

'*And she told me this, my friend from long ago. And things will never be the same.*'

Simon didn't look any different. The shoulder-length fair hair, the pointed nose, the slender fingers. Carina had heard him sing and play the guitar hundreds of times, just like now, and yet it was as if he had suddenly been transformed, become someone else altogether.

'*I'll see you by the waters. The dark and lonely waters.*'

When he reached the second chorus, Tanya joined in. Her voice was surprisingly deep, and Simon quickly adapted and sang the upper part instead of the melody, making the song even more beautiful. Carina and the others simply sat in silence, listening. Even Joe, although he was trying to maintain his ironic expression. Simon and Tanya's voices blended perfectly, echoing out across the old quarry.

'*The dark and lonely waters.*'

Carina tried to join in the final chorus, but without much success. Her voice was too weak, so feeble that it could hardly be heard. When they stopped singing, there was total silence.

'That was amazing,' Carina said, squeezing Simon's arm.

'Thanks,' he replied, without taking his eyes off Tanya.

Alex spat over the edge of the rock, clearly pissed off.

'Fantastic,' Bruno said. He looked as if he'd like to say more, but one look from Marie silenced him.

Joe got to his feet, stretched exaggeratedly and winked at Carina.

'I'm getting bored now. How about a dip? Or are you kids too scared to swim in the dark?'

11

Autumn 2017

The railway station in Nedanås is a beautiful building from the early 1900s, with tall pillars, a rendered façade and a clock tower right in the centre. Inside Anna can see a small waiting room, the obligatory newspaper kiosk, and a large sign informing her that Espresso House will be opening here very soon.

It is almost five o'clock, and the bus depot in front of the station is full of people on their way home from work or school. Anna parks in the drop-off/pick-up zone, gets out of the car and tries to spot her daughter. The air is thick with exhaust fumes and cigarette smoke. There is no sign of Agnes, so she decides to head for the platform. As she steps onto the pavement, she hears a voice shouting behind her.

'You can't park there!'

A patrol car has pulled up with the window down. Jens Friberg is sitting in the passenger seat, and at the wheel is the snappy, short-haired woman she met in the kitchen earlier.

'Hi, Jens,' Anna says. 'I'm just picking up my daughter.'

'The traffic regulations apply to everyone,' Friberg says. 'And it looked as if you were about to leave the vehicle. If you leave the vehicle, it's parked.'

Anna doesn't say anything for a few seconds; she is trying to work out what's going on. Is this just a bad joke on a new colleague, the kind of thing that used to happen in Stockholm? She can't see any indication of that in Friberg's rigid expression. However, Frida is smiling in a way that is anything but pleasant. There are several empty spaces both behind and in front of Anna's car; she considers pointing this out, but refrains. This discussion is not about traffic regulations at all. Out of the corner of her eye she sees Agnes, chatting to a group of people her own age. Anna feels curiously vulnerable. She takes a deep breath. 'My d . . . daughter is here now,' she says, unable to stop herself from tripping over the second word.

Friberg stares at her, his eyes grey and cold, his face still expressionless.

'Good,' he says, and closes the window.

Agnes isn't particularly talkative in the car. The open, friendly girl Anna glimpsed over the weekend has disappeared; all her attention is on her phone. This would normally irritate Anna, but today it suits her very well. It gives her the chance to calm down and analyse what just happened. The more she thinks about it, the more convinced she is that Friberg followed her from the police station, looking for an opportunity like this. A chance to catch her in the gap between her professional role and her private life, and to challenge her authority. And his annoying female sidekick would definitely make sure that everyone heard about how Friberg had put the new boss in her place. As they begin to climb the ridge, she realises that she herself will have no opportunity to respond.

One: she shouldn't have parked in the drop-off/pick-up zone, and Friberg was only doing his job by pointing this out. In fact, he was demonstrating his professional integrity by not differentiating between a police officer and a member of the public.

Two: she hasn't yet taken over officially. She and Morell are working in parallel for the rest of the week, so if she wants to hit back, send Friberg down to the archive or get him cleaning patrol cars for a few days, she will have to involve Morell, which of course is out of the question.

Three: after Morell's little speech in the car the other day, it is clear that the sympathies of the station are already with Friberg. If she attempts to squash him as soon as she takes command, it might look as if she's punishing him for being her rival for the post.

All she can do is grit her teeth and put up with the situation. Wait for the right moment to repair the gash Friberg has just inflicted on her authority. Hopefully, it will come along very soon. After meeting his gaze through the car window, she is quite certain that what happened was neither a coincidence nor a one-off.

When she sees the sign for Tabor, she decides to let go of work, at least for tonight.

'Who was that you were chatting to?' she asks.

'Nobody. A couple of girls from school. We were on the same train,' Agnes mumbles, eyes fixed on the screen.

'Do they live in Nedanås too?' She knows it's a stupid question, and expects to have her head bitten off. Instead, she gets a neutral 'Mm' in response, which encourages her to try again. 'So, what were you talking about?'

'Nothing special. There's some kind of party in the park on Friday. Caia Bianca is coming, so everyone's really excited.'

'Who?'

Agnes looks up and sighs. 'Seriously, Mum? Caia Bianca. She's a reality TV star, turned blogger, turned businesswoman. She's got her own makeup brand; she often appears as a judge on TV talent shows.' She fiddles with her phone, then shows Anna a picture of a platinum blonde with pouty lips, cheeks that owe a great deal to fillers, and a smooth, shiny forehead – thanks to Botox.

'Oh, her,' Anna says. She still hasn't a clue who Agnes is talking about.

'Apparently, she grew up in Nedanås, but she doesn't seem to come here very often. Like I said, everybody's really excited. They couldn't talk about anything else on the train. Big deal.'

'Right – well, we don't have any plans for Saturday, if you want to go?'

Agnes gives a snort of derision. 'No chance.'

Anna parks right by the door. She can hear Milo barking in the kitchen. He is beside himself, bouncing up and down around

Agnes as soon as the door opens before shooting off into the forest like a small white arrow.

'Milo!' Agnes calls anxiously. She looks as if she's about to go after him.

'Leave him for a while,' Anna says. 'He hasn't eaten since this morning, so he must be hungry. We'll give him ten minutes, and if he's not back by then I'll help you catch him, OK?'

Agnes bites her lower lip the way Håkan used to do, sending a pang of loss through Anna's heart. Sometimes they're so alike it hurts.

Anna's prediction turns out to be correct; within ten minutes Milo is back. He looks as if he's grinning with satisfaction when they open the door; there is a dead rabbit next to him on the step. He is covered in mud, and the two of them give him a bath in the big sink in the utility room. When they've finished, he has a good shake and sprays water all over the place, which makes Agnes burst out laughing. Anna enjoys the sound, the normality of it all.

The feeling lasts almost all the way through dinner. Agnes talks about her new school and class; she doesn't say much, but it's something. However, when darkness has fallen and they are sitting in front of the TV, something happens. Agnes has her iPad on her knee, and Anna is watching the news – yet another report claiming that the healthcare system is on its knees, with pictures from an oncology ward. A row of beds, white curtains, yellow blankets. Anna's stomach contracts, she fumbles for the remote, but it's fallen down between the sofa cushions, and it's almost thirty seconds before she manages to swap the cancer patients for a harmless American sitcom. Much too long, as it turns out. When she glances at Agnes, it's clear that the atmosphere has changed. She searches for something to say, anything to defuse the situation, but it's too late.

'You were there, weren't you, Mum?' Agnes says quietly. 'When Dad died. You were there.'

'Yes,' she replies, without giving herself time to think or compose herself.

'Why wasn't I allowed in?'

ANDERS DE LA MOTTE

Agnes has asked the question before. Never in words, but in looks, gestures, and long, painful silences. And just like before, Anna doesn't have an answer.

Håkan is keen to respond, and she quickly turns up the volume on the TV so she doesn't have to listen to him.

After Agnes has murmured goodnight and closed the bedroom door behind her, Anna goes out onto the top step and picks up the dead rabbit by its hind legs. It's lighter than she expected, and she soon realises why. Its belly gapes open and its innards are missing. At first, she thinks this is somehow down to Milo, and is disgusted at the memory of him licking Agnes's face earlier. However, when she holds the body up to the light, she sees that the belly has been neatly slit from top to bottom, and the animal has been completely gutted. She stands there for a moment trying to work out what this means, but can't find an explanation. Milo must have taken the rabbit from somewhere, maybe over at Änglaberga, but the distance and the time he was away don't make sense.

She carries the rabbit over to the bins by the outbuilding, and after some hesitation chooses the one marked GENERAL WASTE. The wind has got up, the trees are swaying, and as she turns her back on the forest and sets off towards the house, she gets the same feeling she had the other day. She knows why – it's because of Agnes's question, and Håkan's whispering. *Is this far enough? Do you really think they won't find you if they want to? You have to tell her, Anna!*

That night the dream comes back, for the first time in months. The claustrophobic hospital room: Anna in the chair, Håkan in the bed beside her. The air is dry and smells of antiseptic, the light is subdued. Machines hum, tubes and wires are wound around one another like larvae, and somewhere underneath it all there is a frail human body. A body that was once Håkan, and is now in the process of slowly wasting away.

'Please help me, Anna,' he whispers. Raises a skinny hand and points to the machine next to the bed with a gnarled finger that

82

ought to belong to a much older man. It is a square box with buttons at the front, an infusion pump sending morphine into his blood.

The tears come as always, blurring the image of the room. She hears his voice.

'I don't want to die, not like this. Please help me, Anna!'

New scene. An interview room.

Two internal investigators on one side of the table, Anna and her defence lawyer on the other side.

'Did you do it?' one of the investigators asks, and it takes a few seconds before she realises that the man is actually Jens Friberg.

She is woken by a noise. Or at least she thinks she heard something; she is suddenly wide awake, her heart pounding. She lies still, listening hard. The room is pitch dark; she can hear the faint sound of the wind outside. She sits up, checks her phone. Two o'clock in the morning – four hours until her alarm goes off. She needs a wee, and gets up quietly so as not to disturb Agnes and Milo. She pauses outside Agnes's door, but all is peaceful.

She closes the bathroom door, pulls down her pyjama bottoms and sits down on the toilet. Underfloor heating makes the tiles lovely and warm beneath her bare feet. She closes her eyes for a moment, but something makes her open them – a faint creaking from above. She stands up, pulls up her pyjama bottoms. Opens the door a fraction. The creaking comes again, and this time she's sure: it's a floorboard. Someone is up in the chapel. An intruder, a stranger in their house in the middle of the night, only metres away from her daughter. She tiptoes into the hallway, grabs her telescopic baton from the chest of drawers. A sharp swing, and three steel rods lock together. She spins around to face the door leading to the stairs, the baton raised in a defensive gesture. The feeling of the rubber handle against her palm makes the panic gradually subside. She listens again.

The intruder seems to be standing still; maybe he heard the sound of the baton. She holds her breath, then exhales slowly to clear her head. She has two choices. She can wake Agnes and Milo, get them into the car and drive away from the house as quickly as possible, then call the emergency number when they're at a safe distance. She glances out of the window. The full moon is illuminating the entire yard. The car is no more than five metres from the door, but whoever is upstairs will hear them, and be long gone by the time the police arrive. The creaking comes again. It doesn't sound threatening; it's more wary, uncertain. Fleeing from her home in a panic isn't going to earn her any Brownie points at the station. She can already imagine the conversation over coffee – how the boss wimped out, ran like a scared rabbit. The other option is to catch a burglar red-handed during her first week in the job. That's exactly the kind of clichéd kudos she needs, plus it's a lot more appealing to her instincts as a police officer. She grips the baton tightly and thinks for a moment.

The element of surprise is probably still on her side. She is armed, trained, and has experience of close combat. She reaches into the drawer again, slips the small leather case containing handcuffs into her pocket. Then she opens the door very slowly and listens again. She hears a creak, then a faint rustle which seems to come from the side where the mural is.

She places her foot on the first step; the wood is cold. Second step, third. She rests the baton on her shoulder. Fourth step, fifth. She is moving silently. Sixth step, seventh. She pauses, listens. Nothing. Two more steps and she will be able to see into the room. Eighth step. She feels the faint vibration a millisecond before the wood creaks. Shit!

She stops dead, holds her breath. Still not a sound from the chapel. Has she been caught out? If so, she is in the worst possible position. The intruder is somewhere above her, the steep, narrow staircase means she can't use the baton to its full potential, and she risks falling down backwards. Keep going or retreat – she has to decide.

She takes a deep breath and runs up the remaining steps with her left arm raised to defend herself as she swings the baton over her head. But there is no attack. She stands in the chapel trying to locate whoever is in here. The full moon is directly outside the huge window, filling the room with it silvery light. There isn't a sound, or any sign of an intruder. The only possible hiding places are the wide staircase behind the organ, or behind one of the screens Agnes uses for her photography. She checks behind the organ, glances over her shoulder in case someone comes at her from behind. Her heart is throbbing in her ears. Nothing. The staircase is also empty. She edges slowly towards the screens by the mural. Stops halfway, tightens her grip on the baton.

'You might as well come out.' Her voice echoes spookily throughout the big room. Nothing happens. 'I'm a police officer,' she says, a little louder. 'Come out!'

Still nothing.

She moves forward until she can see behind the first screen; the space is empty. Only one place left – the screen in the other corner.

She pauses, listens. All she can hear is her own breathing. Her mouth is as dry as dust, the handle of the baton is sticking to her sweaty palm.

'Come out!' she says again. No response.

She reaches out with her left hand until she can touch the side of the screen. It is light, consisting mainly of aluminium and fabric. She jerks it towards her, backs away and lets go so that she has the space to swing the baton. The screen teeters briefly, then crashes to the floor.

The corner is empty. Anna lowers the baton, lets out a long breath.

Could she have imagined the whole thing? Was the noise she heard just the old house settling down for the night? It's entirely possible, although she's not ready to accept that explanation. But if there was an intruder, where the hell has he gone? She walks down the main staircase, checks the door leading to the yard. Locked and barred on the outside, just as she'd expected. She returns to the chapel. The big window doesn't open. The view is almost as beautiful at night. Far away on the horizon, the sky has a faint, pink shimmer.

There is something different about the chapel, and it takes her a few seconds to work out what it is. A faint smell that doesn't belong here; it grows stronger as she gets closer to the mural, but she can't quite identify it.

The painting looks even more sinister in the moonlight. The autumn colours are more subdued, the sky darker, the rain more gloomy. Just like earlier, the distorted reflections in the surface of the water almost seem to be alive, subtly shifting as she approaches – separating, coming together, separating again, forming new patterns, new shapes. Something that resembles . . .

The moon passes behind a cloud, and for a few seconds the chapel is in semi-darkness. Anna stops dead, not taking her eyes off the painting. She is so focused that she doesn't hear someone coming up the narrow staircase.

Moonlight floods the room once more and she inhales sharply. The reflections in the water have flowed together to form the outline of a young man. His arms are stretched out and his face is turned up to the sky. His skin is pale, his blond hair surrounds his head like a halo. There is something incredibly beautiful about the image, yet at the same time it is deeply tragic, because it is very clear that the young man is dead.

'That must be Simon Vidje,' Agnes says from behind her, almost frightening the life out of her mother.

12

28 August 1990

Carina watched as Simon stood up, propped his guitar against a rock and set off towards the path – going for a pee, no doubt. She waited until no one was looking in her direction, then got up and slowly followed him. She didn't really know why, just that something had happened, something that meant she needed to talk to him. It was dark among the trees, but she'd taken this path many times before. It went all the way to the ruins of the old workmen's huts that had once belonged to the quarry; nobody went there anymore.

'Simon?' she whispered. 'Where are you?'

'Here!'

She heard a noise to her right, and he emerged from the trees zipping up his fly. They stood opposite each other, a little closer than they would have done in daylight, as if the darkness was pushing them together. The proximity gave Carina a little tingle in her belly, which was ridiculous. This was Simon Vidje, whom she'd known since preschool. And yet, in some strange way, it wasn't the same Simon, but a completely different person.

'I was thinking ...' She shuffled uncomfortably. 'It's fantastic news about the tour – congratulations again.' The weed was making her slur her words slightly. They tasted ... burned.

'Thanks.'

'When are you leaving?'

'On Monday.'

'Right.' Carina took a deep breath, hesitated. Her attention was caught by the sound of a branch breaking somewhere in the forest.

'What was that?'

'I've no idea.'

'Do you think there's someone there?'

'Like who? All the others are still by the fire, aren't they?'

'Not them. Someone else . . .' They listened for a few seconds, but all they could hear was their own breathing, and the general hum of conversation from the rest of the group.

'Probably the same killer deer as before,' Simon said with a grin. 'It probably wonders what the fuck we're doing.'

'You think?' She tried to shake off the fear, but without success.

'Absolutely. What's wrong with you, anyway? Has something happened?'

Carina didn't answer. Instead, she chewed at her upper lip, still listening.

'It's silly,' she mumbled. 'I'm just a bit drunk and paranoid.'

'What are you talking about?'

She shook her head.

'Tell me!' Simon took her by the arm. His touch wasn't unpleasant – quite the reverse, in fact. Carina took a deep breath and held it for a few seconds. 'OK, so the week before school finished, Marie and I were on the bus home. We were bored and started talking about our favourite '80s hits.'

Simon laughed. 'Which one of you went for "Never Gonna Give You Up" by Rick Astley?'

'Fuck off.'

'Sorry, sorry. Go on – you were on the bus talking about '80s hits.'

'I happened to mention that I really like "When Doves Cry".'

'Prince – good song!'

'It is!' Carina's face lit up. 'Anyway, we started humming the bit that goes *do do-do. Do do do-do*. After a while it became a thing. We'd be talking about something else, and suddenly one of us would start humming and the other one would join in.

Do do-do – we'd laugh until we nearly wet ourselves. Not very mature, but you know what that last week was like. It was such a relief to be finishing school.'

Simon nodded.

'The next morning—' She broke off. 'Promise you won't laugh.'

'Scout's honour.' Simon saluted with his right hand.

'So . . . no, it sounds really stupid.' Carina could feel her cheeks burning.

'Just tell me.'

'OK, but don't laugh!' She pulled herself together. 'The next morning there was a dead bird on my windowsill. A white dove.'

There was a brief silence, then Simon burst out laughing.

'Fuck's sake, Simon, you promised!' Carina punched him in the chest.

'Sorry, it just sounds so . . .'

'Stupid. Yes, I know. I'm a blonde bimbo.' She folded her arms and turned away.

'I didn't mean it like that. I really am sorry. You're anything but stupid, Carina. You don't think the dove had just crashed into the window?'

'No, because the noise would have woken me up. It wasn't battered at all – it was just lying there. It looked as if was asleep. It was almost beautiful, but in a horrible way. I got the idea that someone had overheard us, followed me home. I've been paranoid ever since.'

'Could it have been a joke? Who else was on the bus?'

Carina thought for a moment. 'Alex's car was being fixed, so he and Bruno were further back. Apart from them it was a load of younger kids – Marie's brother and his classmates. You were there too, but you had your headphones on as usual, so you wouldn't have heard us.'

'In which case Alex is definitely the main suspect,' Simon said. 'You do know what he did after we'd watched *The Godfather* on video?'

'Stuffed horse shit into Bruno's pillowcase. The whole village heard that story.'

Simon gave a wry smile. 'He said it was instead of a horse's head. Bruno didn't speak to him for two weeks. Immature, but pretty cool.'

Carina gazed at him and sighed. 'You could be right. It does sound like one of Alex's ideas.' She tried to sound convinced, but couldn't fool herself. 'Or maybe it's just my bored brain trying to make life more interesting. Sometimes I just feel so tired of everything – do you know what I mean?'

Simon nodded.

They stood in silence for a few seconds, looking at each other in the darkness. Her heart was still pounding, but not only because of fear. There really was something different about Simon tonight. He seemed so mature, so exciting, so . . .

Impulsively she stepped forward, put her arms around his neck and kissed him. Their tongues met, their breath fused into a thrilling taste of saliva, weed and alcohol. Their bodies were pressed together, and she felt him harden immediately.

'Take me with you,' she whispered breathlessly in his ear. 'Take me to Stockholm. We can share an apartment; I've put money aside. Just you and me, Simon.'

She tried to kiss him again, but he suddenly pulled away. He placed his hands on her shoulders and took a deep breath.

'And what about Alex?'

'Alex!' she snorted. 'Alex is a fucking idiot. He'll never get away from here. Olympics or no Olympics, when did you last hear about a wrestler's fantastic luxury lifestyle?' She stumbled over her words, spat out the last two in order to catch up with herself.

She slid Simon's hands down to her waist, pushed herself against him. He was still hard.

'Forget Alex, forget Nedanås, forget all this. We'll go away together, just the two of us.' She made a fresh attempt to kiss him, but he moved his head to the side, which annoyed her even more.

'You know you want to,' she said, grinding her body against his crotch. 'I can feel it.'

Simon took a step back, held up his hands. 'Carina, I just can't—'

He was interrupted by the sound of rapid footsteps, gravel tumbling down the slope. The beam of a torch dazzled them.

'There you are!' Bruno shouted. 'What are you doing? We said we were going swimming – we've set up lamps and stuff. Come on!'

'We're coming.' Simon shaded his eyes against the light and glanced at Carina.

The expression on his face shocked her. It wasn't excitement, or fear that Bruno had caught them. It was something else, something that stabbed her in the belly like a rusty knife. Pity.

Simon fucking Vidje, the stupid little music nerd who'd been panting over her for years, who'd definitely fantasised about her while he was wanking several times a week, felt sorry for her.

How dare he!

13
Autumn 2017

When Anna attended a leadership course at the beginning of the 2000s, her tutor had been a very experienced murder investigator. He often said that the most dangerous thing you could do when conducting an investigation was to make up your mind too early. The second you did that, your brain immediately began to interpret every piece of information from that point of view, to the extent that it would sometimes actually ignore anything that hinted at a different conclusion.

'Hang on to your doubts,' he would say. 'Keep an open mind. That's what differentiates a good investigator from a bad one.'

The mural fits in well with that mantra. If you think it depicts a small dark pool surrounded by trees and steep cliffs, then it does. You can look at it a hundred times and see nothing but reflections in the water. But as soon as you realise there is something else, an outline just beneath the dark surface, it is impossible to look at the picture without seeing the figure.

Anna and Agnes have been talking about the painting, Karl-Jo and Simon Vidje all morning. Agnes has been so captivated that she hasn't even asked about the possibly imaginary intruder, which suits Anna perfectly. She certainly doesn't want Agnes to feel unsafe in her own home, especially not now, when they've finally found a way to get closer. A common interest. They've already decided to make a fresh attempt to find the location of the quarry so that Agnes can take some photographs. The mere thought of the expedition puts Anna in a good mood, in spite of the tragic undertone.

She should start the morning by preparing for her conference call with the commissioner, but instead she fills her coffee mug, closes her office door and clicks on the Wikipedia link Agnes has just sent her from the train.

Karl-Jo was born Karl-Johan Pettersson in Malmö in 1943. Studied at the University of Arts, Crafts and Design in Stockholm, then spent a couple of years in Paris. His early works feature streets, cabs and backlit representations of Sacré Coeur. A promising start, according to many. In 1971, when he was twenty-eight years old, Karl-Jo unexpectedly married twenty-three-year-old Elisabet Vidje in the town hall in Lund. They had met only a few months earlier. Maybe he thought Pettersson was too ordinary, because for some reason the couple took Elisabet's surname. Later that same year, their son Simon was born. There is no date, but marriage and a baby in the same year, combined with the civil ceremony, suggest that the wedding may have been a necessity.

Karl-Jo produced very little during the early '70s. Maybe life as the parent of a small child got in the way, or maybe he just lost his inspiration. Whatever the reason, he started up again in 1975, but his style had changed radically. A hill with a lone tree, the fields and forests of Skåne, always with a melancholy, dreamy air. This new style gave Karl-Jo his big breakthrough, and his paintings were seen everywhere.

When Anna clicks on one of the links to his work, a familiar motif comes up over and over again – the view from Tabor. Morning, afternoon, night. She finds several paintings of small dark pools, but just as Agnes said, none is a match for the mural. The palette doesn't fit either. During the '70s and '80s Karl-Jo used bright, intense colours. His work got better and better, and towards the end of the '80s he began to receive international recognition. He exhibited in Berlin, London and New York, to great critical acclaim. Then, just as Gunnel in the shop had said, everything took a significantly darker turn.

Karl-Jo and Elisabet's only child Simon died in August 1990 in a tragic drowning accident not far from the family's home. In that same year Karl-Jo was diagnosed with retinitis pigmentosa, a genetic eye condition that leads to loss of vision. Although his popularity continued to grow – he was regarded as one of the leading artists of his generation – no new pieces were exhibited during the '90s or 2000s, and it's not clear whether any were even completed. In 2010 a spokesman for the family announced that Karl-Johan Vidje was suffering with Alzheimer's, and had given up painting completely.

A dull rumble makes the windows rattle. Anna still hasn't got used to the blasting over at Glarea. The floor vibrates, as does the coffee in her mug. Tiny rings form on its dark surface.

She finishes work at exactly five o'clock. Agnes has texted to say she's got a lift home, so Anna doesn't need to go via the railway station. She wonders if it's one of the girls from yesterday, or maybe one of their parents? She wrestles with the idea of calling her daughter to check, but the counsellor made it very clear that Agnes needs space, so she reluctantly refrains.

She has searched the police database for Simon Vidje, but as expected she found nothing. The system wasn't computerised back in 1990, so if she wants to read the case file she will have to venture down into the archive. She considers it, but decides there are other, more important matters in need of her attention.

Like the fact that your solicitor still hasn't called, Håkan whispers. *We both know what that means: the internal investigation is still ongoing. It isn't over.*

Running away hasn't done any good at all . . .

In order to shut him up, she goes for a walk around the station making small talk with her colleagues. It doesn't go all that well. She doesn't bump into Jens Friberg or his annoying female sidekick, but it's obvious that word has already spread about yesterday's little incident. The older officers grin openly when she appears, while the younger ones at least have the decency to answer her questions in a politely neutral tone. She needs to come up with some kind of strategy over the next week or so, a way to show them who's in charge.

She is so caught up in the problem on the way home that she almost has an accident. On one of the many hidden bends she meets another vehicle, realises that it has crossed over onto her side of the road. She swerves at the very last second. Her right-hand wheels slip over the edge of the tarmac, sending a clattering warning against the mudflaps before she manages to straighten up. She glances in the mirror and sees the rear lights of a white pickup truck with the Glarea company logo and some kind of telescopic crane on the back, before it disappears around the next bend. The land drops away steeply and is crowded with thick tree trunks on both sides of the road; Anna knows how serious the situation could have been if she'd gone over the edge. She promises herself that she will be much more alert in future.

When she arrives at Tabor, there is another car in her usual parking spot – a Land Rover that must be at least twenty-five years old, maybe more. The green paintwork has been bleached by the sun, and the metal has been patched and repaired in several places. However, this is no old banger. The inside is tidy, the upholstery clean and in good condition. Whoever owns the car seems to care about it.

She goes into the house and hears voices from the kitchen. There is a pair of Wellington boots next to Agnes's shoes; for a moment she thinks they are Klein's, but realises they are too small. The wood-burning stove has been lit, the room is warm and welcoming. Agnes is sitting at the table with a cup of tea. Opposite her is a thin woman in her seventies; she is wearing glasses and a headscarf. Her oilskin jacket is not unlike Klein's, and the similarities don't end there; the woman's facial expression is equally reserved, controlled. The contrast between the older woman and Agnes, with her ripped jeans, pink hair and exaggerated makeup couldn't be greater, and yet they seem to be getting along very well.

'This is Elisabet,' Agnes says. 'She's the one who gave me a lift.'

The woman stands up and holds out a skinny hand with prominent blue veins on the back. 'Elisabet Vidje – I'm your landlady.'

She has a strong accent, like a Skåne nobleman in an old film. 'You have a delightful daughter.'

'Thank you,' Anna replies. 'And thank you for bringing her home.'

'No problem. We bumped into each other at the station, and Tabor is on my way.'

Elisabet sits down, perching on the edge of her chair. She holds the handle of her teacup between her index finger and thumb, as if she would rather not touch things unnecessarily. Her voice is clear.

'Agnes tells me she wants to be a photographer, and that her father encouraged her. I believe your ex-husband is dead?'

'Yes.' Anna is surprised by the other woman's directness, and by the fact that Agnes has already opened up to a stranger. At the same time, she can't help being annoyed; as usual, Håkan is the hero, according to Agnes.

'How did he die?'

'Cancer.' If she says any more, she is bound to stammer.

'My condolences. My father was about the same age when he died – heart attack.' She turns to Agnes. 'He also thought education was important.' She takes a sip of her tea. 'His dream was that my older sister, Ebba, and I would go to the University of Lund. Make something of ourselves.'

'And was that what you wanted?' Agnes asks.

Elisabet tilts her head on one side, and she compresses her lips into a thin line. Anna is about to steer the conversation away from such a personal question, make an apologetic gesture indicating that Agnes is still a little too young to understand social norms, but to her surprise Elisabet speaks first.

'I enjoyed studying,' she says. 'I worked hard in school. Ebba found it more difficult. She wasn't remotely academic, and eventually she married Bengt Andersson instead. She preferred to be looked after. That was just the way she was – she suffered with her nerves, if you know what I mean.' She grimaces. 'I started to study law, but then my father died and I had to take care of my mother, Ebba and the farm. Sometimes things just don't turn out the way you expect, do they?' She takes another sip of her tea. 'You're replacing Henry Morell.'

'Yes – next Monday, technically.'

'Good. I assume he's warned you about me. Dragged up that old hunting story and told you I'm one sandwich short of a picnic. No, you don't need to answer – I know how he operates.' Elisabet raises her free hand.

'Henry Morell and I have known each other since we were young. He's an intelligent man, charming too – when he wants to be. He and my brother-in-law Bengt Andersson have done a lot of positive things for this community, and many people admire them.' Her eyes narrow. 'Let's just say I'm not one of those people, and with good reason. But this isn't about something as simple as an injured deer.' Elisabet looks as if she would like to say more, but then she glances at Agnes and seems to change her mind.

'By the way, I have a little welcome gift for you in the car. Could you fetch it for me, Agnes?'

'No problem.'

As soon as the front door closes behind Agnes, Elisabet goes on: 'I'll get straight to the point. My son died in 1990, as you perhaps already know.'

Anna nods.

'Good, that saves time. The police concluded that his death was an accident, but I don't believe that.'

'Why not?'

'Mainly because although the former chief of police was responsible for the investigation, everyone knows that Henry Morell was really in charge. The thing is . . .' she leans across the table, 'Henry's son was part of the group up in the quarry that night.'

'Alex?'

'So, you've already met him.'

'He was with Henry at the police station yesterday.'

Elisabet compresses her lips again. 'That was no coincidence, I'm sure. Henry's cunning. Has he introduced you to any of the others? Bruno? Marie? Carina Pedersen?'

'Yes . . . well, I've met Bruno, but I've only heard about his wife. Henry invited me to lunch at the Italian restaurant.'

Elisabet leans even closer.

'Simon's death was no accident, Anna. Something else happened that night. Something that Henry, my brother-in-law and maybe also that slippery little restaurant owner Sordi managed to keep quiet.'

The front door opens, and Agnes comes in.

'Henry Morell is manipulating you,' Elisabet whispers. 'He probably started the second he met you. The reason why he's clung onto his job for all these years is to make sure that the truth about what actually happened to Simon never comes out. But I want you to look into it, Anna. Find out what really went on the night my son died. Promise me you'll do that.'

14

28 August 1990

Marie had been waiting impatiently for Simon for several minutes after Bruno came back up the slope, followed by Carina.

'What's wrong?' she asked, because Carina looked furious, but her friend merely shook her head angrily and headed for the tents.

'Time for a dip!' Marie heard Alex yell as he turned up the volume of the boombox. Hard rock again. She hated hard rock.

'I want ttto tttalk ttto you,' she said, grabbing Simon by the arm as soon as he appeared. Her head was full of thick fog, her mouth refused to co-operate fully. Certain letters were . . . chewy, they needed extra help from her tongue to make it past her lips. She realised she was stoned, or drunk, or both, but it didn't matter.

Simon shook off her hand; he was watching Carina.

'Not now, Marie.'

'Yes, right now!' She stood in front of him and poked him in the chest. She was taller than him, and her fingers were strong.

'Ow – pack it in!'

'You pack it in!' She prodded him again, even harder this time. He knocked her hand away. 'What the fuck is wrong with you?'

'What the fuck is wrong with you?' she parroted.

'Stop it, Marie. You're stoned!'

'Yes, I am. For once. Stoned, drunk and furious. How the fuck can you . . .?' She spat, licked her lips. Her anger was beginning to clear the fog inside her head. 'How can you just up and leave? We were supposed to be doing this together. The apartment, Lund . . .'

Simon looked away. 'I told you, it was only confirmed today.'

'But you knew you had other plans.'

He didn't answer.

'For fuck's sake, Simon, we've known each other since we were kids. We're like brother and sister . . .' Her tone slipped from angry into pathetic, but she couldn't help it. 'And yet you said nothing.'

He spread his hands wide.

'I've changed my mind. There's no going back.'

For some reason the words and the nonchalant gesture made Marie even more furious. She'd spent so much time organising everything for the two of them, and so far Simon had done nothing to help. He hadn't even said thank you. And now, just days before they were supposed to be leaving, he'd dumped her. He didn't have the decency to apologise; instead, he was standing there telling her that what was done was done. She was suddenly overwhelmed by an intense desire to puncture that smug 'prodigal child' bubble, stick a pin right through it to make him feel the same pain that she was experiencing.

'And is Aunt Elisabet OK with you taking off for Stockholm?'

'Dad supports my decision,' Simon replied, a little too quickly.

'But not Aunt Elisabet?'

He refused to meet her gaze. 'We haven't told Mum yet.'

'Marie laughed scornfully. 'Because she wants you to study in Lund. Get your degree.'

Simon tried to sound as if he didn't care. 'I'm going anyway, whatever she thinks.'

'As if,' Marie snorted. 'Your mother makes all the decisions. Just look at your dad, sitting in the house painting all day. He wasn't good enough to be a farmer, so your mother and Klein locked him away at Tabor . . .'

'Shut the fuck up.'

'But why? It's true. Everyone knows your dad's not right in the head.'

'At least he doesn't interfere in my life like your father does in yours. And just look at your poor kid brother. Bengt doesn't give a shit about Mats – you're the only one who matters. Daddy's precious little girl . . .'

'You do know that your mother and Klein are having an affair? Screwing each other behind Karl-Johan's back?' Rage and drunkenness made the words fly out of her mouth, and Marie immediately realised she'd gone too far. However, it was too late to backtrack now. What was done was done, just as Simon had said. She raised her chin, met his eyes, but he didn't react as she'd expected. Instead of exploding, he simply shook his head slowly and gave her a condescending smile.

'It's true!' she went on. 'Everyone knows that Aunt Elisabet and Klein set Karl-Johan up at Tabor so they could be alone. They've been together ever since they were young. Karl-Jo was a mistake – you were a mistake!'

Simon stared at her, then shook his head again. This time his expression was one of pity.

'Marie—'

'Hi!' Tanya appeared from nowhere and took Simon by the hand. 'I was wondering where you'd got to. Won't you play a little more?'

Marie glared at her. 'We were having a private conversation,' she snapped.

'No,' Simon said. 'You and I are done, Marie.'

He sounded sad, but not in the way she wanted. Not because he was hurt, not because she'd crashed into his fucking fairy-tale world, but for some other reason. A reason she was too drunk or too stoned to work out. Whatever it was, it made her want to slap him across the face over and over again, wipe off that expression until she was certain, one hundred per cent certain, that he was feeling the same pain as her.

15

Autumn 2017

The staff kitchen is deserted and quiet. The TV is on, but some-one has muted the volume so that the actors in *Emmerdale* are mouthing silently.

'Well, that's just about it,' Morell says as they sit down at the table. 'Anything else you'd like me to explain?'

'No, everything seems perfectly in order.'

'Good. I'd really like to hand over the ship with the flag flying high.' He takes a sip of his coffee.

They've spent most of the day going through everyone's per-sonnel files, and Morell has shown that he has his finger on almost every detail, which has increased Anna's respect for him.

'By the way, my retirement presentation has been postponed for a week,' he goes on. 'The county governor wants to be there, so we menial civil servants have no choice but to fit in with her schedule. However, that means this Friday is free, so Eva-Britt and I were wondering if you and your daughter would like to come to dinner at our place instead?'

'That would be lovely!'

'Good – shall we say six thirty? Casualwear, nothing formal. I'll be the chef for the evening. Alexander and his girls are coming too.'

'Six thirty is fine.'

'Excellent.'

Anna is genuinely pleased, and she is slightly ashamed of her earlier concerns about Henry Morell. Apart from the first few minutes of their acquaintance, he has been nothing but helpful and welcoming, and now he's invited her and Agnes to his home. She's been wondering whether to mention Elisabet Vidje's visit to him. She was tending towards yes anyway, and the invitation has tipped the scales.

'Elisabet Vidje called round yesterday.'

'Did she now.' Morell puts down his cup. 'Let me guess – she wanted to discuss Simon.' He sighs. 'I should probably have warned you, Anna. I was intending to do it the other day, but I didn't want to bring up the old story in front of Alexander. He's already suffered enough over something that happened when he was only nineteen.'

Morell scratches his beard, sighs again.

'I can only guess at what Elisabet said to you, but the investigation proved beyond any doubt that Simon's death was purely accidental. It had rained heavily during the night, visibility was poor, and the rocks up in the quarry were treacherous. Presumably, he went out for a pee, slipped and banged his head, then fell in the water. The sound of the rain hammering on the tents meant that Alexander and the other three, who were sleeping, didn't hear him or notice that he was missing. But as you've realised, Elisabet refuses to accept that conclusion. She's convinced that someone is hiding what really happened, and that I'm part of the coverup.' Another sigh, another bout of scratching. The gesture is familiar, yet there is something about his body language that makes a faint alarm bell start ringing in Anna's head.

'Over the years Elisabet has written to the chief prosecutor, the police commissioner, and the ombudsman. She's done her best to get me transferred away from here. Did she mention Bengt Andersson?'

Anna nods, tries not to give away the fact that she is observing him closely as he continues.

'Of course she did. He's her brother-in-law. They've been at loggerheads ever since Bengt sold off some land from the property old man Vidje had given them. According to Elisabet, as I'm sure she told you, Bengt and I are behind "the great conspiracy".' This time Morell actually draws quotation marks in the air. She didn't think he was the type; it doesn't match the way he usually expresses himself, and increases the volume of the warning bell.

'I'm sorry you've been dragged into all this, Anna. I had a bad feeling when I heard you'd be renting Tabor. Simon's tragic death is Elisabet's lifeblood. On a purely human level, one has to sympathise with her, of course. She and her husband lost their only child, and soon afterwards Karl-Johan became ill. Elisabet is certain there's a connection; she believes that grief made Karl-Johan go blind, and stop painting. What she forgets is that what happened was a tragedy for many others, not just the Vidje family.'

He shakes his head slowly, which makes him look like a sad old bear. Both the words and the body language seem genuine, and yet ... there is a faint dissonance that Anna can't quite put her finger on.

'Simon, Alexander, and Bruno Sordi had been best friends since primary school. They all spent a lot of time at our house, along with the two girls.'

Morell takes another sip of coffee. 'Simon was able to play several instruments from a very young age. A child prodigy, according to his music teacher. One in a million. As he got older he was often asked to perform at weddings and funerals. He played and sang so beautifully it would break your heart.'

Another sad-old-bear shake of the head.

'He'd got a place at the Music Academy in Malmö, although that was just the beginning. Everyone knew he was going to be something great, but then the accident happened. The death of such a young person is obviously tragic, but the fact that it was Simon made it even more shocking. Shortly afterwards the post office and the bank closed down, and the following year the jam factory went the same way. It was as if Simon's death knocked all the stuffing out of Nedanås. Unemployment shot up, people started to move away, and property prices slumped. It took many years for the community to recover, and Bengt Andersson was a big part of that recovery. He was the one who attracted new employers to the area, and brought the inter-urban trains here. He's also made Glarea profitable once more, and we're keeping our fingers crossed for the long-distance trains. If you add in Marie and Bruno's conference centre up on the ridge, you can see that the community is about to enter a new golden age, not unlike the 1960s.'

He puts down the cup and brushes a few imaginary crumbs from the table. His body language is different now, more relaxed. The little discrepancy Anna thought she sensed is gone.

'That's what makes it somehow doubly tragic that Elisabet insists on clinging to the past,' Morell says in conclusion. 'It's as if she's constantly reminding everyone of a difficult time that the rest of us have worked hard to put behind us.'

He empties his cup and puts it down with a little bang.

'So – shall we get back to it?'

Anna would really like to continue the conversation. She knows that four other people were present when Simon died: Alex, Bruno Sordi, Marie Andersson, and another girl whose name Elisabet mentioned yesterday – Catrin? – whom Morell seems less inclined to talk about. She wants to ask why, dig into what it is about his story that doesn't quite fit, but Morell's tone makes it clear that he has finished discussing Simon Vidje's death. Reluctantly she decides to let it go – for the time being.

After work she picks Agnes up at the railway station and drives to the bike shop as agreed. She has promised Agnes a moped, one of many bribes aimed at softening the blow of the move.

The shop turns out to be a large yard on the outskirts of the village, with two converted barns full of bicycles and mopeds. The strong smell of rubber, oil and grease has replaced the odour of animals. Agnes immediately spots a white Vespa very similar to the one Audrey Hepburn rode in *Roman Holiday*. Needless to say, it's one of the most expensive models.

Anna gives in, of course; the money isn't a problem. The house in Äppelviken sold for four times the price she and Håkan originally paid, plus she received a large life insurance payout from the policy he had with the police officers' union.

At least something good came out of all this, Håkan says with a grin. *I bet you were surprised that you were still the beneficiary, even though we were divorced. Then again, you know why. You know it was my way of saying—*

She closes her eyes, rubs her fingers over her ears. The trick works, and Håkan's voice disappears.

A powerfully built bald man with impressive sideburns appears and introduces himself as the owner. He has a large plug of *snus* beneath his top lip. He is open and talkative in the way that some salesmen are, and she lets him chat for a while. Lets him add in a helmet, gloves and a lock that she was intending to buy anyway, then counters by negotiating a reduction of a thousand kronor, plus home delivery and a full tank of petrol, which seems to impress him.

'We can have it ready for the weekend,' he says in a strong local accent. 'Where do you live?'

She gives him the address. He frowns, then the penny drops. 'Oh – you're the police officer who's renting from Elisabet Vidje.'

'Do you know her?'

The man shrugs. 'I used to, but it's many years since I spoke to her. However, I do bump into Bror Klein from time to time. He takes care of most things to do with the estate and the business.'

'And Karl-Johan?'

'The poor guy is in a nursing home in town – has been for many years. He doesn't really know what's going on, or so I've heard.' He clicks his tongue sympathetically. 'But no doubt Bror Klein takes good care of Elisabet.' He winks suggestively, then takes out his receipt book. 'You've got yourself in a bit of a pickle there.'

'What do you mean?'

'You're renting from Elisabet Vidje and working for Morell.'

'I'm not working for Morell – I'm replacing him.' Anna hears the irritation in her voice.

'Of course. But you are aware of the situation?'

'You mean Simon Vidje's accident?'

'Yes. If it was an accident . . .'

'You don't believe it was?'

He shrugs. 'All I know is that twenty-seven years have passed, and people still don't want to talk about it when anyone else is around. That has to mean something.'

'But you don't mind talking?'

The man grins so broadly that the plug of *snus* is visible.

'I'm an old-fashioned pedlar, as you've no doubt realised. People like me can never keep our mouths shut, even when we probably should.' He turns his attention to the receipt book. 'Will you be paying by card, or cash?'

Anna raises her eyebrows. 'Does anyone really pay thirty thousand in cash?'

The plug of *snus* makes another appearance.

'Are you asking in your professional capacity, officer?'

She smiles. 'I'll be paying by card.'

On the way home they stop off at the supermarket, passing the obligatory beggar by the door, who makes Anna feel uncomfortable. She has spotted Call-me-Lasse's Passat in the car park, and they bump into the solicitor by the milk. He is with a boy only a year or so older than Agnes.

'Hi, Anna, good to see you again,' Call-me says; he both looks and sounds as if he means it. 'This is my son, Erik.'

Erik seems nice; he has inherited his father's aura and self-confidence. He holds out his hand and greets them politely.

'Hi, Erik – I'm Anna, and this is Agnes.'

Agnes glares at her, making it clear that she is soooo embarrassing, but Anna doesn't care.

'How are you settling in up at Tabor?' Call-me asks, a little too cheerfully.

'Very well, thank you.' She is about to draw Agnes into the conversation, but notices the way that her daughter and Erik are eyeing each other up, and decides against it.

'And you're finding your way around the village?'

'We are. We've just been to buy a Vespa for Agnes.'

'Oh, so you've met Göran.'

She must look a little confused, because Call-me adds: 'That's the owner's name.'

'Right.' The topic is exhausted; there is an awkward silence. 'Anyway, we'd better—' Anna begins, but she is interrupted by Erik.

'Are you coming to the party?'

'What party?'

'The homecoming party in the park on Saturday.' The question was addressed to both of them, but Erik's attention is fixed on Agnes.

'We hadn't actually planned to . . .' Anna replies.

'Of course you must come.' Call-me's face lights up. 'There'll be people from all over the place, food, drink, dancing – at least for those who don't have two left feet, like me.' He smiles, and just as on the last occasion when they met, there's something about him that means Anna can't help smiling back.

'You're welcome to come with us,' Erik says. Anna glances at Agnes. She knows her daughter is already less than happy about being dragged along to the Morells' tomorrow, and she is just about to decline politely when Agnes surprises her.

'Great – what time shall we meet, and where?'

They actually talk to each other in the car on the way home. They even enjoy speculating on the dress code for a homecoming party in a park in Skåne. Agnes goes for a shirt and jeans, while Anna suggests a fleecy top, which makes her daughter burst out laughing. Anna's heart skips a beat.

Agnes falls silent, looks away as if she's caught herself doing something wrong. Anna wants to tell her it's OK, that it's all right to be happy even when you're grieving. That Håkan would have wanted her to have fun, and that she herself would do almost anything to hear that laugh every single day. As usual, she can't find the right words. Instead, they move on to the mural and Karl-Jo, and after a while she decides to tell Agnes what Morell and Göran in the bike shop had to say about Simon's death. She hesitates, then mentions the fact that the other evening, Elisabet Vidje asked her to take another look at the case.

Agnes is very excited. 'You have to do it!'

Anna shakes her head.

'Why not?'

'Partly because the incident has already been investigated, and partly because any possible crime, except possibly murder, is well beyond the statute of limitations after all these years.'

'But what if it was murder? What if Elisabet is right, and someone killed her son? There could be a murderer out there who's got away with it for twenty-seven years!'

Of course, Anna ought to make it clear that she has far more important things to think about than an old case of accidental death. The only problem is that she still hasn't told Agnes the real reason why they're here. *Internal Affairs suspect that I had something to do with your father's death.* She simply can't tell Agnes, because she wants to avoid the inevitable follow-up question at all costs. *Did you?*

Instead, she keeps the mask in place and once again rejoices that they are talking to each other without her having to be constantly on her guard.

'We'll see. By the way, did you manage to find out where that quarry is?'

Agnes nods. 'I asked a girl on the train; she lives in Mörkaby. She said it's the third turning on the left if you're coming from Änglaberga. There's a narrow logging track with a barrier.'

'Good – maybe we can go there at the weekend?'

It's dark when they reach Tabor, and the outside light is on. They can hear Milo barking an eager welcome in the hallway, and Agnes hurries over to the door. Stops dead a foot or so away.

'Look,' she says, pointing.

There is a dark shape on the top step. A dead rabbit with its belly sliced open. It has been disembowelled.

16

28 August 1990

Alex had helped Joe move his motorbike right by the shore so that the front headlamp shone out across the water, its beam creating ghostly shadows on the rocks as he and Bruno ran down the track in their swimming trunks, towels over their shoulders. Carina was following them, looking distinctly pissed off. Alex knew why, of course. She was no longer the only pretty girl in the group, and she didn't like it.

The night air was cold; it even made Alex shiver. Joe, who had suggested the late swim, was still fully dressed. He was standing at the edge of the water on the flat rock they always called the bathing stone, a joint dangling from the corner of his mouth as he moved his torch around, allowing the light to linger on Carina. Alex still hadn't made up his mind about Joe. Admittedly he'd provided weed and rode a motorbike, which was cool, but Alex couldn't shake off the feeling that the guy was somehow making fun of them. Plus, he didn't like the way Joe looked at Carina. However, at last he had a chance to impress Joe's attractive sister. He'd had his eye on Tanya from the minute she turned up; she reminded him of one of the girls in a Whitesnake video. He ran towards the edge of the rock and somersaulted into the dark water, with Bruno right behind him.

'Come on in, Joe!' Alex shouted. Joe crouched down and put his hand in the water.

'Jesus, that's cold,' he said. He looked up at Marie, who was weaving her way down the track. 'Are you going in?'

Marie nodded, took off her top and jeans and kicked off her shoes, then jumped in wearing only her bra and pants. Carina joined her.

'Give me some light, Joe!' Alex called out as he scrambled out and began to scale the rock face. Joe obliged.

'Come down, Alex! It's too dangerous in the dark!' Carina shouted as she and the other two clambered out and grabbed their towels. Alex continued to climb. He stopped about halfway from the highest point, the spot he'd jumped from earlier in the day.

'Too scared to go any higher?' Joe said, but Alex pretended not to hear. He wanted to impress Tanya, but he wasn't stupid.

'Drum roll!'

He stepped out onto the outcrop and looked over towards the group; as he'd hoped, Tanya had moved to the edge. He waited for a few seconds until he was sure she was watching him.

'Geronimo!' he yelled. He jumped, executing the same dive as before, folding his body in half like a pocketknife. This time he misjudged his entry. The cold took his breath away; it was considerably more painful than in the afternoon.

He surfaced, pushed his hair out of his eyes and looked up expectantly. Tanya had disappeared, and the boombox wasn't playing anymore.

'What the fuck happened to the music?' he bellowed.

'Tanya switched it off,' Joe said dryly. 'I did tell you that guitarists are her thing. Listen!' He held up his index finger. Alex could hear Simon and Tanya's voices coming from the campsite – the same song as before.

'*I'll see you by the waters. The dark and lonely waters.*'

He swore quietly to himself, then swam quickly to the side and heaved himself out of the pool. Carina threw him his towel without meeting his gaze. Marie was shivering, trying to wrap herself in her top. 'It's too cold,' she whimpered. 'Can't we go back to the fire?'

'Come on,' Joe said, sweeping the beam of his torch slowly over Carina for at least the third time. 'One more dip. I haven't been in yet, and nor have those two up there.'

Alex slung his towel over his shoulders. His legs were trembling, and not only because of the chill. 'He's right, this is the last swim of the summer,' he said. 'Everyone has to go in.' He took a few steps towards the camp site. 'Simon! Simon!'

The guitar fell silent and Simon peered over the edge. 'What?'

'Time for a swim.'

Simon pulled a face. 'No thanks.' Tanya appeared beside him, holding a lit joint.

'Come on!' Alex insisted angrily. 'You didn't go in earlier on. The last swim of the summer, OK?'

He turned to the others for support. 'Come on, Simon!' Bruno echoed Alex's words, then Marie joined in too. 'It's a tradition, Simon – you can't let us down!'

Joe pointed the torch at Simon, started a chant.

'Simon, Simon, Simon . . .'

Simon still looked reluctant. Tanya whispered something in his ear, stuck the joint in his mouth. He took a deep drag and they both gazed at each other in a way Alex didn't like at all.

Then Simon's lips curved in a mysterious smile and he set off down the track. He pulled off his top but kept his jeans on. Joe kept the beam of the torch on him, as if he were a rock star heading for the stage. The chant grew louder: 'Simon, Simon, Simon . . .'

Much to Alex's surprise, instead of joining them on the bathing stone, Simon began to climb the rock face. The chant continued, but Alex dropped out when Simon passed the place from which he'd just jumped, and kept going. There was anxiety in their voices now, until Tanya joined in, giving them fresh energy.

'Simon, Simon, Simon . . .'

Simon was still climbing, the beam of the torch tracking him like a spotlight. Foot after foot, until he reached the highest outcrop. Alex suddenly felt sick. The chant bounced off the walls of the quarry, over and over again, until the place was filled with noise.

'Simon, Simon . . .'

Simon moved to the edge and looked down. Joe held the torch steady, illuminating his slim, pale body high above the water.

Alex licked his lips. He ought to say something. Simon had never jumped from that height before, and doing it in the dark when he was drunk could be lethal. He glanced over at Tanya. Her eyes were fixed on Simon, and Alex felt a pang deep inside, an unpleasant iciness that was completely new. It felt a bit like fear, but it was something else. Simon looked hesitant now. He looked around, as if he'd sobered up, grasped where he was, and realised this wasn't a good idea.

Alex knew exactly how that felt, how alone you were up there. Simon was bound to bottle it. The sickness passed and he was overcome by a wave of relief.

'No way he's got the nerve!' he yelled, loud enough for Tanya to hear.

Simon was still hesitating. The chant lost its impetus, but Joe joined in again and got everyone clapping along.

'Simon, Simon, Simon . . .'

Simon took a deep breath, looked at Tanya, then closed his eyes.

Took two rapid steps, leaped straight out into the darkness.

Shit, Alex thought.

Shit shit shit!

17

Autumn 2017

The dream is back again. The claustrophobic hospital room, the smell of the yellow blanket, medication, death. The hum of the infusion pump that delivers relief through Håkan's blood, making the unbearable fractionally less unbearable. A grey box with smooth rubber buttons that only need to be pressed in a certain order for the morphine to flow freely, without any restrictions, lulling him into the final sleep. She can see the sequence in her mind.

Three, three, seven, five, nine, two. Select.

That's all it would take.

'Help me, Anna!'

She suddenly realises that something in the dream has changed. The voice from the bed is not Håkan's. It is not his sunken face on the pillow, but someone else's. A young man with blond hair, surrounding his head like a halo. His eyes are staring up at the ceiling, which is now a lead-grey morning sky. Black water is seeping from beneath the covers, a trickle at first, then gathering force until the floor turns into a dark pool that swallows up the bed. The walls disappear and are replaced by rocks and trees in autumn colours.

'Help me!'

She is standing in the water, close to the edge. It reaches her knees. A couple more steps and she will have to start swimming. Simon Vidje's body is floating out there just beneath the surface, exactly as in the mural, but the water is moving, its shifting nuances making the face change constantly – from a pale young boy to an emaciated man, clinging on to life with the last of his strength.

'Help me, Anna!'

She takes a step towards him. The bottom of the pool is made up of sharp stones. She stumbles and almost loses her balance. The water has reached her waist now; the cold makes her gasp.

'Mum!'

Someone is shouting behind her, and when she turns around she sees Agnes standing on the shore with Milo beside her. The dog has a dead rabbit in his mouth, and Anna already knows that it has been slit open and disembowelled. The trees are swaying gently in the wind, making a faint sound that reminds her of the hum of an infusion pump. 'Sometimes you have to do the right thing,' Agnes says, pointing to the body which is both Håkan's and Simon Vidje's at the same time.

'Promise me you'll do the right thing.'

Three, three, seven, five, nine, two.

Select.

She waits until shortly after five before closing her office door and heading down to the archive in the basement. The entire day has passed, yet the dream still lingers and refuses to give her the peace of mind at work that she had been hoping for.

Morell's office is dark and silent, as is most of the station. She doesn't really need to creep around; she will be in charge from Monday, and already has the right to take an interest in any case. However, she knows that Simon Vidje's death is a sensitive subject, and she doesn't want anyone asking why she's looking into it. Particularly as she doesn't have a good answer, or at least not one that sounds sensible. Is she seriously using something that happened almost thirty years ago to get closer to her own daughter? Is she that desperate?

She has to pass the cloakroom to get to the archive. There is no one around, the radio is off, which means the squeaking of the soles of her shoes sounds even louder. She unconsciously speeds up.

There is no pass card reader on the door of the archive; she has to use the master key that Morell gave her when she arrived. The steel door slams shut behind her with an unnecessarily loud bang. The fluorescent light is motion-activated, and comes on before she has time to start groping for a switch. The windowless room is as dry as dust, and smells of old paper and printing ink. It houses nothing but six double shelving units, very close together. The end of each shelf is labelled with years, and there is a black wheel beneath the labels. The shelf she is searching for is the one almost furthest away, and it is a real effort to turn the wheel and make the shelves move. They reluctantly open up to reveal a narrow passageway lined with blue files.

She works her way along until she reaches 1990. Most of the files contain several different cases. She chooses one at random. Drunk driving, July. Breaking and entering, also July. The type-written documents have gone yellow with age. She moves on to the next file. Domestic abuse, driving without due care and attention, both August 1990. The remaining three cases are of a similar calibre – not what she's looking for. Even before she takes out the next file, she knows it's the right one. According to the information on the spine, it contains only one case. It is lighter than she'd expected.

On the night of 28 August 1990 car 3495 was called to Mörkaby quarry to investigate a death.

Bingo! She carries on reading as her pulse rate increases.

On arrival the body of Simon Vidje was found floating on his back in the water. There were four witnesses in the immediate vicinity of the scene.
   Alexander Morell, Bruno Sordi, Marie Andersson and Carina Pedersen, all nineteen years old and all friends of the deceased.

Carina, not Catrin, that was the name of the fourth person – or fifth, depending on your point of view. She is about to read on when the light goes out and the room is plunged into darkness. The motion sensor is over by the door and she is hidden by the shelves, which means the wretched thing thought the room was empty. She tucks the file under her arm and feels her way along the shelves with her free hand. An unexpected noise makes her stop dead: the squeak of a rubber sole on a vinyl floor. She stays where she is, listening.

A key turns, the door opens and the light comes on, bathing her in a harsh white glow.

'What are you doing here?' Jens Friberg asks.

'Looking for some old cases.' She tries to sound nonchalant. 'Actually, it's a good job you turned up.' She feels a stammer coming, waits, then goes on. 'The light had just gone out and I was trying to find my way to the door.' She gives him her best smile, which has no effect whatsoever.

'Which cases, if you don't mind my asking?' His eyes move to the file under her arm, then to the shelf behind her. The dates are clearly visible. She sees his brain trying to make sense of the details, then his eyes narrow as the penny drops and he realises what she is doing. She presses the file a little tighter to her side and takes a deep breath.

'Thanks for your help, Jens. I'm heading back up to . . .' She nods in the direction of the doorway behind him.

He makes no attempt to move. Instead, he simply stares at her. She meets his gaze, does her best not to show any sign of hesitation. Takes a step forward; the distance between them is now considerably less than comfortable.

'If you'll ex-cuse me,' she says, separating the third word to avoid a stammer.

Friberg remains where he is for a second or two, his eyes locked on hers. Anna feels as if the oxygen in the cramped room is running out. She raises her eyebrows a fraction to indicate that she wonders what he's doing. His eyes dart from side to side, then he clears his throat and moves aside.

'Have . . .' – breathe – 'a nice evening,' she says over her shoulder as she walks out and along the corridor with the file still clamped to her side.

Back in her office she locks the door then flops down in her chair with an enormous sense of relief. Spends a couple of seconds congratulating herself on the way she handled the whole situation with Jens Friberg, then turns her attention to Simon Vidje's case file, which comprises only a handful of documents – seven, to be precise. There is the report itself, written by the police officer who was first on the scene; his name is not familiar to Anna. Then four short interviews with the witnesses, the pathologist's report, and a final note.

It takes her only a few minutes to realise that the contents of the file don't tell her much more than she already knows, but at least it gives her a summary, helping her to put together the scattered pieces she has acquired so far.

Simon Vidje and his four friends are camping in the former quarry at Mörkaby up on the ridge. Alex and Bruno arrive in one car, the girls in another, while Simon, who lives at Änglaberga only about a mile away, comes by bike. Apparently camping out overnight is a tradition, something they've done many times before, which means they are all very familiar with the area. They build a fire, talk, eat, drink alcohol, and eventually retire to their three tents. Alex and Bruno are sharing, as are Marie and Carina, while Simon is on his own. During the night it begins to rain, and just as Morell said, the rocks become slippery, and the rain hammering on the tents drowns out any other sounds. Early the next morning Simon is found dead, floating on his back in the pool.

The autopsy report shows several crush injuries to his body, all consistent with a fall. The most serious is a wound to the back of his head, which according to the pathologist almost certainly killed Simon instantly. This conclusion is backed up by the fact that his lungs didn't contain any water, which means that Simon had already stopped breathing when he ended up in the pool. The pathologist also states that the cold water has made it difficult to establish the time of death; his estimate is between 01.00 and 03.00 on the morning of 29 August.

Anna does find some new information. There were two other people at the quarry earlier in the evening: a man called Joe and a woman called Tanya, both a few years older than the five friends, and not local. They joined in the party for a couple of hours, but according to all the witness statements they left on their motorbike at about eleven thirty, when the rain started. Their full names and identity numbers are given on a separate sheet of paper at the back of the file. There is also a note stating that shortly after one, Joe was involved in an altercation at a petrol station in Reftinge, thirty miles away, which resulted in him spending the rest of the night in police custody. This means he couldn't possibly have been at the quarry at the time of Simon's death. The four witness statements are very short, and virtually identical. It started raining, Joe and Tanya left, the others went to bed at about half past midnight. They all claim to have slept deeply, and neither heard nor saw anything during the night.

Marie Andersson was the one who found the body at about five o'clock, and she immediately shouted to the others. They tried to get Simon out of the water, but without success. Bruno drove Marie's car to the grocery store in Mörkaby and used Gunnel's phone to call for help. The first police car arrived at 05.54, followed shortly afterwards by the fire service and an ambulance.

She closes the file and leans back in her chair. Exactly as Henry Morell said; there doesn't seem to be anything suspicious here. Rain, darkness and treacherous rocks, perhaps combined with too much alcohol – a perfectly natural, if tragic, explanation for Simon Vidje's death.

For some reason, this conclusion leaves her feeling a little disappointed.

18

28 August 1990

Bubbles. All around him. Tiny silver spheres surging out of his clothes, hair, nose and mouth before disappearing into the darkness. The sound of his body entering the water is still ringing in Simon's ears, vibrating through every fibre of his being. The cold pressed against his skin made his blood vessels and lungs contract and his heart pound. And yet he didn't move, he simply hung there, still and weightless. Closed his eyes and allowed himself to be embraced by the darkness.

Is his how it feels to die? he thought as he gradually began to see patches of white behind his eyelids.

Then he opened his eyes, kicked out with his legs. Once, twice, three times, began to use his arms. Shot up towards the faint light above until his head broke the surface of the water. He'd done it!

Simon gasped for air, then let out a yell of pure joy. Tanya immediately responded, followed less enthusiastically by the others.

Bruno helped him out, before being pushed aside by Marie. 'What is wrong with you?' she shouted in his face. 'You could have killed yourself!'

'You were the ones who wanted me to swim,' Simon said with a broad grin. 'The last dip of the year – isn't that what you said?' This was directed at Alex, who was standing a short distance away with his arms folded. It was one of their standard jokes, but Simon regretted it as soon as he'd closed his mouth.

When Alex didn't respond, Joe shone the torch right in his face. 'Looks as if someone's braver than you, Mr Alpha Male!'

'Fuck off!' Alex raised his hand to avoid being dazzled, and turned away.

Tanya came running down the track, pushed in between Bruno and Marie, and immediately made Simon forget about Alex's bad mood.

'You did it! How fucking cool was that!'

She flung her arms around his neck and kissed him. She tasted sweet, of weed and something else, something exciting that made Simon pull her close. This was his second kiss in ten minutes, and coupled with the adrenaline kick from the jump, he felt as if his head was about to explode.

There was a brief embarrassing silence as the others looked away – except for Joe, who moved the spotlight onto the couple as they kissed with increasing intensity, as if he was encouraging everyone else to watch.

'Congratulations to Simon, this evening's winner,' Joe said in a voice dripping with irony. 'Many thanks to all those of you who took part, and goodnight!'

Tanya removed one hand from Simon's neck and gave Joe the finger, then finished off the kiss.

'Let's get you out of those wet clothes,' she said to Simon, taking him by the hand and heading up the track. Simon felt as if his face was frozen in a huge grin.

'I'm so cold,' he heard Marie say just before they left. She sounded pathetic.

Tanya led him past the tents, beyond the plateau. She began to giggle, then burst out laughing. Simon couldn't help joining in. His jeans were sodden and cold, plastered to his legs. Tanya kept going, on into the forest. They stumbled over the uneven ground, and once she almost fell over head first, but luckily he caught her. Neither of them could stop laughing – not until they reached a big oak tree. She stopped and threw her arms around him and kissed him again. His hands found a life of their own, exploring her body.

They pressed close together, then somehow they'd taken off their jeans. Tanya's legs were wrapped around his waist, her back was against the tree. He felt her take hold of him and guide him into a soft warmth that embraced him in the same way as the darkness in the water. She dug her nails into the back of his neck and thrust her hips against his. She gave a loud moan, then made him join her in an increasingly frantic rhythm until the whole world – or maybe it was just his head? – dissolved into a cascade of atoms.

19

Autumn 2017

The Morell family home is a single-storey house with a base-ment, probably built in the late 1960s. The garden is incredibly neat, with barely a fallen leaf to be seen on the lawns, in the flow-erbeds or among the various figures dotted around. Anna counts three gnomes, two statues and an entire family of deer at the front of the house. A large dark blue BMW is parked outside the gate, and for a moment she wonders if it's Morell's private vehicle. Then she sees the Glarea sticker in the back window and guesses that it probably isn't.

Agnes isn't happy about being dragged along, but at least she hasn't kicked off or slammed any doors. The fragile truce engendered by the story of Simon Vidje seems to be holding.

Morell's wife, Eva-Britt, turns out to be an elegant, pleasant woman in her mid-sixties, with a sense of humour and a mind of her own. She hugs them both as if they are already friends, and in no time wins Agnes over by offering her the same drink as everyone else.

'Henry always makes them too weak,' Eva-Britt whispers as she shows them into the living room.

The smell reminds Anna of her maternal grandparents' house – an unmistakable hint of mustiness that gets into your clothes and accompanies you home. The living room is cool, as if the central heating has only just been switched on. Henry Morell is there, along with two other people.

'My apologies, Anna, but Bengt and Marie have just got back from Stockholm, and they really wanted to meet you,' Morell says, nodding to the unexpected guests.

The man holds out his hand. 'Bengt Andersson. Welcome to Nedanås, Anna.'

She had imagined him as a typical short fat Skåne civil servant with a combover, but in fact he is tall and skinny, like a long-distance runner. His hair is receding, but instead of fighting the inevitable he has shaved it off. The eyes behind the designer glasses are alert, and his suit is anything but cheap.

'Thank you,' she says, not quite sure how to continue.

The woman sitting next to Bengt solves the problem for her.

'Marie Sordi,' she says, warmly squeezing Anna's hand. 'We're really looking forward to working with you, Anna. You're such a role model – woman, boss, mother, police officer!'

Marie is almost as tall as her father, and has the same elongated equine face. The glasses and dark trouser suit she is wearing merely serve to reinforce the impression. Her hair is presumably naturally curly, just like her younger brother Mats's tousled mop, but it is kept in check by a short, fashionable cut.

'I met Bruno at the restaurant,' Anna says. 'Your husband is an excellent chef.'

'That's good to hear,' Marie replies. 'Just wait until he has free rein and doesn't have to stick to his father's boring old menus!'

'Oh, I don't know,' Bengt says with a smile. 'Sometimes it can be good to lean on the experience of the older generation, wouldn't you say?' At first Anna thought the comment was aimed at Marie, but when Bengt winks and jerks his head in the direction of Henry Morell, she realises he's speaking to her.

'Henry's been a great help,' she murmurs, eliciting a satisfied smile from Morell. She's about to say more, then she recalls the meeting at the restaurant, and Alex Morell's arrival in her office. The feeling is the same. This apparently accidental encounter has been arranged. Marie is the third of the four surviving friends from the quarry she has met within just a few days. She can't help hearing Elisabet Vidje's voice.

Henry Morell is manipulating you!

'So, you've been in Stockholm?' she ventures in an effort to get her brain to change tack. Marie nods.

'We had a meeting with the party and one or two others. Is it OK if I tell her, Dad?'

Bengt Andersson nods and smiles.

'It's not yet official, but the infrastructure minister has approved the new railway initiative for southern Sweden,' Marie says, sounding delighted. 'Towards the end of next year, the long-distance trains will stop at Nedanås. We've also signed a declaration of intent with one of the big e-commerce companies; they're planning to build a logistics centre, hopefully with the help of state development funding. That will bring lots of new jobs, and fresh opportunities for the community.'

'Congratulations,' Anna says. 'That's excellent news.'

'The information minister and I used to be on the same committee,' Marie informs her. 'It's always good to have contacts.'

'Marie was in parliament for a while,' her father chips in. 'But it was hard to make it work with the family.' His tone is conciliatory; an almost imperceptible, involuntary micro-expression is the only thing that betrays his underlying disappointment. Anna is aware of it, and she's pretty sure that Marie is too.

'We also had a few words with Stockholm's police commissioner,' Marie goes on. 'She spoke very highly of you, Anna. She said you'd be a great asset both to the Skåne police and the community, and that they'd miss you in the city.'

Anna's stomach turns to ice. Is Marie hinting at something? Does she know about Håkan, about the investigation? Marie sips her drink, which makes it hard to read her face. Anna glances at Bengt, but sees nothing to confirm her fears.

'That's nice,' she says, but the feeling of unease lingers.

After chatting for a few more minutes and insisting that she must come to the next Rotary breakfast, Bengt and Marie take their leave.

Eva-Britt has been entertaining Agnes in the meantime, and the two of them seem to be getting along very well.

'Agnes has promised to give Henry a few tips. He had a fantastic camera for his sixty-fifth birthday, but in the two years since I haven't seen a single photograph.'

'There's something wrong with it,' Morell mutters as he gathers up the glasses. 'Everything comes out blurred.'

'Have you tried setting it to autofocus?' Agnes suggests.

'I think so. Excuse me, I'll just go and call Alexander.'

'I'm pretty sure he hasn't even read the handbook,' Eva-Britt says quietly when he's gone. 'He's a bit embarrassed now, but I'm sure he'd love a lesson from the expert after dinner.' She gives Agnes a conspiratorial wink.

Alex and his two daughters join them. The eleven-year-old is open and curious, asking Agnes why she's coloured her hair, and whether it hurts to have so many ear piercings. Agnes answers warmly and patiently. The fourteen-year-old peers out from beneath her fringe; she seems to find the whole thing embarrassing. However, after a while the three of them end up on the sofa with their heads close together, watching a video on Agnes's phone.

Alex is more relaxed than he was at the police station. He smells of Kouros, and is wearing dark blue 501s and a red Lacoste polo shirt that shows off his muscular upper arms. His short hair is still damp, and a tiny piece of red toilet paper just above his collar suggests that he shaved in a hurry. The ear that sticks out has one of those blisters at the top that wrestlers get, and Anna can't help finding it quite attractive.

She is seated next to Alex at dinner, and Eva-Britt steers them skilfully through the obligatory small talk. They get through both the weather and the seasons before the starter is cleared away. Morell serves fillet of beef with a potato gratin for the main course, with a special vegan dish for Agnes. The atmosphere is warm and friendly, the conversation flows, and Morell is so generous with the wine that Anna has to point out more than once that she's driving home, which doesn't stop him from topping up her glass.

Alex is a charming companion. He is amusing and has an infectious laugh; she found him quiet and reserved at the police station the other day, but revises her opinion of him this evening. Maybe it's the wine, but both she and Agnes are really enjoying themselves.

Morell turns out to be a keen gardener, and towards the end of his third plant-related anecdote, Alex catches Anna's eye and raises an eyebrow, which makes her like him even more.

'You look as if you work out, Alex,' she says.

'As often as I can – maybe three or four times in the weeks when I don't have the girls.' He unconsciously rubs his bare ring finger, and at the same time Anna realises that she is fiddling with her hair. What the hell is wrong with her? Is she seriously sitting here flirting with her predecessor's recently divorced son, in her first week in her new home town? She lowers her hand, straightens her shoulders, decides not to drink another drop of wine, however insistent Morell might be.

'Alexander was a very promising wrestler,' Morell says. 'He almost made the Olympic team.'

'Wow,' she says. 'Which year?'

'Barcelona 1992. I injured my knee just before the final selection process, so there were no more chances.' Alex shrugs. 'Plus, I'd got into the building trade, found myself a decent job, which was probably just as well. I mean, when did you last hear about a wrestler's fantastic luxury lifestyle?'

The words sound awkward, as if they're someone else's, and his smile doesn't quite reach his eyes. *1992 – two years after Simon Vidje's death*, Anna thinks to herself.

Just as Eva-Britt had predicted, Morell brings out his camera when coffee has been served. It looks like the same top-of-the-range model as Agnes's, and Anna tentatively asks who gave him such an expensive birthday present. The answer turns out to be Bengt Andersson. He and Henry seem to be close friends, just as Elisabet Vidje said.

Agnes sits down beside Morell on the sofa, and with practised ease she goes through the different settings and finer points of the camera. Anna takes the opportunity to pop to the bathroom. It's occupied, but Eva-Britt directs her to the basement.

'It's on the left, through the curtain,' she says.

At the bottom of the stairs is a pine-clad hobby room. Two leather sofas with a patina acquired over several decades, a glass coffee table with a matching drinks trolley, and of course the essential slightly-too-large flatscreen TV on the wall. She follows Eva-Britt's directions, pulls aside a bead curtain and finds herself in a narrow hallway. There is a faint smell of mould, combined with disinfectant. The bathroom is the first door on the right. The walls are tiled from floor to ceiling in green, and there is a shower cubicle in one corner. She can just see a bottle of blue shower gel through the glass, which is still wet. The cabinet contains foot cream, a pack of out-of-date ibu-profen, an open packet of disposable razors, and a can of cheap shaving foam. She is slightly embarrassed by her nosiness, but tells herself that it's one of the qualities that makes her a good police officer. That and the ability to remain sceptical, and yet she is becoming increasingly convinced that Elisabet Vidje has a point: Morell, possibly with the help of his good friend Bengt Andersson, is trying to steer her in a certain direction. Get her to accept their version of Simon's death as the truth. There could be many reasons for this. The wounds from the tragedy have clearly not fully healed, and maybe Morell doesn't want them opened up again, either for the good of the community or the four survivors. At the same time, Anna can't ignore Elisabet's criticism of the investigation, and her suspicions that Morell has clung to his job for all these years to make sure that the truth about what really happened to Simon never comes out.

She is about to go back upstairs via the hobby room when she sees that the door opposite the bathroom is slightly ajar. By the light from the hallway she catches a glimpse of something that could be a display cabinet, and she can't resist taking a peek. The room is spacious, and has stained-glass windows just below the ceiling. She is able to make out a dozen or so cardboard boxes piled on top of one another. Beyond them is a desk with a stereo system that must be at least thirty years old, including a record player and double cassette deck. Right at the back she sees a messily made bed. The air smells of fitted carpet and Kouros, which immediately transports her back to a peer-group party towards the end of high school. Fumbling hands, the taste of Hubba Bubba bubblegum, 'Take My Breath Away' on the record player.

She is sure of two things before she switches on the light. One: this was Alex Morell's room when he was a boy, and two: he is living here now.

The display cabinet is crammed with medals, plaques and cups, mostly for wrestling, although there are a few from various school championships in different sports from the mid-'80s. Beside the cabinet there is a display of pictures – young men in wrestling gear and hockey strips. Alexander is in every one; he was very good-looking back then. He is almost always smiling, gazing confidently into the camera – except for the last photograph, in which he seems distracted, not really present. Anna looks at the date: 1991. The year after Simon's death. The year before he injured himself and missed out on the Olympics.

The box of LPs beneath the stereo contains nothing but '80s rock – Bon Jovi, Europe, Bryan Adams, Iron Maiden, AC/DC.

In one corner of the room she finds a framed collage of images – young men and women dressed in white, with their student caps. Signs proclaiming HIGH SCHOOL GRADUATION 1990, enlarged baby pictures, miniature champagne bottles, garlands of flowers. Dazzling, perfect smiles, sparkling eyes. Even though the occasion was almost thirty years ago, she can almost hear them singing the traditional songs at the tops of their voices.

One of the pictures is slightly bigger than the others: Alexander Morell in a dinner jacket, with his arm around the waist of a curvaceous woman in a low-cut dress, with curly blonde hair. Anna assumes it was taken at the graduation ball, and guesses that the woman is Alex's girlfriend – maybe even the mother of his two girls?

In the bottom right-hand corner there is a group photo: three boys and two girls, all in their white student clothes and peaked caps, arms around one another, seemingly roaring at the camera.

FRIENDS FOREVER, it says in one of those stuck-on speech bubbles that was popular at the time.

Anna immediately recognises Alex and his blonde companion; the shorter boy beside him must be Bruno Sordi. A tall girl with curly hair and an elongated face is on the other side of Bruno. There is no mistaking Marie Andersson, now Sordi, though she isn't wearing glasses, and looks considerably more cheerful than she does nowadays. On the far left is a young man with shoulder-length fair hair. He is pale, his skin seems almost transparent, but his eyes are bright and lively, and he looks happy. This must be Simon Vidje.

'There you are!'

Alex is in the doorway with a drink in each hand. His tone and expression are largely amused, but there is the tiniest frown between his eyebrows.

'I saw the display . . .' she pauses to avoid the stammer, 'cabinet from the hallway. Impressive!'

He relaxes, hands her a glass.

'I must have told Mum and Dad a hundred times to put everything away and convert this place into a guest room. I think Mum likes the idea, but Dad refuses. He wants everything to stay exactly the same as it's always been. Time travel straight back into the '80s . . .'

'And you've moved back in?' She nods towards the cardboard boxes.

He blushes, which she finds quite sweet. 'Joss is staying in the house – we thought that was best for the girls. They're happy there – they've got a pool, a basketball court, the lot.'

His face contorts for a brief moment, suggesting that the divorce wasn't entirely straightforward.

'I'm in the middle of building four houses on Smedjevången – one is for me. But the project is delayed, so I've touched down here, so to speak.' He makes an apologetic gesture; his cheeks are still slightly flushed.

'Here's to touching down!' Anna says, raising her glass. 'And the '80s.' After a couple of seconds he manages a wry smile in response.

'And to Mum and Dad's basement,' he adds.

'I noticed your high school graduation photos,' she says. 'The boy you were compared to the man you've become.'

'What does that mean?'

'Nothing in particular – it's just something I read somewhere.'

'I see.' His smile is a little uncertain this time. 'So, what were you like when you were nineteen?'

Anna laughs. 'Unbearable, I should think – weren't we all at that age?'

He counters with another question.

'Did it turn out the way you expected?'

'What?'

'Life, everything. Did it turn out the way you thought it would when you were young?'

'Yes and no.'

The topic bothers her, so she points to the photo from the ball.

'Is that your ex-wife?'

'No, that's Carina Pedersen. We were together from junior school ... everyone thought we'd get married. But it ended after ...' The pause is brief, but audible. And telling. 'A few years.' That's not what he means.

She ought to have worked it out for herself. Carina Pedersen, the fifth person from the quarry. Five friends in the photo, the same five people who were there that night. She blames the wine.

Alex smiles again, and she feels a little tingle in her tummy, a faint vibration that finds its way south. She gives herself a mental shake and tries to think of how she can exploit the tension between them to move on to the subject of Simon Vidje. She is too slow.

'I wanted to ask you something, Anna.'

'Go on.'

'There's a homecoming party in the park tomorrow. A talent show, a funfair, market stalls – and probably a bouncy castle, if you're in the mood.' She can't help smiling back at him. 'In the evening there's a dinner and dance – I wondered if you'd like to go with me?'

She's about to say that she'd love to, then she suddenly remembers she's promised to go with Call-me. Alex misinterprets her silence.

'It's fine if you don't want to . . .' He sounds embarrassed.

'No, it's not that. I'd love to go with you, but I've already agreed to go with someone else. Call . . .' She pauses, tries to remember what the solicitor is actually called. 'Lasse Gunnarsson. His son and Agnes know each other.' That's not strictly true; a white lie to save Alex's pride. 'But I hope to see you there.'

He nods, finishes off his drink. There's something about Alex Morell that she can't quite work out. One minute he's flirting, full of fun and self-confidence; the next he's quiet and unsure of himself. It could be down to the divorce, of course. Men find it much more difficult than women to handle separation, and moving back into Mummy and Daddy's basement at the age of forty-five isn't exactly an ego boost. And yet she doesn't think that's the full explanation.

She glances at the photograph of the five friends with their arms around one another in that frozen moment almost thirty years ago.

Friends forever.

20

28 August 1990

When Simon and Tanya had disappeared, the others remained standing on the path. Carina looked at Bruno, Alex and Marie; their expressions were wary, almost doubtful, as if they couldn't quite believe that what they'd seen had actually happened. This was a moment they would return to for the rest of their lives. It would become another of the magical tales surrounding the quarry – Simon Vidje once jumped from the highest cliff in the middle of the night.

A legend indeed – and yet the atmosphere was subdued.

'This is all your fault!' Carina snapped at Alex. His only response was a shrug.

'I'm freezing,' Marie whined.

Joe switched off the torch.

'OK, kids – what now?'

Nobody answered him. Without warning, Marie turned and threw up into the dark water.

They made their way back up to the tents. There was no sign of Simon and Tanya, but no one mentioned it. Bruno piled more logs on the fire before everyone except Joe crawled into their tents to take off their wet clothes. The flames sent a shower of sparks up into the sky, where the clouds had now almost completely obscured the stars. Carina was out first. She put the mix tape back in the boombox, pressed play, then sat down on a rock by the fire next to Joe. The music lightened the weird atmosphere a little. She was still angry with Simon – even angrier now, to be honest.

Alex had been showing off to Joe's sister all evening, which was to be expected, but the fact that Simon had chosen that trailer-trash slut over her was considerably more painful. Her fury at his rejection had grown into a burning lump behind her breastbone.

'Have you got a cigarette?' she asked Joe.

'Sure.' He handed her one and lit it for her between his cupped hands, then rummaged in the cool bag and opened a can of beer for each of them.

'Are you at college?' Carina asked. 'You and your sister?'

'College!' Joe snorted with laughter.

'So, what do you do, then?'

'Me and Tanya do whatever we feel like.' He took a deep drag, blew the smoke out through his nose.

'Where do you live?'

'So many questions,' he said with a grin. 'Why, do you want us to move in together? We've only just met!' He took another drag. 'I have a kind of cabin at my stepfather's place, but we can usually find somewhere to live. Tanya's good at getting us invited to stay with people. There are plenty of parties in the summer.'

'Your stepfather? Not Tanya's?'

Joe raised the can of beer to his lips without answering, shuffled closer so that their arms were touching. Carina could feel his eyes roaming over her body.

'So, what are you going to do when the summer's over? Seriously.'

Joe looked as if she'd said something amusing.

'You're all the same,' he said, shaking his head. 'Little kids who think you're so fucking unique. You can't imagine that anyone has ever felt or thought the way you do, but you're nothing more than extras in your own self-obsessed show. Your dreams are so childish.'

He drew a circle in the air with the glowing end of his cigarette. 'Look at you. In thirty years the five of you will be at some pathetic class reunion talking about how simple everything was when you were young, wishing you could do it all again, but really enjoy it this time round.'

One final drag, then he flicked the butt into the fire.

'Me and Tanya, we do whatever we want. Unlike you, we'll never get old enough to have regrets.'

He grinned, and once again Carina found it difficult to work out whether he was serious, or simply teasing her. She thought probably the latter. It was nowhere near as much fun being on this end of the joke.

The others gradually emerged from the tents. Marie's eyes were red-rimmed, and she firmly refused when Joe offered her a beer. Alex opened a can and knocked back the entire contents in one, finishing off with a loud belch that made Carina turn her back on him in disgust.

As usual, Bruno looked vaguely unsure of himself. He put another log on the fire and sat down next to Marie, who was leaning forward with her head resting on her knees.

'Are you OK? Can I get you anything? Some water maybe?'

Marie shook her head. Nobody spoke for a while; they stared into the flames as Madonna played in the background.

'Jesus, this party's lost its sparkle,' Joe said, nudging Carina with his elbow, then gesturing towards Alex with his can of beer. 'Look at the alpha male. His whole world has been turned upside down. Pushed off his throne by a skinny little musician.'

'Shut the fuck up.' Alex turned away and spat into the darkness.

'And the lovesick cook over there looks confused more than anything,' Joe went on, pointing to Bruno. 'Don't worry, kids, Uncle Joe will explain what's happened. Your friend Simon, the sweet little troubadour, has grown away from you. And just a little while ago, he realised that himself. Realised that he's too gifted, too attractive and too smart for this dump, and to hang out with losers like you.'

Silence fell once more, an unpleasant, oppressive silence that somehow drowned out the music. The burning lump in Carina's chest kept on growing. She really wanted to tell Joe to shut up and remove his hand from the base of her spine. Tell him to get on his fucking motorbike and go to hell. But she didn't do it. She was somehow paralysed by the whole situation, and the others seemed to be in the same boat. Joe's words slithered around her brain, a snake of letters and syllables, taboo yet at the same time so very true.

Simon had always been the outsider in their group. He ought to be grateful that they'd let him hang out with them all these years, grateful that they'd put up with him always showing up late and playing crap music. It also annoyed her that people's voices softened when they talked about Simon fucking Vidje – unlike her own family – as if he was so special just because he could play and sing.

Marie suddenly stood up and pointed at the others. She looked at each of them in turn, but seemed to be having some difficulty in focusing.

'Pissed,' she slurred. 'He's pissed on all of us . . .' She swayed, looked as if she had more to say, but instead she ran between the tents and threw up again. Bruno followed her. 'Black Velvet' came on the tape player – one of Carina's favourites. Without really knowing why, she got to her feet, turned up the music and began to dance, closing her eyes and nodding in time with the bass line. She sang along, cigarette in one hand, can of beer in the other. After a little while Joe joined her, slipping his arm around her waist and pulling her close. He pressed his crotch against hers, and she felt him harden in seconds.

She glanced at Alex – no response. Instead, he was glaring at the path, as if he still couldn't understand why he wasn't the one who'd gone off with Tanya. Joe drew Carina even closer, rubbed his cock against her as the suggestive bass line kept on pumping.

Carina looked over at Alex again, wanting him to react. A part of her realised how ridiculous this whole thing was. She'd regressed to a Year 10 kid trying to make her boyfriend jealous by dancing with another boy, but right now she needed that, needed to know she was desirable. She had to find a way of damping down the anger that was still burning inside her.

Alex stood up, and for a second she was sure there was going to be trouble. He would come over and knock away Joe's hand, which had found its way to her bottom, and punch him in the face. She was excited, pleased. But then Alex mumbled that he needed a pee, and tottered off towards the path leading down to the turning area.

As soon as Alex was out of sight, Joe started kissing her neck. She let him carry on for a few seconds before pulling away. 'Oh, come on, Carina . . .' He caught her, held on to her.

'No – pack it in!' She pushed him hard, but he refused to let go, tried to kiss her on the lips.

'Stop it!'

'Don't be such a fucking tease – you've been coming on to me all evening!' He made another attempt, and this time she half-heartedly returned his kiss, attempting to satisfy the childish part of her that wanted to be loved, desired.

'Let's go in the tent,' he whispered. 'I've still got a joint we can share.'

21

Autumn 2017

Anna sleeps late on Saturday, doesn't wake up until Milo is barking and scratching at the front door. She wraps herself in the old dressing gown she should have got rid of before the move; the fabric is threadbare, and the hotel name embroidered on the front is barely legible these days. And yet she can't bring herself to part with it; it's as if the memories of that weekend – Paris, the autumn leaves, the younger, better versions of Håkan and herself – would disappear along with the dressing gown, fade away like the letters on the breast pocket until all that remained were tiny fragments of what used to be.

Fragments of us, Håkan whispers as she stands in the doorway inhaling the fresh air. Milo has raced over to the nearest tree. He is so desperate for a pee that he hobbles along on three legs for the last couple of metres, and Anna can't help laughing. Milo seems to notice; he gives her a dirty look as he trots back across the yard and slips indoors past her legs. Anna remains outside for a little while longer. Watches a skein of geese flying across the sky in a V-shaped formation. No more disembowelled rabbits have appeared on the step, thank goodness. Agnes seems to find the mystery intriguing rather than horrible, which is something of a relief. Anna takes another deep breath, appreciates the smells, the beauty, the vivid colours, the faint cries of the geese, high above. Tries not to hate everything, but it's hard.

I loved you more than anything in the world, Håkan whispers. *And you felt the same way about me, didn't you?*

She didn't dream last night, at least not that she remembers. And yet there is something niggling away in the back of her mind, a lingering thought or feeling that she can't quite pin down. Something to do with the mural and Simon Vidje's tragic fate. She ought to think about something else; she definitely ought to call her solicitor. He'd promised to get in touch as soon as the preliminary investigation was over, but more than a week has passed since they last spoke. *Monday*, she tells herself. *If I haven't heard anything, I'll contact him on Monday.*

After breakfast she helps Agnes to load her photographic equipment into the car. Agnes is very keen, and keeps showing her mother the satellite image on her phone.

'There, look. The little black pool in the middle of the forest – that's the old quarry. You can even see the rocks if you zoom in.'

They get in the car; Milo settles down on Agnes's knee as usual, and looks deeply hurt when Agnes shoos him down onto the floor. He glares at Anna as if she is somehow to blame for this terrible rejection.

'You have to drive a couple of miles before you reach the turning.'

Anna does as she is told. She is so pleased that she and Agnes are talking to each other and doing something together. The strange landscape of the ridge whizzes by on both sides – deciduous trees, small enclosed fields and low stone walls. A little sawmill right by the roadside, before the vista opens up.

'Look!' Agnes is pointing to a herd of deer over by the edge of the forest.

Dark clouds have moved in, but there is no fog, and the white, stepped gables of Änglaberga are clearly visible. A vehicle pulls away from the lodge at the end of the tree-lined avenue; it is Bror Klein's pickup, and Agnes waves to him as they pass.

'How far is the quarry from here?'

Agnes checks her phone. 'About a mile.'

Close enough to cycle, Anna thinks. She gazes out over the freshly ploughed fields, tries to picture Simon cycling along.

The rain comes with no warning. As they enter the forest it begins to hammer down; it is almost too much for the windscreen wipers in spite of the shelter from the treetops. She slows down, but doesn't see an unexpectedly sharp bend and almost comes off the road.

'Take it easy, Mum!' Agnes grabs the handle above the window and glares at her.

'Sorry.' Anna slows down even more.

'There!' Agnes points to a narrow dirt track between two bends. Anna stops, makes sure no other car is approaching before she turns left. The track soon begins to climb. The surface is uneven, and she has to negotiate large potholes. The trees thin out, and the top of the hill is bare. The rain is coming down even harder now; she has no choice but to creep along.

Agnes is leaning forward, trying to see. Anna cautiously negotiates the next bend, but still ends up bouncing in and out of a deep hole. They are on a logging track now, hardly wide enough for one vehicle, with a green strip of vegetation down the middle that is so overgrown she can feel it scraping against the undercarriage.

'Stop!' Agnes says, but Anna has already seen the barrier. It is made of galvanised steel and extends right across the track, with a faded yellow sign in the centre. Wind and weather have obliterated its message, apart from one word in capital letters.

DANGER!

They stay in the car for a few minutes until the rain eases. Agnes has put away her phone, and Milo is sitting quietly on her lap. Twenty metres beyond the barrier the rocky landscape gives way to dense coniferous forest, which swallows up both the light and the logging track.

Milo whimpers, places his paws on the dashboard and presses his nose against the windscreen as if he's spotted something. The rain patters gently on the roof, then stops.

'Shall we go?' Anna says, and Agnes nods.

The track on the other side of the barrier slopes gently downwards among the fir trees. The smell here is completely different from a deciduous forest; it carries a darker hint of decay. Combined with the faint light, the atmosphere is distinctly creepy.

After about half a mile they reach an overgrown turning area. The ground consists of tightly packed stone chips, which is presumably why it hasn't been completely taken over by the forest. They catch a glimpse of the pool, but the shore is so overgrown that it's impossible to get an overview. Here and there, between roots and fallen branches, small puddles of rainwater have formed, with pond skaters dancing on the surface. Agnes photographs them while Anna thinks back to the case notes.

She knows that the place where the five friends camped is above the quarry to the left. Eventually she finds an old path. Agnes and Milo follow her, and after a brief tussle with brambles, undergrowth and an increasingly steep climb, they reach an open plateau. This must be the campsite. The view is beautiful – and familiar. The trees are taller, the vegetation denser than in the mural, but there is no mistaking the pool and the steep rocks. Anna is struck by what an incredibly skilled artist Karl-Jo must have been. Not only has he captured every detail and carried off the amazing optical illusion with the surface of the water, but he has also recreated the atmosphere that pervades this place, a kind of melancholy that is reinforced by the fiery yellow dying leaves and the black water. Agnes seems to be aware of it too.

They stand there for a while gazing at the pool. Anna pictures the outline of a body floating just below the dark surface. She can't explain why, but gradually a new feeling comes over her. The feeling that something other than an accident happened here, something tragic and terrible that cannot be explained by seven yellowing documents in an old file.

When they get back to Tabor, a van is waiting for them. The back doors are open and a small ramp has been lowered. The talkative motorbike dealer is busy wheeling out Agnes's Vespa, but stops when Milo starts barking at him.

'There you are,' Göran says as they come closer. 'I was start-ing to wonder if something had happened – we did say I'd deliver today, didn't we? That's what I put in the diary.'

He takes a tin of *snus* out of the pocket of his overalls and tucks a plug beneath his upper lip, then nudges it into the right place with the tip of his tongue.

'Sorry, my fault,' Anna says. 'I'd actually forgotten you were coming today – it's really kind of you to deliver on a Saturday. Coffee?'

'Please!'

While she sets the coffee machine going, Göran talks through the Vespa with Agnes. He shows her how to start and stop, and what the various buttons are for. They finish just as the coffee is ready. Agnes puts on her helmet and sets off along the track with Milo trotting along behind, and Göran joins Anna in the kitchen.

'So, this is what Tabor looks like,' he says, glancing around curiously. 'I've only ever seen the house from the outside, and that must be twenty-five or thirty years ago. I see the slide is gone.'

Anna frowns and tries to work out what he's talking about, but to no avail.

'Karl-Johan knocked a hole in the wall at the gable end of the house and built a slide – a blue metal one,' he explains, making a gliding motion with his hand. 'Everyone thought it was for the boy, but actually Karl-Johan used it himself. Because walking down the stairs was so tedious, he said. Karl-Johan had his own way of look-ing at the world.'

Göran laughs as he continues to inspect the kitchen.

'How did he end up here?' she asks as she fills his cup. The com-bination of pouring-coffee-asking-questions works well, as always.

'Karl-Johan and Elisabet met when she was at university in Lund.' He leans forward, lowers his voice. 'She fell pregnant pretty quickly, and they were in a hurry to get married. Old man Vidje dropped dead soon afterwards. Some people said it was the shock that killed him.' Göran grins, revealing the *snus* plug. 'Elisabet had to give up her studies and move back to Änglaberga to help her mother with the farm. Karl-Johan came with her, and fell in love with the place. It was the '70s and the so-called green wave – lots of city-dwellers who decided to change direction and become farmers. Learn the kind of thing that takes generations in just a matter of weeks.'

He grins again, discreetly removes the *snus* before sipping his coffee.

'So, Karl-Johan wasn't much of a farmer?'

'You could say that. He had plenty of ideas, each one crazier than the last. He tried to cultivate vines; for a while he kept llamas in an enclosure behind the house. Llamas, in Skåne – can you imagine? What was he going to do with them? Organise a spitting contest?'

Göran is so taken with his own witticism that he almost chokes on his coffee. When he has recovered, he goes on:

'What's surprising is that Elisabet let him carry on for as long as she did. After a few years the bank was threatening to repossess the whole of Änglaberga, so Elisabet had Tabor converted into a studio for Karl-Johan, and persuaded him to start painting again. Which was very smart, and not only because his work is worth a fortune today. Thanks to Bror Klein, Elisabet is now one of the largest landowners on the ridge. He's looked after Änglaberga for all these years as if the place was his own.'

Göran seems to have finished his tale, so Anna brings out the box of cakes she bought earlier.

'How well did you know Karl-Johan?' she asks as he finishes off the first raspberry tart.

'Well, I ran into him occasionally. Chatted about the weather and so on, but that was all. He tended to keep himself to himself up here; he really only spent time with Elisabet and Klein. Especially after they lost the boy . . .' He grimaces, reaches for another tart. 'A terrible tragedy – for all concerned.' He falls silent, takes a bite.

Anna pictures the five young friends in the group photograph, shouting for joy. *Friends forever.* She recalls the feeling she had up in the quarry earlier.

'Simon was a good kid,' Göran continues. 'He played and sang in the church at my mother's funeral. Even I was moved to tears.' He smiles again, this time more sympathetically. 'I actually helped him collect egg boxes. My brother-in-law works at the chicken factory . . . Could I have a top-up?'

She refills his coffee cup and sneaks in another question to keep him talking.

'Egg boxes?'

He nods. 'To improve the acoustics. Simon had kitted out the room above the garage at Änglaberga as a music room. Or studio, I suppose. I delivered two hundred egg boxes only a couple of months before the accident. It looked great – he had tape decks, microphones, all kinds of stuff he'd saved up for. Thousands of kronor, and it all went up in smoke.'

'What do you mean?'

'The whole lot was destroyed in the fire.'

She raises her eyebrows.

'The garage at Änglaberga burned down to the ground,' he clarifies. 'The night after Simon died. He'd set up amplifiers and a whole load of other equipment, which overloaded the electrical system. At least that's what the fire chief said.' He shakes his head almost imperceptibly, but Anna's trained eye immediately picks up the movement.

'You don't believe that's what happened?'

He looks surprised, as if she's read his mind, when in fact she's merely interpreted his body language.

'God knows,' he mumbles, munching on another raspberry tart. 'But there are those who say that the fire was a way of shutting Elisabet up.'

Anna is curious now. This is completely new information, and it's probably important, but she is experienced enough not to let her interest show.

'Are there many people who don't agree with the conclusions of the police investigation – that Simon's death was an accident?'

He shrugs. 'Most people just don't talk about it. Almost everyone knows someone who was involved. Alex, Bruno and Marie still live around here, and both Henry Morell and Bengt Andersson are pretty powerful men.'

'But you're not afraid of them?'

Göran grins again. 'I'm probably too stupid to be afraid. Or maybe I feel safe because my little business attracts customers from all over northern Skåne. Helps to put Nedanås on the map, so to speak. And if there's one thing you can say about Bengt Andersson, it's that he really cares about the community. To the point of obsession, if you ask me.'

Anna stands on the step watching the van until it is swallowed up by the forest. She is trying to fit the new pieces of the puzzle with the ones she already had. Henry Morell never mentioned a garage fire at Änglaberga, even though it seems to have happened in connection with Simon's death. Why not? And why does the incident still make people so uneasy? Twenty-seven years have passed. And perhaps even more importantly: why is she so interested? The whole thing started as a way of getting closer to Agnes through finding out more about the fascinating mural and its history, but even though she now knows the background, and has plenty of her own concerns to think about, she can't let the case go. The mural and the visit to the quarry have touched something within her, in a way that she can't really explain.

22

28 August 1990

Alex had gone down to the turning area. He was drunk and stoned, and as he reached the lower part of the slope he stumbled and fell to the ground head first. A sharp pain in his knee took his breath away. He scrambled to his feet, brushed off the dirt and tentatively flexed his leg. The pain gradually subsided. He let out a long breath, his cheeks burning with embarrassment as he glanced over his shoulder to make sure no one had seen him. The whole evening had gone wrong, and he didn't really understand how. Carina, talking about going away without him. Bruno, wandering around like a lost soul. Marie, getting drunk and throwing up. Fucking Joe, winding him up all the time, and his hot sister who for some incomprehensible reason didn't seem to be impressed by Alex at all. And then there was Simon, who'd suddenly become the hero of the hour. Alex took a few uncertain steps towards the trees and started fiddling with his zip.

The night of their graduation from high school, the strangest feeling had come over him. Without any warning he'd started sobbing helplessly; he'd locked himself in the toilet so that no one would notice. He'd blamed it on too much bubbly and the ensuing drunken sentimentality, but the same thing had happened a couple of times since then. Tonight, the feeling was back, and twice as strong – the feeling that everything was slipping through his fingers. Tears burned behind his eyelids. The next step was snivelling, followed by sobbing. He had no intention of going down that road. Not tonight.

He pulled out his cock and pissed straight into the bushes in an impressively high arc, squeezing his eyes tight shut. It worked, oddly enough.

He was Alex Morell, sports star and future Olympic medallist, and no one was going to walk all over him. Not fucking Joe with his sarcastic smile and his wandering hands, or his toffee-nosed sister who didn't know how to pick a winner. And no other fucker either. Joe had moved his motorbike away from the shore and put it next to Simon's bicycle. Alex stopped in mid-flow, took a couple of steps to the side, then pissed all over the tank and the handlebars.

There you go, you fucker, he thought contentedly, before directing the last spurt at Simon's bicycle.

Suddenly he heard agitated voices from above. He tucked his cock away and zipped up his jeans. The voices were getting louder. Someone was shouting his name. He set off up the path, clenching his fists. With every step it was as if the sense of powerlessness began to ease. Step by step, bit by bit, until all that remained was burning, white-hot rage.

23

Autumn 2017

C all-me-Lasse's Passat arrives in the yard at exactly three o'clock. His timing is so precise that Anna suspects he's been parked up around the bend, waiting for the right moment. Erik jumps out and chivalrously holds the back door open for Agnes, while Anna climbs into the front passenger seat.

Call-me is as pleasant as always. He looks nice, he has a good job, and a son who obviously gets on well with Agnes, yet after a little while Anna realises she is thinking about Alexander Morell and what Göran told her. The group photograph comes into her mind again: Simon Vidje, Alex Morell, Marie Andersson, Bruno Sordi – and Carina Pedersen, Alex's blonde and slightly too pretty girlfriend, whom he didn't marry. She wonders why, and at the same time she feels pleased, which is weird to say the least. Carina is the only one of the four surviving friends that she hasn't met. Not that it matters; Anna isn't carrying out any kind of investigation.

Of course you're not, Håkan says with a laugh. *Shall we have a chat about whether Santa Claus exists as well?*

She doesn't answer him, partly because he has a point, and partly because he's bound to answer back. But mainly because he's dead.

They take the four hairpin bends heading down the hill; by now she feels a lot more comfortable with the terrain. On the third bend they meet a white Glarea pickup truck, exactly like the one she almost hit the other evening; as before, the driver is partly on the wrong side of the road, and Call-me has to swerve. She hears him swear quietly through gritted teeth.

'Same thing happened to me, although I was going in the opposite direction,' she says. 'That guy drives like an idiot.'

'Mm. When was this?'

She thinks back. 'Wednesday evening.'

'And you're sure it was the same truck?'

'I didn't see the registration number, but it looked identical, and it had one of those telescopic crane things on the back. Why do you ask?'

'No particular reason.'

There is a brief silence while she tries to work out why he's lying to her. The presence of the pickup means something to Call-me. Something important.

'It's a drilling machine,' he adds. 'That thing on the back. Glarea use it to take samples.'

'I presume they're looking for a new source to replace the one down in the village,' Anna says, keen to show that's she's already up to speed with local issues.

Call-me doesn't answer. He is frowning slightly, which she hasn't seen before. Even though he changes the subject and chats away for another ten minutes, the frown still lingers when they reach the park.

The festivities are just the way Alex Morell described them. A travelling funfair with a shooting range, chocolate wheel and three rides that all look lethal. Nedanås's sports association is running the tombola, plus a coffee and hot dog stall. Even the promised bouncy castle is there on one side of the large gravelled courtyard. The other three sides are occupied by an outdoor stage, a dance floor and a party room. Up on the stage the accordion club are playing a jolly tune, and the smell of candy floss, popcorn and doughnuts fills the air. The place is packed – there must be a thousand people here.

Erik and Agnes soon disappear among the crowds, leaving Anna alone with Call-me. She nods a greeting to two uniformed officers, and congratulates herself on remembering their names.

The accordion group has finished, and a voice informs the audience that they were the final act in the talent show. Three people, presumably the judges, begin what looks like an amused discussion at one corner of the stage. The first judge is Bengt Andersson, the second his daughter, Marie. The third, however, is something else altogether. From a distance she looks like a Hollywood star, with hair extensions, lip fillers, high-heeled boots and a fake fur coat – totally out of place, both on that stage and in Nedanås in general.

'Who's that?' she asks Call-me.

'Caia Bianca – I thought you'd recognise her.'

She shakes her head, realising this is the woman whose picture Agnes showed her.

'Caia was in one of the very first reality TV shows in the early '90s. Personal appearances, magazine shoots, the usual. Then she married a financier and used the money she inherited when he died to build her own makeup brand. These days she's married to the biggest car dealer in southern Sweden, and often pops up in the gossip columns.' He raises his eyebrows quizzically.

'Nedanås's very own celebrity,' she says, silently thanking Agnes for the information.

'Exactly. She hardly ever agrees to come to this kind of thing anymore, so it was quite a surprise when she said yes.'

Anna murmurs something vague in response, and takes a closer look at the woman on the stage. After a while she re-evaluates Caia Bianca. Admittedly, she still looks like a pub singer who's seen better days, but in spite of the nature of the event, she carries herself with confidence and pride. She is the one who takes the microphone and announces three young girls as the winners of the talent show, then conducts a very professional interview without in any way stealing their thunder. It takes a minute or so for Anna to work out that one of the girls is Alex Morell's younger daughter. She steers Call-me a little closer to the stage, and eventually spots Alex right at the front, filming the whole thing on his phone. Bruno Sordi is standing next to him. She catches a glimpse of Alex's expression: pride, of course, but there is a hint of something that reminds her of the way he looked in the photo collage.

'I'm assuming Caia Bianca is a stage name,' she says, turning to Call-me. 'What's her real name?'

'Carina – Carina Pedersen.'

The final piece of the puzzle falls into place. Caia Bianca is Carina Pedersen, who used to be Alex Morell's girlfriend, his date at the graduation ball. The last person in the group photo. Anna repeats the names to herself, working from right to left in the group photo as she looks at those same faces now, almost thirty years older. Marie Andersson, now Sordi, on the stage next to her father. Bruno Sordi, her husband, waiting down below. Carina Pedersen, alias Caia Bianca, waving to the audience and acknowledging the applause. And almost directly in front of her Alex Morell, who can't take his eyes off her. All the old friends gathered together. Except for Simon Vidje.

24

28 August 1990

S imon and Tanya slowly made their way back to the campsite hand in hand. Halfway up the path they heard angry voices.

'You pig!' Marie shouted. Simon increased his speed, pulling Tanya along with him.

Carina and Marie were standing next to the fire with their arms around each other, while Bruno and Joe seemed to be involved in some kind of shoving contest before they suddenly started rolling around on the ground. Bruno seemed to have the upper hand, but then Joe stuck his fingers in Bruno's eyes, and took the opportunity to press down on Bruno's throat with one arm. Bruno gasped for air, his face contorted with the effort.

'Alex!' Marie and Carina screamed. 'Alex!'

Bruno tugged at Joe's arm, but Joe refused to ease the pressure.

There was the crunch of gravel as Alex hurtled into the little circle. He lifted Joe's arm with ease, twisted his wrist and yanked him backwards, giving Bruno the opportunity to scramble away. Joe grabbed a handful of gravel and threw it in Alex's face, using the element of surprise to get to his feet and attempt to deliver a kick. However, there was no strength behind it, and Alex simply stepped aside before seizing Joe's shoulder and the back of his neck, hooking his leg around Joe's and throwing Joe over his hip in one smooth movement. Joe landed on his back, knocking all the breath out of his body. He went limp. Tanya gasped, tried to pull away, but Simon refused to let go of her hand.

'He tried to rape Carina!' Bruno said, pointing to Joe. 'If Marie and I hadn't come along . . .'

Joe attempted to protest, but all that came out of his mouth was a dry cough.

'You fucking bastard,' Alex hissed through gritted teeth. He stepped forward and kicked Joe hard in the side, a vein throbbing at his left temple.

'Stop it!' Tanya wrenched her hand free, ran over and dropped to her knees next to Joe. Alex hesitated, unsure of what to do.

'Get out of the way, you little slut,' Marie hissed. 'Take him, Alex – ignore her!'

Simon reluctantly pushed his way into the circle and positioned himself beside Tanya. 'What the hell is going on?' he said.

'That fucker tried to rape Carina,' Bruno reiterated.

'Rubbish . . .' Joe stumbled to his feet, knocking aside Tanya's helping hands. His face was streaked with dirt and tears, and blood was oozing from a nasty graze on one cheek.

'She was the one who wanted it.' He coughed, took a deep breath. 'Tell the truth, for fuck's sake!' He pointed to Carina, who hid her head against Marie's shoulder.

Alex clenched his fists and took a step towards Joe and Tanya.

'Wait!' Simon moved between them. 'Can someone tell me exactly what happened?'

Marie glared at him. 'I'd been in the bushes throwing up. When Bruno and I got back here we heard noises from our tent, then Carina suddenly started screaming.'

Simon turned to Joe, who was bent over with his hands on his knees, Tanya's arm around his shoulders.

'And what's your version?'

'She asked me for more weed.' Joe spat out a gob of saliva. 'I'd saved half a joint, so we shared it in her tent. We were snogging, then we heard someone coming. All of a sudden she started screaming.' He shook his head.

Carina's head was still buried in Marie's shoulder. She didn't say a word. Simon looked at her, then at Joe, then Tanya. The mix tape changed to Roxette; the cheerful beat and bright voices made the whole situation seem utterly absurd.

'The thing is,' Simon said slowly, 'we're all pretty drunk and tired . . .'

'Don't tell me you think she's lying!' Marie snapped.

Simon held up his hands.

'I just mean it's easy to get the wrong end of the stick when you're stoned.' He glanced at Tanya. 'Joe and Tanya are leaving now, but first he's going to apologise, OK?'

Tanya nodded. 'If Joe's said or done anything inappropriate, he apologises – don't you?'

Joe avoided her gaze, straightened up and brushed the dirt off his jeans.

'Don't you?' Tanya said, more sharply this time.

Joe raised his head, his lips compressed into a thin line. He forced his features into a grimace that was meant to express regret. 'Sorry.' He grabbed his leather jacket. 'Sorry you're a bunch of immature kids.'

He shrugged his jacket and set off down the path to the turning area.

Tanya lingered for a moment. 'I really do apologise,' she said to Marie and Carina, but they refused to look at her. She took a couple of steps towards the path, then stopped and glanced over her shoulder at Simon. 'Sorry,' she said. He stood there watching her go, then suddenly he dived into his tent and dug a cassette tape out of a pocket in his guitar case. He caught up with Tanya and gave it to her.

'Here – you said you liked my song.'

She looked at the tape. '*Property of Simon Vidje*,' she read out loud. 'Thanks.' She stood on tiptoe and kissed him on the lips. 'You're going to be a star, Simon.' Then she ran to join Joe; the motorbike roared into life. Tanya swung her leg over the saddle; she barely had time to sit down properly before Joe shot away along the forest track. The last sight of them was Joe's arm raised above his head, middle finger extended to make his opinion clear.

Simon went back to the campsite. Roxette weren't sounding too good – a sure sign that the boombox's batteries were running out. Raindrops pattered against the tents – just a few at first, then more and more. Cold rain, different from the showers that had fallen during the summer; it soon extinguished what remained of the fire. The others were waiting for him. The rain was heavy now, transforming the world into sharp lines.

'So, that's that,' he said with a shrug. 'Shall we call it a night?'

Carina peeled herself away from Marie and went up to Simon.

'Traitor,' she hissed. Her face was bright red with rage, and her mascara had run.

'What?'

Carina slapped him across the face. The pain and shock made him raise a hand to his cheek. 'But I was just trying to . . .' He floundered, couldn't find the right words. The rain was hammering down now.

Marie came and stood next to Carina. 'How could you? How could you defend a rapist?'

'I just . . .' Simon held up his hands.

'Did you fuck her?' Carina demanded. 'You did, didn't you?' She turned to Alex and Bruno. 'Simon fucked that little whore while her brother was trying to rape me. That's why he let them get away.' Her voice had almost risen to a scream.

'You bastard,' Bruno growled. 'You think you're so much better than us, don't you? We ought to teach you a lesson.'

Simon was still standing there, holding up his hands. 'Can we all calm down?' he said, with fear in his voice. The tape suddenly stopped, and in the ensuing silence the rain was deafening.

25

Autumn 2017

The party room is bigger than it looks from the outside, and has a faded air of times gone by about it. The ceiling is high, allowing for a horseshoe-shaped balcony that extends around three walls, almost all the way to the stage where a trio is playing jazz music. Cigarette smoke from seventy years of parties has impregnated the walls, mingling with the smell of fried food from the buffet, and guests' aftershave and perfume.

Call-me has bought dinner tickets for both Anna and Agnes, and refuses to let Anna pay him for them. Erik and Agnes still seem to be getting along very well, exchanging cheerful banter as they help themselves to food. Each dish is labelled, and as at least half of them have Italian names, Anna assumes they come from the Sordis' restaurant. Her suspicions are confirmed when she sees Bruno looking stressed and ordering the staff around.

Alex Morell is sitting at the top table with his two daughters, his parents, Bengt Andersson and the Sordis. At one point they make eye contact and she almost waves, but settles for a small smile and a nod.

Agnes and Erik disappear after the main course, and Anna seizes the opportunity to try and get some sense out of Call-me.

'Elisabet Vidje,' she begins.

'Yes . . .' He waits to see where she's going with this.

'Why did she suddenly decide to rent out Tabor? I believe it was empty for years.'

156

'As I said, she thought it was high time the place was occupied.'

'But why now? And why us?'

'Why not?' Call-me attempts a winning smile, a tactic that would doubtless have worked on almost anyone. But not Anna.

'Answer the question, please. Why was Tabor done up so quickly, and why was it rented to us?'

His expression grows serious. 'Elisabet called me about a month ago, roughly when it became clear that you would be taking over from Henry Morell. She asked me to contact you and tell you about Tabor.'

'And you didn't ask why?'

He shakes his head. 'I've been dealing with Elisabet for long enough to know there's no point.'

'But you have your suspicions. You think you know why she wanted me there. Because of Simon.'

'Elisabet Vidje is my client,' he says after a brief silence. 'I'm sure I don't need to tell you about the duty of confidentiality . . .'

'OK.' Anna accepts that she isn't going to get any further with that. 'So, let me ask you this: why did she ask you to deal with renting out the house? Surely normal practice would be to use an estate agent?'

He considers his response.

'There are very few people that Elisabet feels she can trust. I'm one of them.'

'You, Bror Klein, and who else?'

He shrugs and leans back, looking slightly hurt.

'I thought we were here to enjoy ourselves, not so that you could interrogate me about one of my clients. Can't we talk about something else instead?' The charming smile is back. 'About you, for example. Why did you leave Stockholm for this backwater, Anna? What is it you're trying to hide from?'

The question floors her.

'We're n . . . n . . .' A huge stammer takes over the sentence, and she clamps her lips tight shut. Shifts her breathing from her throat to her diaphragm. Does he know something? If so, who has he spoken to? Maybe he knows her solicitor?

'OK, you got me ...' She slowly raises her hands above her head. 'Agnes and I are on the run. We're actually sisters, wanted for robbing a bank.'

Alex Morell would have got the joke straight away, but with Call-me it takes a few seconds for the penny to drop.

'Ha ha – I knew there was something dodgy about the pair of you! You're actually Selma and Louise!' He throws his head back and laughs.

Thelma, Håkan whispers. *But don't correct him. Nobody likes a smartarse!*

'I love your sense of humour,' Call-me says. 'Can I get you another glass of wine? Just don't rob anybody while I'm gone.'

She forces the corners of her mouth up into a smile. Waits until he turns his back on her before she allows herself to exhale.

Bengt Andersson gives a speech when coffee has been served. He has a natural gravitas, and even though the guests are well refreshed by this stage, the room falls silent as soon as he steps up to the podium. He talks about how Nedanås has gone from a small industrial community to become what he refers to at least three times as 'a dynamic meeting place'. Presumably, this is a catchphrase that some PR firm has come up with. Behind him a series of 'then and now' slides shows the progress Nedanås has made.

'Shouldn't Marie be making the speech?' Anna whispers to Call-me.

'Yes, but the community has a lot to thank Bengt Andersson for. It was in the doldrums for many years, but now it's thriving. The number of residents is going up year on year, as are the property prices. So Marie is happy to let Daddy have his moment in the limelight. A smart move, if you ask me.'

Anna thinks about the conversation at the Morells'.

'Marie said she'd been in parliament for a while?'

'Yes, but only for half an electoral term.' Call-me's tone suggests that there is more to tell.

'Why?'

'She found it too difficult to combine family life, running her own business and spending time in Stockholm. At least that was the official explanation. As I understand it, she was burned out – she was signed off sick for a long time.'

'That's sad.' Anna thinks about Bengt Andersson's dissatisfied expression when the subject of parliament came up. It is clearly a sore point between father and daughter that has yet to be resolved, but tonight there is no sign of discord.

At the end of his speech Bengt calls Marie up onto the stage, and together they deliver the good news about the trains and the logistics hub.

'Is Bengt completely out of local politics?' Anna asks during the warm applause.

'Officially, yes. But Bengt is the chairman of the board at Glarea, which means he still has a finger in the odd pie.'

'So, he's the one who'll be responsible for winding down the quarry. Putting a stop to the noise and the smell,' Anna says.

'Exactly.' The worried frown has reappeared, and as Marie and Bengt leave the stage, he gets to his feet. 'Excuse me, I won't be a minute.'

Anna uses the time to look around for Alex Morell, who is no longer sitting at the top table. After a while she spots him in a corner talking to a plump woman, who is at least five years younger than her. The discussion seems heated, and when one of the girls goes up to them and the woman puts her arm around her, Anna realises this must be Alex's ex-wife.

One of the waiters gently taps her shoulder.

'Excuse me – I'm afraid we have to move these tables to make room for the dancing.'

Anna grabs her bag and walks towards the door. Alex has returned to his seat. She sees him knock back a drink as Bruno puts a hand on his arm and whispers something in his ear. For a moment she wonders whether to join them, but quickly decides against it. Instead, she goes out into the foyer and heads for the toilets. About halfway there she meets a group of distinctly tipsy women in dresses that are just a little too tight; she swerves to the right and finds herself outside behind a row of wooden pillars running along the front of the building. She almost bumps straight into two men engaged in a discussion. Fortunately, they are facing away from her.

'You promised not to carry out any investigations up there.' The voice belongs to Call-me. 'Permission or no permission, Elisabet will not allow a quarry at Änglaberga – you know that as well as I do.'

Anna is partly hidden by one of the pillars; neither of the men appears to have seen her.

'Calm down, Lasse,' says the other man, who turns out to be Bengt Andersson. 'You're a good lad, loyal and conscientious, just like your father. Elisabet has a great deal to thank you for – both of you. Her health isn't the best these days. God forbid, but if Elisabet should leave us, it doesn't do any harm to be prepared. I mean, we don't want Sydsten, Swerock or some other outside firm moving in and stealing our community's natural resources, do we?'

Call-me turns his head and Anna quickly takes a step back. Unfortunately, she is out of earshot and misses his response. She is also embarrassed to be eavesdropping, and decides to go inside. As she slowly makes her way to the toilets, she thinks about what she heard. It must have something to do with the pickup truck they met on the hill, the one that caused the little frown between Call-me's eyebrows. Glarea is carrying out some kind of investigation up on the ridge, presumably to replace the operation they're being forced to shut down in the village. Judging by Call-me's angry reaction, it must be taking place on Änglaberga's land. She knows this is perfectly legal; the landowner doesn't automatically control underground natural resources. Elisabet Vidje must be aware of this too, but presumably she is not prepared to accept it. That's probably one of the reasons why she is a thorn in Bengt Andersson's side.

After visiting the toilet she catches a glimpse of Alex Morell on his way outside. She decides to follow him, and finds him around the corner of the building lighting a cigarette.

'Can I cadge one?' she says.

He glances up, seems both surprised and pleased. 'Hi, Anna – of course.' He holds out a newly opened packet. She takes a cigarette and he lights it for her between cupped hands.

'I didn't know you smoked,' he says.

'I don't – it's expensive and it kills you. Plus, you get yellow teeth. Only idiots smoke . . .' She takes an exaggerated drag, manages to tease a little smile out of him.

'Absolutely – smoking is for losers.' Alex also takes a deep drag. Anna feels as if the burgeoning connection between them has been restored.

'I saw your youngest daughter won the talent show,' she says. 'Congratulations!'

Before Alex has time to answer, the group of giggling women reappear. They seem to know Alex; a couple of them fling their arms around his neck and shower him with sympathetic babbling. 'Poor you!' 'Joss has no idea what she's throwing away!' 'It's so nice that you're staying on good terms for the sake of the girls.'

Alex plays along, but glances in Anna's direction from time to time, making it clear exactly what he thinks of the situation. The autumn air is cold and damp, and she shivers. She jerks her head in the direction of the party room, and Alex nods. He extricates himself from the women and accompanies her inside.

'So, how's the date going?' he asks, keeping his tone light.

'Brilliant. Lasse Gunnarsson is a real catch!'

He stops, apparently not realising that she's joking; he looks quite crushed. She frowns and shakes her head, and he breaks into a grin. Only now does she realise that he's pretty drunk.

'You're divorced too, aren't you? How long have you been on your own?'

'Two years.' She waits for Håkan's comment, but fortunately he's keeping quiet at the moment.

'Can I ask whose decision it was?'

'Mine.'

'I see . . .'

He sounds so sad that she goes on:

'Håkan and I met at the police academy. We got married in 2000 and Agnes came along the following year. He was my best friend; I really thought we were together forever. But then I found out he was having an affair with a female colleague. It's not unusual among police officers.'

'I see,' Alex says. 'What an idiot. No wonder you kicked him out – you must have been furious.'

Anna shakes her head. 'It wasn't really about anger. Actually, that's not true . . .' She pauses, navigates her way past a stammer. 'At first I was livid. Håkan was devastated – he begged me to forgive him.'

She falls silent again, takes a deep breath. She's never told anyone this, and yet she's standing here, baring her soul to someone who was a complete stranger only a few days ago. But she goes on:

'I honestly tried, but the wound was too deep.'

He doesn't say anything, which she appreciates. He merely nods slowly as if he understands her thinking, even though she doesn't really understand it herself. She shivers.

'And what about you?' she asks.

'I'm not sure,' he replies, although his body language tells another story. 'Joss was the one who wanted a divorce.' He looks away. 'We do our best to get along, for the sake of the girls – but it's hard. Are you and Håkan still friends?'

'We were. He died a year ago from li . . . liv . . .'

Alex has that look on his face that so many people get when they realise she stammers – as if they're unsure whether to keep quiet or help her to fill in the tricky word.

Alex makes the right choice, giving her time to catch her breath, change things around.

'Cancer of the liver.'

'I'm so sorry.' They stand in silence for a little while, about ten metres from the main door. 'Do you ever wish you could go back?'

'To the time when we were married? Sometimes, yes.'

Alex shakes his head. 'Further back. Before marriage and a mortgage and all those obligations. Before everything got so complicated.'

She senses where he's going, and gently nudges him along.

'I suppose everyone does from time to time. Life was pretty simple when we were teenagers. Full of possibilities.'

'It was.' He looks down at the ground. 'I'd give anything to have that feeling again. To get back . . .'

He doesn't finish the sentence.

A shiny, expensive SUV drives into the courtyard and stops directly in front of the entrance. The driver's door opens and Caia Bianca steps out. She is immediately surrounded by fans wanting selfies. Alex straightens his shoulders and his expression changes completely. He watches Caia until she's disappeared inside, then smiles foolishly at Anna as if he's forgotten what they were talking about.

'Maybe we should go in,' she says dryly.

He nods and shoots off at such a speed that she ends up several metres behind him. She considers running to catch him up, then realises how stupid that would be. Instead, she lingers outside for a few minutes. Back inside she sees Caia over by the top table being hugged and air-kissed by Marie and Bruno Sordi, while Alex stands nearby, sheepishly waiting his turn. Caia has swapped her fake fur for a tight white dress; she clearly spends many hours in the gym, and her breasts are considerably younger than the rest of her.

Anna doesn't quite know what to do now. Her table is gone, and there's no sign of Call-me. People are milling about, some heading outside, others coming in, while the staff quickly and efficiently get the room ready for the dance.

A man is leaning against the wall by the door. His face is gaunt, and he has a bushy beard. He is wearing tinted glasses. Anna's instinct as a cop kicks in, and even though she's only seen him for a couple of seconds, she's convinced he's up to no good. He doesn't look like a mugger – he's too skinny. He's more of a small-time thief, waiting for the right opportunity.

He's probably about fifty years old. His stance is casual, with the sole of one foot pressed against the wall and a can of beer in his hand. He seems to be staring at one of the few tables that haven't been cleared away, but with the tinted glasses it's hard to tell exactly where his focus is. It could be an unattended handbag, or a jacket with a phone in the inside pocket. Anna approaches slowly so that she can cut him off if necessary, but he doesn't make a move. Sips his beer, gaze still fixed on whatever he's looking at. The hand holding the can has a large, ugly tattoo on the back, which only serves to strengthen Anna's suspicions.

She's about five metres away when he spots her. Their eyes meet briefly, and she can see that he immediately knows she's a police officer. His lip curls in a half-smile, he pushes himself away from the wall and slips out through the door. Anna follows him into the foyer, but he's disappeared. She wonders whether to go looking for him, but she hasn't seen him do anything illegal, and after all she's off duty. She makes a mental note of his appearance.

She hears her name, and finds Call-me, Agnes and Erik involved in a discussion about Caia Bianca, whom everyone in the whole wide world, with the exception of Anna, seems to have heard of.

Before long the DJ kicks off his set with traditional dance band music, and Agnes and Erik wander off together.

'Would you like to dance?' Call-me asks.

She'd prefer to say no, find a quiet place to continue their earlier conversation, but unfortunately politeness dictates that she has to accept.

She's a pretty good dancer; the only problem is that she tends to start leading after a while. Or at least she used to with Håkan, and he didn't like it at all. Call-me doesn't seem to mind; in fact, he looks quite grateful for her help.

'Did you hang out with that lot when you were younger?' she asks, nodding in the direction of the top table, where Caia's arrival has definitely heightened the atmosphere. Anna waves to Henry and Eva-Britt Morell, but they're both too busy to notice her. The four friends from the group photo are sharing a toast. Alex's eyes are sparkling, and he doesn't take them off Caia for a second.

'No. They were a tight-knit group; they didn't let anyone else in.'

'It looks as if that's still the case.'

'It is for Alex, Bruno and Marie. We don't see Caia here very often.'

'No?'

Call-me shakes his head.

'She and her new husband built a huge villa on the coast outside Helsingborg a few years ago. There was a bit of trouble about it – not all the neighbours were keen on the style. Old money meets new, if you know what I mean.'

'You said her first husband died – was he a lot older than her?'

'No – only a couple of years, I think. He was found dead in their summer home in France. This was right in the middle of the financial crisis, so there were rumours, but I have to admit that Caia did a good job of managing the money after he was gone.'

Someone at the top table says something funny; the whole group bursts out laughing so loudly that they drown out the music. The DJ turns up the volume, and soon the dance floor is so crowded that there is no chance of talking. Call-me draws her closer; she can smell his aftershave. He seems to be trying to put his cheek against hers, and Anna doesn't quite know how to handle the situation. She lets him carry on, and at the same time she steers them a little closer to the top table, where there is still much hilarity.

As they reach the end of the table, she realises that things aren't quite as they seem. The voices, the expressions, the laughter – everything is forced, as if everyone is making a huge effort to show what a wonderful time they're having.

Alex gets to his feet and leads Caia onto the dance floor. Anna watches them over Call-me's shoulder, sees Alex draw her closer, sees her move her hand up to the back of his neck. Their cheeks touch, and Anna feels a pang of – what?

Pull yourself together, Håkan whispers. *You're not fifteen, for God's sake.*

'Shut up,' she hisses between gritted teeth. Call-me gives a start.

'Did you say something?'

She shakes her head, but doesn't take her eyes off Alex and Caia.

'And now a song you'll all recognise,' says the DJ, a man aged about thirty-five, with glasses and a nose piercing, from his booth in the middle of the stage.

The lively dance band set gives way to a slower track, a gentle ballad accompanied by a solo guitar. The singer sounds like a young man.

'*I saw a friend today, someone I knew long ago. But I still recall her name . . .*'

The voice is clear and beautiful, the guitar soft and melodic, but after a couple of steps Anna notices that something has changed in the room. Alex is the first to react. He stiffens, raises his head as if he can't believe what he's hearing, then others begin to do the same.

'*And she told me this, my friend from long ago. That things will never be the same,*' the young man sings, and the hum of conversation grows louder.

Alex has stopped dancing. He stands motionless, his face ashen. Caia looks unsure of what to do, then she too stiffens. Another burst of laughter from the top table. One of the women, probably Marie Sordi, is laughing louder than everyone else, but with a sharp dissonance that makes it sound almost like a scream.

'*I'll see you by the waters,*' the voice sings from the loudspeakers. '*The dark and lonely waters.*'

Total chaos breaks out.

26

28 August 1990

S imon couldn't quite work out what had happened. Only a few minutes ago he'd been so happy. Stockholm, the tour, the jump from the highest rock, Tanya.

Somehow he was now standing in the middle of a circle, surrounded by his best friends. Although they weren't behaving like friends.

Marie was still very obviously drunk, her face bright red. Bruno was standing in front of her and to one side, clenched fists raised. Alex's expression had darkened in the way that usually meant somebody was in trouble, and Carina's lips were white with rage.

And then there were the words they were throwing at him, spitting them out of their mouths, almost matching the tempo of the rain. The viciousness ate through his skin, burrowed deep down inside him.

'Traitor!'

'Do you realise what he did?'

'How could you defend a fucking rapist?'

'How could you?'

'With that whore!'

'Who the fuck do you think you are?'

Simon held up his hands, tried to get away. He glanced over his shoulder, down at the turning area where he'd left his bike. The rain was coming down harder and harder.

'Listen, I think I'll head home . . .'

He was about to leave – he managed one step.

'Simon tried to kiss me,' Carina announced.

Suddenly there was total silence, apart from the rain.

'What?' Alex and Bruno said almost simultaneously.

'Earlier this evening, down on the path!'

Simon stopped and turned back. Carina's eyes flashed in the darkness.

'It wasn't like that,' he began. He discovered that his voice was far from steady. Alex's eyes were black now; Simon felt scared for the first time. Scared of Alex, scared of the others, of what might happen.

'Did you kiss my girlfriend?' Alex growled, taking a step towards Simon.

'She was the one who . . .'

Simon didn't know how it happened; it was as if his brain missed a couple of seconds in the course of events. All at once his body was flying through the air. Terrified, he tried to extend his arms to break his fall, but it was too late. The hard ground came rushing straight at him.

27

Autumn 2017

A nna has experienced this on several occasions in the past, usually in the course of her job. At certain critical moments time seems to slow down, making it possible to pick up on even the smallest details.

Alex Morell hurtles towards the DJ booth, barrelling forward like an American football player and knocking people over on his way. Bruno Sordi is also heading for the stage from the top table. His wife is on her feet, and her chair has fallen over. The Morells and Bengt Andersson are all staring at Marie as she stands there with her lips clamped together, her face contorted in a mixture of fear and disgust. Caia Bianca is left alone in the middle of the dance floor. A space has opened up around her, as if the people who seconds ago wanted to get as close to her as possible have now withdrawn. One of the spotlights colours her white dress blood-red, and the beam has caught her with her mouth half-open in what looks like a silent scream.

'*The dark and lonely waters,*' the beautiful voice sings again, and for a brief moment Caia's lips move as if she is joining in.

Anna notices all of this before Alex Morell reaches the DJ booth. There is a crash and the music stops abruptly. Time resumes its normal rhythm, releasing a cacophony of voices.

Anna lets go of Call-me and races to the stage, pushing her way through the crowd that has gathered below what used to be the booth, but is now a collection of broken wood, cables and parts of a computer. Alex is lying in the middle of the wreckage on top of the DJ; he has the man's neck in a wrestler's hold. Alex's face is bright red, his eyes almost black, his lips drawn back like a predator. Bruno Sordi is standing over him, legs apart, fists clenched, but instead of trying to drag Alex away he bends down and yells something in the DJ's face. The same words, over and over again, but the hubbub around her is too loud for Anna to make out what he's saying.

The DJ offers no resistance; his face is turning blue and he is gasping for air. His eyes begin to roll back in his head. Anna heaves herself up onto the stage.

'Let go, Alex!'

Bruno steps in front of her. 'Not until he admits it.'

Bruno is about the same height as Anna, and judging by his complexion and the way he is moving, he is pretty drunk. Anna goes straight for him, gripping his chin and upper arm. While he is busy trying to twist his face free, she kicks his legs out from under hm. Bruno crashes to the floor; she doesn't wait to see how he reacts, but throws herself at Alex instead. The DJ's body has gone limp, but Alex still hasn't loosened his hold. She grabs his hair and face and yanks him backwards. Alex lets go of the DJ, but instead of giving in he whirls around, pushes his arm under her shoulder and wrestles her to the floor. He is almost six feet tall and weighs over fifteen stone. He used to be an elite wrestler, so Anna doesn't have much of a chance. The impact as her knees hit the stage makes her cry out in pain. Her upper body is about to follow, but she resists with all her strength. She can hear him panting above her head. The room begins to spin, sounds and voices and movement combined. *You know what to do*, Håkan hisses inside her head. *Go on – do it!*

She jerks her head back and hits Alex squarely on the nose. He groans and his shock enables her to put one foot on the floor, giving her the strength to turn and knee him in the groin. He gurgles, his legs give way and he collapses, both hands clutching the family jewels.

'You fucking bitch!' Bruno is on his feet, his face is purple, fists clenched, eyes two narrow slits. He takes a step forward, ready to punch her, and she automatically raises her arm to protect herself. But the blow doesn't come. Jens Friberg has appeared behind Bruno – in full uniform. Anna sees a black line whizz through the air, she hears a whoosh followed by a crack as Jens's telescopic baton hits the back of Bruno's knees, sending him crashing down for the second time.

The main lights come on and the room is bathed in harsh white light. The noise level falls slightly.

'Here!' Jens throws her a pair of handcuffs, presumably the spare pair that amused her only a few days ago when she saw him and all his kit for the first time. Jens bends down and cuffs Bruno with his regular pair. Alex Morell has curled up in the foetal position, and has a small pool of blood beneath his nose. Anna meets no resistance as she secures his hands behind his back. She straightens up, brushes the dust off her trousers and turns her attention to the DJ.

He is lying on his back among the wreckage of his equipment. His face is a better colour now. He coughs, rubs his throat and tries to sit up.

'Are you OK?' Anna asks, and he nods slowly.

'How do you want to do this?' Jens asks, jerking his head towards the crowd, where hundreds of pairs of eyes are following their every movement. Henry Morell is at the front with Eva-Britt beside him. His expression is grim, and he makes a point of catching Anna's eye. Marie Sordi and her father are there too.

She looks away, turns to Jens.

'I want both of them brought in,' she snaps. 'Charge Alex Morell with violence and assaulting a police officer, and Bruno Sordi . . .' She stops, tries to work out exactly what crime Bruno has committed. Decides to take the easy way out for now. 'Bring him in so he can sober up.'

Jens remains silent for a few seconds; he glances at the front of the stage, then nods. He gestures to two uniformed colleagues who have materialised behind him. 'Take them both in.'

Alex and Bruno are escorted from the building, and Anna helps the DJ to his feet. She asks if he needs an ambulance, but he shakes his head. 'OK then, I have to ask you to accompany me to the police station.' A nod.

She finds his glasses and accompanies him down the steps. She sees Henry Morell marching determinedly in the direction of the door; he isn't even looking at her now. Unlike plenty of others, including Caia Bianca, Marie Sordi, Bengt Andersson and Call-me.

There is no sign of Agnes; presumably she didn't see what happened, which is a relief.

The hum of voices is growing louder now as she and the DJ approach the door. She is able to pick up the odd phrase:

'. . . took down Alex Morell.'

'And Bruno.'

'No sign of fear at all.'

'What the hell got into them?'

'Didn't you hear?'

Just as they are about to leave, she spots the skinny, bearded man with the tattoo on his hand. As before he is leaning against the wall with a certain arrogance, a grin on his face, and in spite of the tinted glasses she is pretty sure that he winks at her as she passes by.

Call-me drives her and the DJ, Kristian Persson, to the station. She asks him to go back and find Agnes. Kristian seems to be a perfectly ordinary guy with an ordinary job, who earns a little extra by working as a DJ. He says he has no idea why Alex and Bruno attacked him, claims he doesn't even know them. There is nothing in his tone of voice or body language to suggest that he is lying. Anna asks him to wait in reception while she goes to the custody suite.

As expected she finds Henry Morell there, engaged in a serious conversation with Jens which stops as soon as they see her. There is no sign of Bruno, but Alex is sitting a short distance away with an ice pack clamped to his nose and his other hand cupped around his crotch. The handcuffs are gone, his shoulders are slumped, his eyes fixed on the vinyl flooring.

'Anna, I'm so pleased you're here,' Morell says with exaggerated warmth. 'I must thank you for a very timely intervention, and I must also apologise for Alexander's behaviour. Totally unacceptable, of course.'

'Why hasn't he been locked up?'

The question is directed at both men, but only Jens looks away.

Morell draws her to one side.

'Between you and me, Anna, Alexander is having a hard time at the moment. The divorce has taken its toll. He invested a lot of money and thousands of hours in the house to provide a good life for his family, and now he's living in his parents' basement and is only allowed to see his daughters at the weekend.' He makes a resigned gesture, lowers his voice. 'Alexander had problems in the past – before Joss and the girls. He spent some time in a psychiatric unit – more than once, in fact. Locking him up can act as a trigger, if you know what I mean.'

He interprets her stunned silence as assent.

'So, this is what we're going to do. Bruno can sleep it off in the custody suite. In about half an hour I'll cancel Alexander's arrest and take him home. That will give us time to interview the DJ. I realise that Alexander put you in an unpleasant situation, but I'm sure you've experienced worse. Plus, you sorted everything out wonderfully well. If you ask me, Alexander got exactly what he deserved, and the whole village could see that you were fully in control of the situation.' He smiles and gives her that fatherly look that she finds so hard to resist.

'S . . . so you want me to convince the victim, whom I've just dragged down here, not to press charges, even though there were hundreds of witnesses?' She tries to keep her voice calm, but doesn't entirely succeed.

'No, no, I would never ask you to do that. Jens will deal with the practicalities. I just wanted to ask you not to file a charge of assaulting a police officer. Look on it as a personal favour to me – a kind of retirement present, if you like.'

She hesitates, waits for Håkan to say something, come up with one of his helpful comments. Morell gets there first.

'Plus of course I am still responsible for this police district,' he adds, his tone not quite so warm now. 'Until Monday morning this is my station, and every officer here works for me. Including you, Anna.' His face stiffens, then breaks into that paternal smile once more. 'But of course I hope we can sort this out between us – between good friends.'

Anna shuffles uncomfortably. On several levels she feels sorry for Alex Morell, not least because of what his father has just told her. And she likes him. Or rather liked him, until about half an hour ago. But he assaulted both her and the poor DJ.

'So, what do you say, Anna? Are we in agreement?' Morell is still smiling, but there is a sharpness in his eyes. A no would probably end their friendship and make her situation considerably more difficult.

Håkan has woken up. She already knows what he's going to say, and as so often, she wishes he would keep quiet. But of course he doesn't, because not even death can shut Håkan up. *Sometimes, darling Anna*, he whispers, *you just have to roll with the punches.*

She slips out the back way so that she doesn't have to face DJ Kristian. Call-me, Erik and Agnes are waiting in the car park. Both teenagers are excited; they've already heard rumours about what happened, and want Anna to tell them how she flattened two fully grown men. She has no desire to go over it all again. Call-me seems to realise how she feels, and gives a quick summary without too many details. She gives him a grateful look, and promises herself that she will be nicer to him in the future.

As they drive into the yard at Tabor it has started to rain. The headlamps light up the front of the house. There is something on the top step. Two rabbits with dead eyes and empty bellies.

28

Autumn 2017

She sleeps badly. The dream about the painting, the quarry and the body comes back, but this time it is neither Simon Vidje nor Håkan floating out there beneath the water. It is Alexander Morell.

'Help me, Anna!'

The rain comes down harder and harder, transforming the whole picture into a thick, acrid fog, and suddenly, in less than a second, everything has changed to a completely different scene, the way that can only happen in a dream. She is sitting in the small interview room with her solicitor on her left, and the two Internal Affairs investigators opposite. One of them places a photograph on the table. 'Do you know what this is?'

She doesn't need to look, but glances down anyway. The photo shows a grey box with wires and cables coming out of the back, and a display on the front. An infusion pump with smooth rubber buttons. If they are pressed in a certain sequence, the morphine will flow freely and Håkan will no longer feel any pain.

Three, three, seven, five, nine, two. Select.

'Did you do it?' the investigator asks. 'Did you murder your husband?'

Anna wakes to find she is holding her breath. It is early in the morning, wet and windy. She pulls on her raincoat and goes outside to get rid of the traces of what Agnes has begun to refer to as the Rabbit Mystery. She was too tired to deal with it last night. She's glad that

Agnes regards it as some kind of joke; she herself is not so sure. She gingerly picks up a disembowelled rabbit in each hand and heads for the outbuilding and the bins. As she gets closer she sees Bror Klein's pickup truck parked around the corner. The door of the outbuilding is wide open, and she can hear someone rummaging around inside. She calls out 'Hello?' knocks on the door frame and steps inside. Presumably this place used to be a garage back in the day, but now it looks like a rubbish dump. The air smells of dampness and rust, and the floor is covered with scrap. The metal shelves lining the walls are crammed with tins of paint, bottles and boxes. At the far end of the room there is a small, dark doorway – that's where the noise is coming from.

'Hello!' she calls out again. The noise stops and Klein appears.

'Oh,' he says, looking uncomfortable. 'I just came to collect a couple of things. I didn't want to disturb you at this early hour.'

'No problem.'

They stand there in silence.

'Er – are you settling in OK?'

Klein's attempt at small talk surprises her. 'We are. It's so quiet, and so beautiful. Exactly what we need.'

Klein nods. 'And how about work? How's it going with Henry Morell? Has he handed over the reins?'

'I think it's gone pretty well so far. I take over first thing tomorrow morning.' The first sentence grates a little; she can't help thinking back to the previous evening's events.

Klein nods again; he seems to have run out of topics of conversation. Anna's eyes have grown accustomed to the gloom, and she can see something large and blue further down the room. 'Is that Karl-Johan's slide?' she asks.

Klein gives a start – almost imperceptible, but enough for her experienced eye to pick up. 'How do you know about that?'

'Göran told me when he delivered Agnes's moped.'

'He talks too much. Always has done.'

Silence falls. All Anna can hear are the raindrops, finding their way through the old roof in odd places.

'The mural,' she says, without really thinking. 'I've seen what it actually represents.' This time Klein's mask remains in place. Nothing in his expression reveals what he is thinking, but she can feel it bubbling away beneath the surface. There is something about him that draws her in, makes her want to crack that stony face and find out whatever it is that he's hiding. 'Karl-Johan never accepted that it was an accident either,' she goes on. 'That was why he spent ten years on that painting, even though he must have been almost completely blind by the end.'

'That's nothing to do with you,' Klein says quietly. The artificial civility from before has vanished. 'You didn't know him; you have no idea—'

He stops in mid-sentence, wipes away a drop of spit that has come out with the words and landed on his chin.

'Excuse me, Anna.' He makes a point of looking at his watch. 'I'm afraid I have to go.'

She accompanies him outside and stands beside him while he secures the side door with a sturdy padlock. His embarrassment is palpable, even when he has his back to her. He gives her a brief fare-well nod, then jumps in the pickup truck and drives off in the rain.

Anna can't help wondering what he was doing in the outbuilding. She takes a walk around. There are two garage doors on the front, a few metres apart, both secured with a metal bar and a padlock. The one on the left must lead to the room with the slide and all the rubbish, and the one on the right to the room from which Klein emerged. The doors are the same size, so she assumes the rooms are too. She searches for a gap to peer through, and finds a loose plank of wood around the back. She jiggles it around until she has made a hole big enough to get her hand through. The smell is even mustier than in the first room – damp, rust, and something else. Something burned. The gap lets in only a small amount of light, but she switches on the torch on her phone and pushes her arm in as far as she can. The beam illuminates several metres of concrete floor, then a dark shape. It takes her a few seconds to work out what she's looking at. It is the charred remains of what must once have been a sports car.

29

Autumn 2017

In the afternoon she heads into the office to check the results of last night's events. The corridor on the upper floor is silent and deserted. She sits down at the computer, types in Saturday's date and searches for reports. She finds a couple, but neither of them has anything to do with an assault in the park. She runs a search for Alexander Morell, but finds no results. She tries Bruno Sordi – nothing. Jens Friberg appears to have carried out his task with exemplary efficiency.

Anna sits quietly for a little while, then types in her own ID number. She knows she is not allowed to carry out a search on herself, but given what happened last night, she can always say she wanted to check if she was listed as having reported the incident at the park. She knows what will come up, but her stomach still flips over when the case number appears on the screen. She doesn't click on it; there's no point. No one outside Internal Affairs can access the case or the suspicions against her.

However, there is one thing she can see, something that makes her stomach flip again. The status box shows the code for 'ongoing', in spite of her solicitor's assurances that everything would soon blow over.

A discreet tap on the door makes her look up. Jens Friberg is standing there. She quickly closes the web page.

'Have you got a minute?' he says. He waits until she says yes before coming in and closing the door behind him. She gestures towards the visitor's chair, but doesn't waste time on small talk. From tomorrow she is his boss and she intends to make that clear to him as soon as possible. However, he surprises her.

'I just wanted to say how well you did last night,' he begins. 'The way you handled both Alexander Morell and Sordi was . . .' He pauses, searches for the right word. 'Impressive,' he says, with so much air that the word almost sounds like a sigh.

'Thank you,' she replies, unsure of how to continue. The situation is both unexpected and difficult to read. Is this some kind of trick, a clever way of putting another dent in her authority? But Jens's tone doesn't seem false, and nor does his body language. In fact, he appears to find it painful to praise her, and yet he's doing it.

'It's lucky you arrived so quickly,' she says, testing the waters.

'We were already in the courtyard when someone shouted that a fight had broken out inside.'

'What happened after I left?' she asks, even though she already knows the answer.

'The DJ . . . decided not to press charges, after some consideration.'

Anna is about to make an acid comment when she sees how uncomfortable he is. She decides to keep quiet instead.

'The thing is . . .' Jens bites his upper lip as if he is trying to stop the rest of the sentence from coming out. 'I have a great deal of respect for Henry Morell. I regard him as something of a mentor.'

But, she thinks. She is trying hard not to show how unexpected this conversation is.

'But what he asked us to do last night wasn't right. Admittedly, I've cleaned up after Alexander a couple of times in the past, but those were only minor matters. This could have ended very badly – plus he assaulted a police officer.'

Once again Anna wonders whether this is a ploy, but there are still no signs of insincerity.

'Were you there when Bruno Sordi was released?' she asks.

Jens nods.

'How long was he held?'

'Not long. He was home before midnight. His wife and father-in-law came and picked him up. They weren't happy.'

'Did you speak to him?' She knows the answer before he nods. Jens is a conscientious officer who doesn't like loose ends. 'So, what did he say?'

'He claims it was a drunken misunderstanding.'

'A misunderstanding?'

Jens straightens his shoulders, glances at the closed door. 'He said the DJ played an old song. They were all shocked and thought he was messing with them, trying to ruin their evening. That was why they attacked him.'

'How could he do that with an old song?'

'Because the person singing was Simon Vidje.'

Anna inhales sharply, tries to recall what she heard. The beautiful voice, the chords, the lyrics. Something about dark and lonely waters. She can't help shuddering.

'Did you ask Kristian Persson about it?'

'No, he was long gone by then. I didn't want to call him and wake him early on a Sunday morning, plus I'm pretty sure that after our little chat earlier on, he would have told me to go to hell. It would be interesting to hear his version, though.'

He takes a folded piece of paper out of his shirt pocket and places it on her desk before getting to his feet, giving her a brief nod of farewell and leaving the room. Anna opens up the piece of paper and sees a mobile phone number.

For the third time she tries to work out if this whole thing is a trick, but in the end, she gives in.

Kristian answers on the third ring and doesn't seem very pleased to hear from her, to say the least.

'Listen, I get it,' he snaps as soon as she's introduced herself. 'Your fascist colleague made it very clear to me last night that it wasn't a good idea to press charges against Alexander Morell. You could have told me that in the first place instead of dragging me down to the station, and you definitely don't need to call—'

She interrupts him, her cheeks burning with shame.

'That's not why I called. I wanted to ask you about the song you played just before it all kicked off.'

There is a brief silence at the other end of the line. 'You mean that demo recording, or whatever it was?' He sounds surprised rather than angry now.

'Yes – how did you come to play it?'

'Some guy gave me a USB stick earlier in the evening – it happens sometimes. It's a kind of 2017 version of requests. I usually say no, because I don't like putting a stick that isn't mine into my computer, but he was very insistent. He gave me five hundred kronor to play the track when Caia Bianca was on the dance floor, and promised me the same again afterwards. The gig wasn't particularly well paid, so I thought what the hell – a thousand extra just for playing one song.'

'Who was this guy?'

'I've no idea. I don't think he was local.'

'What did he look like?'

Kristian thinks for a moment. 'A bit scruffy. In his early fifties, maybe. Skinny, with a beard. Tattoos on his hands.'

'Was he wearing glasses?'

'Yes – with tinted lenses. I could hardly see his eyes.'

Anna knows exactly who he means.

'Do you remember anything else about him? Anything he said or did?'

Silence. 'No, he just said the song was an old favourite that would go down really well, and that Caia and her friends would recognise it right away.'

They certainly did, she thinks. *They recognised it only too well.*

181

30

Autumn 2017

A nna has just walked in through the door at Tabor when her new work phone rings. Agnes has already texted to say that she's gone to Erik's, and as usual Milo seems moderately pleased to see her.

'Hello, this is Olsson in the patrol car,' says a voice in her ear.

'Yes?'

'We're over at Glarea – one of the team leaders called us. They've found a dead body in a tree.'

'What?'

'A jumper,' the officer clarifies. 'There's a steep drop where the quarry meets the northern end of the ridge. We had another suicide there a while ago.'

'OK, I'm on my way. Can you tell me exactly where you are?'

It is dark by the time Anna reaches the main entrance to Glarea, where a white Jeep with a security company logo is waiting for her.

'Follow me – it's a bit tricky to find,' the driver says.

This turns out to be something of an understatement. After the gates and the office buildings, the road slopes steeply downwards. The heaps of gravel on either side grow higher and higher until Anna reaches the bottom of the immense quarry. The smell of burning that sometimes pervades the village is so strong that she switches off the air con.

The road opens out into an area the size of four or five football pitches. They pass several large buildings and tall metal towers which she assumes are crushing plants, along with a row of heavy machinery and trucks parked up for the night. Floodlights heighten the sense of a lunar landscape.

The security vehicle veers off to the right between two huge piles of gravel, ploughs through a pool of water, then turns left. Anna realises that the quarry is not a gigantic rectangle, as she'd imagined. It is more like a wheel; the section they've just left is presumably the hub, with various ravines running off it like spokes in all directions. However, when the ravine they're following keeps splitting into several new branches, she can see that that comparison doesn't work either. At the fifth division she understands that she would never have found her own way, and is very glad that all she has to do is follow the rear lights of the Jeep.

She is almost completely disorientated by the time they reach another flat, open area, with the ridge forming a high, steep cliff on the far side. Three vehicles are parked in a semi-circle, their headlights focused on a solitary birch tree. Rain hangs in the air, the odd drop already slicing through the beams.

She parks a short distance away and walks over. One of the vehicles is the patrol car whose driver called her, the second is a large digger. The third is Henry Morell's car. He is talking to the uniformed officer and a man who, judging by his high-vis jacket, is the Glarea team leader who made the original call.

'Hi, Anna,' Morell says. 'I'm afraid he's not a pretty sight.'

He switches on a torch and shines it high up into the tree, where the headlights don't quite reach. The scene is horrific, yet bordering on the absurd. A long wound of broken branches reaches all the way from the top of the tree down to about four metres from the ground, where something that looks like a rag doll has got stuck in a V-shaped cleft. The dead man's limbs are contorted at unnatural angles, and his clothes are ripped. One branch has gone straight through his chest and is sticking out between his shoulder blades. The leaves, the trunk and the ground below are dark with blood.

'We had another suicide here about ten years ago,' Morell informs her. 'A business owner from the city who'd ruined both family and friends, but he actually landed on the ground. This poor bastard has made things a little more difficult for us.'

He directs the beam of his torch at the cliff behind the tree. It is at least fifty to sixty metres high.

'There's a viewpoint at the top. People often go there in the summer, take a picnic and watch the sunset. Technically, unauthorised persons are not allowed access, but nobody bothers to keep people out.'

The rain sets in and Anna fastens her jacket. She's glad she got herself a proper, classic raincoat that keeps out the wet. Morell switches off his torch.

'I've spoken to the duty officer at the regional control centre. We've decided to wait until first thing tomorrow morning to bring in the technicians. It's Sunday evening, the guy in the tree is going nowhere, and it's not necessary to call anyone in on overtime. The budget is already under enough pressure. Glarea has offered to help guard the body overnight, but it's not as if anyone can get at it up there. Maybe you and I could drive up onto the ridge, see if we can find his car? I think I know roughly where it should be.'

She isn't sure what to say. Morell is behaving as if he's still in charge, with an authority in his tone that irritates her. He notices her expression, which is some small consolation.

'Listen, I'm sorry for jumping in. Olsson called me first, no doubt out of habit. I don't live far away, so I thought—'

'Who found the body?' she interrupts, perhaps with unnecessary sharpness.

'One of the drivers. This is one of the oldest parts of the quarry, and it's been closed for many years. The driver decided to take a leak behind the tree, poor guy.'

'Is he still here?'

Morell shakes his head. 'Olsson had a chat with him, then sent him home to his family. He was very shocked – obviously.'

He switches on the torch once more, directs the beam at the body in the tree. A flash of light, a reflection, catches Anna's eye.

'Can you shine it right next to the trunk?' she says.

She takes out a pair of blue plastic shoe covers she slipped into her pocket before she left home, and pulls them on. Then she switches on her own smaller but more powerful torch and moves towards the tree. The rain is hammering on her coat. The metallic stench of blood grows stronger, almost defeating the smell of burned clay.

She stops half a metre from the thick trunk, just outside the patch of blood-spattered leaves, and crouches down. Directs the torch towards the point where she saw the flash. Something has got stuck between the tree's roots, diagonally below the body; she assumes it has come loose from his clothing, or fallen out of his pocket. She sees a piece of plastic and suspects she knows what she's found.

She puts on a pair of disposable gloves and takes a pen out of her pocket. She uses it to fish out the item. Just as she suspected, it turns out to be a pair of badly damaged glasses. The frame is bent and one lens is missing. She holds them up to the light. The remaining lens is tinted. She stiffens, looks up at the body. It is hanging face down, the features battered and contorted; one eye socket is empty. However, she immediately recognises the dead man. It is the bearded stranger from the party.

She replaces the glasses and slowly retraces her footsteps. She takes off the gloves without looking at Morell, then calls over the officer who rang her.

'Olsson, get these vehicles out of here then cordon off an area of at least fifty square metres around the tree. No one sets foot there until the CSIs have arrived.'

Olsson looks confused. 'But he's a jumper,' he says a little too loudly, glancing over Anna's shoulder. She doesn't need to turn around to understand that he's seeking guidance from Morell.

'We are treating this incident as a suspicious death until we have evidence to the contrary, so get the vehicles out of here and set up a cordon. Is that clear?' No stammering, no hesitation. *Good!*

Olsson hesitates, looks over at Morell again.

'Is that clear?' she repeats in a tone that brooks no argument.

'Yes,' he mutters, heading reluctantly for his car.

Morell has crept up on her; he obviously heard the whole thing.

'So, Anna . . .' He bounces up and down on his heels. 'As I said, it's your district now, and your budget. But is this really the best use of resources, in view of—'

'I'm afraid I have to ask you to leave, Henry,' she interrupts him, trying to sound pleasant but firm. She takes a deep breath before delivering her final sentence. 'Right now, please.'

31

Autumn 2017

Anna's first murder investigation was relatively straightforward. A standard Swedish murder involving two alcoholics partying in a seedy flat. At the beginning of the evening they were best friends and brothers, eating hot dogs and drinking Explorer Vodka with grape tonic. At some point just before midnight, things went wrong. They'd run out of booze earlier than planned, and one guy stuck a bread knife in the other's chest before crashing out next to his victim on the sofa. Fingerprints, DNA, the suspect discovered half a metre from the victim. An open-and-shut case, as they say on TV.

However, she did learn something important: that the motive for the most serious crimes can be that you make your own drink a little stronger than someone else thinks is reasonable. Over the years that knowledge has served her well. No motive, however petty it might seem, can be ignored.

Jens Friberg arrives about thirty minutes after she called him. He has three uniformed officers with him in the VW van, and two more following in a patrol car. Henry Morell left the scene some time ago, screeching away with gravel spraying up around his tyres, and the rain is more persistent now. Anna is pleased to see that Jens makes no attempt to lift the police tape and go tramping over to the birch tree to look at the body. He parks the van right behind her car, then flips open the back as a protection from the rain and spreads out a large map.

'I thought you might need to orientate yourself.' He shows her the spot where they are standing, then moves his finger a centimetre or so to the contour lines marking the ridge. 'There's a forest track up here that people tend to use to reach the viewpoint. If the deceased travelled there by car, then that's probably where his vehicle is. If it's OK with you, I was thinking of taking two men and going to look for it. We also need to cordon off the viewpoint and protect the area from the rain as best we can. We brought a couple of tarpaulins.'

'Good thinking. The CSIs are on their way from Helsingborg, but it's likely to be at least an hour before they get here.'

'OK.'

'There's something you need to know,' she says as he's about to turn and leave. 'Our victim was behind the fight at the party on Saturday. He gave the DJ a USB stick with a song by Simon Vidje on it, and gave him money to play it when Caia Bianca was on the dance floor. It was that song that triggered the whole thing.'

'Shit!' Jens is clearly taken aback. 'Have you told Henry?'

She shakes her head. Jens chews his upper lip, but says nothing. Anna is still not sure of him; only a few days ago she regarded him as a rival, possibly even an enemy. However, right now he is her only real resource. *Sometimes you just have to roll with the punches*, she thinks before Håkan can pipe up.

'I saw the victim on Saturday night,' she says. 'He was watching the fight, and seemed to find it all very amusing. With hindsight I'm increasingly convinced . . .' She falls silent, tries to read Jens's face, but without success. She decides to keep going. '. . . that the whole thing was planned. That he was there with the intention of starting something.'

Jens nods slowly, then glances over at the birch tree. 'In which case he succeeded beyond expectations, wouldn't you say?'

Jens calls her after about forty minutes to tell her that they've found a battered old Saab 900 only a few hundred metres from the viewpoint.

'According to our records, it's belonged to a scrapyard in Klippan since 2005. It's deregistered and not insured. It hasn't been reported stolen, but of course it could be. The scrapyard probably doesn't keep a close eye on its vehicles. As far as I can see, there are no visible signs that it's been hot-wired, but it's hard to tell from the outside. We're talking about a thirty-year-old car, and as I'm sure you know, you can more or less start a 900 with an ice lolly.'

She notes that he hasn't opened the car, which pleases her, and she also gives him credit – somewhat belatedly – for thinking of the tarpaulins. Whatever she thinks of Jens Friberg as a person, Morell's assessment of him was correct: he is an excellent police officer.

'What does the car look like in general?' she asks.

'Like a typical old banger. I'll send you a couple of pictures.'

'How about the viewpoint?'

'As far as evidence goes, it's not great. The ground consists mainly of wet leaves and earth, and the rain is making it worse, of course. We'll cordon off the area and cover it as best we can, then the CSIs will do their bit. I'll call you if we find anything interesting.'

They end the call, and seconds later her phone beeps. Coverage in the quarry is poor, so it takes a while for the pictures to download. She moves around, searching for a better signal, and glances up at the top of the cliff where she can see the torch beams moving around among the trees.

The first image shows a rusty white Saab 900 that has come off the track. The second shows the driver's seat seen through the side window. The upholstery is dirty and torn, and two furry dice and a faded air freshener dangle from the rear-view mirror. The ignition is hidden by a McDonald's bag, making it impossible to see if there's a screwdriver in it. The third image is of the back seat. The flash is reflected in the rain-soaked windows, but she sees two large blue IKEA bags and lots of clothes. She would really like to go up and take a closer look. There is still no sign of the CSIs, which makes her feel frustrated and restless, but also strangely excited. She knows why, but would prefer not to admit it. As usual, Håkan sees straight through her.

ANDERS DE LA MOTTE

Because you love this, Anna. You love the challenge, the hunt, the excitement. You love the fact that you're good at it. That's why you never stammer when you're talking about work.

She takes a deep breath, closes her eyes and visualises a volume control. Turns it all the way down to zero. The trick works and Håkan falls silent, at least for the time being. She decides to make the call she's been putting off for the last half hour. She needs to tell Agnes that she won't be home tonight.

32

Autumn 2017

At about seven in the morning Anna nips home to Tabor to change her clothes and give Agnes a lift to the station. She is met by a less than happy Milo, who shoots between her legs and disappears among the trees. There is a note on the kitchen table.

Staying the night at Erik's.

Five words, no signature. Nothing more than the information she needs to prevent her from worrying, and yet the brief note tells her something else: the fragile truce between them is probably over. It's her fault; she promised Agnes that she would no longer work nights and leave her alone.

However, by the time she sets off for the police station, she is angry. She considers calling Agnes, telling her it's not OK to sleep over at a friend's without talking to her mother first, but Håkan has something to say.

There are more important things, aren't there? Things you ought to tell her before she hears them elsewhere. The investigation is still ongoing . . .

She tries to shut him up, tries to explain to him that the status code on the computer screen doesn't necessarily mean what he's implying. It could just be that the prosecutor has been very busy, and hasn't yet got around to dismissing the case. This could happen any day now, then Håkan can stop worrying. Leave her in peace and concentrate on being dead.

Her internal dialogue with her ex-husband is still going on when she arrives at the station. Several vehicles that she recognises from last night are parked outside, including the CSI van, back up from county HQ, and Jens Friberg's VW. She follows the smell of wet clothes and finds the whole team in the kitchen, chatting to Henry Morell. The room is jam-packed, the atmosphere is relaxed, and she walks in on the end of a burst of laughter.

'There you are, Anna,' Morell says. 'We were just sharing old memories – nothing about current cases, so you don't need to worry.' He smiles, his tone is almost too friendly, which of course is another way of showing his displeasure at the way she treated him last night.

She ignores the challenge, simply stands there in silence, waiting. She notes that he is still in uniform, even though he's now officially retired. After a few uncomfortable seconds he gives in, picks up his coffee cup and gets to his feet.

'Well, it's high time I made a start on that chapter I promised the police academy. After all, they've already paid me the advance! Good luck everyone.' He raises his cup in a farewell toast and heads for his office.

Anna waits until she hears his door close.

'I am aware that most of you know Henry Morell,' she says slowly. 'He has many years of service behind him, and the police . . .' she pauses, breathes, 'authority has a great deal to thank him for. However, as of yesterday he is no longer in active service, and cannot be allowed access to any information covered by the requirement for confidentiality. This includes all information relating to this case – is that clear?'

The CSIs and the officers from county HQ don't seem to have any objections, but she sees a couple of her own officers exchange meaningful glances. Jens Friberg, however, doesn't react at all.

'Good. If you'd like to top up your coffee cups, I'll see you down in the briefing room.'

She doesn't start the meeting until the door is firmly closed. There is no hint of a stammer as she goes through the circumstances in which the body was found, then hands over to Grönwall, the senior crime scene investigator, who has just linked his laptop to the overhead projection system.

'The victim is a man in his early fifties,' he says, bringing up a picture of the man's battered face.

'Height five feet five inches, and at the time of death he weighed approximately eight stone. According to the forensic pathologist's preliminary assessment, death is thought to have occurred between ten to twelve hours before the body was discovered. This wide time frame is down to the cold and the rain, but it leads us to the early hours of Sunday morning. More on that after the autopsy.'

He takes a sip of coffee, then continues: 'As you've probably already worked out, the primary cause of death is severe trauma to the entire body, consistent with a fall. Again, the autopsy will provide further detail – there are a great many injuries that will need to be examined more closely.'

He clicks onto the next slide, a photograph of the man lying on his back on top of a tarpaulin. His arms and legs have been straightened, yet there is still something unnatural about their position. The branch that had penetrated the body has been sawn off and still protrudes from the chest, which combined with the angle of the limbs and the empty eye socket makes the corpse look like a macabre marionette. It is so unpleasant that it takes a moment for Anna to realise what is really bothering her.

'Wasn't he wearing any shoes?' she says.

'No – they were in the car. It is a little odd, although we did have a jumper over at Kullaberg the other year who was stark naked apart from a Santa hat.'

Grönwall makes the most of the expected laughter before continuing.

'We haven't yet identified the deceased. We didn't find an ID card or any other documentation, either on the body or in the car. However, we did find other traces that should help us to establish his identity before too long.'

His next picture is a collage of several tattoos distributed over the victim's hands, arms and chest. Anna recognises the one on the back of his hand, which presumably represents a seaman's grave. Grönwall changes to an image of the man's arms; the crook of each elbow is marked with a series of small white scars, forming a familiar pattern.

'The victim has a number of prison tattoos, plus scarring from drug abuse, which means he is probably on our database. We'll try matching fingerprints first, because that's the quickest method. As you know, DNA samples are processed by the National Forensics Laboratory.' He pauses, sighs. 'Of course, I mean the National Forensics Centre, as our friends in Linköping are known these days. The bright sparks who came up with that name ought to be locked up for life.'

Once again he waits for the laughter to subside.

'Anyway, if he's had his fingerprints taken in the past, then we could have a match by this afternoon. Unfortunately, it's not quite as fast as on TV.'

Yet another predictable burst of laughter.

'Any sign of a mobile phone?' Anna asks before Grönwall can continue his comedy routine.

'No. We searched with a metal detector around the body and up at the viewpoint, but no luck. There's a charger plugged into the cigarette lighter in the car, but as I said, no phone yet, which is surprising these days. This is the viewpoint, by the way.'

A low wire fence in a poor state runs along a plateau. Beyond it the view stretches into the distance. A rusty sign with the word DANGER! attached to the fence reminds Anna of the one she and Agnes saw on the barrier at the old quarry. The next few pictures were taken a metre or so into the forest. The ground is covered in wet leaves and small piles of earth, which could have been kicked up by people or wild animals.

'As you can see, it's difficult to find any concrete evidence in this kind of terrain. Our best chance is probably the fence. You have to climb over it to reach the edge of the cliff, so we might find clothing fibres. My team is working on that right now. I'd also like to award a gold star to the colleagues who protected the area with tarpaulins last night.'

He gives Jens Friberg a nod of appreciation before moving on to the white Saab. He goes through the information that Anna already knows: model, year, registration number, the name of the firm that owns the car, the fact that it hasn't been reported stolen.

'We still can't formally link our victim to the vehicle, but given its location, we're working on the hypothesis that it belonged to him. We've had it brought in for forensic examination; we'll get on to that as soon as we've finished outdoors. OK, so that's about it for now. To summarise: at the moment we don't have anything to confirm either suicide or murder. We're waiting for fingerprint analysis, and for the results of the autopsy.'

They discuss the investigation for a few more minutes; apart from the digger driver, there are no witnesses to question, and no houses along the last few miles leading to the viewpoint. Anna thanks everyone for their hard work overnight, and sends them home to get some sleep. Personally, she has other plans.

She makes her way down to the underground car park and finds the Saab tucked away in a corner, surrounded by police tape. Just as she'd hoped, the CSIs haven't got around to emptying the vehicle or dusting for prints.

She puts on her nitrile gloves and carefully opens the driver's door. She is met by the smell of cigarettes, dirty, old upholstery, petrol, a dried-up air freshener, and the other more or less pleasant smells an old car accumulates. She stands there for a moment, trying to picture the bearded man inside the vehicle. Without touching the seat, she reaches in and picks up the McDonald's bag. Jens Friberg was right. A fragment of what looks like a broken piece of a hacksaw blade has been pushed into the lock to serve as an ignition key. Just as Grönwall said, there is a charger cable dangling from the cigarette lighter, and on the floor on the passenger side there is a pair of trainers so muddy that it's almost impossible to tell what colour they are. Why did the man take them off?

She turns her attention to the back seat. One IKEA bag contains a cheap toiletries bag on top of a pile of crumpled clothes; in the other is a sleeping bag and a pillow. The odour of an unwashed human body is pretty strong here. The torch jammed between the roof and the handle above the door convinces her; the bearded man had been living in this car.

In the boot she finds a selection of rusty tools, several metres of garden hose and a plastic can. Judging by the smell, the last two items have been used to siphon petrol from parked cars.

She steps back and stares at the Saab, tries to put together what she has just learned with the information from Grönwall and what she already knows about the dead man. After ten seconds she is convinced that something isn't right. Another twenty and she knows what it is.

The bearded man is, or was, five feet five inches tall, only slightly taller than she is. He was also thin, bordering on emaciated. But the driver's seat is pushed back as far as it will go.

She leans in, looks at the rear-view mirror and attempts to work out the angles. It is important to keep an open mind, but she can't find anything to contradict her original conclusion. If the victim had sat in the driver's seat as it is now, it would have been extremely difficult for him to operate the pedals effectively, or to use the mirror. There are two possible explanations for the position of the seat: firstly, the car does not belong to the bearded man. This doesn't fit in with their hypothesis, which is not a reason to ignore it. The other option seems far more likely. The car does belong to the bearded man, but someone else drove it to the viewpoint – someone much taller, someone who has also taken the victim's phone in order to hide his own involvement.

In spite of her best efforts, an image of Alex Morell immediately pops into her mind and refuses to go away.

33

Autumn 2017

Before Anna leaves the station to go home and rest, she feels the need to sort out the awkward situation with Henry Morell. The door of his office is ajar, and she taps gently on the frame.

'Come in!'

He is sitting at his desk with his reading glasses on. 'Anna, I'm so glad you're here. This damned cursor won't go where I want it. I've tried everything.' He waves helplessly at the screen.

'Let's see,' she says, hiding her surprise.

She leans over his shoulder to fix the problem. As usual he smells of aftershave with a hint of musty house.

'There you go.' She straightens up.

'Thank you so much – you're a lifesaver, Anna.'

She stays where she is, looking down on him. His glasses are perched on the end of his nose, which makes him look kind and slightly absent-minded. She wishes she hadn't been so short with him down at the quarry, and decides to tell him.

'Henry, I really didn't mean to—' she begins, but he holds up his hand to stop her.

'You don't have to say anything, Anna. To be honest, I'm the one who owes you an apology.'

He slowly removes his glasses, shuffles in his seat.

'I've worked at this station for the whole of my career. The people of Nedanås have become my extended family. To suddenly be excluded . . .' Anna is about to speak again, but once again he

197

holds up his hand. 'No, no. You did absolutely the right thing. This is your jurisdiction now, your station, your colleagues, and, not least, your decisions. I have no doubt that you will do an excellent job, and I hope you can forgive an old dinosaur who's finding it a little difficult to let go. With the benefit of hindsight, and to quote my clever wife, maybe staying on here wasn't such a good idea.'

Anna doesn't really know what to say. Part of her is pleased about Morell's sudden self-awareness, while another part feels sorry for him.

'It's fine,' she says in a conciliatory tone. 'I really appreciate everything you've done to help me feel at home here, and it's good to have you around if I need—' She stops as the stammer alarm bell begins to ring before the word 'help' – that wouldn't sound right. She considers changing to 'support', but rejects that too. 'Advice,' she says instead, which makes his face light up.

'You can always turn to me, Anna, whatever it's about.'

'Thank you, Henry.'

There is a brief silence; neither of them seems to know how to bring the conversation to an end.

'Anyway, I'm going home for a couple of hours. It was a long night,' she says eventually.

He nods. 'Yes, I realised that – the team looked pretty tired. But they're all good officers – I'm sure you'll get to the bottom of what's happened.' He pauses, considers what to say next. 'Would you allow me one question out of curiosity, Anna?'

'Of course!'

'Have you found anything to suggest that it wasn't suicide?'

She thinks about the position of the driver's seat, but chooses to keep that little detail to herself.

'Not yet,' she replies with exaggerated slowness.

Morell nods; the kindly, ageing bear is back. And yet she thinks she detects a hint of relief.

On the way home she turns on the GPS on her phone to help her locate the viewpoint, but as before it works only sporadically as soon as she reaches the ridge. It tells her to turn right by two signs; one is old and says KOTORP, the other is newer, with the words NORRBLICKA BED & BREAKFAST. After that the GPS becomes confused about which road she should take. Eventually she comes across another sign pointing to a place called Vargadalen, but she knows she would have remembered such an unusual name from Jens's map, and decides to carry straight on. Fortunately, she meets the CSI vehicle and waves it over to the side. She recognises the two men from last night.

'Have you found anything?' she asks.

The driver, who looks exhausted, nods. 'We secured a number of clothing fibres from the fence right by the edge, and part of a footprint next to the same spot.'

'Anything else?'

The men glance at each other. 'Not exactly,' says the man in the passenger seat. 'It's been raining for several days, so the ground is soft, and there are no footprints in the forest, only little piles where the leaves have been kicked up. This is largely speculation . . .' they exchange another glance, 'but both Börje and I have seen similar locations over the years, and we think this happened very fast.'

'What do you mean?' She turns back to the driver, who is evidently called Börje.

'We mean that it looks as if he was running. Started off in the forest, leaped over the fence and carried straight on into thin air. The footprint supports that theory.'

'It's only the front part of the sole,' the passenger clarifies. 'The way your foot lands when you're running as fast as you can.'

She thanks them for the information and asks for directions to the viewpoint before letting them go.

She finds the right logging track and weaves between the pot-holes. She parks just in front of the tracks left by the Saab and the truck that picked it up.

There is dense, deciduous forest on both sides of the track. The trees have tall, straight trunks, just like those around Tabor. The ground is covered in a thick layer of wet leaves – this year's on top, last year's in the middle, then older and older layers in varying stages of decomposition, until you reach the soil beneath. She glimpses light between the trees, and follows the slope downwards. After about a hundred metres, she reaches the viewpoint.

The plateau is only three to four metres wide. It appears all of a sudden, and the only warning is the light from the sky. The view is impressive, although nowhere near as beautiful as the one from Tabor. Glarea's lunar landscape extends from the bottom of the cliff – an ugly, dirty brown wound with ragged edges that has chewed its way down through the earth's crust and stretches all the way to the outskirts of Nedanås. She can see the huge machines moving around, and smoke rising between the ravines. In spite of the height and the wind, she can also smell burning clay. The houses she can see in the distance on the edge of the quarry must really suffer from both the blasting and the stench. It's hardly surprising that the place is going to have to close down.

The wire fence from Grönwall's pictures appears to be in even worse condition in reality. It's no more than a metre high, and sags in several places. If you came running down the slope in the dark and the rain, it wouldn't provide much of a barrier. She cautiously moves forward and peers over the edge of the cliff. Fifty or sixty metres below she can see the damaged crown of the birch, and a pale scar of broken branches.

So, could it have been an accident rather than a suicide? She considers the possibility. It can't be ruled out, of course, but an accident doesn't explain why the bearded man was up here, or why he ran down the slope with no shoes on. Nor does it explain the absence of his phone, or the position of the driver's seat. To summarise: the scene itself provides no clear evidence for either scenario. All doors are still open, at least for the time being.

She gets back in her car and heads home. Her mind is elsewhere and she takes the wrong turning, but doesn't realise until she drives into someone's yard. The house itself is a beautiful old Skåne long house, but right now it looks anything but inviting. A huge trench has been dug out in front of the door. A wooden pallet serves as a bridge, and building materials cover half the yard: concrete drainage pipes, piles of wood, bricks and tiles, and beyond them a huge diesel tank next to a digger. She recognises the company logo from Morell's basement. Alexander Morell's construction firm is working here, and for a second she wonders if she risks bumping into him. However, even though it's Tuesday afternoon, there doesn't appear to be any activity going on, and the builders' hut is secured with a sturdy padlock.

She turns the car around and ends up with her back wheels in a pool of water. She doesn't realise how deep it is until the suspension complains. She is about to change gear in order to get out when someone emerges from the house – a tall, slim figure in overalls and a cap, with two large German Shepherds on the leash. Both dogs are on full alert, ears pricked up, eyes fixed on her car.

It takes her a few seconds to recognise Marie Sordi, who looks uneasy.

Anna lowers the window and sticks her head out.

'Hi, Marie – it's only me. Anna Vesper.'

'Oh, hi.' Marie's expression softens slightly, but she doesn't relax completely. Hardly surprising, in view of what happened the last time they met. She walks over to the car, and as soon as she stops, the dogs sit down, one either side of her.

'Sorry about the reception – I didn't recognise the car. This place attracts all kinds of weirdos.'

'Is this Kotorp?' Anna asks.

'It's call Norrblicka nowadays,' Marie says, with a small but noticeable grimace. 'Were you looking for Bruno? Is it about Saturday night?' She sounds worried.

'No, I just took a wrong turning.'

Marie is clearly relieved. 'It's easily done – there are so many dirt tracks up here.'

One of the dogs lets out a low growl, but a sharp word from Marie silences him.

'Would you like to come in? It's a bit of a mess – as you can see, we're living on a building site at the moment.'

Anna shakes her head. She isn't feeling particularly sociable after the events of last night, and longs to get home for a shower and a nap.

'Not today, thanks – some other time, maybe? This is quite a project.' She nods in the direction of the house. 'I hear it's going to be a conference centre.'

Marie smiles wearily. 'Well, that's the plan – right now it feels like hard work. We only have water and electricity in half the house, and the fact that Bruno and the architect keep altering the design doesn't exactly help.'

'I'm sure it'll be amazing when it's finished.' Anna doesn't know why she says that, but she can't help feeling a little sorry for Marie, living in the middle of this mess with her family.

The other woman nods. 'That's what I keep telling Bruno. Just between the two of us, he moans more than the kids about having to shower in the cellar.'

They exchange a smile.

'Anna, before you go . . .' Marie tilts her head to one side. 'Bruno has a lot on, with the build and his father's restaurant. Fabbe thinks he spends too much time here instead of doing his job. Bruno and Alex had too much to drink, and combined with the stress and everything else . . .' She makes an apologetic gesture which makes both dogs look up at her.

'I realise that's no excuse, merely an explanation, but I wanted to apologise, and to thank you for your help. We've already sent the DJ a gift hamper to try and smooth things over, and needless to say we'll replace all the equipment that was damaged,' Marie concludes with an artificial smile.

'According to Bruno, it was the song that triggered the whole thing,' Anna says. 'An old track by Simon Vidje that the DJ played?'

Marie is still smiling, but the reaction provoked by the name is clear to see in her face – anxiety, disgust, even fear.

'I don't know anything about that. It was so noisy I could hardly hear myself think.'

A lie, a very obvious one; the signs are there in Marie's voice and body language. Just like her friends, Marie definitely recognised the song, so why lie about it? Anna knows the answer; she has come across the phenomenon before. Unnecessary small fibs are a defence mechanism, a way of distancing yourself from something unpleasant that you really don't want to be associated with.

'You and Simon were cousins, weren't you?'

Marie looks uncomfortable. 'That's right. Elisabet Vidje is my maternal aunt.'

'So, you and Simon knew each other well?'

One of the dogs whines, as if it has picked up on its mistress's unease.

'We were like brother and sister,' Marie says quietly.

The rain begins to fall again, pattering into the puddles around them. Somewhere far away a bird croaks, a harsh monotone that echoes faintly across the treetops.

'Well, I must get on.' Marie rediscovers her politician's face and straightens her shoulders. Both dogs immediately get to their feet. 'As I said, Anna, both Dad and I are very grateful for the discreet way you handled things on Saturday. We're really looking forward to working with you in the future.'

34

Autumn 2017

Back home at Tabor, Anna lets Milo out and has a quick shower. She really wanted a nap, but there are too many thoughts whirling around inside her head. She makes herself a sandwich, sits down on the kitchen sofa and goes through the events of Saturday night again, tries to recreate exactly what happened. She remembers yelling at Alex to let go of the DJ, and that Bruno said something when he positioned himself in front of her. Something about admitting it. She closes her eyes, pictures Bruno. The bright red face, the fury in his eyes, his lips moving. *Not until he admits it* – was that it? Admits what? That he played the track? There was no doubt about that, so what did Bruno mean? His wife gave no clues at all; it was very obvious that she didn't want to go anywhere near the subject of Simon Vidje.

Sooner or later Anna is going to have to speak to Alex and Bruno. At the moment only she and Jens Friberg know that the dead man in the tree is the same person who caused the fight at the party, and she'd like to keep it that way for a while longer – at least until she knows his identity, which might make his motives a little clearer. Best to hold off on the interviews until then. It also gives her time to think about how best to handle Henry Morell.

Exhaustion hits her like a sledgehammer. She leans back and closes her eyes – just for a couple of minutes, she tells herself.

Her phone wakes her, buzzing around on the table like an oversized angry insect before she manages to catch it.

'Hello?'

'Hi, it's Grönwall. We've identified the body – I thought you'd want to know right away.'

'Absolutely. How?' She grabs a piece of paper and a pen.

'A match on the fingerprints, just as we thought.'

'So, what's his name?'

'Kent Joakim Rylander, date of birth 16.06.1960. He has a whole lot of aliases, and his record is as long as your arm – drugs, theft, burglary, a series of driving offences. The latest entries involve petty fraud and the misappropriation of funds.'

'Address?'

'He's registered at the same address as the scrapyard that owns the Saab, so I think we can assume that the car is his. We've just finished going through it for fingerprints and DNA. I'm waiting for the results, but it's really a formality.'

'Good.' She thinks for a moment. 'Still no phone or wallet?'

'No. Rylander doesn't have a driving licence, so he might not even possess a wallet. There were a couple of crumpled hundred-kronor notes in one of his pockets.'

'OK.' She suppresses a yawn. 'We need to search his home address; do you have anyone who can come along?'

'Not until tomorrow. My team worked late last night, and I need to send them home as soon as they've finished with the car. And myself, come to think of it.'

Anna looks at the clock: almost two thirty. She can hear Milo barking agitatedly; he's been out in the drizzle for almost an hour and a half, and must be cold and wet.

'Of course,' she says to Grönwall. 'I'll see you at the station at eight in the morning and we'll travel together.'

She ends the call and goes to open the door for Milo, who is still barking. Mats Andersson is crouched on the top step, playing with the dog.

'H-hi,' she says, taken aback.

The big man glances up and frowns, keeping Milo at arm's length to stop him clambering up.

'Is Agnes home?'

'No, she's at school.'

'Oh.' Mats looks disappointed. Milo slips past his defences and tries to bury his nose in the scruffy leather backpack on the ground behind Mats.

'Anything I can help you with?'

'No.' He shakes his head, shoos Milo away and stands up. 'I brought something for her. A present.'

'Would you like a cup of coffee?' She knows why she's asking; there is something about Mats that makes her curious. The fact that he is Marie Sordi née Andersson's brother and only a year or so younger than Simon Vidje is probably part of the explanation. She steps aside, gestures invitingly towards the kitchen.

Mats's face lights up, but then he hesitates, as if the appealing thought of coffee is wrestling with something else.

'I don't know. Aunt Elisabet said that nobody's allowed to go inside Tabor . . .' He shuffles his feet uncomfortably. Milo is still skittering around his legs, eyes fixed on the backpack.

'What if I bring us both a cup out here?'

Mats thinks for a moment, then nods. Anna goes in and sets a tray with two Höganäs cups, milk, sugar, and a packet of biscuits that she finds in a cupboard. She pulls on a jacket before going back outside. The drizzle is still hanging in the air, but Mats doesn't seem bothered. He takes a cup, thanks her politely and helps himself to milk and sugar, then stirs with such concentration that she thinks he must be counting. Five clockwise, then five anti-clockwise.

'Your aunt was here the other day,' she says as a way of starting off the conversation.

'So I heard. Klein wasn't happy about that.' He takes a sip of his coffee.

'No?'

Mats shakes his head. 'Aunt Elisabet isn't well. She shouldn't be driving around.'

'Is Klein in charge at Änglaberga?'

Mats pulls a face, but Anna's not sure if it's a reaction to the question or the coffee. He doesn't answer, so she tries a different tack.

'I met your sister, Marie, earlier. We saw each other in the park on Saturday as well.'

'The homecoming party,' he says, wiping a drop of coffee from his beard. 'I expect my father gave a speech as usual. He likes to be the centre of attention.'

'But you weren't there?'

He shakes his head. 'I'm happiest up here in the forest.'

Milo has sat down and is now giving Mats his full begging routine. Head tilted on one side, spontaneous dribbling, a sweet little whimper. Anna throws him a biscuit, but he gives her a dirty look as if that wasn't what he wanted at all. Then he eats it anyway.

'How come you're living with your aunt?'

'When my grandfather died, Aunt Elisabet had to take care of Änglaberga. When my parents got married, they were given Kotorp, but my father sold off almost all of the land to Glarea in the '80s. Have you been down to the quarry?'

'Yes.'

'A lot of it is Kotorp's land. It looks terrible.'

'Like a lunar landscape,' Anna says, and Mats nods in agreement. 'So you and Marie grew up at Kotorp?'

'Mm, but our mother was often ill, so we spent a lot of time at Änglaberga.' He shakes his head, his expression sceptical. 'When my father sold Kotorp to Marie and bought a house down in the village, he and Aunt Elisabet decided that I should move into Änglaberga. My collection was already there, after all.'

Mats takes a biscuit and nibbles at it without explaining what he means by the last sentence.

'How long ago was that?'

He thinks for a moment. 'Mother died in 2007, so it must be ten years.'

'Your father, Bengt – I gather he and Elisabet don't get along.'

'They can't even be in the same room. It's always been that way. Elisabet doesn't like the fact that he sold Grandfather's land to Glarea.'

'And Henry Morell?'

'They definitely don't get along. Elisabet can be difficult. To be honest, Klein is the only one who can talk to her.'

'I assume it's because of Simon?'

Mats stares into his coffee cup. Anna decides to stop asking questions and allow the silence to do its work, but Mats doesn't say another word – he just carries on munching his biscuit. Anna tries a different angle.

'When Göran delivered Agnes's moped the other day, he told me that Simon had built his own recording studio above the garage at Änglaberga. Did you see it?'

Mats looks up with a wry smile.

'I was the one who built it, not Simon. He was no craftsman. I made a booth which we soundproofed with egg boxes, and a window so that you could see in. It turned out well.' He smiles again, as if it's a pleasant memory.

'Were you there when he recorded his music?'

Mats nods. 'He'd saved up for a proper reel-to-reel tape recorder. Sometimes he asked me to press the buttons while he was in the studio. He had a lovely voice. Everybody thought so. Everybody liked Simon.' Mats falls silent, stares into his cup once more.

'Did the rest of the gang come to the studio? Your sister, Alex, Bruno and Carina?'

He shrugs. 'No. Simon didn't like having people around. Only me and Karl-Johan were allowed in.'

'Not your aunt or Klein? Why not?'

'He said it bothered him.'

'Was Karl-Johan often there?'

'Now and again. His summer car was in the garage down below.'

'Summer car?'

'That's what he called it. A red cabriolet with the steering wheel on the wrong side. It was beautiful, but it needed a lot of work. Karl-Johan used to open the door at the bottom of the stairs when he was tinkering with the car so that he could hear Simon playing. Simon would yell at him to shut the door and Karl-Jo would yell back, "OK," but he'd leave it open.'

Mats inhales deeply as if all this talking has left him breathless. He empties his cup, glances at the track. 'Do you think she'll be back soon?'

'Agnes? I've no idea.' She tries to remember Agnes's schedule, and immediately feels like a bad parent. 'Would you like me to go inside and have a look?'

Mats shakes his head. 'I need to go home. I'll catch up with her another day.' He puts his cup down on the tray, picks up his backpack.

'I believe the studio was destroyed in a fire?' Anna says.

Mats freezes. 'Yes. The studio, the tape recorder, the summer car. All of it. There was nothing left.'

'Nothing?' She is thinking of the charred skeleton of a car she saw in the outbuilding, and can't help glancing in that direction. Mats follows her eyes.

'Almost nothing,' he adds.

'Karl-Johan kept the car – or what was left of it.'

Mats nods. 'I suppose he intended to renovate it, but he never got around to it. He had his hands full with . . .' He raises his hand a fraction, indicating either the chapel or his own head.

'The mural,' Anna says. 'Have you seen it?'

'No.' The answer comes a little too quickly, and he looks slightly uneasy.

'But you know what the subject is?'

No response.

'Your sister was there that night. Does she ever talk about what happened? About Simon?'

'Nobody talks about Simon. Not my father, not Marie, not Bruno or Alex. Nor does anyone else, at least not in public. It's as if he never existed. But Simon did exist. I liked him.'

He stares at the ground. Milo whines, edges closer, tilts his head to one side again, as if he's picked up on the big man's sorrow.

'There's one thing I don't understand,' Anna says quietly. 'Your Aunt Elisabet – she's angry with your father, Henry Morell, Alex, Bruno and Carina because she thinks they're lying about what went on that night. But she talks to your sister, even though Marie was there too. Why is that?'

'Her clothes,' he mumbles.

'Her clothes? What do you mean?'

He glances in the direction of the forest as if he really wants to get away.

'When they saw Simon in the water that morning, Marie jumped in to try and get him out. Only her, none of the others. They stayed on the shore. Marie was soaking wet – their clothes were dry.'

'So your aunt's interpretation is that they didn't think it was worth jumping in, because they already knew that Simon was dead.'

Mats shrugs. 'The water in the quarry pool is freezing cold. They knew that from the previous evening – Carina was shivering, her lips were blue.' He shuffles his feet. 'I have to go. Thanks for the coffee.'

He gives Milo a farewell pat, then lumbers off across the yard and in among the trees. It's only after he's disappeared completely that Anna realises there's something in his story that doesn't make sense.

She finds it difficult to get to sleep that night. She and Agnes are barely talking, and she's forgotten to call her solicitor to ask what's going on with the internal investigation. And yet that's not what's occupying her mind.

How does Rylander fit in? Why did he turn up in Nedanås for the homecoming party? Where did he get Simon Vidje's music from, and why did he ask for it to be played when Caia Bianca was on the dance floor? Where is his phone, why wasn't he wearing his shoes, and most important of all: who killed him? Even though she doesn't have anything specific on which to base her hypothesis, she is convinced that Rylander's death was neither suicide nor an accident. There is something missing, something that will tie everything together. Something that she is going to do her utmost to find out.

Tiredness begins to take over. She thinks back to what Mats said earlier: Carina was shivering, her lips were blue. How could he know that? Maybe his sister told him, but it seems unlikely. Mats and Marie seem to be anything but close.

She slowly drifts away to the no man's land between sleep and wakefulness. Just before she drops off, she thinks she hears the sound of a creaking plank up in the chapel.

35

Autumn 2017

Anna is in her office at seven o'clock the following morning. Agnes is going to ride her Vespa to the train station, so they haven't even seen each other, let alone tried to talk things over.

Grönwall, or possibly a member of her own team, has printed out the information from the criminal records database on Rylander, including a photograph, and put everything in a file on her desk. She appreciates the efficiency, but decides it's probably a good idea to lock her door from now on. The photo is eight years old and he's wearing ordinary glasses, but there is no doubt that the body in the tree and Kent Joakim Rylander are one and the same person.

She leafs through the file. Rylander started with petty theft and minor drugs offences in his late teens, then advanced to car theft, burglary and various degrees of receiving stolen goods. A slightly more serious narcotics crime put him behind bars for a few years. As soon as he came out, the merry-go-round began again. He drifted from place to place in southern and central Sweden, changing his address virtually every year. Gradually he moved from narcotics into fraud and document forgery, crimes that carry shorter prison sentences but require greater skill, which suggests that Rylander wasn't stupid. Like so many other criminals, he used many different names. He called himself Kenta, Kekke, Jocke and similar variations on his two first names. He also changed his surname no fewer than three times before settling on Rylander.

Anna searches for relatives and discovers that his parents are dead and he's never been married. However, there are three children, all by different women. The first child, a daughter, was born at the beginning of the '90s when Rylander was only in his early twenties. The other two didn't come along until he was well over thirty, and are still minors. She decides to ask one of her team to inform the eldest daughter of his death, and find out what she wants to do with the body when it's released. She closes the file. Kent Joakim Rylander lived as a parasite feeding off other people, avoiding all responsibility, and even though he had three children, he lacked close family. He also died as he lived – alone. Anna thinks of Agnes. Their relationship is back to square one, and she has to find a way to deal with that. Try to get back to how things were over the weekend.

Tell her, Håkan whispers. *You know you have to.*

She pushes him away, takes a snap of Rylander's photo with her phone and sends it to DJ Kristian. Then she calls him and asks him a straight question.

'Yes, that's the guy who gave me the USB stick.'

'Are you absolutely sure?'

'As sure as I can be. The photo looks as if it was taken a while ago. Why do you want to know – I thought you'd dropped the case?'

'Have you ever heard of Kent Joakim Rylander?'

'I don't think so. Is that his name?'

'Yes.'

'Like I said, I'd never seen him before. Why is this so important?'

'Rylander was found dead yesterday, over in the quarry at Glarea.'

'Shit!' His tone changes from slightly put out to curious. 'What happened?'

'That's what we're trying to establish. At the moment it seems as if you were the last person to speak to him, so I'd like you to think carefully about what he said and how he seemed.'

There is silence on the other end of the line for a few seconds. 'As far as I remember, he just showed up. Held out a USB stick and a five-hundred-kronor note and asked me to play the track when Caia Bianca was on the dance floor. He said I'd get the same amount again afterwards. I thought it was a bit weird, but stranger things have happened. I did a season in Ibiza—'

'Where's the USB stick now?' she interrupts him.

'I don't know. I went back to the park on Sunday to pick up my stuff, and it was gone.'

'And you can't think of anything else? Something you forgot to mention before?'

Another silence. 'Actually, there is something.'

'What?' She presses the phone closer to her ear.

'When Alex Morell was holding me down, the other guy was yelling something in my ear. The cook – what was his name?'

'Bruno Sordi?'

'That's him. He kept shouting that I had to admit it.'

'Admit what?' Anna remembers Bruno saying the same thing to her.

'I've no idea – at the time I was too busy trying not to be strangled, but thinking back I'm pretty sure it was to do with an email.'

'An email? What kind of email?'

'Again, I've no idea, but I think that's what he said. Admit that you sent the email – something along those lines.'

Anna wonders where an email fits in.

'Thank you for your time,' she says. 'One of my officers will contact you to arrange a more formal interview, but please don't hesitate to get in touch if anything else occurs to you.' She gives him her mobile number before ending the call.

She opens the file and glances through Kent Joakim Rylander's criminal record one more time, then focuses on the last year of his life. He was released from prison in November 2016. Between that date and his death he is listed as a suspect in seven cases involving fraud on internet auction sites, getting people to pay for goods that don't exist. In order to carry out that kind of crime you need a computer, a tablet, or a smartphone at the very least. One that had at some point been charged in Rylander's battered old Saab.

She makes a note to look for IT equipment during the house search. Adds the word 'EMAIL' in capital letters, then enters the address of the scrapyard into Google Maps. The satellite image shows a remote location next to a lake. Three buildings in a horseshoe formation, and a smaller structure a few hundred metres away. Everywhere – along the narrow access road, all over the yard and behind the house – she sees pale and dark rectangles. When she zooms in, they turn out to be scrap vehicles. The satellite pictures are so good that she can sometimes make out tyre tracks and pools of mud. She zooms out again. The nearest village is Klippan, just under three miles away. She continues zooming out. In the opposite direction it's over ten miles to a place called Reftinge. Something about that name rings a bell; she's heard or read it somewhere quite recently.

She says it out loud a few times, rolls the 'R' to imitate a Skåne accent, but realises that she sounds ridiculous. She decides to leave it for the time being and enters her own ID number into the computer. The case comes up, the status box still shows 'ongoing'. *Shit!*

She calls her solicitor.

'Good to speak to you, Anna. I was actually going to contact you later today.'

'Right.' She takes a deep breath. 'Good or bad news?'

The brief silence answers her question.

'Internal Affairs want to interview you again. Apparently, a different prosecutor has taken over, and the new incumbent isn't willing to drop the case just yet.'

'You said everything would go away if we waited. Kept a low profile.'

'I also said there were no guarantees.'

She sighs. 'When?'

'As soon as possible. When can you come up to Stockholm?'

'We're in the middle of a major investigation . . .' She pauses to give herself some thinking time. 'Can't they do it over the phone?'

'I'm afraid not. You have to attend in person. They were very clear on that point.'

'Oh . . .' Her heart is pounding.

'Text me a couple of dates to put forward – preferably today, so they don't get the idea you're trying to wriggle out of it, OK?'

She tries to sound calm.

'Is it that serious?'

'Hard to say. I'm going to call the new prosecutor, try and suss things out. The important thing is that we are as co-operative as possible, OK?'

'OK.' She puts down the phone, closes her eyes and leans back. For a second the tears burn behind her eyelids.

You thought we were safe, Håkan murmurs. *If you could just get away, if no one saw you in the corridors of the police station, then they would forget about you. Find someone else, easier prey. That was what you thought, wasn't it?*

She waves him away, presses her fingers against her eyelids until the feeling of despair passes. She has to pull herself together, keep her head up, concentrate on the job. Both for her own sake and for Agnes'.

Jens Friberg appears at ten to eight. He puts his head around the door and asks if she'd like a coffee. She still hasn't got used to his new, friendlier persona, but accompanies him to the kitchen. Morell's door is closed, his office in darkness, which makes her feel slightly better.

Small talk isn't exactly Jens's strong point. They sit in silence at the table for a while until she decides to sound him out.

'I know it was long before your time, but I assume you've heard about Simon Vidje's death in the pool at the old quarry?'

He nods and sips his coffee without taking the bait.

'Was it an accident?'

He looks at her over the rim of his cup, then puts it down.

'As you say, it was long before my time. I've never had any reason to doubt Henry's account.'

'And what did he say?'

He pulls a face. 'Anna, I'm not comfortable passing on second-hand information like this. Talk to Henry, or go through the case notes.'

'I've already done that.'

He nods slowly, as if he'd already worked that out.

'Did you find anything to give you cause for concern?'

She notices that he's turned the tables – he's the one questioning her.

'Would you like a top-up?' She fetches the coffee pot, refills their cups. 'There is one thing that strikes me as a little strange,' she says when she's replaced the pot and sat down again.

'Oh?' Jens is trying not to sound particularly interested, but Anna is too experienced to be fooled.

'It's the fact that Marie Andersson was the only one of the four who jumped in the water. The only one who tried to get Simon out.'

'There could be a perfectly natural explanation,' he says, revealing that he knows exactly what she's talking about, and is a lot more familiar with the case than he would like her to think.

'Go on.'

'Maybe Marie discovered Simon before the others, and managed to get the body to the shore before they had the chance to jump in.'

Anna shakes her head. 'There's nothing to indicate that in the interviews.'

'No?' He is pretending he doesn't know this already, but she can see right through him.

'And besides, it was the firefighters who recovered the body. Apparently, the terrain was very difficult.'

'Well, maybe there's your explanation. Marie realised that Simon was dead, and that there was nothing to be done; it was impossible to get him out without professional help.'

'Maybe.' She maintains eye contact.

They hear footsteps on the stairs, then Grönwall appears in the doorway with one of his colleagues. 'Good morning – are we ready for a house search?'

Jens leans across the table. 'I wanted to ask . . .' He pauses, waits until Grönwall comes over to join them. 'Is it OK if I come along?'

She thinks for a moment. The easiest thing would be to say no, but Jens is a good police officer, and has already impressed the CSIs with his actions at the scene of Rylander's death. Snubbing him now in front of Grönwall would lead to raised eyebrows; she doesn't really have a choice.

'Of course – we have room for one more, don't we?'

'Certainly,' Grönwall says. 'The more the merrier. We need to fill up on the way – Klippan is quite a distance. Anyone know where the nearest petrol station is?'

'There's one down on Reftingevägen,' Jens says, and at that moment something clicks in Anna's brain.

Reftinge

Petrol station

Klippan

She gets up without a word and goes back to her office. Unlocks the bottom drawer of her desk, takes out Simon Vidje's case file and begins to leaf through the yellowing pages. Swears quietly to herself – why didn't she see the connection before? It takes her only a few seconds to find the right sheet of paper – the note Henry Morell made twenty-seven years ago.

Two other individuals were present at the quarry during the evening – Joakim Jonsson, referred to by the others as Joe, and Tanya Savic, both aged 20 and resident in Klippan.

However, according to statements from all four witnesses, Jonsson and Savic left the quarry just before midnight when it began to rain. Jonsson and Savic were apprehended by police officers at 01.36 that same night after an altercation at 24-hour petrol station outside Reftinge. Jonsson was arrested on suspicion of possession of drugs, joyriding, and illegal driving. He spent the rest of the night in the custody suite. Therefore, neither Jonsson nor Savic were at the quarry at the time of Simon Vidje's death.

Eagerly she retrieves the information on Rylander and places it on the desk next to Morell's note. Circles two lines near the top of the first page. The missing piece of the puzzle.

Kent Joakim Rylander, born Kent Joakim Jonsson. Alternative first names: Kenta, Kekke, Jocke – Joe.

Joakim 'Joe' Jonsson.

She exhales slowly.

Joakim Rylander and his girlfriend were at the quarry the night Simon Vidje died. Twenty-seven years later, he uses Simon's music to provoke the four friends, to start something. Less than twenty-four hours later, he is dead. Broken and impaled on a tree after plunging down a steep slope on the same ridge where Simon's life ended that autumn night. It can't possibly be a coincidence.

36

Autumn 2017

J ust as Google Maps has already revealed, the scrapyard was once a horseshoe-shaped farm. These days the buildings are in a poor state, and dozens of cars at various stages of decay litter the yard. The autumn air is filled with tiny water particles, something between mist and rain, which intensify the smell of oil, rust and neglect – a smell that finds its way straight through your clothes, with the help of the wind.

There is a barrier across the muddy track, with a sign warning visitors that guard dogs are on the loose. As they approach the main building on foot, they hear barking. Both CSIs and the officer Anna has brought with her exchange anxious glances. She understands how they feel; she herself is afraid of dogs, even though she has one in the family. She could have revealed the connection between Rylander and Simon Vidje's death during the drive, but after some consideration she has decided to wait, at least until after they've searched the house. This is mainly because of Jens Friberg. She's still not quite sure where she stands with him, and until she is, there is no reason to apprise him of every detail of the investigation. Irritatingly, right now it feels good to have him here, especially when the barking grows louder and a big Rottweiler blocks their path.

They all stop dead, apart from Jens who keeps on walking without the slightest hesitation. The dog's hackles are raised, its teeth are bared, and a low growl is coming from deep inside.

As Jens gets closer the Rottweiler darts forward and snaps at thin air, then backs away as the distance between them diminishes. Jens still keeps on walking, without even glancing at the dog. With three metres to go, the powerful animal decides to go for Jens's legs. Jens doesn't slow down, he simply delivers a well-aimed kick. The Rottweiler whimpers, staggers backwards then limps away, managing the odd half-hearted bark. It is impossible not to be impressed by Jens's composure. He doesn't stop to receive the accolades of his colleagues, but continues towards the house.

The impression of neglect is even stronger when they round the corner of the main building. The yard is full of muddy puddles with dark, rainbow-coloured surfaces. Scrapped cars piled on top of one another lean against the wall, presumably placed there by the yellow Volvo wheel loader parked at an angle in front of a door marked OFFICE.

The door opens and a man in his early seventies emerges. He is wearing a pair of stained green trousers and a flannel shirt that might once have had a check pattern, but these days has degenerated into fifty shades of shit. His hair is long and greasy, he hasn't shaved for at least a week, and even though he is some distance away, Anna's nose detects that he probably hasn't showered for quite a while.

'Whatdoyouwant?' he says, running the words together.

'Kent Joakim Rylander,' she replies.

'Jocke? What's he done now?'

'Can we go inside?'

After a brief hesitation the man reluctantly steps aside and lets them into a cramped little room. Virtually every surface is occupied by plies of paper and filthy car parts. The stench is so overwhelming that Anna has to breathe through her mouth. The Rottweiler is lying on a disgusting blanket in one corner; it must have slunk in through the crooked dog flap in the door. It lets out a low growl, but lowers its head and falls silent when Jens takes a step closer.

'How do you know Rylander?' Anna asks. The man sits down behind his cluttered desk. He doesn't offer them a seat, which is hardly surprising since all the chairs are occupied.

'I was with his mother for a while in the '80s. You could say I'm his stepfather. Or I was. As I always say to the police, whatever Jocke's been up to, it's nothing to do with me.'

'But he does live here?'

'He's still got his old cabin. He comes and goes as he pleases. I intended to clear out all his crap years ago, but I never got around to it. I didn't realise he'd given this place as his address until his post started arriving.'

The man gestures towards the chaotic room.

'I told him I had my hands full – it was up to him to take care of his own affairs. But he didn't give a shit about what I said – as usual.'

Anna takes out her phone and shows him a photograph of Rylander. On an impulse she chooses a recent one, taken after his death. His face is black and blue, but because the picture was taken at an angle from one side – the empty eye socket isn't so visible. The old man picks up a pair of reading glasses, perches them on the end of his nose and reaches for the phone. His hands are black with ingrained oil, his nails long and yellow. Anna quells the urge to look away and holds the phone at a distance so that the worst details can't be seen. People don't usually want to speak ill of the dead, so she is keeping Rylander's fate to herself for the moment.

'Yes, that's Jocke. Looks as if someone's given him a beating. Well deserved, no doubt.'

'Why do you say that?'

The man snorts, takes off his glasses.

'Jocke cons people – that's one thing. But he likes to mess with them too, provoke them, often for no reason. He's done it ever since he was a kid. Have you heard the story of the scorpion who asks a frog to give him a lift across a lake? He promises not to sting the frog, because then they'll both drown, but he does it anyway. That's Jocke. Somewhere deep inside he knows he's fucking things up for himself, but he just can't help it. That's not the first time he's taken a beating, and it won't be the last.'

A gob of spit accompanies the final word.

'It sounds as if you're speaking from experience.'

Another snort. 'I've known Jocke since he was a kid. I'm immune to his tricks.'

'Yet you still allow him to live here?'

The old man shrugs. 'His mother and I were happy together. He was a nice little boy. Back then this place was buzzing . . .' He falls silent, his gaze turns inward.

Jens Friberg interrupts his train of thought. 'Rylander's cabin – where is it?'

They find the cabin at the end of a gravel track, some three hundred metres behind the main buildings. It's more of a hut than a cabin. The muddy yard is full of puddles and tyre tracks, and half of the low roof is covered with a tarpaulin. The wooden walls are so rotten and mouldy that it's impossible to tell what colour it might have been. The door is padlocked, but the old man has a key.

'Don't tell Jocke,' he mutters. 'He doesn't like people poking around among his stuff.'

Anna tells him the truth. He takes it well, with little more than a grim nod.

'I think I've always had the feeling it would end that way. Poor bastard.' The old man clears his throat, spits in the direction of a patch of nettles. Turns his head away so that she won't see the tears in his eyes.

The cabin consists of a single room. There is a kitchenette at one end with a sink and hob, and at the other end a toilet behind a broken sliding door. A sticky carpet can be seen here and there between heaps of newspapers, cardboard boxes and clothes. Every surface is piled high with car stereos, mobile phones and other electrical items; Anna presumes they are all stolen goods.

There is a sofa in the middle of the room; judging by the blankets and pillow, it also functions as a bed. The coffee table is littered with overflowing ashtrays, pizza boxes and empty beer cans. On the wall opposite is a flatscreen TV that is much too large and expensive to belong in here. The smell is entirely predictable – dampness, cigarette smoke, dirt, rotting rubbish, poor hygiene, and – most of all – loneliness.

She nods to the CSIs to make a start, then turns to the old man once more.

'Did Jocke have a mobile phone?'

'Loads.' He points at the sink, which contains parts of at least three phones.

'Have you got his number?'

The old man shakes his head. 'Not his new one. He changed it all the time. The last number I have stopped working about a month ago.'

'But you're sure he had a phone?'

'Doesn't everyone?'

Anna thanks him for his help and sends him away. He looks as if he's about to protest, but then he turns and ambles back to the house, head down.

'Anna!' Jens beckons her. Underneath one of the pizza boxes there is a laptop with a sticker on the lid: PROPERTY OF VÄSTERVÅNG SCHOOL. Two cables run over to the wall, one to a plug socket and the other to a classic old double cassette deck, the kind that was popular in the '80s before CD players came along. Anna pulls on a pair of nitrile gloves and presses the eject button, revealing a cassette tape. She carefully removes it. Something is written neatly on the label in ink, as if someone tried hard to make it look nice.

Property of Simon Vidje.

'Rylander used Audacity to copy the music from the tape to the USB stick,' says Jens, who has got the laptop working. 'I use the same program at home for my vinyl collection.'

He pauses, seems almost embarrassed, as if he's accidentally opened a window into his private life. He quickly resumes his professional role.

'The file is dated just over a week ago.'

Grönwall and his colleague have made a start at the far side of the room and are methodically working their way through everything. Anna wants to get her head around the cabin. The sofa and the coffee table seem to have been the centre of Rylander's activities, but there is one other place that could be of interest.

She pushes open the broken bathroom door. The narrow space is every bit as unpleasant as she'd expected. There is no door on the shower cubicle, and some of the tiles have fallen off, exposing a large area mottled with mould. She had hoped to check out the bathroom cabinet, but all that remains are two holes in the wall where the screws once sat. The toilet is making a constant rushing sound. She lifts the lid of the cistern and finds that the ballcock is obstructed by a bag containing a couple of hundred grams of what is probably marijuana.

When she has fished it out, she discovers a basket pushed between the toilet and the wall. It is full of Donald Duck comics and porn magazines. The corner of a white envelope is sticking out. She removes it from the basket. It is made of thick paper, and has Rylander's name and address printed on the front. Rylander seems to have opened it with his fingers; the edges are torn and ragged, partly obscuring the name of the sender, which is pre-printed on the upper left-hand corner. However, she manages to work it out.

Gunnarsson & Son Solicitors.

She inhales sharply. Why has Call-me been in contact with Rylander?

She cautiously opens the envelope and takes out a single sheet of neatly folded paper.

Dear Joakim,

Twenty-seven years have passed since our dear Simon left us. He was a wonderful son, a good friend and an incredibly gifted musician who touched all those he met. Even though his death was written off as an accident, we are convinced that the truth never came out. That is why we are turning to you and everyone else who was at Mörkaby quarry that night with the following request:

If you have anything to tell us — a detail that you happened to miss out, a memory that came back to you long after the event — or if you simply want to take the opportunity to unburden your heart at long last, please contact Detective Inspector Anna Vesper at the police station in Nedanås. Anna will be taking up her post as district chief of police on 9 October. She has no connections to anyone in the area; she has an excellent reputation as an investigator, combined with many years' experience. We are very hopeful that she will be able to discover what really happened to Simon, providing us, his parents, with long-awaited peace of mind.

Your help in this matter would be very much appreciated.

With best wishes,

Elisabet and Karl-Johan Vidje

Änglaberga

The envelope is postmarked 17 September – only a few days after she signed the lease on Tabor. Newly renovated Tabor, which has never before been rented out. Karl-Jo's studio, which houses his final and possibly most important piece of work. Anna had already had her suspicions, but now they are confirmed – literally in black and white. She has been manipulated, not only by Henry Morell, but also by Elisabet Vidje.

'I think you'll want to see this,' Jens says. Something in his tone makes her put the letter in her pocket and go over to the sofa.

'Here.' He turns the laptop so that she can see the screen. An email program is open. He moves the cursor to the last message in the Sent box.

'On 25 September, Rylander sent an email to Alex Morell, Bruno and Marie Sordi, and Caia Bianca.' He double clicks to open the message. 'The account was created the same day – look at the username.'

'Simon Vidje,' she reads aloud. 'What did he write?'

Another click and the message fills the screen. It is one single line. Seven words, seven syllables, but more than enough to constitute a motive for murder.

Time to pay for what you did!

37

Autumn 2017

Anna remains silent during the drive back to Nedanås. Searching Joe Rylander's rundown cabin has occupied most of the day. They have taken away a considerable amount of material – mainly suspected stolen goods and drugs equipment, but also the laptop and cassette tape, each in its neatly labelled evidence bag. She has asked Jens to keep the contents to himself until tomorrow morning because she needs to work out a strategy overnight, which is perfectly true. For the same reason she hasn't mentioned the letter to him or anyone else; it is tucked away in her jacket pocket. The journey gives her the opportunity to go over everything in her head, and to interrogate the chain of events with all the scepticism she can muster. However, the chain still holds, from the day she applied for the job in Nedanås until Henry Morell announced at the scene that Rylander's death was definitely suicide.

Anna knows that she is going to have to interview the four friends, asking questions not only about Rylander, but about the initial investigation – what really happened on that August night in 1990? But before that she has a number of points to clarify, and she also wants to talk to the person whose spirit hovers over everything.

When they arrive at the station, she turns to Grönwall. 'Can you make sure the laptop and cassette are logged and locked away in the evidence room?'

'I can take care of that,' Jens offers. 'Would you like me to make a copy of the song and send it to you as an MP3 file?'

She hesitates for a second, sees that he has noticed.

'Good idea,' she says, but the damage has already been done.

Anna drives along the winding road up the ridge unnecessarily fast, and has to remind herself of the close shave with the Glarea truck the other day. However, she realises that she keeps speeding up as she approaches her destination. The weather is about to change; sunbeams are beginning to poke through the grey cloud cover here and there, making the tarmac sparkle so that she has to flip down the sun visor.

The tree-lined avenue beyond the lodge feels longer than it looks from the main road. The trunks and treetops all lean slightly to the left at almost exactly the same angle because of the wind.

The original section of Änglaberga consists of four large whitewashed buildings. Straight ahead is the grand two-storey manor house with stepped gables and several chimneys. On the left are two long, low structures that she assumes are stables, with attractive wrought-iron window frames. On the right the stables are mirrored by an identical building, but judging by the large doors it is probably some kind of lodge. The space on the far right is empty. It looks as if a fifth building should be there, but there is only a large area of neatly raked gravel, which somehow makes the well-maintained estate look unbalanced, as if something is missing. It takes her a few seconds to work out that this was where the garage used to be. The place where Simon set up a studio upstairs, and where Karl-Jo kept his sports car.

She slows down, looks up at the gable of the lodge but can't seen any trace of fire damage. Hardly surprising – they've had twenty-seven years to fix things.

There is no sign of any parked cars; she is wondering whether to leave her car there anyway when she sees a track running between the left-hand stable and the main house. It leads her to a lower courtyard surrounded by much newer stables and a machine shed with roller doors on the sides. One of them is open, and she can see two men, each pressure-washing a tractor. She recognises the man nearest the door – he's one of the Poles who helped her and Agnes move into Tabor. She waves to him as she passes by, but gets no response. At the far end of the yard there is one of those ubiquitous low-level temporary buildings. A couple of cars with foreign number plates are parked outside, and she guesses that it is used as accommodation for the workers. Klein's pickup truck and Elisabet Vidje's green Land Rover are parked in a carport. She pulls up behind them, gets out and follows a gravel path leading back to the main house. The air smells of earth and animals, with a faint hint of overripe apples.

The path cuts through a thick hedge and opens out into a lovely arbour featuring a fountain with an angel in the centre. Anna glances up at the house; an upstairs window is ajar. She is about to round the corner and head for the front door when she almost bumps into Bror Klein, who is busy fastening his oilskin.

'What the fuck are you doing here?' The language is unexpected and doesn't fit in at all with Klein's usual calm and collected approach. Nor does the stressed expression.

'I need to speak to Elisabet.'

'She doesn't want to see you.'

The venom in his voice takes her by surprise. And him, apparently.

'I mean . . . she's not feeling well. She doesn't want any visitors.' He fastens the last button on his coat and regains his self-control. 'It would be better if you came back another day.'

'It's about Simon,' she informs him. 'The original investigation.'

Klein's face is impassive, yet she thinks she can detect a hint of lingering unease in his eyes.

'Elisabet . . .' He pauses, searching for the right word. 'She's ill. Very ill. The last thing she needs right now is for someone to start poking about in—'

'Klein!' The upstairs window is now wide open. Elisabet's face is pale, and she is wearing a white nightdress. 'Show Anna into the drawing room. I'll be down in a few minutes.'

The window slams shut before Klein has time to answer. He mumbles something, turns away and beckons Anna to follow him.

The main entrance is at the top of a number of steps. The dark oak double doors are impressive. Klein leads her into a large hallway with a high ceiling. He turns left along a narrow passageway and opens another door. The drawing room has an open fire, with four armchairs arranged around it. A phone with extra-large buttons attracts Anna's attention; small sticky labels read 1 – KLEIN, 2 – MARIE, 3 – MATS. The walls and ceiling are a faint shade of yellow from years of cigar smoke. The window at the back overlooks an extensive, beautifully cut lawn surrounded by a tall beech hedge.

'Wait here.' Klein nods towards the armchairs and immediately leaves the room. The chair is soft, and Anna sinks down a few centimetres more than is comfortable. She sits and listens. All she can hear is the ticking of the gilt pendulum clock next to the fire. After a while she begins to think there is something about the energy in the old house. It might be her imagination, something she has come up with because of what she knows about the Vidje family, and yet she can't help believing that in spite of its grandeur, there is a sadness about Änglaberga.

The mantelpiece is lined with photographs; the ones on the far left are black and white. A man and a woman in their forties, with the same grim appearance as Elisabet – presumably her parents. The next one shows the same woman standing between two smartly dressed little girls – Elisabet and her sister? The third is slightly bigger: Elisabet Vidje and a man whose photo Anna has already seen on the internet. Karl-Johan.

They make an attractive couple. Elisabet is wearing a simple but elegant white dress and holding a bouquet of flowers. Karl-Jo is stylish in a well-fitting suit. They are both smiling into the camera and look happy, as you do when you are young and don't know any different.

Anna gets up and moves closer. The couple are standing at the top of an impressive stone staircase. She guesses it's at the town hall in Lund. She can see the shadow of the photographer on the steps to their right. The young Elisabet is very beautiful, yet Anna's eyes are drawn to Karl-Johan. He has a special aura that not even a black-and-white photograph from the early '70s can suppress. His eyes, his smile, the way his long blond hair falls at an angle over his forehead.

Beside the wedding picture is a colour photo of a blond, tousle-haired little boy aged about two sitting on his daddy's knee. It is summer, they are having a picnic in a meadow. The child has his arm around Daddy's neck, and the sun is making them both screw up their eyes. In the next photo, Elisabet is there too; Simon is in the middle, one chubby arm around each parent's neck. Once again the shadow of the photographer can just be seen.

The last picture on the far right is of Simon in a white jacket and his student cap. He has long fair hair, and is gazing into the lens with the same slightly amused expression his father has in the wedding photo twenty years earlier. Anna can't help picking it up, trying to compare the face with the figure in the water in the mural. The clock strikes, tinkling chimes like a mixture of glass and metal, and she doesn't hear the door open.

'He has his father's eyes, don't you think?'

Elisabet Vidje has put on a dressing gown and sheepskin slippers. She looks tired; her face is grey, and she has dark circles under her eyes. However, her expression is just as sharp and alert as the last time they met. There is no sign of Klein, but Anna is sure he's not far away.

She puts down the photo. 'How did you and Karl-Johan meet?'

Elisabet smiles.

'At a patisserie in Lund. I was there with some friends, and he was sitting at a table all by himself. When he came to pay, he'd forgotten his wallet. He was so embarrassed that I felt sorry for him. At first he refused to let me pay, and didn't give until I promised he could take me to the cinema. We saw *Catch-22*, I remember that. It turned out we'd both read the book. He invited me back to his little flat for a glass of wine and we spent all night talking about books. Shall we sit?'

Elisabet gestures towards the armchairs and sinks down with an air of relief.

'How are you, Elisabet?'

Anna has really come to get some answers, but Elisabet seems so frail that she can't bring herself to press the woman. Elisabet waves the question away.

'Don't take any notice of Klein, he's a real mother hen. I'm just a little tired. Tell me why you're here.'

Anna takes out the letter, unfolds it and places it on the table. 'You told Lasse Gunnarsson to send this.'

Elisabet nods, showing no hint of embarrassment. She clearly doesn't feel the need to apologise.

'In the letter you refer to me and suggest that I am willing to revisit the investigation into Simon's death.'

'I don't suggest anything.' Elisabet purses her lips. 'I'm merely asking those involved to think back and search their consciences. That's not illegal, is it?'

'But you want the case reopened. That's what you've been fighting for all these years, but Henry Morell has always blocked your request.'

'Henry Morell should never have been involved from the start. He's incompetent.' Her voice is calm, but there is no mistaking her anger.

'You tried to get rid of him, and when you didn't succeed you had to wait him out. For twenty-seven years.'

Elisabet lets out a snort. 'To be honest, I never imagined that he would cling on for as long as he did, but it proves I'm right – he has something to hide.'

'So you had Tabor renovated in double quick time, and got Gunnarsson to contact me, offering a fantastic place to live at a low rent, to make sure I'd get dragged into the whole thing. You knew I'd see the m . . . mm.' She stops herself, but a fraction too late. Elisabet raises her eyebrows. 'M . . . mmural.'

'You have a stammer.' An assertion, not a question.

'Only sometimes.'

'Does it bother you?'

'Not really. I'm used to it.'

Elisabet nods slowly. 'Karl-Johan had a stammer too – worse than yours. He was teased about it when he was a child. Did that happen to you?'

'No.' Elisabet has made her lose her thread, and she searches for a way to get back on track.

'You were lucky,' the older woman goes on. 'Children can be horrible. Vile. Karl-Johan was afraid the stammer might be hereditary, and that Simon would have it too, but he was worrying unnecessarily.' Elisabet smiles at the memory, then grows serious once more.

'Karl-Johan spent almost ten years working on that mural. Towards the end he could hardly see at all. Klein had to lead him to and from Tabor. I thought that if you saw it, you'd understand the depth of his grief.'

'You manipulated me,' Anna says as calmly as she can. 'Used me and Agnes as your pawns – didn't that occur to you?'

'Of course it did. And don't imagine I took any pleasure in it, but my father always said that sometimes you have to sink to the depths in order to reach the heights. There's something in that.' She pauses, then laboriously gets to her feet. 'Come with me – I want to show you something.'

They follow the path slowly all the way to the far end of the garden. It is a distance of about a hundred metres, and Elisabet does her best not to show how exhausting she finds it. Klein, who supplied her with a jacket and boots, is hovering anxiously, but he stays in the background. The sun is beginning to go down.

Behind a large fir tree there is a gap in the hedge that leads out through an iron gate. Elisabet asks Anna to open the gate, and they emerge on a patch of level ground. An undulating fairy-tale land-scape is spread before them, with low green hills and dales, trees and bushes extending all the way to the edge of the forest, which must be about a kilometre away. A herd of white cows has settled down to rest in one of the valleys. Two birds of prey hover high in the sky, against clouds coloured pink by the setting sun. The whole scene is breathtakingly beautiful, and Anna recognises it at once. It is one of Karl-Jo's favourite motifs.

'Over there.' Elisabet points to an old oak tree on their left, with a wooden bench beneath it. 'Let's sit down.'

Anna is so busy helping Elisabet that she doesn't notice the gravestone beside the tree until they are settled. It is made of pale marble with gold lettering, and there is something about the small, perfect stone that brings a lump to her throat.

Simon Karl-Johan Vidje 22.06.1971 – 29.08.1990
Loved. Missed.

'Karl-Johan and I used to sit here on summer evenings. Simon too, when he was a little older. This was our place.' Elisabet waves a hand in the direction of the valley. 'My father started a quarry here at the end of the '40s. There was a need for gravel and tarmac for construction after the war. When I was little, it looked terrible – nothing but brown, black and grey. Dust, fumes and noise from crushing the stone. Not as bad as what Glarea has done on Kotorp's land, but close. My father didn't like it either. As soon as he'd made enough money to buy more land, he shut down the quarry, filled in the worst of the craters and sowed grass everywhere. People thought he was crazy, walking away from a profitable business, but he loved the ridge and couldn't bear the thought of destroying it.'

Elisabet pauses to catch her breath. She is shivering in spite of the thick jacket.

'Karl-Johan loved the ridge as much as my father did. I've promised him that he and I will rest up here together when our time comes – that all three of us will be together again. But before that I have to decide what is going to happen to Änglaberga.'

She falls silent, as if talking to Anna has drained all her energy.

'And you can't do that until you know the truth.'

Elisabet doesn't answer right away. She remains silent for a moment before continuing.

'The doctors say that Karl-Johan's illness began even before Simon's death, but that's nonsense. I know it was triggered by grief. He knew he would go blind, and yet he spent almost every waking hour on that painting. I assume you've seen what it's hiding?'

Anna nods.

'It's the best thing he's ever done. He redid it hundreds of times, worked day and night and used the last of his strength to make it perfect. All to do our son justice.' Elisabet looks Anna in the eye, her voice soft and filled with sorrow now. 'So, tell me, Anna – how could I settle for doing anything less?'

38

Autumn 2017

Twilight is falling as they slowly make their way back to the house. Just as before Anna tucks her arm beneath Elisabet's, but something has changed. Her grip is both firmer and softer, the distance between them has diminished. Anna tells her about the fight at the homecoming party and Rylander's death, but doesn't mention the threatening email. However, Elisabet comes to the same conclusion as her.

'You think he was murdered.'

'We still don't know how he died—' she begins, but the older woman waves away her reservations.

'You think this Rylander knew something about Simon's death, and he tried to blackmail whoever was to blame. And that was why they killed him.'

'That's one theory, but we're keeping our options open.'

'Nonsense,' Elisabet snaps, but a second later her sour expression is replaced by a contented smile.

'So now you'll have to reopen the old case. Question Alexander Morell and the others. Henry Morell will hit the roof. So will Bengt Andersson.' The smile grows broader.

'There's one thing I don't understand,' Anna says. 'You and Marie Sordi seem to be on good terms, but Marie was there that night, and you've accused her father of colluding with Henry Morell to hide the truth.'

Elisabet looks pensive.

'Marie is my niece; I've known her since she was born. She and Simon were like brother and sister – they were going to share an apartment in Lund. I can't imagine that she would wish him any harm.' She smiles wearily. 'She's been a great support to both me and Karl-Johan over the years. She goes to visit him in the nursing home in town once a month. I have my doubts about her husband, though – not to mention the other two.' The smile becomes a thin line. 'Kalle Pedersen was a drunkard and a petty thief who beat both his wife and kids black and blue. His daughter Carina was always a little too calculating for my liking. As you perhaps know, her first husband died under mysterious circumstances. And then there's Alexander Morell – his wife threw him out. I assume she couldn't cope with his temper.' She shakes her head. 'As far as Bengt Andersson goes, his attempt to hide the truth is more to do with the reputation of Nedanås than with Marie. He's always put the community first – before his own family, in fact. My sister chose the wrong man, but his children shouldn't have to suffer because she made a bad decision.'

'Is that why you allow Mats Andersson to live here?'

Elisabet purses her lips.

'Poor Mats is a little . . . different, as I'm sure you've noticed. I was pleased when Marie bought Kotorp from Bengt, even if I don't like the change of name. Norrblicka sounds so pretentious, and Marie knows exactly how I feel. Mats became a kind of spare part, so we agreed that he would live here. Klein and I have plenty of room, and Bengt couldn't care less about his boy.'

Klein is waiting for them at the front door. He looks concerned, but Elisabet pats his arm reassuringly.

'You don't need to worry, you silly old thing. Anna and I have had a good talk, and I think we understand each other. But now I need to rest.'

They say their goodbyes and Anna walks slowly over to her car. The conversation didn't exactly go as planned. Does that mean she's chosen her side? That she believes Elisabet when she claims that the truth was suppressed? She wants to say no, wants to insist that she's keeping her options open, but she's not sure that applies any longer.

When Anna is leaving the newer part of the estate and driving between the old stables, she sees an old muddy pickup truck parked by the lodge. She catches a glimpse of something white sticking out from beneath a tarpaulin on the back, and a few seconds later she realises what it was. She brakes and slams the car into reverse. She parks behind the pickup, jumps out and lifts the tarp to see Agnes's white Vespa. Her first thought is that there's been an accident, Agnes is lying injured somewhere. Her heart is pounding, but then she sees that the Vespa is undamaged. What's going on?

She looks around, but there isn't a soul in sight. The bonnet of the pickup is still warm, so it can't have been here for long. She takes out her phone and calls Agnes, but it goes straight to voicemail. *Shit!*

She walks around the building to find herself in an apple orchard. Beyond it, at the end of a gravel path, is a low building in the same style as the stables. There is a light in one of the windows, and she breaks into a run, her anxiety increasing with every step.

When she reaches the front door she tries to peer in through the windows, but can't see anything. She thinks she can hear the sound of hammering, which stops as soon as she knocks. Someone approaches the door, then hesitates. The key rattles in the lock, and Mats Andersson is standing there. He doesn't say a word, he just glares at her. He is wearing a leather apron over his normal clothes; here and there Anna can see big brownish red stains which are probably blood.

She hears claws pattering along the floor of the dark hallway and something white appears – Milo. He has a rabbit in his mouth, and a cut along the dead animal's belly is clearly visible.

'Wh-where is Agnes?' she snaps, without bothering about her stammer. She takes a step forward, forcing Mats to back away. 'Where is she?' A spot of saliva lands on his chest, making him take another step back. In spite of the fact that he is a lot taller and at least fifteen kilos heavier than Anna, he looks scared. He shuffles his feet, fixes his gaze on the floor.

'S-sorry . . .'

She follows him inside. Her anxiety has given way to anger, blowing away any hint of caution.

'What have you done with my daughter?'

Mats holds up his hands, fear in his eyes.

'I didn't mean to . . .' He bumps into the wall and Anna raises a hand to slap his face, sees him recoil.

'Mum!' Agnes appears beside Milo, looking both shocked and furious. 'What the hell are you doing?'

Anna lowers her hand as her anger is replaced by relief. Mats is still standing with his back pressed against the wall, palms outward as if he's expecting a blow. Anna is ashamed of her behaviour.

'I'm sorry,' she says. 'I thought . . . I d-didn't know . . .'

Agnes goes over and gently touches Mats on the shoulder, which makes him lower his arms. She gives Anna a filthy look.

'I saw the V-Vespa. You d-didn't answer your ph-phone.'

She is gasping for air, trying to compose herself. Make sense of the situation, find a logical explanation. She fills her lungs with air, breathes in through her mouth, out through her nose several times before turning to Mats.

'I do apologise,' she says with exaggerated care. 'I saw Agnes's Vespa on the back of your truck and I thought something had happened to her. She didn't answer her phone, and when I saw you and Milo with that . . .' She points to the dog who is sitting quietly with his head on one side, the rabbit still clutched in his jaws.

Mats stares at her as if he can't quite decide whether she's telling the truth. He looks at Agnes, then at Milo, then back at Anna.

'I'm sorry, Mats,' she says again. 'I'm a mother hen.'

He nods, then gives a wry smile. 'Hens aren't too bad. Wild boar are worse. You don't want to get between a sow and her young.'

'No?' She returns his smile.

'No, that can be fatal.' He nods wisely.

Anna turns to Agnes. 'Sorry. Why is your phone switched off?'

Agnes holds up her phone; there is a large crack across the screen. 'Milo was in such a hurry when I got home that he tripped me up. I dropped my phone on the step. Then Mats arrived – he's the one who's been leaving the rabbits for Milo.'

Mats is grinning now. 'I have a smoker at the back. My sister's dogs love smoked rabbit. Something to gnaw on – good for their teeth.'

'Right,' Anna says; even she can hear how foolish she sounds. 'Well, at least the mystery of the rabbits is solved.' She ventures a smile at Agnes; no response. 'So, what are you doing here?'

'Mats wondered if I'd like to photograph his collection. I had nothing better to do.'

'Collection?'

Agnes has no intention of explaining, but Mats steps forward and opens a door. 'Down there. You're welcome to take a look.'

The cellar appears to be several hundred years old, and consists of one long rectangular room. No doubt it was originally used for storage. The floor is made of the same reddish brick as the walls. Mats is able to stand upright only in the centre beneath the vaulted ceiling. The air is not damp as Anna had expected, but cool and dry. A large square dehumidifier in the middle of the room explains why. There is a chemical smell she recognises but can't quite identify.

A passageway is lined on either side with what she assumes are storage units, but turn out to be hand-made display cabinets. Various nature scenes and motifs are painted on the back and side walls, and each cabinet contains stuffed animals. Hares, badgers, and further along larger animals like deer, even a stag. All frozen in positions that make them look as if they are still alive – a fox in mid-leap, a bird of prey with wings outstretched, about to sink its talons into a rabbit, a flock of geese grazing on grass while glancing anxiously at the sky.

The lighting is skilfully placed to enhance the impression of life. It makes the animals' glass eyes shine, and brings out the textures of their fur and feathers. The whole thing reminds her of something she saw on a school trip a very long time ago.

Mats switches off the overhead lights; it feels even more like a museum now. Agnes and Milo lead the way between the cabinets, heading for the far end of the room.

'I've been doing this ever since I was a boy,' Mats says. 'I started with birds. Karl-Johan helped me. He was the one who said I could use this place.'

They pass a badger with bared teeth, plundering the eggs from a bird's nest.

'Do you shoot the animals yourself?' Anna asks, mainly to be polite. There is something horrible about Mats's collection. Killing animals for food is one thing, but stuffing them and expending huge amounts of time and energy to make them look alive is just weird.

'Some – although I catch most of them in traps, like that one. I'm good at setting traps.'

He points to a large lynx that has clambered up a tree trunk. One hind leg is caught in a gin trap attached to the trunk by a chain. The teeth of the trap are buried deep in the poor animal's flesh; it has snapped shut with such force that the broken bones are visible. Even though the lynx has been dead for many years, it is still possible to see the pain on its face.

'That's my biggest predator,' Mats says, almost tenderly. 'But I am hoping for a wolf.'

Anna raises her eyebrows, and he immediately picks up on her scepticism.

'The odd wolf does find its way down here. Last year one made it to Österlen, and only three weeks ago a truck driver photographed a wolf over by Perstorp. I've got gin traps out in a couple of good places, including where I caught the lynx.' Once again, he points to the animal in agony. Anna suppresses a shudder. She can't understand what Agnes finds so fascinating about this revolting cellar.

'Isn't it dangerous? What if a dog or a child steps on the trap?'

'I only put them out where no one goes walking,' Mats mumbles. 'And I put up warning signs. It's not my fault if people don't read them.'

Agnes has her photographic equipment set up in front of the last display case, which contains three white doves arranged

ANDERS DE LA MOTTE

side by side on a branch, half turned away from the observer. The fairy-tale landscape painted on the back wall looks familiar – low green hills and dales, trees and bushes extending all the way to the edge of the forest, which must be about a kilometre away. The clouds are coloured pink by the setting sun. It is the view from the bench where she and Elisabet were sitting a little while ago.

'Did Karl-Johan paint this?'

Mats nods and straightens his shoulders. 'This one and two more. I did the rest myself.'

Anna admires the arrangement for a few seconds. There is something lovely about the three doves, admiring the sunset together. After a while the beauty actually outweighs the unpleasantness.

One of the doves is slightly smaller than the others. Are they meant to represent Elisabet, Karl-Jo and Simon?

'It's beautiful,' she says truthfully, earning an appreciative nod from Mats. Agnes moves one of her screens a fraction before she starts clicking away, the flash illuminating the doves and the painted sunset.

Flash, flash.

After a few seconds the rhythm becomes almost hypnotic.

Flash, flash.

'I'm best at doves,' Mats murmurs. 'I've had the most practice on them.'

Flash.

'How come?'

Flash.

'There was a girl I liked, a long time ago. She liked doves, so I did them for her.'

Flash.

'She was so beautiful. Everyone thought so.' His voice softens.

Flash.

'Almost like a white dove.'

Flash.

A white dove, Håkan whispers in her ear, then he begins to hum 'Una Paloma Blanca' in an ironic tone. Suddenly Anna realises who Mats is talking about.

White dove, Blanca-Bianca.

'Carina Pedersen,' she says. 'That's who you mean, isn't it?'

Mats doesn't answer, but his silence tells her she is right.

39

Autumn 2017

The following morning Anna makes a big fruit salad for breakfast even though it's Wednesday. However, her gesture of reconciliation falls flat. Agnes does eat something, but she is still angry about the way Anna behaved the previous day, and the fact that her phone isn't working doesn't help. The silence between them is oppressive, and after a while Anna can feel her own irritation rising. She allows Agnes to take her vegan hot chocolate into her room to avoid a quarrel.

No doubt Håkan has plenty to say on the matter, but today she has no desire to listen to him. Since it's raining she offers Agnes a lift, drops her off at the station without receiving a thank you or anything other than a mumble in response to her goodbye, which doesn't improve her mood. When she opens the door of Lasse Gunnarsson's stuffy office, she isn't far from boiling point.

'Anna – how lovely to see you!' Call-me is wearing a pair of reading glasses, which he quickly whips off and hides in a drawer. The room feels too small, too dated, as if it belongs to someone from a different age. The yellowing photographs and faded diplomas on the walls reinforce this impression.

'Take a seat,' he says, gesturing towards the visitor's chair. She is already sitting down.

She doesn't waste any time on small talk, she simply places the letter she found at Joe Rylander's cabin on the desk in front of him. He grimaces, but doesn't look surprised. Presumably he's spoken to either Klein or Elisabet.

'Right . . .'

He leans back, looking nowhere near as relaxed as usual. His chair squeaks in protest.

'I think I owe you an apology, Anna.' He blushes slightly, and forces another squeak out of the chair. 'Elisabet Vidje is my client. Our dealings are confidential. Unfortunately, I found myself in a rather difficult position when you and I . . .'

He looks at her in a way she doesn't like, as if he's suggesting that there's something going on between them, and he's expecting her to confirm it.

'You and Elisabet exploited me,' she snaps, although she'd intended to keep quiet. 'You dragged me into this business and sent out a letter that very likely got a man killed.'

Call-me stiffens.

'All we did was ask the people who were at the quarry to take the opportunity to ease their consciences . . .'

'But one or more of them didn't want to do that. Instead, they killed the person who probably knew something.'

Call-me continues to look affronted. 'If that's true, you can hardly blame me or Elisabet.'

'No? How many dead witnesses were there before the letter was sent out?'

She realises almost immediately that the question is slightly ridiculous. However, it seems to have worked, because Call-me's face contorts into a tortured expression.

'Between you and me, Anna . . . Elisabet is seriously ill. She doesn't have long left. So, when an old friend of mine who works in the office of the chief of police told me you'd applied for the job, Elisabet saw it as a sign. One last chance to get to the truth.'

He glances over at the closed door as if he's afraid that someone will come in.

'Änglaberga and its land are worth a great deal of money, and Elisabet is thinking about what will happen to the estate after her death. She has no direct descendants, so her niece and nephew, Marie Sordi and Mats Andersson, are her closest relatives. Elisabet almost regards them as her own children. Their father Bengt, however ...'

Anna waves a dismissive hand. 'Elisabet told me all this yesterday. She said she trusts Marie.'

'She does, but she's also convinced that the whole truth hasn't come out, and that some people are prepared to do whatever it takes to keep it that way. She realised that the day after Simon's death.'

'You mean the garage fire.'

Call-me nods.

'It was before my time, but my father has told me the story often enough. Elisabet tried to get Green, the former chief of police, to exclude Henry Morell from any involvement in the investigation; she wanted him to bring in officers from outside, who didn't have a connection to anyone in the village. Green agreed at first, but later that afternoon he suddenly changed his mind. It was obvious that someone had put him under pressure. Elisabet took my father with her and went down to the police station to confront Green, but Henry Morell and Bengt Andersson were also there. In the end Elisabet and my father were thrown out, and that same night the garage at Änglaberga was burned to the ground.'

He pauses and manages to regain something of his normal composure.

'With all of that in mind, maybe it's understandable that Elisabet is still clutching at straws. We should of course have spoken to you right from the start, in fact I suggested it, but Elisabet refused to listen. She said you would form your own opinion – we were just setting things in motion.'

'By installing me and Agnes at Tabor and sending out letters to the six people who were involved?'

He sighs. 'I guess so. By the way, it turns out only five of them are still alive. Tanya Savic died in 2002.'

Anna had intended to run a check on Tanya as soon as she was back in the office, but now she didn't need to. So Tanya had died before she turned thirty-five.

'I spoke to her daughter on the phone,' Call-me goes on. 'It was an overdose. Tanya had just been discharged from a rehab centre. Apparently, she was in and out all the time; she'd had problems with drug addiction for many years, so it wasn't entirely unexpected. The daughter wanted her mother's letter from Elisabet anyway, so I sent it on to her. This whole story is just so tragic.'

As soon as Anna unlocks and opens her office door, she can feel that something is wrong. She is certain she pushed her chair all the way in, so that the seat was right underneath her desk. Now it's a few inches short. The same applies to the papers on the desk. Everything is where she left it – but not quite. She checks the bottom drawer where she keeps Simon Vidje's case file. It is still locked. She opens it with her key; the file is still there, and a quick flick through tells her that nothing is missing. She thinks for a moment, then looks in the wastepaper basket. It has been emptied, which means the cleaner has a key to her office, so it's possible that he or she moved the papers. And yet she isn't completely convinced. She picks up her coffee mug and heads for the kitchen. Morell's office door is open, and he is absorbed in something on his screen.

'Hi, Henry.'

'Hi, Anna.'

She continues to the kitchen and pours herself a coffee, even though she doesn't really want one. Morell takes the bait, just as she'd hoped, and appears in the doorway after only a few seconds.

'So, how did it go yesterday? Did you find anything at Rylander's place?'

She shrugs, pretends she isn't studying him closely. 'We've got a few things to work on.'

'Forgive my curiosity, Anna. We haven't had a murder in Nedanås for many years. Has the cause of death been established?'

'Not yet.'

She tries to compare his body language and expression with his tone and the words coming out of his mouth. Does he know who Joe Rylander really is? And if so, does he know about the blackmail message, and the fact that she has retrieved Simon Vidje's file from the archive? If he does, it means that there's a leak. Her money is on the crown prince, Jens Friberg.

There is nothing suspicious about Morell. No tiny shift in his expression, no tics or unconscious grimaces to suggest that he might be hiding something. Instead, he simply gives her the fatherly smile that she finds so hard to resist as he scratches his beard.

Back in her office she closes the door and settles down with the Rylander file. The next step is crystal clear: question the four people Rylander presumably tried to blackmail. However, the first rule of interviewing is that you do your homework and have as much information as possible before confronting a suspect. There are still pieces of the puzzle missing. The autopsy hasn't yet been carried out, and even if the cause of death seems obvious, unexpected details can sometimes emerge – details that may prove critical to the case. The same applies to the car and the forensic examination of Rylander's home. Her instinct is to speak to the four friends as soon as possible about the email and their alibis for early Sunday morning, but her experience tells her to wait.

Her mobile rings before she has time to consider her next move. It's her solicitor. As usual he doesn't waste any time on small talk, which she particularly appreciates today.

'I've just spoken to the chief prosecutor who's dealing with the internal investigation. His name is Tord Santesson, and he's personally taken over the case.'

'Why?'

'I didn't get a clear answer. He claims that new information has come to light, and that you must be interviewed as soon as possible. It could just be a shot in the dark, of course. Santesson is a slippery bastard, if you'll excuse the expression, and he's perfectly capable of something like that. But it does seem as if he means what he says.'

'So, what are the implications in practical terms?'

She hears him take a deep breath.

'Well, if you don't get yourself down here within a very short time, there is a strong possibility that Santesson will have you brought in for questioning. And if that happens, we won't be able to keep it out of the press. A murder detective suspected of murder – that's big news. And I'm pretty sure that Santesson wouldn't mind that at all.'

He pauses for a moment, and Anna can hear her heart pounding.

'I suggest that you drop everything and get on a plane to Stockholm – today if you can.'

She stays in her office for the rest of the day, sending her team brief instructions by email. Then she books the first flight to Bromma tomorrow morning.

She makes every effort to stay calm, tells herself that this is all down to a new prosecutor hungry for results. Internal Affairs haven't really come up with anything new. She has the situation under control.

But what if you're wrong? Håkan whispers. *What if they know? What if you're arrested, what if Agnes has to read all about it in the papers, what if—*

She tells him to shut up, she knows what he's doing, it's not going to work this time either. But he's not listening, he keeps going on and on at her. He is determined to break down her defences, sentence by sentence.

She deserves to know, Anna. She deserves the truth. You've put it off long enough. She's strong. You're strong. You can both cope.

Eventually she has to give in. She puts the Vidje and Rylander files in her briefcase, locks her office door and heads for her car. The emissions from the clay burning hover over the rooftops like a faint cloud of smoke. She doesn't start the engine immediately, she just sits there.

So – what's your decision? Do you want Henry Morell to go and tell Agnes you've been arrested? Or Jens Friberg? Do you want . . .

'OK, OK!' she screams, beating the wheel with her hands. 'You can have it your way, but please shut the fuck up for a little while. Give me a chance to think things through in peace.'

Håkan doesn't say another word. Anna takes a minute to compose herself, then starts the car and slowly sets off. Since the confrontation with Mats, her relationship with Agnes is back to square one – or worse. If they're going to talk to each other, then she has to open with a peace offering. She drives over ten miles to the nearest shopping centre, finds the obligatory phone shop and buys the latest ridiculously expensive iPhone in a colour she thinks Agnes likes. She picks up two portions of sushi for dinner and makes it back to Nedanås just in time to collect her daughter from the train station.

Agnes is still sulking, but she accepts the present. When they get home Agnes transfers the SIM card from her old phone, and after messing with the new one for a while, she mumbles something that could possibly be interpreted as a thank you. Agnes takes Milo out while Anna sets the table. She spends most of their silent meal trying to gather her courage.

Can she do this?

Of course you can. You're the strongest person I know, Håkan whispers. *Do it now. For my sake.*

As the moon appears, she goes into Agnes's room and waits patiently until her daughter lowers her phone and gives her that now-what-do-you-want look.

'The man who started the fight in the park has been found dead,' she says. 'It turns out he was with the others in the quarry the night Simon Vidje died.'

Agnes is interested. 'Wow!' The sullen expression disappears. 'Can you tell me any more?'

Anna nods. *But first I'm going to tell you about your dad. How he died.* That's how she was intending to go on. She promised Håkan. She knows he is eagerly waiting for her to say those words, but at the last second her courage fails her.

Instead, she goes into Elisabet Vidje's bitter conflict with Henry Morell and Bengt Andersson after Simon's death. She explains about the letter, and how Joakim Rylander's death seems to have stirred everything up.

She knows she shouldn't be doing this; much of what she has told Agnes is covered by the rules regarding confidentiality. And yet she draws out the story for as long as possible, partly because it seems to fascinate Agnes, and partly because she wants to avoid silence. She is desperate to shut out Håkan's reproachful words.

I'm sorry, she thinks when she finally gets to the end of her story. *I couldn't do it. It's too hard. I need more time. Please don't be angry.*

Håkan doesn't answer.

40

Autumn 2017

Internal Affairs does not fall under the jurisdiction of the police authority, and is therefore housed in a separate building rather than the main police HQ in Kungsholmen. The last time Anna was here was in June. Her solicitor had more or less promised that that interview would be the last. It is clear from his slightly embarrassed expression when he turns up at five to nine that he remembers exactly what he said. His shirt is freshly ironed, his teeth are dazzlingly white and his suit is ridiculously expensive, which is hardly surprising given how much he charges. However, Anna has no desire whatsoever to be represented by some spotty novice, and she can afford his fees. She doesn't care if that makes it look as if she has something to hide.

At precisely nine o'clock the door opens and one of the investigators she met the last time emerges. He is a short man with an underbite that makes him look like a bulldog, and she has chosen not to remember his name. The bulldog shakes hands with both of them, then leads the way through the security doors and shows them into the same windowless interview room they used on her previous visits. There are cameras in two corners, so she avoids talking to her solicitor. Instead, they merely nod grimly to each other.

They sit in silence for almost fifteen minutes, exchanging meaningful glances as the time ticks away. It seems unlikely that Santesson would have planned another meeting or interrogation before nine o'clock on a Thursday morning, so the delay is meant to unsettle her, a sly little psychological pinch to put her off balance. She has used the same trick herself on many occasions, and yet she is surprised at how effective it is. A poor night's sleep and the uncomfortable early flight have already left her out of sorts; she is tense and on her guard.

Calm down, Håkan would have said to her, but after the previous evening's betrayal he is no longer speaking to her. She is alone now.

The door is flung open and the bulldog comes in, accompanied by a slightly overweight man in a suit, with a thick case file under his arm. He introduces himself: 'Tord Santesson, Chief Prosecutor.' He is in his early fifties, and just like Bengt Andersson, he deals with his baldness by shaving off his remaining hair. His handshake is firm and a fraction too long.

'So, Anna . . .' He sits down opposite her and places the file on the table. Drums his strong fingers on it as he stares at her. His eyes are dark grey, shining with intelligence.

'The previous lead investigator was ready to drop the case, but I decided to take another look. Leave no stone unturned. Fortunately.' The fingers stop drumming. Anna feels a reflexive urge to swallow, but manages to stop herself.

'We have discovered fresh information that doesn't look too good for you.' The powerful index finger taps the file.

'First of all, we have a new witness. A nurse.'

Santesson pauses, allows his words to sink in. 'She transferred to a different department just before your ex-husband passed away, which is why she wasn't questioned earlier.'

The drumming begins again. Anna feels his gaze on her, and makes a huge effort to meet it.

'According to this nurse, you asked her a number of detailed questions about how an infusion pump works. So detailed that she remembers the incident almost a year later.'

Santesson pauses again, gives her a wry smile.

'Plus, we have this.' He opens the file without taking his eyes off Anna. 'My colleagues have already examined your work computer and your personal laptop without finding anything, but I requested a search of every computer in your former place of work, and guess what?'

He places a sheet of paper in the middle of the table, equidistant between Anna and her solicitor, so that they both have to lean forward.

'A search had been carried out on a co-worker's computer for a manual for an infusion pump – the same model that was used in the care of your ex-husband. The time of that search was just after midday, and your co-worker has told us that he doesn't always log out of the system when he goes for lunch. He has also said that because you were his team leader, you often had a good reason to be in his office.'

Santesson pauses again, exchanges a quick glance with her solicitor, then delivers the killer blow with a smug little smile.

'One more thing. The infusion pump that gave your ex-husband the overdose that killed him . . .' That horrible finger taps the file again. 'We've re-examined it. Can you think of any good reason why your fingerprints should be on it?'

The finger executes a little dance of triumph. Out of the corner of her eye Anna sees her solicitor straighten up, but before he can speak, Santesson leans across the table, his tone softening.

'Håkan didn't have long left, Anna. A week maybe, no more. Helping someone out of their suffering is neither murder nor manslaughter; it's an act of mercy. Love, even.' Santesson's smile is sorrowful and sympathetic this time. Anna doesn't manage to quell the swallow reflex.

'I think I speak for everyone in this room, when I say that we can all put ourselves in your position. It's possible that one or more of us would have done exactly the same.' He tilts his head on one side. 'That's what it was, wasn't it, Anna? An act of mercy?'

The silence in the room is intense, the atmosphere so thick that she can barely breathe.

'I . . . I . . .'

The stammer comes at exactly the wrong moment. It's a big one, the kind that only affects her once or twice a year. She gasps for air, tries to employ the usual methods to regain control, but to no avail. Her vocal cords cramp uncontrollably and refuse to stop, even when she clenches her fists and stares down at the floor. The lack of oxygen is making her head pound.

She feels her solicitor's hand on her shoulder, holds up her own hand before he can suggest a break. 'W . . . wait!' she manages to say.

She swallows hard and finally the cramping stops. She fills her lungs with air. Once, twice. The pressure on her temples slowly eases. She looks up, meets her solicitor's troubled gaze, then Santesson's. His bald head is still tilted on one side, and his smile is still full of false empathy. The bulldog leans forward as if he has scented blood. Anna closes her eyes, takes another deep breath.

'Think of your daughter,' Santesson says softly. 'Doesn't Agnes deserve to know the truth about how her father really died?'

Agnes's face comes into Anna's mind. Her daughter, her little girl, whose name Santesson is using as if he knows her. She opens her eyes, licks her lips. The camera lenses are staring at her. Santesson leans even closer, as if he's desperate to hear what she has to say.

'Which year did you do the course?' she asks with exaggerated calmness.

'What?'

Santesson's fake sympathy disappears in an instant, and one eyelid twitches.

'The FBI course on interrogation techniques. Which year did you do yours? I did mine in New York in 2010.' She feels the anger constricting her throat, but keeps it in check.

Santesson's eyelid twitches a little faster. He narrows his eyes, but can't stop it.

'You're very good,' Anna goes on. 'First there's the file, which you've stuffed with papers so that it looks full. The last time I was here it wasn't even a quarter of that thickness.' She demonstrates with her finger and thumb. 'Then there's the discreet way you drum on it intermittently with your fingers, to make sure I keep thinking about what it contains. All the evidence piled up against me. Nicely done.'

Santesson's mouth is a thin, hard line, not unlike the expression Elisabet Vidje frequently adopts.

'That little trick was also nicely done,' she goes on. 'You didn't actually say you'd found my fingerprints on the infusion pump; instead, you asked if I could think of any good reason why my prints should be on it. It sounds the same, but it isn't. However, if a person is stressed, he or she doesn't pick up on the difference.'

Santesson doesn't move a muscle, but the bulldog hasn't mastered the necessary poker face. His eyes dart from side to side, avoiding her gaze and glancing at his boss for guidance.

'The dot over the "i" is your final masterstroke, when you minimise the significance of the act itself in order to make it sound more acceptable. Not murder, but an act of mercy. Not manslaughter, but an act of kindness and love. Because it's so much easier to confess to an act of love. After all, that makes you a good person, not a real criminal, doesn't it?'

Santesson sits up straight; his lips have practically disappeared now. A tiny, almost imperceptible bead of sweat has broken out on one temple, and he irritably wipes it away.

'Listen to me, Santesson,' Anna continues, her voice firm and steady. 'Yes, I did ask one of the nurses about how the infusion pump worked. There's nothing strange about that. Morphine was the only thing that helped Håkan to get through those final weeks, so it was hardly surprising if I was interested in how the pump worked and what dosage he was on.'

She falls silent, realises she hasn't stammered once. She takes another deep breath, slows down a little just to be on the safe side.

'With regard to the online search on my former colleague's computer, I have no explanation whatsoever. Nor do I need one. It's up to you to prove that I was the one who carried out that search. Can you do that? Is there anything at all in your big fat file to link me to that computer?'

She reaches out and taps the file with her index finger, just as Santesson did. The bulldog turns his body, moving away from his boss and the table just a fraction, as if he wants to distance himself from what is going on. Santesson is still staring at Anna, no longer attempting to hide the anger in his eyes. She holds his gaze for a few seconds before leaning back on her chair. Theoretically, Santesson could arrest her without any evidence and lock her up for forty-eight hours just to be difficult, so it's best if this pissing contest doesn't go on for too long. She decides to give him an acceptable way out rather than continuing to humiliate him.

'The fact is . . .' She spreads her hands wide and inhales. 'The fact is, I have no idea how Håkan acquired that final dose. Maybe one of the staff took pity on him, or maybe the pump malfunctioned. Or maybe a higher power intervened. Whatever happened, I'm grateful.' She lowers her head, allows the grief to show through. It's easier than expected. 'Håkan was incredibly strong-willed,' she says quietly. 'He fought hard, lived longer than most others with such advanced cancer, but in the end even he couldn't take any more.'

Santesson is still staring at her, while the bulldog and her solicitor are motionless. Once again, the atmosphere in the room makes the air feel thick. She keeps looking at Santesson, and somewhere deep in his eyes she thinks she sees a glimmer of genuine sympathy. Beneath that tough exterior he is also a person with feelings, with a family, with empathy.

'Håkan was the father of my child,' she adds quietly. 'We might have been divorced, but he was the love of my life and my best friend. Not a day goes by when I don't think about him. Talk to him. Miss him.'

She swallows, composes herself. 'I wanted him to die. Longed for it to happen.' She draws a jagged breath. 'But I did not kill him.'

41

Autumn 2017

They are asked to wait in reception while Santesson consults with his colleagues. As soon as they are out of sight and earshot, Anna's solicitor lets out a huge sigh.

'That was either the smartest or the dumbest thing you could have done.'

She shakes her head. 'I went too far. But when he brought Agnes into it—'

The nausea comes from nowhere, starting deep in her stomach and finding its way upwards.

'Excuse me, I just need to ...' She sets off for the toilets as calmly as she can, breaking into a run only when she is two metres away. She drops to her knees in the cubicle and throws up.

She sleeps through the flight home and lands at Sturup late in the afternoon. Her mind feels slow, and it isn't until she's in the car that she is able to summarise the day. She has done her best and she hasn't been arrested, which of course is a plus. However, the investigation is still going on, and humiliating Santesson in front of the bulldog hasn't done her any favours. The chief prosecutor is not the type to take something like that lying down, and he is bound to welcome the first opportunity for revenge. The question is when and how, but she can't think about that right now. She just wants to get home.

That's how she has started to regard both Nedanås and Tabor. She and Agnes have lived here for only a few weeks, but the place already feels like home.

She has two missed voicemail messages on her phone. The first is from Rylander's stepfather. The unpleasant scrap dealer whines about Rylander's mail, and mumbles something about 'sending the whole pile of crap to the police' before he hangs up. The second message is much nicer. A soft female voice introduces the caller as Lisa Savic, Joakim Rylander's eldest daughter. She says she will be coming to Nedanås next week to collect her father's belongings, and will be in touch then.

Anna is still not thinking straight, and it's a good few miles before the penny drops. The surname is the same as the woman who was with Rylander at the quarry and later at the petrol station – Tanya Savic, who died of an overdose in 2002. Call-me said he'd spoken to the daughter about the mother, but Anna hadn't made the connection until now. Joakim Rylander and Tanya Savic had a child together – a daughter called Lisa. Does that have any relevance to the case? After a while she concludes that it doesn't.

She continues along the main road, and eventually passes the sign for Reftinge. Before long she comes across a large petrol station. Was this the place where Rylander was arrested on the night Simon died? She decides to check it out. The woman on the checkout is about twenty-five, and turns out to be the owner's daughter. Anna shows her ID and explains why she's there. The woman calls her father and asks if he remembers the incident. She's in luck – it's the right petrol station and the right person. The woman hands her the phone.

'The two of them turned up on a motorbike, just after one in the morning,' the man on the other end says. 'A man and a woman. I could see straight away that there was a problem. The guy was drunk. He was aggressive towards the woman – I think he actually hit her once, so I rang the direct line to Reftinge police station. They filled up the bike, and when the guy came in to pay, he tried to steal a cigarette lighter – just a cheap one from the display by the till. I asked him for the money and he started mouthing off. He faced up to me and started knocking things over, as if he wanted a fight. The woman tried to calm him down, but he wouldn't listen. The police arrived and took him away.'

'And the woman?'

'I felt sorry for her. I gave her a lift to catch the night bus to Klippan; it was due to leave at two. She seemed like a nice girl who'd ended up in the wrong company.'

Anna buys an energy drink and knocks it back standing by the car. She soon feels more lively and in a better mood. The wind coming off the plain nips her cheeks and blows new life into her mind and body. She uses the rest of the journey to shake off the trip to Stockholm by focusing on Joakim 'Joe' Rylander. Neither he nor his girlfriend Tanya Savic were at the quarry when Simon Vidje died, at least according to the four witnesses, yet in his email Rylander hints that he knows something about Simon's death and wants to be paid for his silence. Which is probably why he was murdered.

So, what was it that Rylander knew? The email was sent to all four friends, so it must be something that touched each of them. Or was it just a trick, a way of putting extra pressure on the person – or persons – who really did have something to hide? Another question: how did Rylander get hold of the cassette tape with Simon's recording? The entire studio, containing all of Simon's possessions, burned to the ground the evening after his death. Was Rylander involved in the fire, or did he acquire the tape some other way?

When she arrives home the house is empty and there is no sign of Agnes's Vespa. Her first impulse is to call her and demand to know where she is, but instead she sends a text asking what she'd like for dinner. She sits there holding her phone for a minute or so, but there is no reply.

She lets Milo out, and as usual the stupid dog ignores her completely. While Milo is out she takes a shower, washes away Stockholm, Santesson and the interview. She tells herself once again that she did what she could, and that there is no point in worrying anymore. She is waiting for Håkan to pipe up, but apparently, he has nothing to say. His absence makes her feel desperately lonely. She lets the water flow through her hair and over her face for a long time, until it begins to run cold.

Agnes has answered her text:

Whatever.

It's not exactly the kind of response she was hoping for, but it will have to do.

She pulls on a vest top and sweatpants, wraps her threadbare robe around her body and slides her feet into wooden clogs. Dusk is falling, and as she steps out onto the porch to call Milo in, she sees a light glinting among the trees. At first she thinks it's the Vespa's headlamp, but then she realises it's a car. Klein's pickup truck stops in front of her, and she sees that Agnes is in the passenger seat.

'Hi, Mum,' she says. Her voice is neither friendly nor unfriendly, but there is no hug, just a crooked little smile. 'I've been to Änglaberga to photograph the rest of Karl-Jo's paintings in Mats's collection. Aunt Elisabet asked Klein to drive me home. He's got some apples for us.'

Before Anna can react to the fact that Agnes has started referring to Elisabet Vidje as 'Aunt', Klein appears with a big wooden box.

'Cox's Orange,' he says. 'We've got plenty.'

'Thank you.' She steps aside and lets them into the kitchen. Klein places the box on the table, while Agnes heads for her room. Milo lingers, transfixed by Klein as always. He doesn't follow Agnes until she calls him.

Klein shifts uncomfortably from foot to foot and glances in the direction of Agnes's door.

'I actually wanted a word with you, Anna. Maybe we could go outside?'

She accompanies him out to the pickup. The evening air is damp and chilly, carrying with it the smell of decay.

Only now does she see Agnes's Vespa in the back of the truck, secured with ratchet straps.

'I'll help you get it down,' she says.

Klein shakes head and nods at her robe and clogs. 'I'll do it. You're not exactly dressed for the job.'

He drops the tailgate and pulls out a wide plank, which he props up against the back of the truck before manoeuvring the moped down the improvised ramp. It looks easy, but she hears him grunt a couple of times. This reminds her that he is considerably older than he looks.

'There you go,' he says, parking the Vespa over by the house. He pushes back his cap, which is made of the same green fabric as his coat, and rubs his brow with the back of his hand. Inside the house Agnes is clattering around in the kitchen; it actually sounds as if she's making dinner.

'So . . .' Klein moves a little closer. His normally expressionless face looks a little troubled. 'Elisabet told me you think the man who was found dead on Monday has something to do with Simon.'

Anna nods slowly, waits for him to go on. He holds his breath, as if he is choosing his words with extreme care, then continues.

'Elisabet has lived for virtually one thing over the past twenty-seven years: to see the investigation into Simon's death reopened.' He adjusts his cap. 'There's no denying that you've made her very happy, and for that I'm grateful. At the same time . . .' He stops, glances at the house and the open front door. 'At the same time I have to warn you,' he says quietly. 'There are those who don't want anyone poking about in what went on. Who are ready to go a very long way to prevent that from happening.'

'You're thinking about the burned-out garage. Simon's studio, Karl-Jo's sports car.' She waves in the direction of the outbuilding where the charred skeleton of the car is hidden.

Klein looks completely taken aback – almost frightened.

'How—' he begins, but breaks off and regains his composure. His voice deepens. 'All I want to say, Anna, is that you need to think carefully before you act.' He leans forward, bringing his face close to hers. 'Elisabet Vidje is the most important person in my life. If she's at risk of being hurt by all this, by something or someone . . .'

He doesn't finish the sentence. Instead, he straightens up, pulls down his cap, then jumps in the truck and screeches away.

Agnes has made a start on dinner. They finish off together, then eat at the table while making polite conversation. The subject of Simon Vidje soon comes up. Agnes is still interested in the mural and the story behind it; she asks questions about the details and about those involved. Anna answers as best she can, trying not to break the rules of confidentiality, but at this stage that's virtually impossible.

After dinner Agnes fetches her camera, transfers the memory card to her computer and shows Anna the pictures she's taken down in Mats's creepy cellar.

'Karl-Jo painted these too.' She brings up photographs of a small display case with a forest motif: tall grey tree trunks disappearing into the mist and becoming barely visible shapes, half trees and half shadow-creatures. Inside the case Mats has built a section of a stone wall. It must have taken him many hours. On top of one of the bigger stones a snake with a zigzag pattern down its back is consuming what is presumably a mouse; only the back legs and the tail are protruding from the snake's jaws. Seen through the lens of a camera, it looks incredibly realistic. It is almost impossible to distinguish the image from the reality itself.

'Did Mats say what Karl-Johan thought of his collection?'

'He said Karl-Jo did the paintings here at Tabor, then Mats came and collected them. He's had his collection down in the cellar since the mid-'80s, but Karl-Johan has never been there. According to Mats, he doesn't like dead animals. It's a pity every-one doesn't think that way,' Agnes says with a little smile.

Anna remembers Morell's story about the injured deer that found its way into the garden at Tabor, and wonders if she should share it with Agnes.

Her daughter leans back in her chair and tucks a strand of hair behind one ear. The gesture reminds Anna so strongly of Håkan that her heart turns over.

'I asked Mats about Simon,' Agnes continues. 'At first he seemed pleased; he talked a lot about Simon's studio and his music. Apparently, he could play five instruments, and everyone liked him. But when I wanted to know about the accident, Mats didn't want to chat anymore. He said all the joy had gone from Änglaberga with Simon, and that it never came back. Then he went up to his room and closed the door. I had to find my own way out. Aunt Elisabet called to me as I was about to start the Vespa and invited me into the kitchen for coffee and cake. Mats is right – the whole of Änglaberga feels kind of gloomy, doesn't it?'

'Mm.'

They sit in silence for a few seconds. 'Do you really think that grief can make you go blind?' Agnes asks.

'I don't know, but certain illnesses can be triggered by traumatic events. I'm not sure about . . .'

'Retinitis pigmentosa,' Agnes supplies. 'I googled it. The first symptom is difficulty with night vision, then a loss of colour and sharpness, then peripheral vision disappears until all that's left is a narrow, grainy black-and-white field of vision straight ahead.' She shakes her head sadly. 'It must be terrible, especially for someone like Karl-Jo, who has lived with colours and pictures. So cruel.'

'Some illnesses are more cruel than others.'

Anna doesn't think about what she's said until the words have slipped out and exploded. Agnes stiffens, her eyes shine with unshed tears, and Anna swears silent to herself.

'I've got something you might want to hear,' she says quickly. 'A recording of Simon Vidje.'

She fetches her phone, opens the sound file that Jens Friberg sent her. Simon's voice emerges from the little speaker.

Some of the tension leaves Agnes's body. She tilts her head on one side as she listens, just like Håkan used to do. Once again, Anna's heart turns over.

'Can you send it to me?' Agnes says. 'I want to listen to it in my room.'

42

Autumn 2017

Agnes is using her Vespa to get to the train station, so Anna decides to have an extra half an hour in bed. At the last moment she remembers that today is Morell's retirement presentation, and quickly irons her uniform shirt before leaving for work.

When she gets to the office she takes the Simon Vidje case file out of her briefcase and reads through it again. She decides to sketch out a timeline.

Bruno and Alex arrive at the quarry at about three o'clock in Alex's car.

Simon shows up half an hour later on his bike, and after another hour or so Marie and Carina turn up, also by car.

Both vehicles are parked down by the barrier. Anna knows from her own experience that this is just over half a mile from the quarry. Simon can cycle all the way there.

They light the fire at around seven, and at some point after eight Joe and Tanya arrive on a motorbike; clearly it was possible for them to negotiate the barrier.

Shortly before midnight – at 23.40 according to Bruno, 23.50 according to Marie – Joe and Tanya leave the quarry. At the same time it begins to rain heavily.

At 01.36 Joe Rylander is arrested at the petrol station near Reftinge. At that stage he and Tanya have been there for less than fifteen minutes.

According to the autopsy report, Simon Vidje dies between 01.00 and 02.00.

By five o'clock in the morning, it has stopped raining. Marie Sordi leaves the tent she is sharing with Carina Pedersen and sees Simon in the water.

After they have established that Simon is dead, Bruno drives off in Marie's car to call the police and an ambulance. Änglaberga isn't far away, but instead of going there, he heads for the grocery store in Mörkaby.

The first police car is on the scene at 05.54, with the ambulance and fire service arriving shortly after.

Anna reads through the timeline twice, but can't find any gaps. It might seem a little strange that Bruno chose to go to Mörkaby instead of Änglaberga, but in fact it's completely understandable. Presumably he didn't want to be the one to tell Karl-Johan and Elisabet that their son was dead.

During the lunch break she slips down to the archive again. It takes her only a few minutes to find the report on the fire at Änglaberga, remove it from the file and take it back to her office. The whole case consists of only two A4 pages. First, there is the incident report, written by an officer whose name she doesn't recognise.

At 02.23 on 30 August patrol car 3485 was called out to Änglaberga because of a fire in a garage. At the scene were the owners of the property, Elisabet and Karl-Johan Vidje, plus the estate manager Bror Klein. Klein, who lives nearby, states that he looked out of his window and saw flames. He contacted the fire service, then went over to try to put out the fire himself.

When the patrol arrived the garage was in flames, and the fire service decided to focus their attention on trying to save the adjoining stable buildings. Klein suffered minor burns to his hands, but otherwise no one was hurt, and no one was at risk because the garage and the room above were unoccupied.

The second page is a brief note written by Henry Morell.

From conversations with the owners of the property it transpired that the room above the garage had been converted into a music studio, containing a considerable amount of electrical equipment that had not been installed by a qualified electrician. According to the senior fire officer at the scene, the fire probably started in the studio, probably because of an overload, which was then exacerbated by the insulation material that had been used. Before long the fire reached the flammable liquids stored in the garage itself, then ignited the petrol tank of the car parked there, which explains the fierceness and rapid spread of the conflagration.

Anna adds both pages to the Simon Vidje file. A death, and less than twenty-four hours later a fire, both affecting the Vidje family. Two incidents, both written off as accidents. And Henry Morell was heavily involved in both.

Morell's retirement presentation in the council offices' dining room is entirely predictable: paper plates, cake, and plastic glasses of cheap Cava. Everyone from the police station is there, along with council representatives and local businessmen and women. A brass quartet from Nedanås music society is playing and the atmosphere is relaxed. The place smells of a communal hall, coffee and Friday.

Anna greets Eva-Britt Morell first of all, then Fabbe Sordi. She receives polite nods in response but neither of them comes over to talk to her, presumably because of the disturbance at the home-coming party. Bruno is there, but seems to be deliberately avoiding her. There is no sign of Alex Morell, which makes her feel both relieved and slightly disappointed.

The first speaker is Marie Sordi. She talks about how she has known Henry since she was a little girl. How she, Alex, Bruno and Carina used to hang out in the Morell family's hobby room. Simon is not mentioned in the anecdote. With a faint tremble in her voice she refers to Morell as 'Uncle Henry', saying that he deserves to step back and take it easy at long last. She finishes off by giving him a big hug.

The next speech comes from Marie's father. Bengt Andersson has a lot to say about working with Morell, and how the two of them have steered Nedanås through the difficult years and into the golden age that now awaits their community. Bengt and Marie then present Morell with a plaque bearing the town's coat of arms and his name. Something rather more unexpected happens next. A large package is handed over; according to Marie, everyone has contributed to the purchase of this present, which turns out to be a robotic lawn mower. Morell's face lights up like a child's on Christmas morning.

Jens Friberg has appeared beside Anna. 'I don't think that falls within the framework of the council's present-giving policy,' he whispers. 'But of course it's well-deserved,' he adds, without a hint of irony.

The police commissioner steps forward. He is a serious little man; Anna has met him only once, when she was interviewed for Morell's job. They exchanged a few words before the ceremony began, but the only thing she's learned about her boss is that his personality confirms the general perception that he is a boring bureaucrat. She knows he's a lawyer with no police background, but he's good at keeping to a budget, which makes him popular with the administrators at national level. Like most non-police officers within the authority, he is clearly delighted to be wearing the uniform. His shoes are impressively shiny, and his jacket appears to have been taken in at the waist. His buttons and epaulettes are dazzling. No doubt he polishes both them and the badge on his cap – which he insists on carrying tucked beneath his arm like a US marine – several times a month.

In a rasping voice he praises Morell for his immense contribution, and for the trust he has built up with the public. He also mentions all the training Morell has apparently initiated over the years, saying that this has enhanced not only the commissioner's own competence and skills, but those of many others.

The final speaker is the county governor, a scrawny woman in her late fifties who quickly reads her audience and keeps her speech admirably short. She too praises Morell, gives a nod to Eva-Britt who will now have to put up with him being at home all day, then finally expresses the hope that officers like Morell are not a dying breed, and that others will follow. Then she leads everyone in three cheers.

Now it is Morell's turn. He is clearly moved. He thanks everyone for their gifts and good wishes, then speaks warmly of his colleagues and his wife before unexpectedly turning to Anna. He wishes her every success, and raises his glass in a toast.

'Here's to you, Anna. I hope you will be very happy here in Nedanås.' His tone is relaxed, his expression warm. But when his eyes meet hers, Anna sees a hardness behind the warmth.

43

Autumn 2017

On Monday morning, Anna wakes feeling rested. She reads the online edition of the local paper, then gives Agnes a lift to the train station with plenty of time to spare. In the car they listen to the radio and chat politely. Their relationship continues to improve gradually, as it has done over the weekend. Even Milo seems to be aware of the change and occasionally acknowledges Anna's presence instead of simply ignoring her as he usually does.

At the police station she says a cheerful 'Good morning' to Henry Morell and makes small talk in the doorway of his office for a little while. He looks happy; the plaque he received on Friday is already on display among the photographs and diplomas covering the walls.

'How's it going with Rylander? Have you found out any more?'

She shakes her head. 'We're still waiting for the autopsy report and forensics.'

Jens Friberg calls into her office half an hour later. His uniform is perfectly pressed as always, and there isn't a hair out of place in his little side fringe. Anna is about to make a comment to Håkan, then she remembers that he isn't speaking to her. Slightly ironic, given that she and Agnes are now on speaking terms at long last.

Her relationship with Jens also seems to be getting better. He asks about the case, and she tells him exactly what she told Morell.

'And when you get the reports, what's the next step?' he asks.

The question is justified, and she's had plenty of time to prepare a response.

'If there isn't an obvious lead, then we need to question Alex, Bruno, Marie, and Caia Bianca.'

Jens grimaces. 'You know that's going to cause all kinds of problems? The son of the former chief of police, the restaurateur, the leader of the local council and our local celebrity, all interviewed about something that happened twenty-seven years ago. Something that most people around here would prefer to forget. And only days after the police commissioner and the county governor were here.'

Anna nods. 'I'm aware of all that, but we are conducting a murder investigation. We can't treat certain individuals differently because of who they are. And this is about Joakim Rylander, not Simon Vidje.'

Jens lets out a snort. 'You're going to have to practise that statement a few more times if you want it to sound sincere. I'm out in the patrol car today, but call me if you need my help.'

'There is one thing I wanted to ask you, Jens. I could do with your advice.'

He gives her a crooked smile. 'You want to know if I think you should share your plans with Henry.' He shakes his head. 'Sorry – I'm going to pass!'

Both reports arrive just after lunch. The forensic examination of the white Saab basically tells Anna what they already know, and she quickly skims through the pages. Joe Rylander's fingerprints are all over the car, and his DNA is on the cigarette butts they found on the floor. There are also half a dozen different sets of prints in various places in the vehicle, most of such poor quality that they are probably quite old. In the most relevant locations – the steering wheel, gear stick and rear-view mirror – there are only Rylander's prints, which means there is no real evidence that anyone else drove the car to the spot where it was found. When it comes to fibres, the results are equally depressing. There are plenty of clothing fibres on the old, sagging seats, plus both human and dog hairs, but as the Saab is thirty years old this is hardly surprising, and it is virtually impossible to say whether any of the fibres are relevant to the investigation. A couple of fibres have been matched to Rylander's trousers and to the wire fence at the viewpoint, but that gets them precisely nowhere.

The autopsy report is extremely well written. The pathologist has divided Rylander's injuries into two categories. The first are those consistent with a fall from a great height – crush injuries, broken bones, the eye that had fallen out of its socket, all listed in alphabetical order with accompanying photographs.

In the second group he has detailed a large number of wounds, from small scratches on Rylander's forehead to the hole in his chest, caused by the branch on which he was impaled. The pathologist states dryly that even though these injuries are not typical of a fall, they can be explained by the fact that the body landed in a tree.

Right at the end there are several pictures that interest her. The first shows a bloodstained bandage that appears to be carelessly wrapped around Rylander's calf.

There was a gauze bandage around the body's right calf. Beneath it was a large, recently treated wound. Closer examination revealed that the fibula (calf bone) was fractured, and there were further injuries to the tibia (shin bone). The right leg of Rylander's jeans was torn and bloodstained, matching the wound. Given the severity of the damage, it is reasonable to assume that Rylander's mobility was severely compromised.

The next two pictures show the wound itself; it is deep, with ragged edges. She thinks back to her brief encounter with Rylander in the dance hall. He spotted her approaching, pushed himself away from the wall and quickly slipped out through the door without the slightest hint of a limp. Therefore, the injury must have happened after the fracas, but before he died.

She turns back to the forensic examination of the car, finds the page she's looking for. Three photographs of Rylander's filthy shoes with an accompanying note.

Trainers, black, Nike. Covered in a thick layer of mud and vegetation. This vegetation consists of dead beech and birch leaves, and fir needles. Inside the right shoe there was a bloodstain so large that it had not completely dried out. Analysis showed that the blood was Rylander's.

Anna sits quietly, trying to process this new information along with what she already knows. At some point shortly after their encounter at the dance hall, Rylander injured himself so badly that he would have had difficulty in walking. Since the wound was bandaged, it can't have been sustained at the time of death, which is yet another indication that he didn't take his own life. Who bandages their leg shortly before they commit suicide? So how did he injure himself? Where did he spend the final hours of his life – and more importantly, with whom? It's high time she found out, but first of all she needs to reveal her plans to Henry Morell.

She knocks on the door frame, then walks into Morell's office and closes the door behind her. He glances up from the screen, raises his eyebrows and takes off his glasses.

'This looks serious.'

She nods. 'I'm afraid it is.' She takes a deep breath. 'Rylander's former name was Joakim Jonsson, and he and his girlfriend, Tanya Savic, were at the quarry on the night Simon Vidje died. Rylander was responsible for the trouble in the dance hall, and he seems to have been trying to blackmail Alex, Bruno, Marie, and Caia Bianca.'

She falls silent, mainly to try and work out to what extent this information comes as a surprise.

Morell pulls a face. 'Jesus Christ . . .' He scratches his beard, considers for a moment. 'And now you think one of them is involved in his death – is that how I'm supposed to interpret your visit?' His voice has hardened. Only a fraction, but she doesn't like it.

'At the moment we're keeping all our options open—' she begins, but stops when he waves a dismissive hand.

'Anna, I've been a police officer for far too long to listen to this nonsense. You have a death which, in spite of the lack of solid evidence, you are treating as a murder. You've also got it into your head that this case is linked to an incident that happened twenty-seven years ago, which was investigated and dismissed as purely accidental. And now here you are, ready to move heaven and earth to prove . . . what? I'm right, aren't I?' Morell shakes his head. 'I have to say I'm very disappointed in you, Anna.'

Something in his tone makes her feel a stab of pain. She has no problem with anger, but disappointment is harder to deal with. Her father used exactly the same tactic. He never raised his voice, he just made it clear that he was 'disappointed in her'.

'I tried to warn you about Elisabet Vidje,' Morell goes on. 'She gives the impression of being old and frail, but behind the façade there is a cunning, manipulative woman who holds a grudge. I thought someone with your experience would realise that.'

He shakes his head again.

'As I told you on the first day we met, in a small town like Nedanås police work is largely about building relationships with people. I thought we were on the same page, that we saw things in the same way. I invited you into my home, I even stood up for you when certain individuals questioned whether you were the right candidate to take over from me.'

His mouth twists, conveying his inner torment.

'The fact that you've started running Elisabet Vidje's errands shows that I've misjudged you.'

Anna searches for a suitable response, but her mind is blank. She hadn't expected him to be pleased at her revelations, but she had at least hoped for some level of resigned understanding.

Morell puts his reading glasses back on. His face is set in grim lines.

'Well, it's your police station, Anna, and of course I can't stop you. You don't need my approval to rip open wounds that have taken almost thirty years to heal, but I have no intention of giving you my blessing, if that's what you're looking for.'

He focuses on the screen once more, with a brief nod in the direction of the door to indicate that the conversation is over. Anna can't think of anything else to say, so she turns to leave.

'By the way,' Morell says sharply, looking up. 'To save you time – Alexander was at home Saturday night. I took him home after the party and he slept in late. He didn't leave the basement during the evening or the night. Both Eva-Britt and I can confirm that.'

'OK, thank you for the information.' She stands for a couple of seconds with her hand resting on the door handle, her eyes fixed on Morell, but he behaves as if she is no longer there.

44

Autumn 2017

Anna knows that she cannot and should not conduct the interviews alone. From a practical point of view it is always better to have another officer present; two pairs of eyes and ears pick up more than one. However, because this case is particularly sensitive in many ways, she also needs a counterbalance. Someone who cannot be suspected of doing Elisabet Vidje's bidding, which is clearly what Morell thinks. The natural course of action would have been to choose one of the investigators, but for one thing she doesn't know them very well, and for another she's far from certain that they won't go running straight to Morell to tell him everything. After due consideration on Monday evening, she plumps for Jens Friberg. Admittedly he's not a detective, but he is respected both within the station and in the wider community. Plus, the two of them haven't always agreed, which strengthens his impartiality. The third and most important reason for choosing Jens is that she's actually begun to trust him.

Just as she hoped, Jens has no objection when she talks to him on Tuesday morning. He suggests that it might be best if he changes out of his uniform, and ten minutes later he reappears in her office wearing a leather jacket, fleece top, khaki-coloured Fjällräven trousers and brown Meindl boots. Anna doesn't say a word, she merely waits for Håkan's amused comment on the fact that a dyed-in-the-wool police officer like Jens wears a kind of uniform even when he's in plain clothes. However, Håkan is still punishing her with his silence.

'So where do we begin?' Jens asks as he starts the car.

'Kotorp. Marie and Bruno are both there – I called and checked.'

Jens drives smoothly and with a hint of aggression, just like most police officers. He knows the route up the ridge well enough to handle the bends with ease. Sunday's high winds have brought down a lot of leaves, and it is possible to glimpse the shining waters of the river at the bottom of the ravine.

Building is under way once more at Kotorp. Several workers in yellow hard hats and grubby high-vis jackets are moving equipment and materials across the muddy yard at a steady pace.

Anna and Jens cross the footbridge over the ditch and knock on the front door. They hear the sound of barking, then a shouted command followed by silence. Marie Sordi opens the door.

'Come in,' she says tersely. 'No need to take off your shoes.'

She shows them into the kitchen, where Bruno is sitting at the table. He nods, but doesn't bother getting up to shake hands. Instead, he seems embarrassed, and looks away. There are piles of papers and drawings in front of him; Anna can see the council's letterhead on several of them, while others are from various companies and look like invoices.

'So, what's this about?' Marie says, without asking them to sit down or offering a drink. The question is entirely unnecessary. Her tone and expression reveal that she knows exactly why they're there.

Anna places the official police photograph of Rylander in the middle of the table, on top of an invoice from a firm of architects. She catches sight of the word 'REMINDER' before Bruno quickly removes the sheet of paper.

'This is Kent Joakim Rylander. He was found dead in Glarea quarry a week ago.'

She pauses, gives them time to look at the picture. She would have preferred to use a post-mortem photo of Rylander just as she did with his stepfather, but she realises that she has to proceed with caution at this stage. She can't afford to leave herself open to unnecessary criticism.

'And what does this have to do with us?' Marie says after only a couple of seconds.

'Have you seen him before?' Jens takes over, just as they'd agreed in the car.

Marie shakes her head. 'No, never.'

'Bruno?'

A shrug. 'Hard to say.'

Anna watches them both carefully, sees Marie twitch briefly, then glare angrily at Bruno. Clearly that wasn't the answer she was expecting.

'I mean . . .' Bruno rubs his lips, 'I meet so many people at the restaurant. I can't remember everyone.' He gives an embarrassed smile.

'You've both met him,' Jens says. 'Twenty-seven years ago at Mörkaby quarry. Back then he was calling himself Joe, and he was with a girl called Tanya.'

Neither of them says anything, and judging by their neutral expressions and body language, this information comes as no surprise. Marie and Bruno have been forewarned, not only about this visit, but also the purpose behind it.

Husband and wife exchange glances, then Bruno clears his throat.

'We had an email, both of us, only a day or so beforehand,' he begins, without taking his eyes off Marie. 'From a sender calling himself Simon Vidje. The message went to Alex as well. We discussed it and decided it must have come from some sick bastard. When the DJ played that song . . .' He spreads his hands apologetically. 'We'd all had too much to drink, and things got out of hand. We really didn't intend to hurt anyone.'

Bruno is trying to come across as spontaneous, but he has practised this little speech. Referring to Rylander as a sick bastard is a subtle way of diminishing him as a victim. Anna makes a mental note, then concentrates on what is coming next.

'Bruno and I went straight home from the police station and stayed in all night,' Marie says, without anyone having asked her. 'We were up half the night talking through what happened at the dance. The children stayed over with Bruno's parents.'

Bruno nods with a little too much enthusiasm, which appears to irritate his wife. Marie isn't happy with Bruno's performance so far, Anna thinks.

'Did you see or hear anything unusual when you drove back from the police station – a car you didn't recognise, for example?' Jens points to the window. 'The viewpoint is just over half a mile from Kotorp as the crow flies.'

'Norrblicka, not Kotorp,' Marie snaps. 'And no, not as far as I remember. I think it was raining quite hard, wasn't it, darling?'

Bruno nods. 'It was pouring down. The ditch out there almost overflowed – I had to go out and do some digging.' He would like to embellish his account, but a look from Marie silences him. He receives the smallest of nods as a reward.

Marie smiles at Jens.

'As we said, we haven't seen this Rylander, or whatever his name is, for the last twenty-seven years. And we both spent all of Sunday at home together.' She turns to Anna. 'Perhaps you'd like to write that down so there won't be any misunderstandings.' The acid comment is entirely free of the fake warmth that characterised their previous conversations.

'Simon Vidje,' Anna says calmly. Even though the name has already been mentioned, Bruno can't help reacting when he hears it.

'You were both present on the night he died. In his email Rylander hinted that he knew the truth about what actually happened, and that he wanted you to pay.' She observes the couple closely; Jens is doing the same thing.

Marie's lips are pursed and she narrows her eyes. Bruno looks uneasy.

'My cousin's death was purely accidental,' Marie says. 'The police investigation has already established that.' Her tone conveys the fact that she finds their questions very unfair. 'As we already stated when we were interviewed, we all went to bed just after midnight when Rylander and the girl had left and it started to rain. Carina and I . . .' She stops, corrects herself. 'Caia and I were in one tent, Bruno and Alex in another. Simon always slept by himself.'

'Why?' Jens asks.

Bruno shrugs. 'He preferred it that way. We had a four-man tent in the first few years when we camped up there, but Simon didn't like it. He preferred to cycle home at night rather than share.'

'Why didn't Alex and Carina sleep in the same tent? They were a couple, weren't they?' Anna asks.

Bruno and Marie look at each other. They were not prepared for that question.

'Their relationship was something of a rollercoaster during the last year of high school,' Marie says after some hesitation. 'It ended for good only a month or so later, when Carina left Nedanås. Sorry, Caia.'

'How did Alex take that?' Anna asks. Jens raises an eyebrow.

Bruno and Marie look at each other again. 'Not very well,' Bruno mumbles.

'Was that when he ended up in the psychiatric unit?'

The silence is deafening. Both Bruno and Marie shuffle uncomfortably.

'We don't know anything about that,' Marie says. Her voice lets her down, and Anna is in no doubt that this is a lie. She allows the silence to continue for a few seconds, then nods to Jens to indicate that he can continue.

'How did Simon seem when he went to bed?'

'Same as usual.' Marie is trying to keep her mask in place, but the questions about Alex have shaken her. 'We said goodnight and . . .' She looks away, bites her upper lip. 'And . . .' Her voice breaks.

Bruno gets up, puts his arm around his wife and rests his head on hers in a surprisingly tender gesture. Marie is considerably taller than her husband, and if it weren't for the sorrow on their faces, the tableau would have looked quite funny.

'And after that we never saw Simon alive again,' Bruno says quietly.

'And neither you nor Alex left your tent?'

He shakes his head. 'No.'

'Are you absolutely certain?'

Bruno is clearly irritated. 'Have you ever slept in a two-man tent?' Jens nods.

'Well, then, you know what it's like. You're lying right next to each other. There are at least two zips to open and close the flap. It's impossible to creep out of or into the tent, especially given that the person who'd been out in the rain would be soaking wet. None of us went outside, not me, Alex, Carina or Marie. Simon slipped on the rocks and died while we were all sleeping just a few metres away. How do you think that makes us feel?' He gently strokes his wife's back.

Jens nods again, with a glance at Anna. She has no intention of giving up, at least not yet. There is at least one more question that needs an answer.

'Why didn't you jump in the water to try and pull Simon out, Bruno? Marie did.'

A flash of anger crosses Bruno's face. He opens his mouth as if he is about to snap at her, then controls himself.

'I was woken by Marie screaming,' he says grimly. 'It took me and Alex a minute or so to put on our shoes and get out of the tent. Carina was still half-asleep and confused, and by the time we'd worked out who was yelling and made our way down to the water, Marie was shaking with cold and had had to let go of Simon. We all helped her out. It was freezing cold; you can't stay in the water for more than three or four minutes even in the middle of summer, and Marie had been in longer than that.' He pauses for a moment. 'Besides . . . it was obvious that Simon was dead, and had been for a while. I can't explain it, but it was as if all the strength went out of us. Of course, we should have jumped in and got the body out, but we just couldn't do it. We were nineteen years old, and our friend was dead.'

'So, what do you think?' Jens asks as they walk towards the car. 'Are they telling the truth?'

Before Anna can answer she spots a familiar figure in the doorway of the workmen's hut. Alex Morell.

She wasn't intending to question him yet, but as the opportunity has presented itself . . .

'Alex.'

He turns and looks surprised, but his expression quickly switches to embarrassment.

'Anna – hi. I meant to call you last week, but . . .' He stares down at his muddy boots.

She waits.

'What happened at the dance . . . to be honest, I don't really know what happened. Everything kind of went black. I'm sorry I . . . I'm sorry you . . .' His torment is unmistakable. 'I was totally out of order.'

Anna nods and gestures discreetly to Jens to stay in the background. He understands immediately – another point in his favour.

'I assume your father called you,' she says. 'Told you about Rylander?'

Alex takes a deep breath, then sighs heavily. 'Yes. What a fucking mess. I haven't given Joe a thought in years.'

'What do you remember about him from that evening at the quarry?'

'Not much. He gave us weed and drank our beer. He was a few years older than us, and at first, we thought he was cool, with his motorbike and so on. Plus, he was from Klippan. Back then it was only the tough guys who came from Klippan.' He manages a little smile.

'And the girl who was with him?'

'I only remember that she looked like a girl from a Whitesnake video.'

'Is that a good thing?'

He nods slowly. 'Well, it was in those days.' He smiles again, and she has to make an effort not to smile back. In spite of the outburst of rage and the scuffle at the dance, she realises that she still likes Alex Morell.

'Simon Vidje?' She raises her eyebrows and lets him fill in the rest of the question. His expression darkens.

'Simon was one of my best friends.'

'Why didn't you jump in the water when you found him?'

Another sigh. 'I've been asking myself that for twenty-seven years. If only I had, then maybe he wouldn't . . .' He spreads his hands wide, but Anna isn't quite sure why.

'Henry says you were at home a week ago last Sunday – all morning and most of the day. Is that true?'

He nods, looks embarrassed again. 'It was mostly because of the hangover. Although it was partly your fault too.'

'My fault?'

He points at his crotch. 'I couldn't walk properly for two days after you kneed me in the balls. I had to sleep with an ice pack. But after what I did to you and that poor DJ, I definitely deserved it.'

He gives her that wry, slightly sorrowful smile that she finds so hard to resist.

'To be honest, I don't think Mum and Dad would have let me out even if I'd wanted to go somewhere. Grounded at the age of forty-six . . .'

This time she can't help smiling.

'Alex?' Marie is marching across the yard, a German shepherd on either side of her. 'We need a meeting,' she says, without so much as a glance in Anna's direction. 'Bruno has a few changes he'd like to discuss.'

'No problem!' Alex shrugs as if to let Anna know that he would be happy to talk further but has no choice.

Jens steps forward to stand beside her. They watch in silence as Marie and Alex disappear into the house. The front door closes with a slam.

45

Autumn 2017

Carina Pedersen, now known as Caia Bianca, lives to the north of Helsingborg in an area that Jens refers to as the Gold Coast. The residential development is situated on a steep ridge that runs alongside the sea, and consists mainly of large houses surrounded by high walls or fences. Only the roofs are visible from the street.

They haven't talked much during the drive, except to agree that Jens will ask most of the questions while Anna listens and observes.

He presses the entry phone, and after they've shown their police ID to the camera and explained the purpose of their visit, the tall wrought-iron gates open smoothly. They follow the steep drive through the grounds, which resemble a park rather than an ordinary garden, until they reach the house. Although 'house' isn't really the right word. The main building, a glass-and-concrete box designed by an architect, must measure well over five hundred square metres. There is also a garage with space for at least four cars, and a large pool house. Anna thinks back to what Call-me said about the build, and the neighbours' complaints.

A woman who introduces herself as Caia Bianca's PA shows them into a drawing room with an amazing view over Öresund and Denmark. It is a windy day; the grey waves are tipped with white. A car ferry has just left Denmark, and is halfway across the sound before Caia appears. She is wearing black trousers and a white shirt, and is considerably more subdued than she was at the homecoming event. She sits down on the sofa with her handbag beside her and takes out a rose-gold mobile phone. She glances at the screen, checking for messages before placing it on the glass coffee table.

'I heard Joe killed himself at Glarea,' she says before either of them has the chance to explain why they're here. 'And yes, I got that email too, but to be honest I didn't pay it any attention. As a woman in my industry, I'm used to weird messages. I can't tell you how many dick pics I get in a week. I could hold my own exhibition.'

She gives the phone a gentle push with one finger, then smiles and winks at Jens, who doesn't appear to know what to say.

'Did you have any contact with Joe Rylander before that?' Anna asks in order to help him out.

Caia shakes her head.

'Not that I'm aware of. We only met for a few hours that evening. I'm usually pretty good with faces, but I doubt I'd recognise him. Do you have a picture?'

Jens places Rylander's photograph on the table. Caia takes a pair of elegant reading glasses out of a check case, puts them on and studies it closely. 'No,' she says after a while. 'I'm pretty sure we've never met before. Well . . . of course we have met before, but not since then, if you know what I mean.'

She fires off another smile in Jens's direction. Her pink lipstick emphasises the perfection of her sculpted lips.

'What do you remember about Joe Rylander from the quarry?' Jens manages to ask.

'That he was a complete shit.' Caia reaches into her handbag for an e-cigarette, lights it with a click and releases a puff of vapour. At the same time, she picks up her phone with the other hand, once again checking for messages. The gesture is not meant to be rude; it's probably unconscious. Her fingers are long, the nails beautifully manicured.

'I'm sure it's past the statute of limitations by now, but Joe and that . . .' she waves her e-cigarette around, 'whore he had with him supplied us with weed.' She pauses, takes another drag. 'I know you shouldn't say that kind of thing about other women.' She rolls her eyes. 'God knows, I've been called all sorts. What I mean is that Tina, or whatever her name was, looked like one of those trashy groupie types with torn jeans and back-combed hair. The kind all the boys were crazy for back in the '80s.'

'And why was Joe a complete shit?' Jens asks, earning himself yet another smile.

'Because he got me drunk and high, then came on to me in one of the tents. Fortunately, Alex dealt with him. Sent Joe and his . . . sister packing.'

'Joe and Tanya weren't siblings,' Anna informs her.

'No?' Caia raises a well-plucked eyebrow.

'No. They actually had a child together.'

'Well, there you go. I can't say I'm surprised. It just goes to show how messed up they were – pretending to be brother and sister so they could both try it on with someone else. Totally fucked-up!' Her hand hovers over the phone, as if it's already time to check again.

'You don't have children,' Anna says, without really knowing why. Maybe Caia's dependence on her phone reminds her of Agnes.

Caia shakes her head. 'No, kids aren't my thing. I had to be a mother to my younger siblings when I was growing up – that was enough for me.'

Jens is keen to get back to the evening in question. 'So, what happened after Joe and Tanya left?'

'It started pouring with rain. The fire went out, and we got into our tents pretty quickly. Marie and I were sharing. I woke up in the morning when she went out to pee, and a couple of minutes later I heard her screaming. I ran out and almost bumped into Bruno and Alex – then we saw Simon in the water.' She lowers her e-cigarette, her eyes filled with sorrow. 'I'll never forget it. None of us will.'

There is a brief silence, then Jens asks: 'What did you do after the party?'

'After the fight I drove straight home,' Caia replies without hesitation. 'I was going to leave early anyhow. We had a concert at the Dunker art centre on the Sunday. I'm on the board and I try to go as often as I can.'

'Did you go alone?'

Caia takes one last drag, then puts away the e-cigarette. Her fingers unconsciously reach for the phone again.

'I was with Martin, my husband. He's not really into cultural events, which is why I drag him along. Sooner or later something's bound to stick – at least that's what I tell myself. He was asleep in bed with the TV on when I got home Saturday night, if that is what you were going to ask me. I didn't bother waking him. Netflix is no good for one's sex life, is it?'

She winks at Jens again, but he's got used to it by now, and doesn't react at all.

'I saw you at the homecoming party with Alex, Bruno and Marie. The four of you still seem close. Are you often in Nedanås?' Anna asks.

'No, hardly ever.' Caia's tone is harsh. 'I mean . . .' she goes on, as if she's suddenly become aware of the change. 'It's not always easy, growing up in a place like that. You know how it works – everybody knows everybody else, you mustn't get ideas above your station and so on . . .'

She looks up, as if she's waiting for them to agree with her.

'My father wasn't the best. He drank, and he was violent towards both my mother and us kids. Everyone knew, but no one did anything about it. He ended up in jail a couple of times, but that was for other things. My mother was never prepared to report him, because she knew it would just make the situation worse. He had a bad reputation, and strangely enough that tainted the rest of the family. My older brothers often got into fights because of their surname. So maybe you can understand why I couldn't get away fast enough.' She picks up her phone, as if the discussion is beginning to bore her.

'And yet you came to the party,' Jens says dryly.

Caia looks taken aback; she wasn't expecting that kind of comment from him.

'Marie invited me. Besides . . .' she pauses, weighing the phone in her hand, 'it's nice to drop by occasionally.' She laughs, showing dazzling white, perfect veneers. 'No doubt you think this is

ANDERS DE LA MOTTE

all down to Martin – the grounds, the house, the cars. But the fact is, I earn a lot more than he does. You might have heard that my first husband left me a lot of money? Well, that's not true. He was up to his ears in debt. I've built up everything you can see. Little Carina Pedersen from Nedanås, the girl people looked down on. I've worked hard, and sacrificed more than most in order to succeed. And sometimes . . .' She stops, gives a wry, joyless smile. 'Sometimes little Carina just wants to come home to Nedanås and shove her success in their faces. Henry Morell, who thought I wasn't good enough for his precious Alexander. Bengt Andersson, who thought my family gave the place a bad name. Nowadays they all line up smiling whenever I show up. They're *so* proud when I grace their pathetic little events with my presence.'

She holds up her phone so they can see all the notifications and messages received on the screen.

'If there's nothing else I need to—'

'Alex Morell,' Anna says. 'How's your relationship with him now?'

Caia lowers her phone.

'Alex and I were together in junior school and high school, but that's a long time ago. We split up in the autumn after Simon died.'

She pulls a sad face.

'Was it because of his temper?'

Caia gives her a searching look, as if she's trying to work out where Anna is going with this question. 'You were the one who fought with him on the stage, weren't you? The one who kneed him in the crotch?'

Anna nods. Caia looks moderately impressed.

'Alex had a terrible temper. He still has, as you've seen. But that's not why we broke up, nor was it because his parents thought I was trailer trash. The thing is, poor Alex turned out to be one of those kids who peak in high school.'

'What do you mean?' Jens wonders.

'I mean that Alex's life reached its high point during the spring term in his last year at high school. You know the type – the boys who were good at football and could do a double somersault on the trampoline. The popular girls who had their own little clique, older boyfriends, and who were invited to every party.' Caia rubs her lower lip as if she's afraid that something is stuck there. 'They're all in such a hurry to grow up, get a driving licence and escape from the little place where they grew up.' She shakes her head. 'But then things start to change. Others take their place – those who weren't strong enough, fast enough, or attractive enough to join the clique suddenly grab the baton, and without understanding how or why it's happened, Alex and his type are no longer cock of the walk. They've been outplayed.'

'You mean by someone like Simon Vidje?' Anna says, holding Caia's gaze. Her eyes are clear and intelligent.

'I mean by someone *exactly* like Simon Vidje.'

'It can't have been easy for Alex when he realised what was going on.'

'No, it wasn't.' Caia turns away a fraction. To the untrained eye, it looks as if she has simply altered her position.

'When did he realise?'

'Realise what?' Caia is playing dumb, clearly trying to buy herself time.

'When did Alex Morell realise he'd been overtaken by Simon Vidje? Was it that evening in the quarry?'

Caia shakes her head. 'I just meant in general terms, not that Alex and Simon . . .' She stops, her expression is cold now.

'I think we're done for today,' she says, getting to her feet.

In spite of the wind, Caia accompanies them to the car. She grabs Anna by the arm just as she is about to get in; Jens has already closed the driver's door.

'I didn't mean to be so nasty about Alex. He's a good guy who's had a tough time. I can't imagine he's involved in Joe's death.'

A strand of blond hair blows across her face and she tucks it behind her ear, just as Agnes does.

'Have you kept in touch?' Anna suspects she already knows the answer.

'He started calling me after his divorce – to talk about old times, he said. But I'm really not interested in the past. All we can influence is the present and the future; I've tried to make him understand that, to stop brooding over what's gone. The last few times he's talked mostly about Kotorp. He and Bruno and Marie have put everything they have into the development, and they wanted me to invest too.'

'Did you say yes?'

Caia shakes her head. 'One thing I've learned over the years is not to do business with friends. It never ends well.' She steps back and raises one hand. 'Give my best to Nedanås,' she says with that wry smile. 'I don't think I'll be back for quite a while.'

She stands in front of her big house with her arms defiantly folded as Anna and Jens drive away, a dwindling figure in the wing mirror until she disappears completely.

'So, what do you think?' Jens says.

'They're lying.'

He raises his eyebrows. 'Who's lying?'

'All of them.'

46

Autumn 2017

On Wednesday morning Anna presses the wrong button on her phone and switches off the alarm instead of setting it to snooze. She has to gobble down her breakfast standing by the sink, then drive as fast as she dares along the steep, winding road down the ridge. When she arrives at the station she is still firing on all cylinders, and it takes her a few minutes to notice that the atmosphere is somewhat subdued. She unlocks her office door and has only just sat down when Jens Friberg appears. He's wearing his uniform, to her surprise.

'Hi,' she says, thinking he's come to discuss the previous day's interviews. Then she notices his stiff expression.

'I think it's best if I revert to my previous duties,' he says tersely. Before she has time to reply, he's left and closed the door. She doesn't understand, and is about to go after him when her mobile rings. It's her solicitor.

'Have you seen the article?'

'What article?'

'In the *Express*. Third article down.'

He gives her a few seconds to find the right website.

CHIEF OF POLICE QUESTIONED ABOUT
EX-HUSBAND'S DEATH

The headline turns her stomach to an ice-cold hollow that grows bigger and bigger as she reads. She isn't named, but as the paper refers to her as a newly appointed chief of police in Skåne with considerable experience of murder investigations, it really doesn't matter.

'That's not all,' her solicitor goes on. 'I've just spoken to Santesson, and of course he insists that his department isn't responsible for the leak. He went on at length about how regrettable it is that the case has come to light – all bullshit. As you can see, he has no intention of dropping the inquiry. Instead, he's requested another forensic examination of the infusion pump, and this time he's not satisfied with the local technicians. He's sent the pump off to the lab in Linköping – top priority.'

He falls silent, waiting for her to say something.

'We probably have a week or so before he gets the results,' he continues when she doesn't speak. 'He hinted that they might reduce the seriousness of the charge in exchange for a confession. That's not how things usually work in Sweden, but as he says there were "extenuating circumstances" in this case.'

Anna still doesn't say a word. All she can think about is that Agnes or one of her friends will see the article on their phone. She has to get to her first, has to—

'My recommendation is that you think it over and come back to me within a couple of days, let me know what you want to do. Whatever decision you make, I will of course do my utmost to achieve the best possible outcome.'

'I'll be in touch,' she says and ends the call. Her fingers are shaking so much that she can barely scroll to Agnes's number in her contacts list. The call goes straight to voicemail. She tries again, with the same result. She sends a text:

CALL ME.

Her phone rings as soon as she's pressed send, and at first, she thinks it's Agnes. Then she hears the commissioner's rasping voice in her ear. Her brain, that seemed so clear and eager just minutes ago suddenly isn't working properly, and she mumbles a noncommittal response to the accusation that she has withheld important information from him, and that he doesn't appreciate finding this out via the press.

'I've also spoken to Henry Morell,' he says. 'According to him, you're using a suicide as a pretext to reopen a twenty-seven-year-old case. To be honest, I found it difficult to believe that an experienced officer like you would use the police authority's limited resources to look into an accident that happened almost thirty years ago, but Henry was very convincing.'

'I . . . I . . . It . . . t . . .' That damned stammer is the last thing she needs right now; it makes her sound incompetent and unsure of herself.

'Morell also claims that you've fallen out with his son, and that the whole thing is some kind of personal vendetta. Is there any truth in that assertion?'

'Alexander Morell and his friend attacked a man at an event in the local park, and almost ki . . . killed him.' *Shit.* She pauses, takes a couple of deep breaths. 'When I intervened, they turned on me instead. If my uniformed officers hadn't turned up, things could have gone very badly.'

'Can you give me the case number of your report?'

She realises she's walked straight into a trap.

'No.'

'May I ask why not?'

'Because a report was never filed. Henry Morell asked me and the attending officers not to make it formal.' She wonders whether to mention Jens Friberg's involvement, but knows he probably won't back her up.

'I see.' In the silence that follows she imagines she can hear the commissioner's fingers drumming on his desk, the way Santesson drummed his fingers on the file in the interview room.

'This is what I think, Anna.' His voice has softened slightly. 'Henry Morell has been chief of police in Nedanås for the past twenty-five years. During that time, we have had no trouble, not one single complaint against him from colleagues. You, however, have been in post for just over a week, and . . .' He doesn't finish the sentence. 'Henry Morell is a good friend. He has an excellent reputation, and plenty of contacts both inside and outside the police service. My advice to you is to make your peace with him right away. When you've done that . . .'

Silence. More drumming.

'When you've done that, I want you to send over all the documentation regarding the death you're looking into. I have the greatest respect for your experience as an investigator, and I'd like you to explain exactly why you don't believe that the deceased took his own life. If I don't share your opinion, I will shut down the case with immediate effect. Do I make myself clear, Anna?'

As soon as the conversation is over, she tries Agnes again. Presses redial over and over again, and eventually leaves a message even though Agnes hates her doing that. 'It's Mum, call me when you get this. It's important.'

She sits quietly for a while, trying to gather her thoughts. First the newspaper article, then the fact that Santesson has no intention of dropping the investigation, then a dressing-down from the commissioner. What a mess! And if she can't get hold of Agnes in time, it will be even worse. She is interrupted by her office phone.

'Reception – you have a visitor.' The woman on the other end hangs up before Anna can ask who it is or what it's about, so she has no choice but to go downstairs. On the way she passes Henry Morell's office. He is staring at his screen and pretends not to see her.

The visitor is a woman in her mid-twenties, with short blond hair. She is wearing jeans, boots and a thick sweater.

'Hi – my name's Lisa Savic. I called the other day about my father.' For a couple of seconds Anna's brain refuses to work. 'Joakim Rylander,' the woman adds.

'Yes, of course, you wanted to collect his things. I'm afraid it's mostly rubbish.'

The woman nods. 'Actually, there was something else.' She casts a meaningful glance towards the other end of the desk, where the two receptionists aren't even pretending to work. Anna steals a glance at her phone. Still nothing from Agnes. *Shit!*

'I'm a bit pressed for time at the moment,' she says. 'Could you come back tomorrow? Are you staying in the village?'

Lisa nods. 'I've booked a room for the week. Nine o'clock in the morning?'

'Great – I'll see you then.'

They say goodbye, and Anna turns and glares angrily at the two eavesdroppers. Both receptionists stare back defiantly.

You're losing your grip on the station, she murmurs to herself, knowing that Håkan would have said exactly the same thing if he were talking to her.

She heads back to her office, checking her phone yet again. Nothing. She wonders whether to contact the school, ask someone to fetch Agnes, but realises that probably wouldn't improve the situation. Better to drive over there herself, but first she must fulfil her promise to the commissioner.

She stops outside Morell's office. She can see him through the glass wall, focused on his computer. She knocks on the door.

'Come in!' he says, in an exaggeratedly authoritative voice.

She takes a deep breath. Time to eat humble pie.

Morell doesn't even glance up when she walks in. He is typing away using only his index fingers, and seems to be in no hurry. Anna intends to sit down in one of his visitor's chairs, but discovers they're gone. It takes a few seconds for her to grasp that this is no coincidence. The intention is to leave her standing there for a while until he deigns to speak to her. She is aware of movement on the other side of the glass wall. The two receptionists have stopped halfway up the stairs, and have been joined by the annoying female officer who made fun of her stammer. Two detectives are shuffling slowly along the corridor in their Birkenstocks, carrying mugs of coffee in order to hide the real reason for their presence, which is to watch Morell put her in her place. She can hear them whispering, and turns to close the door.

'You can leave the door open,' Morell says, removing any lingering doubts she might have had about his intentions. She feels her anger rising, and a tiny vein at her right temple begins to throb. But she has to control herself, has to obey orders. Morell still doesn't look up.

'I thought we ought to clear the air, Henry,' she begins. She glances towards the door; the whispering has stopped. The humiliation makes her cheeks and the back of her neck burn. Morell raises his head and takes off his reading glasses.

'Anna. So, what is it you'd like to discuss?'

'We seem to have ended up on the wrong foot with each other, and I . . . I . . .' She pauses, takes a deep breath to quell the stammer, but instead it makes it worse. She hears a snigger from the stairs.

Morell leans forward, nods to her with that fatherly look that is no longer appealing.

'I . . . I . . .' The stammer refuses to give up, her constricted vocal cords leave her gasping for breath. She tries focusing on one of the photographs on the wall behind Morell. It's a trick designed to make the brain engage a new, more effective connection between thought and speech.

The photograph shows three men in suits and one in uniform. The man in the middle is Morell. Next to him is a familiar figure, almost bald, handing over a plaque – presumably the one displayed beside the photo. FOR OUTSTANDING WORK IN THE SERVICE OF THE LAW, it says in gold letters beneath the logo of the Prosecution Service. The familiar figure is Chief Prosecutor Tord Santesson.

Suddenly everything falls into place. The renewed interest in the case against her, the newspaper article, the call from the commissioner. Not bad luck, not an unfortunate coincidence, but three co-ordinated attacks planned by someone who wants to get to her. The throbbing at her temple spreads through her skull and becomes a dull roar.

'What is it you want to say to me, Anna?' Morell says, with a quick glance through the glass wall. The corners of his mouth turn up in a triumphant smile, which freezes the second her meets her gaze.

'You have exactly ten minutes to pack up your shit and get out of my police station, Henry,' she says as calmly as she can. 'If you're not gone by then, I will personally drag you down the stairs.'

She doesn't wait for an answer, but turns and leaves the room. Stops in the doorway and glares at the officers on the stairs, who are standing there open-mouthed.

'You there – Frida, isn't it?' She gestures to the woman who made fun of her stammer. 'You and your little gang of vultures have thirty seconds to get back to work, unless you want to be fired right now. Is that clear?'

The woman mumbles something unintelligible.

'Is that clear?' Anna repeats. She is surprised at how firm she sounds.

'Yes,' Frida mutters a little louder, eyes fixed on the floor.

Fifteen seconds later the staircase is empty.

47

Autumn 2017

She would like nothing more than to get in the car and go and find Agnes, but the incident with Morell means she has to stay in the station until the working day is over. She makes a point of walking the corridors at regular intervals to ensure that there is no doubt about who's in charge.

She has spoken to the colleague responsible for the station's security system and had Morell's pass card barred. She then ordered the considerably less disrespectful women on reception to empty Morell's office, and have anything he hasn't taken with him packed up and sent to his house. The last she saw of Morell was his back view as he angrily marched towards his car carrying a box full of papers.

She spends the rest of the afternoon putting together her conclusions in the Rylander case, then sends them to the commissioner as agreed. She stresses the importance of the blackmail message, the incorrect position of the driver's seat in the Saab, the missing mobile phone and the recently bandaged wound on Rylander's leg – all reasons why his death shouldn't be written off as a suicide, in her opinion. She knows that Morell will have contacted the commissioner on his way home; she is on tenterhooks waiting for another call, but nothing happens.

At exactly five o'clock she leaves her office and drives to the train station in an attempt to intercept Agnes when her train gets in. The Vespa isn't parked among the other mopeds, which means she is too late. As she drives into the yard at Tabor she sees that the Vespa isn't there either, and as Milo is eagerly waiting to be let out, it's clear that Agnes hasn't been back since they left the house this morning. So where is she?

Anna tries her mobile again, but as before it goes straight to voicemail. The Find My iPhone app is no help either, because Agnes seems to have deactivated it. When six o'clock comes and goes and dusk begins to fall, Anna is on the verge of panic. Even Milo knows that something is wrong; he keeps whimpering and wandering restlessly back and forth in the hallway. She wonders whether to contact the duty officers to check if there's been an accident, but instead she takes Milo with her and goes out in the car to conduct her own search. She has just reached the main road when her phone rings. She slams on the brakes and grabs it. The screen is displaying a landline number that she doesn't recognise.

'Hello?'

'Hello – is that Anna? It's Elisabet Vidje.'

'Hi.' She peers through the windscreen, looking for Agnes's Vespa.

'Agnes is here with me. At Änglaberga.'

It takes a little while for the words to sink in.

'With you?'

'Yes, she's in the kitchen. She's pretty upset, poor soul. She read the article about you. And her father.'

Anna feels the icy hollow in her stomach open up again.

'Anyway, we've had coffee and a chat. She's a little calmer now, so I thought I'd better give you a ring. Can you come over?'

Anna parks in the same place as last time. She leaves Milo in the car and hurries along the gravel path. Elisabet is waiting for her by the arbour with the angel fountain. She is wearing a thick coat with a shawl draped around her head; it makes her look even thinner than usual, if that were possible.

'Agnes turned up just after five,' she says, her voice warm and gentle. 'She'd tried Mats, but he hasn't been in the mood for talking lately, and didn't answer the door. He gets that way from time to time. I could see something was wrong, so I invited her in. Klein had shown me what was in the paper. About you . . .'

Elisabet stops, and Anna waits for the obvious question. But it doesn't come.

'We talked for quite a while, Agnes and I. About grief and loss. As you know, I have a certain amount of experience in that area.' She smiles sadly, then nods towards a gate leading to the back of the house. 'Do you mind if I take your arm again? I'm a little wobbly these days.'

Anna nods and links arms with Elisabet. They go through the gate and follow the path along by the house.

'Karl-Johan loved Änglaberga.' Elisabet waves in the direction of the generous garden and the valley beyond. 'But in the end, he was too ill to be able to stay here. He was almost blind, and was becoming more and more confused. He'd get up in the night and wander around the estate and into the forest, looking for Simon. In the end I had no choice but to move him into a nursing home in town.' She slowly shakes her head. 'I know he's well looked after there. He never complains, and he's always pleased to see us.'

She falls silent as they pass below the terrace, heading towards a small flight of steps at the far end. There is an old bench next to them, like the one by Simon's grave.

'That's what I told Agnes. I explained that sometimes you have to do things for those you care about. Difficult things, things that might break your heart. But you do them anyway – out of love.'

She stops and points to the steps. 'Agnes is in the kitchen. I'm sure you'd like to be alone for a while, so I'll wait here.' She sits down on the bench, shoos Anna away with one hand when she doesn't react quickly enough.

'Go on, in you go. I'll be fine.'

Anna slowly walks up the six steps and places her hand on the kitchen door handle. Agnes is sitting with her back to the window with her hair tucked behind her ear, emphasising the line of her jaw which is so like Håkan's.

Tell her, he whispers without any warning. Her heart gives a little skip of joy. *Do it now. Tell her the truth. The whole truth.*

She doesn't answer him, she simply stands there for a while, gazing at their beautiful daughter. Agnes becomes aware of her presence, and turns her head.

It's obvious that she's been crying, but at the moment she seems composed. She doesn't look angry or even contemptuous, just sad. Anna opens the door and stands there, unable to move.

'Did you do it, Mum?' Agnes asks. 'Did you kill Dad?'

Anna takes a deep breath and closes her eyes.

'No,' she says, gently pushing Håkan right to the back of her mind. 'No, I didn't.'

They don't talk much in the car. Agnes sits with Milo on her knee, and as always he has picked up on her mood and does his best to cheer her up, burrowing his head beneath her chin, whimpering and licking her throat and cheeks. Agnes doesn't push him away; instead, she wraps her arms around him and hugs him so tightly and for so long that eventually he gets fed up and tries to wriggle free. When they arrive home, she heads straight for her room. Anna hears the opening chords of Simon Vidje's song before Agnes plugs in her headphones.

Klein has followed them to Tabor with the Vespa on the back of his truck. He unloads the moped without a word, and parks it by the house.

'Thank you,' Anna says, but receives only a curt nod in response.

'I . . .' She hesitates. 'I've chucked Henry Morell out of the police station.' She's not sure why she feels the need to tell him this. Maybe she doesn't want him to go just yet, leaving her alone with Agnes.

'Right.' Klein's voice is rough, but there is a glint in his eyes.

'He tried to interfere in my investigation. Tried to stop me taking a fresh look at Simon's death.'

Klein nods thoughtfully. 'That was brave of you. Brave but stupid.'

His words annoy her. 'Why have you kept Karl-Jo's sports car?' she asks, nodding in the direction of the outbuilding. 'The summer car – wasn't that what he called it?'

Klein gives a slight twitch.

'He wanted to restore it,' he mumbles. 'I even helped him to make a start, but that got in the way.' He jerks his head towards the upper floor of Tabor.

'The mural?'

'It became an obsession, took up virtually every waking hour. He was never satisfied, he kept on redoing it, over and over again. Painted fresh layers on top of the old ones. If you ask me, it was that painting that made him blind, not grief. If it had been up to me we'd have burned down both Tabor and the mural a long time ago. Nothing good comes from an obsession, not Karl-Johan's . . .' he pauses, 'or anyone else's, for that matter.'

It takes a moment for Anna to realise that he means her.

48

Autumn 2017

S he decides not to wake Agnes before leaving for work. Yesterday was tough for both of them, and Agnes needs to sleep more than she needs to go to school.

Anna knows she should have taken the opportunity this time, told her daughter the truth. Håkan makes his opinion very clear by reverting to stubborn silence, and yet she still can't bring herself to speak out.

In her office she sits down and stares at the phone, waiting for the commissioner's call. With the benefit of hindsight, she shouldn't have let herself be provoked by Morell, shouldn't have exploded. It's the second time within a few days that she's allowed her temper to make life difficult for her. Having Morell and his pal Santesson against her is bad enough, but now she's managed to add the commissioner to the list. The question is whether her outburst gives him sufficient grounds to sack her. Probably not. She's only just taken up her post, and had a good reputation within the service – at least until that article was published. Plus, she's a woman – a factor that mustn't be underestimated. Sacking her because she stood up to a man who is no longer employed by the police, and who challenged her authority, could easily backfire on the commissioner himself. She thinks he will wait for stronger grounds, for example if she is formally suspected of having been involved in Håkan's death.

She is in no doubt about what will happen to the Rylander case. The commissioner is a desk jockey, not a real police officer.

He has never interviewed a suspect, and he certainly hasn't led a murder investigation. He'll be looking for things he recognises from TV: a murder weapon, fingerprints, DNA. Mobile phone tracking, blood spatter patterns and other forensic evidence that is always so plentiful in TV cop shows. He won't spend a single krona of his precious budget on something as simple and unscientific as good old police officer's intuition. She can already imagine how the conversation will play out.

So, Rylander's phone is missing – maybe he lost it earlier on? Or perhaps he'd sold it, who knows? And as for the position of the seat, well maybe Rylander liked driving around half-lying down, without being able to use the mirrors or pedals properly. The leg injury? What makes you think that has anything to do with his death?

The worst thing about this imaginary dialogue with the commissioner is that certain points might well be valid. She still has no definite proof that Joe Rylander's death is murder. She's convinced that the four friends are lying, but she has no means of exposing their lies. And worst of all, she's run out of leads to follow up.

The phone rings. It's one of the women on reception, who introduces herself by name and sounds both pleasant and polite.

'You have a visitor, a Lisa Savic. Apparently, she's arranged to see you – would you like me to bring her up?'

Once again Lisa Savic makes a very positive impression when they shake hands. She's wearing the same sweater, jeans and boots, but today the outfit is complemented by a scarf wound around her neck to protect her from the autumn wind. Anna had completely forgotten the meeting after the chaos of the previous day. She tells herself it's better to be doing something rather than staring at the phone.

'I'm not just here because of my father,' Lisa begins when she's settled in one of the visitor's chairs. Her voice is soft and pleasant, her accent from somewhere in central Sweden. 'My mother died when I was eleven. I was born when she was only twenty, and she wasn't ready to have a child. It might have been because of the drug abuse, or something else. Whatever the reason, she handed me over to a foster family when I was a baby. She didn't abandon me,' Lisa adds before Anna can say anything. 'When she was drug-free and feeling well she came to see me, and she sent presents on every birthday. She and my foster parents were in regular contact, and when she died, they even cleared out her apartment.'

Anna leans forward; in spite of everything that's going on, she wants to know where this narrative is heading.

'And your father?'

Lisa shrugs. 'He came with Mum to see me a few times when I was little, but I don't remember anything about it. There are a couple of old photographs of the three of us sitting in the garden. We weren't exactly playing happy families, if I can put it that way.'

She smiles sadly; Anna can't help smiling back.

'When my mother died, the link between us disappeared. However, a few years ago I started to wonder who I was. It's not unusual in children who have been adopted or grew up in foster care. I think I really wanted to find out more about my mother, all the stuff she hadn't told me. Who she was when she was young, what she dreamed of . . . Why things turned out the way they did. So, I contacted my father.'

Her smile is a little shy this time, as if she is waiting for Anna to say something, but then she goes on:

'He was in jail, so I wrote to him, asked about him and my mum, how they met and so on. To my surprise, he actually replied. Not in any detail, but he did agree to meet. When he was released, we had lunch now and again. He told me that he and my mum came from the same area here in Skåne, and that they got to know each other in a children's home. They became so close that they often pretended to be brother and sister instead of girlfriend and boyfriend.

'He was sent to jail for two years just before I was born. They drifted apart, but carried on having some kind of on/off relationship until Mum's overdose in 2002. According to him, she was the love of his life, but I think that was just something he said for my sake.'

A wry smile.

'After those initial meetings he got in touch two or three times a year, almost always because he needed help. He usually wanted to borrow money.'

'Did you help him?'

'When I could afford it – and no, I wasn't stupid enough to think I'd ever get it back. He was no saint, but my foster mother often said that sometimes you have to do good deeds for people who aren't that good.'

Anna nods. She instinctively likes Lisa – her voice, her gentle aura, her positive attitude towards other people. Her mother gave her away and her father didn't want anything to do with her, and yet the young woman doesn't seem to be at all bitter. Was she the same at Lisa's age? Probably not. She was already a police officer by then, and most of her belief in the goodness of humanity had been severely dented.

'A little while ago my father called and said he'd like to meet up. He wondered if I'd kept any of Mum's stuff, and if so, could he take a look at it? I saw this as a chance to find out more about Mum, so I invited him over. It was actually very pleasant; we had dinner, drank some wine and went through Mum's things. There were a couple of boxes of books and bits and pieces that my foster parents had gathered up from her apartment – nothing of any value.'

'So, when was this?' Anna asks. She is beginning to suspect where Lisa's story is leading.

'Around 20 September.'

'Just after you received the letter from Elisabet Vidje?'

Lisa nods. 'That's right – maybe a week or so after that.'

'Do you happen to remember if there was a cassette tape in one of those boxes?'

'There was quite a pile, actually. Michael Jackson's *Thriller* ... Joe and I ...' She pauses. 'I call him Joe, not Dad. Anyway, we joked about Mum's taste in music. I work for a record company, so music is both my job and my hobby. Joe thought that sounded exciting. He asked me lots of questions.'

'Did you happen to notice whether any of the tapes went missing? Whether Joe took one with him?'

'No, why?'

Because that's probably where he found the tape Simon Vidje had recorded, Anna thinks. But why did Tanya have it in the first place?

'Anyway – that letter from Elisabet Vidje,' Lisa continues. 'Joe had had one exactly the same, so I asked him to tell me what it was all about.'

'And what did he say?'

Lisa picks at one sleeve of her sweater.

'That's partly why I'm here. He suddenly became very secretive. He said something about he and Mum being at a party in an old quarry, and that he hadn't worked out what really happened that night until recently. He refused to say any more, but I realised that money was involved somehow. That was nearly always the case with Joe.'

'And your mother? Did she ever mention the quarry?'

Lisa shakes her head. 'Never – not to me or my foster parents. It was before my time, of course – I wasn't born until the following year, but I was wondering . . .' She falls silent, looks a little uncomfortable. 'I was wondering if you could tell me a little more about what happened when that boy died. Do you think it had anything to do with my parents? I mean . . .' She sighs. 'Joe always thought that he was a little bit smarter than everyone else, that the world ought to fit in with him. I've met his type before – they're not uncommon in the music business.'

Lisa's ironic grimace makes Anna smile.

'What they have in common is that they believe the whole world is made up of idiots – apart from them. It might sound stupid, but I can't imagine Joe taking his own life. He was much too fond of himself to do something like that.'

Anna is about to respond when her mobile rings. Normally she would have rejected the call and switched her phone to silent, but it's Agnes. 'Excuse me, I have to take this,' she says, slipping out into the corridor.

'Hi, sweetheart!' she says. *Too much*.

'Hi, Mum – are you busy?' Agnes doesn't sound angry or accusatory.

'Kind of – why?'

'Mats is here. He says he wants to talk to you, it's important.' There's a crackling noise as if she's covering the phone with her hand, and she whispers: 'I think it's about Simon Vidje.'

'I'm on my way.'

She ends the call and explains to Lisa that she has to deal with an urgent matter. She takes Lisa's phone number and promises to be in touch.

Mats and Agnes are sitting on the top step playing with Milo. Agnes should of course be in school, but Anna decides to ignore that for now. As soon as Anna gets out of the car, Mats stands up and tugs at the hem of his jacket, looking embarrassed.

'Agnes said you wanted to talk to me?'

He doesn't answer; instead, he glances up at the roof of Tabor.

Agnes stands up too and takes him gently by the arm.

'Mats was wondering if he could have a look at the mural, Mum.'

Anna raises her eyebrows. 'I got the impression we were going to talk about . . .'

Agnes flashes her an angry glance and shakes her head slightly.

'Of course, Mats,' Anna says, even though she has no idea what's going on.

All three of them make their way to the chapel. When Mats isn't looking, Anna frowns at her daughter, but to no avail.

The big man stops a couple of metres away from the painting, and admires it in silence. After a while his expression grows troubled.

'That's the quarry,' he murmurs to himself. 'But where is he? I can't find him.'

Agnes has placed her photographic lamps at each end of the wall, pointing at the mural. She goes over to one of them and presses a button. The light brings out Simon Vidje's body in the dark water.

Mats gasps and steps back, raises his hand towards his eyes as if to protect himself from what he is seeing.

Anna remembers what he said – that the water in the quarry pool was freezing cold, that Carina's lips were blue. This is the right moment to ask the question that's been bothering her.

'Were you there, Mats?' she says quietly. 'Were you at the quarry that evening?'

He nods slowly, tears trickling down his cheeks.

'To spy on Carina Pedersen?'

He nods again, wiping away the tears with the back of his hand. 'She was so beautiful. Long, fair hair, almost like an angel.' He blushes.

'Did the others know you were there?'

'No. Marie always chased me away if she spotted me. I had to creep around. I hid in the forest. There's a place where you can see nearly everything with a good pair of binoculars.'

'How . . .' she tries to contain her eagerness, 'how long were you there, Mats?'

'Until it started raining. Until they . . .' He falls silent, shuffles his feet, looks at the mural again.

'Until they did what?' Anna prompts him, as gently as she can.

'Until they started quarrelling,' he mumbles.

'Who?' Agnes can't suppress her curiosity.

Mats spreads his hands. 'All of them – Alex, Marie, Carina, Bruno. It was just after the motorbike had left. Then there was a fight.'

'Who was fighting?' This time it's Anna's turn.

'Alex and Simon, but Simon didn't stand a chance. Alex was too big and strong. I didn't like it, so I sneaked back to where I'd hidden my moped. It was pouring with rain, and I skidded and came off on the way home.'

'What was the last thing you saw before you left?'

Mats pulls a face, as if the memory is painful. 'Alex threw Simon to the ground in a wrestling hold. He landed badly. The others were yelling at him.'

'At Alex?'

Mats shakes his head. 'At Simon. They were yelling horrible words, calling him terrible names, so I left. I should have said something, shouldn't I? I should have told Alex to leave Simon alone. Told the others to stop yelling.'

He falls silent, glances at the painting, rubs his chin and mouth. His eyes shine with unshed tears.

'Do you remember anything else?' Anna says after what seems like an eternity.

'No,' he mumbles, without taking his eyes off the image of Simon Vidje's body floating in the dark water. 'Just that I came off my moped on the way home.'

Anna leaves Mats and Agnes in the chapel. She goes downstairs and out into the yard. Her heart is pounding with excitement, so she forces herself to take several deep breaths before she calls Jens Friberg.

'I want you to bring Alexander Morell in for questioning first thing tomorrow morning,' she says as soon as he answers. 'Pull him over between his home and Kotorp, in a place where no one can see you. It's essential that only you and I know he's been brought in, OK?'

Silence.

'Are you really sure about this, Anna?' Jens sounds just the way he did when they first met – wary, sceptical, bordering on hostile. Disappointment forms a hard lump in her chest; has she acted too hastily? 'Henry's going to—' he continues, but she interrupts him.

'Just do as I say, Jens,' she snaps and ends the call.

49

Autumn 2017

The interview room at Nedanås police station is considerably more pleasant than the one in the Internal Affairs department in Stockholm. There is a window opposite the door through which you can see a tree, bearing fewer and fewer leaves. On the other walls a series of blue-and-white posters from the Crime Prevention Agency are displayed. There are no cameras or hidden microphones, just a good old tape recorder on the table in the middle of the room. Anna has had the whole of Thursday evening to mull over the situation. She regrets speaking to Jens yesterday afternoon. She knows she acted in haste, but she also knows why. She has come to appreciate Jens more and more, and she wants him back on her side. She needed to show him how good she is, which of course with hindsight was a ridiculous thing to do. She hardly slept last night, and had more or less expected Jens to call in sick in order to avoid the task she'd set him, and any further involvement in her inquiry. Or even worse – he might have called Henry Morell and warned him about what was going to happen. However, when she arrived at work shortly after seven, Jens's car was already there, and one of the patrol cars was gone. At seven forty-five he called and informed her that he had picked up Alex Morell and was on his way back to the station, which was a relief. Jens Friberg remains a mystery to her, but right now she has other things to focus on.

She inserts a new tape in the machine and checks the sound. She's sat in rooms like this hundreds of times, questioned every possible kind of suspect. This is her home turf, her territory, and yet she can feel the tension rising.

There is a knock on the door, and Jens Friberg appears with Alexander Morell in tow.

'Sit down.' Jens points to the chair opposite Anna, waits until Alex is seated then turns to leave.

'I'd like you to stay, Jens.'

He stops, looks surprised for a second, then sits down beside her.

'So, what's this about?' Alex Morell begins. 'Doesn't my alibi hold?'

The crooked smile can't hide his nervousness. She can almost smell it through the building dust and sweat that pervade his clothes. She switches on the tape recorder.

'Interview with Alexander Morell, date of birth 17-01-1971, in the matter of . . .' She pauses, decides to keep that information to herself. She remains silent, studying the man opposite her. Alex is still smiling, but his Adam's apple is bobbing up and down beneath the stubble on his throat. One heel is jiggling. He might be the son of a former chief of police, but he's certainly not comfortable in a police station. She glances sideways at Friberg, but he is giving nothing away.

'Why did you and Simon Vidje have a fight that night at the quarry?' she asks, leaning forward. Her voice is gentle, the movement slow, but Alex recoils as if she'd slapped him across the face. His mouth opens, he gasps for air.

'You said he was your friend,' she continues before he has time to compose himself. Leans forward a little more. 'And yet you beat the shit out of him while the other three egged you on. The big, strong, Olympic-standard wrestler versus the skinny little musician. It was only ever going to go one way, wasn't it?'

'I . . .' Alex is as white as a sheet, his tongue moving over his lips as if it's searching for the right words. Anna sees Jens also lean forward, and raises her right hand a fraction from her knee to indicate that she'd like him to keep quiet.

'We . . .' Alex's brain and mouth still can't agree on what comes next. He's obviously struggling, desperately searching for an escape route. So she gives it to him.

'Tell us what really happened that night, Alex.'

His eyes dart from her to Jens and back again. He looks down, his shoulders slump, and for a second, she thinks he might pitch forward, but he places both his forearms on the table and props himself up. He sits like that for a few seconds, gathering his thoughts. Then he takes a deep breath and begins.

50

28 August 1990

The rain was hammering down.

Alex had flattened Simon with a headlock, and was using his body weight to keep him on the ground. He was in charge now, he was the one who was in control, and the rage boiling up in his body was mixed with the satisfaction of having regained the advantage. The others were standing around him yelling at him to go in harder, to give Simon what he deserved.

Alex grunted, braced himself and shifted Simon's whole body, just as he did with an opponent in the ring, so that his face ended up in a hollow that was rapidly filling with rainwater. Landing on the hard ground had knocked the breath out of Simon's lungs, but grit and gravel dug into his skin and revived him.

'Let go of me!'

He fought back, tried to turn his head, but Alex held him down. The water entered Simon's nose and mouth, made him cough.

'Let me go,' he ventured again, but it came out as little more than a gurgle. The other three were still yelling, egging Alex on.

Alex tightened the headlock until he could hear Simon's joints protesting. The water had reached the top of the hollow, and Simon was gasping for air. In spite of the encouragement from the other three, Alex decided that enough was enough. He'd made his point, shown Simon what happened when someone strayed into his territory.

He released his grip and slowly got to his feet, hearing the disappointment in the others' voices.

Simon rolled away from the hollow, spitting out brown rain-water. He tried to get to his knees, but was immediately pushed over.

'You think you're so fucking special.' Alex hardly recognised Bruno's voice; it was so full of hatred. 'You think you can do whatever you like, don't you?'

Once again Simon made a wobbly attempt to stand up, this time facing in a different direction, but once again he was pushed over. It was Carina's turn now.

'You're nothing but a little shit, Simon. You know that, don't you?'

Simon rolled sideways and tried a third direction, only to be knocked back by Marie. She hit him with such force that he banged his head on a stone.

'Letting me down with no warning – we're like brother and sister!'

Simon rubbed the back of his head, and his face contorted.

'Look, he's crying!' Alex shouted. 'What a fucking baby!'

'Fucking idiots,' Simon managed to say. His voice sounded fragile, desperate.

He was still trying to stand up, but Alex was having none of it.

'You're the one who's an idiot, Simon,' he said with a grin. The sense of power filled his body, made him feel better than he'd done for a long time. 'Say you're an idiot and we might let you get up.'

Simon shook his head. There were tears pouring down his face, tears of rage, tears of humiliation. He rolled over again, but the headlock and the brief wrestling match had used up most of his strength. Alex signalled to the others to close the circle. They formed a dense forest of legs, blocking any escape route.

'Say you're an idiot!' Alex repeated. 'Say you're a fucking cry baby and we'll let you go.'

Simon pushed himself up with his arms and was rewarded with a kick to his cheekbone, so hard that his teeth rattled.

'Say it!' Alex yelled.

Simon collapsed, rested his forearms on his knees and lowered his head.

'I'm an idiot,' he mumbled.

'Louder!' Carina shouted.

'I'm an idiot.'

'Say you're a traitor!' Marie chipped in.

'I'm a traitor.'

'Say your dad should be in the loony bin!'

Simon looked up. His hair was soaking wet, the pouring rain was running down his face. There was a strange sheen to his eyes.

'Say it,' Bruno hissed. 'Say your dad should be in the loony bin.'

There was a brief silence; the only sound was the rain hammering down. Simon got on all fours in the middle of the circle, then slowly stood up. He glared at them one by one as he wiped the tears from his cheeks. Marie took a step back, looking as if she wished she hadn't joined in. Simon made use of the gap. He walked slowly past his cousin and continued towards the forest.

'Friends forever,' he yelled over his shoulder, and something in his voice made Alex's heart turn over.

51

Autumn 2017

'Everything got out of hand,' Alex says quietly. 'We were high, drunk and angry. Things came to a head and turned nasty, and it was all aimed at Simon.' He shakes his head sadly. 'A total group psychosis – I can't come up with a better explanation.'

'What happened next?' Anna asks. 'After Simon managed to get up and headed for the forest?'

Alex lets out a long sigh. His expression is troubled.

'After a few minutes the rain kind of sobered us up, made us realise what we'd done. The girls started calling Simon's name, they even went into the forest behind the quarry to look for him.'

'What about you and Bruno?' Jens says.

Alex lowers his head. 'We stayed by the tents, tried to get the fire going again, but it was impossible. Then the girls came back. Simon wasn't answering, and it was too dark and wet to carry on searching. We assumed he'd gone around the side of the pool and made his way down to the turning area via the path at the back, and cycled home to Änglaberga. We decided we'd go and see him in the morning, apologise.'

'You didn't think of checking if his bike was gone? Or even going after him?' Jens again, but Anna doesn't stop him. He's doing well. *Simon's bike?* she jots down on her pad, without really thinking about why.

Alex spreads his hands. 'By that stage we were all tired, soaking wet and ashamed of ourselves. None of us was in a fit state to drive,

317

certainly not in the dark and the rain. So, we went to bed.' His voice almost breaks at the end.

'And you didn't hear anything else? No noises, no one else who was up and about?'

Alex shakes his head. 'No. As far as I remember, it was raining so hard that you could barely hear yourself think inside the tent, and yet I fell asleep right away. I didn't wake up until the morning, when Marie started screaming.'

He stares at his hands, slowly turns them over and separates his fingers, as if he is searching for something on his callused skin.

Suddenly, the door flies open and Henry Morell comes storming in. His face is chalk-white, his eyes black. Jens immediately stands up and places himself directly in front of Morell.

'What the hell are you doing, Anna?' Morell roars over Jens's shoulder, spraying his former colleague's face and perfectly ironed shirt with saliva. Jens doesn't move a millimetre.

Before Anna can speak, Morell spins around and grabs hold of his son's arm.

'Come with me, Alexander – you don't need to stay here for one more second.' He points his index finger at her. 'If you wish to speak to Alexander again, then both I and a solicitor will be present. Do you understand?' Morell tugs at his son's arm, but Alex stays exactly where he is.

'Calm down, Dad.' His tone is gentle, almost tender. Morell doesn't seem to have heard; he is still tugging at Alex's arm. The inflamed skin visible beneath his beard is an angry red.

'Come with me! You don't need to say one more word to that . . . to that . . .' He waves a hand in Anna's direction without even looking at her. Alex merely shakes his head sadly.

'I've been carrying this for almost thirty years, Dad. I want to get it out. Take responsibility for what I did. For what we did to Simon.'

Morell lets go of his arm. 'Alexander, you can't . . .' He is pleading now. 'You mustn't ruin your life like this. I won't let you.'

Alex stands up, pats his father's shoulder. 'It's my life, Dad. My responsibility.' He turns to Anna. 'We let our friend down,' he says. The pain in his eyes is so deep that it's impossible not to feel sorry for him.

'We humiliated him and chased him off into the forest. Forced him to wander around in the rain and the dark, battered and bruised, alone and at rock bottom.' Alex takes a deep breath, exchanges a quick glance with his father. Henry Morell's face is still ashen, his arms dangle helplessly by his sides.

'It was our fault,' Alex goes on quietly, speaking to Henry as much as to Anna. Tears have begun to trickle down his cheeks. 'Me, Bruno, Marie and Carina. It was our fault that Simon died, and it's high time we admitted it.'

Anna and Jens return to her office to discuss what they've just heard, leaving Henry and Alex in the interview room. The receptionists and three other colleagues are whispering in a little group, but fall silent as soon as they see Anna.

'Which one do you think called Henry?' she says on the way up the stairs.

Jens shrugs. 'Does it matter?'

'Maybe not.'

She's glad he's back in her corner.

'So, what do we do now?' he says as soon as the door is closed. 'As far as I understand it, Alex Morell has admitted that he and the others attacked Simon Vidje both physically and verbally, but that's all. Do you think he's lying? Confessing to a minor crime in order to get away with something more serious?'

Anna has been considering this for a while now. It's not unusual for suspects to go down that road, but she hasn't seen anything to suggest that's what Alex is doing.

'No. I believe he's telling the truth. How about you?'

'Same here. In which case the four of them are guilty of assault and possibly causing the death of another person.'

Anna nods.

'I'm not sure of the statute of limitations off the top of my head, but I'm assuming that twenty-seven years is way too long to be able to bring a case?' Jens raises an enquiring eyebrow.

'Five years,' she replies. 'Ten if the crime is regarded as serious. Whichever it is, we're seventeen years too late. We need to focus on Rylander.'

Jens pulls a face.

'At least the motive is clear now. The question is – how did Rylander find out what happened? Did he and Tanya go back? Did they see something?'

Anna shrugs. 'Maybe, although my guess is that Rylander knew nothing.'

'No?'

She takes out the letter from Elisabet Vidje and gives him a moment to read it.

'I've been thinking about this quite a lot,' she says when he's finished. 'I think Rylander received this letter and saw a business opportunity. He took a chance on the possibility that something really had happened that night, and that one or more of the four friends would be prepared to pay to keep it quiet. So, he sent the blackmail message, then turned up at the homecoming party.'

It is Jens's turn to nod. He doesn't ask why she didn't show him the letter earlier.

'In which case he was partly right, wasn't he? Someone wanted to make sure that whatever took place that night didn't come out, but they weren't going to pay. Within a very short time Rylander falls to his death. Thanks to Alex Morell we now know why – we just don't know who was responsible.'

Anna holds up her right thumb.

'Alex Morell has an alibi, plus he's admitted to the events in the quarry.'

She moves on to her index and middle fingers.

'Marie and Bruno provided each other with an alibi. We also know that they and Alex are involved in a major building project, and that the financing is an issue.'

She raises her ring finger.

'Caia Bianca says that she was at a concert, but we haven't checked her alibi. From a purely theoretical point of view, she's the one who has the most to lose if the circumstances surrounding Simon's death are made public. A dead nineteen-year-old bullied to death by his friends would be a disaster for her brand. Plus, she already has a suspicious death in her past.'

She pauses, frowns, then holds up her little finger.

'Then we have the fifth option. Someone else took care of Rylander. Someone who will do anything to keep the lid on the truth about Simon Vidje's death.'

'Like who?'

Before she can answer, the phone rings. The call is from a Malmö number; Anna has a good idea of who it is before she hears the commissioner's rasping voice.

'I've just had Henry Morell on the phone, and judging by his state of mind I'm assuming I'm not the only one he's contacted.' He sounds tired rather than angry.

'Could you please explain to me, Anna, how my order to make your peace with Morell resulted in your throwing him out of the police station where he's served for more than thirty years, then having his son arrested?'

'Alexander hasn't been arrested. He's been brought in for questioning.'

The commissioner sighs. 'Morell's friends will be calling me all afternoon, and you're not exactly making it easy for me to defend you, Anna.'

She takes a deep breath, then summarises Alexander Morell's confession. She explains that she thinks there's a connection with Joe Rylander's death. The commissioner listens without interrupting.

'Undeniably interesting, and definitely a possible motive for murder,' he says when she's finished. 'I can see only one problem.'

'Which is?' The question is unnecessary; she already knows what he's going to say.

'I've gone through the case file, and there is still no irrefutable evidence that Rylander was actually murdered. In spite of a number of possible anomalies, his death could have been suicide or an accident.'

She can hear his fingers drumming on the desk as he considers his next move.

'In light of Alexander Morell's confession, I'm prepared to let you continue for a while longer. Bring the other three in for questioning on Monday.'

'We have to keep going now,' she says. 'Before Henry Morell has time to call the others and tell them what Alex has said. We have to seize the opportunity and surprise them.'

'I'd be wary of airing those kind of views around Morell if I were you. He's already accusing you of conducting a personal vendetta against him, and an accusation like that would add grist to his mill. I can't see any justification in using the police authority's limited resources over the weekend, not to mention the unnecessary fuel you would add to his merrily blazing fire if you bring in three well-respected citizens for questioning while they're enjoying a pleasant Saturday.'

The commissioner pauses for a few seconds. When he continues, his tone is kinder.

'You're a good police officer, Anna, and it's not impossible that you're onto something here. But that newspaper article has damaged you, and I'm afraid neither you nor this investigation can cope with any more unpleasantness. Release Alexander Morell as soon as possible, and prepare meticulously for Monday. Meanwhile I'll try to keep Henry's allies at bay for a few more days. And Anna . . . good luck.'

52

Autumn 2017

Anna lets Jens inform the Morells that Alexander is free to go. As father and son walk towards Henry's car, she stands at an upstairs window watching them. They are both the same height, they have the same gait, and the only thing that distinguishes them from each other is that Henry stoops slightly, and has a heavier tread. The sun, which is peeping through the clouds for once, lends the gloomy scene an inappropriate beauty.

As the two men get into the car, she catches herself wondering if either of the front seats in the Volvo is pushed as far back as it will go.

At three o'clock she decides to go home. She drives slowly up the ridge. After a certain amount of messing around she has managed to get Simon Vidje's song on her phone, and listens to it through the car stereo. His voice is soft and pleasant, the words beautiful yet frightening.

'*I'll see you by the waters. The dark and lonely waters.*'

The trees have lost more than half their leaves by now, and the steep slopes are covered with an orange carpet so bright that it almost hurts her eyes. She turns off towards Tabor, then stops and sits there for a few minutes, thinking things over.

Alexander Morell has told the truth about what happened that night – she and Jens know it, as does the commissioner. And Henry Morell, which probably means that the rest of the world will be informed shortly. It's only fair that those most closely involved should also be told. She puts the car in reverse, drives back onto the main road and heads for Änglaberga.

When she reaches the avenue she sees both Klein's and Elisabet Vidje's vehicles by the lodge. She parks her car by the side of the road. The lodge is surrounded by a hawthorn hedge so tall that all she can see is the low roof. Next to the two parked cars is an opening in the hedge. The wooden house is painted green, with an abundance of decorative white woodwork around the porch and above the windows, and yet there is something desolate about the place. It's as if it is hiding away behind the hawthorns right at the end of the avenue, and prefers to keep itself to itself.

She hears voices from behind the building. As she rounds the corner she sees a storage shed. The double doors are wide open, and a deer is hanging in the middle of the room. A hook has been inserted beneath the animal's chin and attached to a chain hanging from a beam. The deer is so big that its hind feet are touching the concrete floor. Anna tries to remember the little she learned about deer in school; she knows there are two kinds, but can't recall which is which. Klein and Elisabet seem to be admiring the creature. They both turn when they hear her approaching.

'Isn't he magnificent?' Elisabet says.

'He is. What kind is he?'

'A red deer.' Klein sounds amused at her ignorance. 'Fallow deer are smaller and have palmate horns. Not like this beast. I got him down at Bensige early this morning. He was worth waiting for.' Klein pats the deer's neck a couple of times. Anna can see dried blood on his hands.

'Klein wanted to shoot him last year, but I asked him to wait,' Elisabet says. 'He's a breeding stag, and I wanted to give him one more season to pass on his genes.' She smiles, but her eyes look tired, and the part of her face not covered by her shawl is pale and lined.

'Why shoot him at all?' Anna asks.

'If we didn't, sooner or later he'd wander further east along the ridge and onto Trolleberg's land. Some trophy hunter would pay a fortune to bring him down, then take his head and mount it on a wall in Germany or Denmark. And the meat would finish up in a food hall in Stockholm.'

Elisabet shakes her head.

'He was born and grew up on the ridge, his children and grandchildren are grazing on its slopes. So we want to keep him here with us, right to the end.' She also pats his neck – tenderly, affectionately.

'Karl-Johan doesn't approve of hunting,' Anna says, without really knowing why. Both Klein and Elisabet raise their heads a fraction when they hear his name. The movement is identical and simultaneous – almost comically so.

'No,' Klein says, glancing at Elisabet.

'Karl-Johan is a romantic,' Elisabet says quietly. 'He loves the thought of nature, but struggles with the practicalities. He's never really grasped that death is a prerequisite for life.'

She pats the deer one last time, and her expression returns to its usual sharpness.

'But you didn't come here to talk about hunting, did you, Anna?'

'Maybe we should go inside and sit down,' Anna suggests.

Just as she'd suspected, the lodge turns out to be Bror Klein's home. An open hallway with the bathroom straight ahead, kitchen and living room on the left, two closed doors on the right. The walls and ceilings are panelled with yellowed pine, and remind her of a cabin that she, Håkan and Agnes used to rent in the mountains. It even smells the same – dry wood and an open fire. The décor is spartan; apart from red deer and fallow deer antlers, she can see only one ornament, a wall hanging with the text: *He who seeks shall find, and to him that knocks the door shall be opened.*

Elisabet sits down at the table, and while Klein is making coffee Anna slips into the bathroom to gather her thoughts. What is she going to say? How much can she reveal?

Klein's bathroom is as minimalist as the rest of the lodge. Toilet, bath, shower, washbasin, metal cabinet which of course she has to peep into. Toothbrush, toothpaste, a couple of bottles of tablets.

One is for high blood pressure, but she doesn't recognise the other. She googles it on her phone and discovers that it's a mild anti-depressant. So stone-faced Klein takes happy pills – that's unexpected. She replaces the bottles and quietly closes the cabinet. As she leaves the bathroom she can hear Klein and Elisabet talking in the kitchen. She still has time to find out a little more about the secretive Bror Klein. The door next to the bathroom probably leads down to the cellar. A faint smell of dampness is coming through the wide gap under the door.

She tries the handle – locked. She crosses the hall and opens the first door on the right. A bedroom with a neatly made single bed and a wardrobe. She steps inside; just like in the rest of the house, there are hardly any personal items, except for a book and a photograph on the bedside table.

The book is Dante's *Divine Comedy*, which surprises her almost as much as the happy pills. It looks like an old edition. She opens the front cover; it was printed in the early twentieth century. There is an inscription in ornate handwriting:

To Bror from Karl-Johan, Christmas 1972.

Not from Karl-Johan and Elisabet, just Karl-Johan. The words and the type of gift suggest that he and Klein were, or are, close friends. You only give an edition like this to someone you know will appreciate it, someone you know well. The photograph strengthens her theory. It's almost the same one she saw on Elisabet's mantelpiece: the picnic blanket, the meadow, two-year-old Simon screwing up his eyes at the sun, one arm around Daddy's neck. However, in this photo it is not Elisabet who is sitting next to Karl-Jo, but a man of about the same age, with an erect posture and a certain severity about his cheekbones and mouth. Even though the picture was taken over forty years ago, she recognises him immediately: it is Bror Klein. She hears a noise from the kitchen and quickly replaces the photo. She hurries out of the room and quietly closes the door behind her. So, Klein was at the picnic too. It is his long shadow that can be seen in Elisabet's photo, and for some reason she is sure that he also took the wedding picture a few years earlier.

She sits down at the kitchen table as Klein pours the coffee. She realises that he is not just a manager, not someone who merely cleaned up after Karl-Jo's mistakes. He is a very close friend – a member of the family, in fact. She thinks about Göran's insinuations, that Klein and Elisabet had conducted a relationship behind Karl-Johan's back for many years. Has she seen any obvious signs of that kind of intimacy? She doesn't think so, but neither of them is the type to go in for public displays of affection. If Klein is actually living at Änglaberga, then the lodge is only for appearances' sake. That would explain its spartan décor, but Klein's medication is here, which suggest that this is his main residence. She ponders the issue for a moment, but gets nowhere.

'I've spoken to Alexander Morell,' she begins when Klein has sat down. She wants him to be part of the conversation in case Elisabet doesn't take the news well.

'He told me what happened in the quarry that night. What they did . . .' she glances at Elisabet, 'to Simon.'

Elisabet nods slowly. Her face is even paler now. She places one hand on top of Klein's and squeezes it as if she is preparing herself. Anna takes a deep breath. 'There was an argument,' she goes on. 'Alex had Simon in a wrestling hold. Bruno, Marie and Carina were egging him on at first, then they encouraged each other to join in. To humiliate Simon . . .'

She falls silent, looks at Elisabet's hand on Klein's. Neither of them says a word.

'They were all high and drunk. Alex Morell described it as a group psychosis. Af . . . af . . .' She pauses, waits for the stammer to go away.

'Simon ran up into the forest behind the quarry. After a while they started to feel guilty, and went looking for him. When they couldn't find him, they assumed he'd cycled home. According to Alex, they were planning to come here the following day to apologise.'

She pauses again.

'And then?' Elisabet says. 'What happened next?'

'Alex and Bruno got into their tent to escape the rain. Alex fell asleep right away, and didn't wake up until the morning, when he heard Marie screaming.'

Elisabet nods calmly and loosens her grip on Klein's hand.

Klein gets to his feet, fetches a glass of water and stands in silence by the table until Elisabet has taken a couple of sips.

'Thank you, that's better. Sit down, Klein. So, where were we, Anna?'

'Well . . .' Anna attempts to gather her thoughts. 'Everything – the letters, Tabor, my involvement – it was all about you wanting one of the other three to reveal what had happened. You needed to find out the truth about Simon's death, to be sure that Marie wasn't to blame.'

Elisabet nods slowly. 'Marie is my closest relative, my only possible heir, and I couldn't leave Änglaberga to her without first resolving the past. I'm very grateful for your help, Anna.'

Elisabet smiles, but Anna is disinclined to smile back. Anger is pounding behind her eyes, making her clench her jaw so hard that she can feel her teeth grinding. She looks at Klein, meets his gaze. His face is as stiff as always, but she can see something bubbling away just beneath the surface. Something is bothering him.

'We're not done yet,' she says firmly.

'No?'

'No. We're still investigating Joe Rylander's death.'

'Oh – have you found anything that rules out suicide?' The question is unnecessary. Elisabet already knows the answer, and her expression intensifies Anna's feeling that she has been utterly manipulated.

53

Autumn 2017

The sun is shining on Saturday morning. Anna and Agnes eat breakfast together, more or less in silence. Their relationship is stranger than ever. They talk to each other in a cautious, unnatural way, testing out every topic of conversation, making sure they're not going to mention Håkan, the case or the newspaper article before they can proceed. Anna used to think of their relationship as a minefield, but that feels much too inflammatory. These days she compares herself and Agnes to the pond skaters she saw up at the quarry, skirting one another with anxious movements without daring to get too close, afraid of breaking the surface tension and being drawn down into the depths.

Yesterday's revelations are going around and around in her mind, and she doesn't know which of them has made the biggest impression: the fact that Simon's friends attacked and humiliated him, that Marie Sordi had already told Elisabet Vidje everything, or that the older woman has manipulated her for her own ends. Probably the latter, she thinks.

At least she now knows the truth about how Simon died, and yet there is something bothering her, a loose end that she can't quite grasp.

She is determined to bring in the remaining three friends on Monday morning and give them a real grilling. They all had a good reason to be worried about what Rylander might have been able to expose.

Caia Bianca certainly wouldn't want her valuable brand besmirched on social media. Marie and Bruno probably couldn't afford to pay a blackmailer, although in Marie's case the motive might be a little more complicated. She has already confessed to Elisabet, and must have realised that her aunt has been pulling strings in order to bring out the truth without putting any blame on her. And Anna still hasn't been able to dismiss the idea that there might be another alternative, apart from the four friends. Someone who took care of Rylander in order to protect them.

Her phone buzzes – a text from Lisa Savic.

> *Have borrowed a bike – going to try and find Mörkaby quarry today. Do you know exactly where it is? No one around here seems to want to tell me. Thanks in advance.*

Anna feels a pang of guilt. She has broken off her meetings with this likeable young woman on two occasions. She glances at Agnes, who appears to be slightly too absorbed in her phone. No doubt she too is conscious of the weird atmosphere between them, but perhaps Anna can do something about it – something that worked before.

'Do you fancy going up to the quarry again? And we could take a look at the viewpoint on the north side of the ridge, if you like.'

They don't say much on the way down, but within five minutes of picking up Lisa the atmosphere has improved significantly. Lisa makes a huge fuss of Milo and asks Agnes about her photographic equipment, which quickly leads them to Karl-Johan. Agnes talks enthusiastically about the mural and the outline of Simon Vidje's body, and Lisa listens with interest. She asks the right questions at the right times, and Anna can't help being fascinated by her. Lisa seems to be a genuinely good person, which is unusual to say the least.

As they drive back up the ridge Lisa and Agnes discuss the autumn colours on the slopes, and when they reach the turning for Kotorp, Anna stops the car for a moment and points. 'In that direction is the viewpoint where your father ... where Joe ...' She hesitates, decides not to finish the sentence. 'I wondered if you'd like to go there first, before the quarry?'

'If it's not too much of a diversion?'

'Not at all.' Anna sets off along the narrow dirt tracks. This time she finds the way easily. The rain over the past week has made the potholes even deeper, and on a straight stretch she drives into what looks like an innocent puddle, but is in fact such a deep hole that the undercarriage of the car hits the ground with an alarming crunch. The impact makes Agnes cannon into Milo. 'Take it easy, Mum!' she snaps crossly, rubbing the dog's head. Anna is more worried that something beneath the car might have been damaged. She turns the wheel, tries the brakes. Everything seems to be OK, thank goodness.

After a little while they reach the spot where Rylander's Saab was found. She tells Lisa about the car, then leads her and Agnes down the slope to the viewpoint. Milo snuffles around among the leaves and barks at a squirrel as it scampers up a tree only metres in front of his nose.

'Here we are,' Anna says, then decides it's best to keep quiet. Agnes's camera clicks away as she takes pictures of the view, then of Glarea's lunar landscape far below them. Lisa goes up to the rusty fence, stands there for a while as the wind ruffles her short, fair hair. Something about the image makes a connection in Anna's mind, and she almost expects Håkan to stop sulking and tell her what conclusion she has just reached. Instead, she hears Milo barking – a different sound this time.

'Mum,' Agnes says. 'Someone's coming.'

Two figures are moving through the trees. Two big German Shepherds are heading straight for them.

Milo is barking angrily now. He looks as if he'd like to rush straight at the dogs, but Agnes manages to grab his collar and pick him up at the last second. He carries on barking like mad as he wriggles and tries to escape. The German Shepherds are completely focused on the little dog. Anna steps in front of Agnes and tries to remember how Jens handled the Rottweilers at the scrapyard. Their tails are up as they run, but it's definitely not a sign of friendliness. Milo is almost hysterical now, snapping at the air, desperate to get down in order to defend Agnes.

The attackers are no more than five or six metres away.

'Mum . . .' Agnes says.

Anna focuses on the first dog and realises that she hasn't even had time to feel scared. Not until now. Three metres to go. Two.

Suddenly the sound of a shrill whistle slices through the air. The German Shepherds stop dead, turn around and run back in the direction from which they came. Milo carries on barking until they are out of sight.

Anna, Agnes and Lisa exchange relieved glances. After a while they hear the rustle of leaves and see two people in hats and long coats coming through the trees, each with a German Shepherd on a leash. It's Bruno and Marie Sordi. Milo starts growling.

'Oh, it's you,' Marie says. 'We heard a loud bang, almost like an explosion.'

'I went into a deep pothole on the track,' Anna explains.

'I'm sorry to hear that – you have to be careful up here. Dad drove into one a couple of years ago when he was searching for a retriever that had run off, and he damaged a shock absorber. Had to be towed home. I hope the boys didn't scare you?' She gestures towards the dog by her left-hand side. 'There isn't usually anyone around at this time of year – it's too cold and windy for picnics.'

'No problem. You seem to have them well under control.'

'Castor and Pollux are both obedience champions.'

The dogs are keeping a watchful eye on the strangers. Agnes is still clutching Milo in her arms. His teeth are bared, his hackles raised. As soon as one of the German Shepherds moves, he growls.

'This must be your daughter,' Marie says, with a friendly nod to Agnes. 'That's a fine little terrier you have there – and brave! How old is he?'

'Two. His name is Milo.'

'Have you taken him to any obedience classes?'

'No. My dad and I were going to take him together, but . . .' Agnes falls silent, glances at her mother. 'We didn't get around to it.'

Marie nods, tilts her head slightly to one side.

'Very sad, that business with your dad,' she says, looking at Anna. Her tone and expression make it clear that she is talking about the internal investigation and the newspaper article.

'If you're interested, both you and your mum are very welcome to the working dogs' club,' Marie goes on. 'We run a beginners' course on Mondays and Thursdays. Bruno and I are trainers.'

Agnes's face lights up. 'That sounds good, doesn't it, Mum?'

Anna nods, wondering exactly how welcome she will be after Monday's interviews.

'And who's this?' Marie turns to Lisa, politely curious.

'My name is Lisa Savic.' Lisa looks as if she would like to step forward and shake hands, but the dogs are putting her off.

'Hi, Lisa. I'm Marie Sordi, and this is my husband, Bruno. I can tell from your accent that you're not from around here.'

Lisa shakes her head. 'No, I'm only visiting. It was my father who . . . died here.'

'I'm so sorry – our condolences for your loss.'

'Thank you.'

'Have you found out what happened to poor Joe Rylander, Anna?'

Anna takes her time before answering. Marie has carried out a successful balancing act for many years, with her aunt and Änglaberga on one side, her friends, her father and Henry Morell on the other. But now that balancing act is over, thanks to Anna.

'Not yet. We're still working on it.'

'Right.' Marie smiles and tries to look unmoved, but doesn't entirely succeed. They stand there for a few seconds; no one seems to know what to say.

'How's the build going?' Anna turns to Bruno, hoping to draw him into the conversation.

'Making progress,' he replies, a little too quickly.

'When are you planning to open?'

Bruno looks at his wife. 'It's too early to say – it's a major project. Anyway, hadn't we better head home, darling? The children are waiting.'

'Yes,' Marie says. 'Let me know if you want to join the beginners' course. It's been running for a couple of weeks already, but you can still jump in.'

One of the German Shepherds moves its feet, and Milo growls again.

'Nice to meet you.' Marie nods to Lisa.

'Marie and Bruno,' Lisa says, as if she's suddenly remembered something important.

'Yes?'

'You were there when Simon Vidje died. You met my mum and dad – Joe and Tanya.'

Bruno and Marie exchange a glance.

'That's right,' Bruno says warily.

'We're on our way to the quarry now,' Lisa informs them, her tone revealing that she hasn't picked up on the tension in the air.

'Are you indeed.' Marie sounds anxious now.

'I didn't grow up with my parents, so I'm trying to find out more about them,' Lisa goes on. 'Where they lived, who they met and so on. It might be an odd question, but do you remember anything about Joe and Tanya from that night?'

Marie looks very small. Her eyes are darting all over the place and her face has lost all its colour. Bruno steps forward, lets out a metre of the leash so that the big dog is free to move towards Milo, who immediately starts barking again.

'No, we don't,' Bruno says firmly. 'I'm afraid we really must get going. Have a nice day.' He takes Marie by the arm and steers both her and the two dogs away.

'Sometimes I talk too much, don't I?' Lisa says.

They head for the quarry. All three of them are quiet at first, but then Agnes and Lisa resume their conversation about the painting.

Anna wonders whether to tell them about Alex Morell's confession. She's already done it once, but Elisabet Vidje is the plaintiff, which means that the breaking of confidentiality is defensible, to a certain extent. She decides to keep the information to herself – at least for the time being.

As they approach the track leading to the quarry, they see a large dark-coloured SUV parked next to the barrier. Anna drives up beside it and stops. There are two people in the vehicle, but the tinted windows mean she can't see who they are until she gets out of her own car and the driver lowers the side window. It is Caia Bianca.

'Oh, it's you,' she says. 'Are we in your way?'

'No, not at all.' Anna leans forward and sees that Alexander Morell is in the passenger seat.

'We were just chatting,' he says, as if he owes her an explanation. 'About the old days, that kind of thing.'

'I see. I thought you didn't like wallowing in the past,' she says to Caia.

'I don't.'

Alex and Caia both look uncomfortable, as if Anna has caught them out. Agnes and Lisa join her.

'I recognise you.' Caia smiles at Lisa, presumably in an attempt to change the subject. 'We've met before, haven't we?'

Lisa shakes her head. 'I don't think so.'

'Are you sure? You look so familiar.'

'I've seen you on TV, but we've never met. Not as far as I remember, anyway.'

'Well, there you go – I must be wrong. I meet so many people that sometimes I get mixed up.' This time Caia's smile is anything but sincere.

'Have you been up to the quarry?' Anna asks. Caia doesn't answer. Instead, she glances sideways at Alex.

'No,' he says. 'We didn't get that far.'

'We're on our way there now if you want to join us.' She doesn't really know why she made the suggestion, but it makes both Alex and Caia shake their heads at the same time.

'No thanks – we need to head back to the village.' Caia starts the engine. 'Good to see you again,' she adds before closing the window.

Anna watches as Caia reverses. Just before they leave, she meets Alex's gaze. He manages a crooked smile, but he still looks ill at ease.

They walk through the forest to the quarry, then follow the path up to the spot where they stood last time. The place is silent and desolate, and the sense of foreboding Anna was aware of before still lingers over the dark water.

Lisa helps Agnes to rig up her camera on its tripod over by the edge of the rock, and seems to be listening with interest as Agnes explains which lenses she can choose between, and what effect they have on the pictures.

Anna contemplates the area with fresh eyes. It isn't particularly large, maybe forty to forty-five square metres, consisting mainly of rocks, flat stones and patches of grass. A circle of blackened stones marks the old fireplace; using that as her starting point, she tries to work out where the altercation happened. There are a few slightly deeper hollows nearby, and she guesses that Alex Morell must have pushed Simon's face down into one of them.

She pictures Alex blocking the route down to the turning area, while Bruno and Carina 'Caia Bianca' Pedersen prevent Simon from getting to the tents. There is only one way he can go: straight up into the forest, just as Alex said. She tries to recreate his escape, but finds that it's easier said than done. Between the forest behind the quarry and the small plateau on which she is standing, there are several metres of steep scree, and it takes her a number of attempts to reach the top. The trees at the edge are birches, but after a short distance the firs are so dense that she has to bend down in order to get through. She tries to go left towards the water, searching in vain for a path that will make her progress easier. The ground slopes upwards and is covered in a thick carpet of rotted needles, but here and there sharp stones protrude. She trips over one of them and

336

bangs her knee on a tree root. She swears and manages to sit up. She can still hear Agnes and Lisa's voices. She tries to imagine what they would sound like in the pouring rain; she probably wouldn't have to go much further to be completely out of earshot. She gets to her feet and continues to fight her way around the back of the quarry. The rough terrain continues to climb upwards, there are more and more treacherous stones poking through, and eventually she realises that she has two choices. Either she can return to the forest, or she can keep going in the same direction and risk having to tackle the steep cliffs on the far side.

She chooses the latter option, and battles on for quite some time before the ground suddenly slopes downwards and she emerges into a small opening behind the top of one of the tallest cliffs.

She can see Agnes and Lisa down below. She waves to let them know everything is OK, then cautiously makes her way to the edge. The cliff is higher than she thought – eight metres, maybe more. The water in the pool is black, but a faint ripple catches her eye. There is a rock just below the surface. If Simon came the same way as she has just done – if he stumbled down the little slope between the trees in the rain and darkness, exhausted from the wrestling match with Alex, feeling angry, upset and humiliated, drunk and possibly high – it's not difficult to imagine him plunging over the edge, striking his head on the hidden rock, then floating out into the water just as he is portrayed in Karl-Johan's painting – on his back, arms outstretched.

'No, it's fine,' Agnes says, presumably in response to a question from Lisa. Her clear voice is carried across the quarry, bouncing off the rocks until all that remains is a melancholy echo.

'Fine . . .'

'Fine . . .'

'Ine . . .'

Anna looks down at the dark water and shudders.

The incline on the far side is less steep, and the trees are more sparse, so it takes her only five minutes to get down to the turning area. If she puts it all together – the inadequate investigation, Alex

Morell's confession and her own observations – the likelihood is that Simon Vidje's death was an accident. Admittedly, it was caused by the altercation between those who promised to be 'friends forever', but still . . . A tragic event where any possible crime has long since passed the statute of limitations. She ought to be satisfied with that, accept that the incident, as Alex described it, was serious enough. The fight is the secret that one of the four friends, or someone close to them, was prepared to kill for.

Caia Bianca has her brand to think of, and then there are the rumours about her first husband. Bruno Sordi is in the middle of a major building project, and is probably on shaky ground financially. Marie is involved in the same project, she is the leader of the local council, and she daren't risk her husband or father finding out that she's already told Elisabet Vidje the truth. Bengt Andersson seems to be obsessed with Nedanås and its reputation. Alex Morell has already admitted his part and has an alibi for the time of Rylander's death, but he has a terrible temper and has already demonstrated violent tendencies. And last but not least there is Henry Morell, who has clung to the same job for twenty-seven years in order to ensure that this whole miserable story never came out.

She has more than enough to do. She ought to focus on Joe Rylander's death, just as she said to Jens Friberg, and yet there is something else that strikes her as she stands in the middle of the turning area. The loose end she sensed before, but couldn't quite grasp. She knows what it is now. The words she jotted down on her notepad during the interview with Alex: *Simon's bike?*

Because if Simon really did stumble around up there in the dark and the rain, if he did fall over the edge and hit his head, then why wasn't his bike down here in the morning? Why wasn't it taken in, or even mentioned in the case file?

They head back to the car. The sun has slipped behind the clouds, and the atmosphere between them has changed. Anna is lost in her own thoughts, and neither Agnes nor Lisa says anything. It's as if the time spent in the gloomy little quarry has made them all somewhat pensive. Agnes has that expression she sometimes wears when she is thinking about her father, and Anna catches herself trying to start a conversation with him for at least the fiftieth time, only to realise once more that he is still torturing her with his sullen silence.

I know I did the wrong thing, OK? So, yell at me for fuck's sake, tell me I'm an idiot who can't keep my promises. Say whatever you like, as long as you say something!

Not a word from Håkan.

They stow Agnes's equipment in the boot of the car. In the middle of all the autumn smells, Anna thinks she can detect something else, an acrid odour that isn't familiar. Milo seems to have picked up on it too; his head is raised, his nose pointing into the wind. Could it be petrol? Has the incident with the pothole cracked the fuel tank? She bends down, runs her hand over the grass beneath the car then sniffs it. Nothing.

They get into the car, with Lisa in the front this time, Agnes and Milo in the back.

'So, what shall we do now?' Anna asks a little too brightly when the silence begins to feel oppressive.

'If it's OK with you, I'd like to go back to my hotel,' Lisa says, sounding tired. 'My train leaves first thing in the morning, and I need to pack.'

'No problem.'

They pass Änglaberga, and she catches a glimpse of Klein's lodge. Thinks once again about how curiously impersonal it is, devoid of anything to suggest that it is someone's home. But presumably that's how Klein wants it. Maybe he prefers to live his life like a monk, with a single book on his bedside table. A book he has kept for over forty years. However, Dante's *Divine Comedy* isn't exactly suitable for a novice reader, and the way he speaks and conducts himself suggests an educated person. He is someone who reads, and yet there are no bookshelves. Unless of course her suspicions are well-founded: the lodge is nothing more than a façade, and Klein actually lives at Änglaberga.

She reaches for her phone, finds Simon's song and presses play. His soft voice fills the speakers as the road curves to the right and begins to wind its way down the hill.

'That's lovely,' Lisa says, and Anna is about to explain who's singing when she realises that something is wrong. The brake pedal, which worked perfectly on the first hairpin bend, feels spongy. She presses down hard, but it doesn't reduce her speed by as much as she would have expected. The next bend is fast approaching, and she keeps her foot down.

Suddenly, there is a metallic bang and the brake pedal hits the floor. Anna is so shocked that she yanks at the wheel, and the car veers across the carriageway. The instrument panel lights up like a Christmas tree, and a warning signal starts beeping.

'Mum!' Agnes says anxiously, but Anna hasn't time to answer; she has her hands full trying to keep the car on the road.

She regains control just before the nearside wheels go over the edge. She hears Lisa gasp beside her. The brake pedal is on the floor, and has no effect whatsoever. She slams the car into a lower gear; the engine roars angrily, almost drowning out the warning beep. At the same time she fumbles for the handbrake, but can't find it. Her speed increases, she is getting closer and closer to the next hairpin bend, and she keeps trying to pull on a handbrake that doesn't exist.

'Mum!' Agnes says again. She sounds very frightened, and at that moment Anna remembers that the car has an electronic brake, a button you press, it's . . . it's . . . Where the fuck is the brake button?

She takes her left hand off the wheel and gropes along the underside of the instrument panel. The roar of the engine is deafening now, the car is moving faster and faster, the sharp bend is almost upon them. She looks up, meets Lisa's terrified gaze.

'Mum!' Agnes yells. 'Brake, Mum!'

Her fingers press every button they find, but nothing happens. The bend is rushing towards them. Anna grips the wheel with both hands and wrenches it to the side. The tyres screech on the tarmac and she steers into the curve, just as she learned on the emergency response driving course many years ago. She almost makes it. She thinks she's done it, but in the middle of the sharp turn the back wheels lose their grip, and she realises that the worst is about to happen.

'Hold on tight!' she shouts. The car leaves the road sideways, the engine roars, and for a couple of seconds it feels as if time has slowed down. Every detail becomes incredibly clear: Lisa's horrified expression, the lights on the instrument panel, the feeling of the smooth leather on the steering wheel pressing against the palms of her hands, the warning beep, the sound of Simon Vidje's soft voice coming through the speakers.

'. . . *dark and lonely waters.*'

The car spins through the air and she sees the ground approaching through the side window. She even manages to close her eyes and prepare herself before the impact makes time switch from slow motion to double speed.

Agnes and Lisa scream, Milo produces something between a bark and a howl, then everything is drowned out by the sound of crunching metal and breaking glass. The car rolls down the slope, over and over and over, up becomes down, the whole world is blurred. They hit a tree, change direction, hit another tree.

A fresh blow crushes the roof above her, and she throws herself across the gear stick to protect her head. Suddenly they are weightless again, and Anna sees something sparkling outside the window. Just as the car plunges into the river, she realises what it is.

Shit, she thinks before the broken windscreen shatters and there is nothing but the dark and lonely waters pouring into the car.

54

Autumn 2017

WAKE UP ANNA WAKE UP ANNA WAKE UP ANNA!
Håkan's voice echoes inside her head and for a millisecond she is filled with joy. He is talking to her again!

Then she remembers where she, Agnes and Lisa are: in a car filled with ice-cold, dark water. She is lying across the gear stick, her head halfway beneath the rapidly rising surface of the water, and when she tries to sit up, she discovers that she is trapped. She wriggles to try and free herself, and feels something pulling across her neck and shoulder. The seat belt. She manages to find the release button, and at the same time she pushes so hard with her feet that she bangs her head on the roof, which has been partly crushed. White light explodes, and she almost passes out again.

AGNES! Håkan shouts. *YOU HAVE TO HELP AGNES!*

She squeezes her eyes tight shut a couple of times and steadies herself. Realises she can breathe. A dwindling pocket of air has formed, and she fills her lungs. Her eyes become accustomed to the darkness, and she can just make out something beside her. She fumbles with her right hand, finds the release button for the passenger seat belt. She presses it, tries to grab hold of Lisa and feels a hand on hers. She drags the young woman up towards the air pocket, which already seems much smaller. She hears a splutter, then a cough.

'The door . . .' Lisa gasps. 'I can't open it.'

'The windscreen,' Anna says. 'You need to dive down and get out through the windscreen.' She is already on her way to Agnes, managing to force her way between the front seats. She takes another deep breath and dives towards the place where she last saw her daughter. She gropes around, finds a leg and thumps it hard with her fist.

Agnes doesn't move. Anna raises her head again. The air pocket is down to a few centimetres now, and she can feel the pressure on her eardrums as the rising water takes its toll. She dives again. It's as if a band of ice is tightening around her temples as she searches desperately for the seatbelt. How long has Agnes been underwater? A minute at least. Probably two.

Three minutes, Håkan informs her, managing to sound both matter-of-fact and worried. *You have three minutes. Not much more.*

She finds the button and presses it, but nothing happens. She tugs at the belt, using so much oxygen that she has to go back up for air. She takes a breath, tries to slow her heart rate. Dives again. Her fingers are freezing cold, she can't get a grip on the belt. Her efforts make the car begin to tilt forwards.

Calm, Håkan says. *Try to keep calm.*

Suddenly, the belt comes free. She pushes it away from Agnes's lifeless body and pulls her daughter close. Manages to drag her up towards the roof. The air pocket is so tiny now that she has to tilt her head to the side in order to reach it. She lifts Agnes's nose and mouth above the surface of the water.

'Agnes!' she shouts. 'Wake up, Agnes!'

No reaction. The car tips and the air pocket moves, finds the highest point inside the vehicle, just above the rear window. She tries to drag Agnes to the right spot, pushes her up towards the roof.

'Agnes!' Slaps her across the forehead. Still no reaction. She takes a huge breath, presses her mouth to Agnes's and blows. She hears bubbling in Agnes's throat. She must have swallowed water; it might even be in her lungs.

You have to get out, Håkan says firmly. *Right now!*

The car shifts again. Anna manages to fill her lungs one last time before the air pocket disappears. She is on her knees on the back seat of the sinking car. The only escape route is through the windscreen,

ANDERS DE LA MOTTE

which is behind them. In order to reach it she will have to wrestle both Agnes and herself between the front seats, avoiding the crushed section of the roof.

It's impossible. She lets go of Agnes and dives down to the side door. The car is full of water now, so the pressure ought to be the same inside and outside, which means she should be able to open the door. Theoretically.

She tugs at the handle, but it's no use. The cold is shrinking her lungs, her movements are getting slower and slower. She braces her body against the driver's seat and pushes the door as hard as she can with one foot.

Gradually it begins to open. White lights flicker in front of her eyes. Her heartbeat is deafening.

Three minutes, Håkan says again in that voice he sometimes used when they were training together. *This is your last chance, Anna. Push, for God's sake!*

She gathers all her strength, opens her mouth and roars into the water, forcing the door centimetre by centimetre until there is a gap wide enough to get through.

She is out of oxygen, the white lights have turned into a multi-coloured firework display, and yet somehow she manages to haul Agnes out of the car. She kicks against the bodywork, propelling them both upwards.

Keep going, Anna. Keep going, you can do this!

But Agnes's lifeless body is dragging her down, and she is on the point of losing consciousness. On the point of being swallowed up by dark, ice-cold water, just like Simon Vidje. She closes her eyes and draws her daughter closer.

Suddenly, the pressure around her head eases, and she is above the surface. She gasps, takes breath after breath. The firework display comes to an end and her vision clears.

The shore is three to four metres away, and she tries to swim in that direction with one hand, keeping Agnes's head above the water with the other. Her daughter's face is ashen, her eyes closed. Blood is trickling from an ugly gash over her left eye.

Their progress is agonisingly slow. The current is forcing them back. Anna shifts her position so that she is swimming on her back with Agnes's head between her hands, as she learned on a lifesaving course. It's a little easier, and they edge towards the shore. Anna coughs and swallows river water, but the adrenaline pumping through her body enables her to keep going, in spite of the cold, the lack of oxygen and exhaustion.

Four minutes, Håkan whispers. *You have to get ashore; you have to check her breathing.*

'Anna!' She looks up and sees Lisa clinging by one arm to a huge rock a few metres from the shore. Her other arm is dangling at an odd angle. The water is swirling around the rock.

'I can't go any further, the current's too strong! My arm . . .' Lisa shouts.

Anna isn't caught in the same current yet, but there is no doubt that she is getting closer to it with every second. She has to reach the shore, has to prioritise her daughter.

She keeps kicking, using all the reserves of strength she can summon up to keep moving forward. Suddenly her shoulders hit rocks. She puts her feet down and manages to take a few steps before she stumbles. Another attempt, then another until she reaches the shore. She grazes her knees on the stones and twists her ankle, but her legs are so cold that she is only vaguely aware of the pain. The bank is no more than half a metre high, but when she lifts Agnes's body out of the river and it is no longer supported by the water, the weight makes her collapse with exhaustion, Agnes in her arms. Her stomach contracts, sending up a cascade of liquid that sears her throat.

Lisa is still calling out to her. Inside her head Håkan is yelling that she has to get to her feet, drag Agnes up onto the bank and start CPR. She tries to crawl, but her legs and arms refuse to co-operate, and she flops on her back next to Agnes. Someone is screaming, the sound is loud and heartrending, a mixture of grief and impotence. It takes a few seconds for Anna to realise that it is her.

All at once someone grabs her shoulders and heaves her up onto the bank. She sees Wellington boots, green hunting trousers and an oilskin jacket. It is Bror Klein.

Without a word he drops her and returns to pick up Agnes. Her face and lips are white.

Hope gives Anna fresh strength. She gets to her knees and hurls herself at Agnes. Pushes away Klein's helping hands and points to the rock where she saw Lisa.

'Out there. Someone else. Quickly!'

He disappears as she pinches Agnes's nostrils and places her mouth over her daughter's lips. She tastes blood, and blows as hard as she can. Hears that horrible bubbling in Agnes's windpipe. She blows again, and again. The bubbling grows louder.

Keep going, Håkan says. *Don't give up!*

She keeps blowing, feels the lack of oxygen making her field of vision narrow, but she doesn't stop. Agnes gurgles, and like lava from volcano, dark green water gushes out of her mouth. Anna rolls Agnes onto her side and bangs her back until the eruption stops.

'Agnes!'

Her voice sounds distant. Agnes doesn't move.

'Agnes!' She can hardly see at all now. She has almost nothing left. With the very last of her strength she pounds her fist on Agnes's back, takes her daughter's head between her hands and presses her face close to hers. Agnes's forehead is sticky with blood.

'Agnes, darling!'

And something happens. A faint twitch across Agnes's face, a spasm in her abdomen, followed by a cough. More water comes up, splashing onto the grass, then there is the wonderful sound of Agnes taking a deep, shuddering breath. The ground moves beneath Anna, she nearly topples over.

Not yet!

She straightens up to give Agnes space. Another burst of coughing, another wonderful breath.

Anna falls backwards. Sees Bror Klein, soaking wet, staggering out of the river carrying Lisa. Sees the tortured expression on his stony face before he slowly slips away, to be replaced by treetops and a high, clear blue sky.

Razor blades. Red, gold and blue.

She spreads her arms wide, closes her eyes. Feels the ground rising to catch her.

Now! Håkan whispers. *Now!* She follows his voice into the merciful darkness.

55

Autumn 2017

S he and Håkan are back in that cramped little hospital room. Everything is exactly the same. The air, the light, the hum of the machines, the tubes and wires wriggling across the covers like plastic snakes. But this time the roles are reversed. Anna is the one lying in the bed, while Håkan is sitting on the chair.

He looks different. This is healthy Håkan – and yet it isn't.

She reaches out to him. It is a huge effort, demands almost all of her willpower.

He takes her hand in his. She feels the warmth of his skin, becomes aware that tears are pouring down her cheeks. Even though she knows this isn't real, she wants to tell him how much she's missed him. How pleased she is to see him.

'You did well,' he says. 'Really well, my love.'

Everything changes.

They are standing hand in hand in the quarry. Her hospital gown flaps in the wind. High above them a skein of wild geese cross the autumn sky, crying out to one another with mournful voices.

'There,' Håkan says, pointing up to the plateau. Anna sees four teenagers, all with their heads lowered. She recognises them from the group photo.

Alex, Carina, Marie and Bruno.

Simon Vidje's body is floating in the black water below them.

The wind passes through the leaves on the trees, rippling the surface of the water.

Somewhere far away, music is playing. A soft voice accompanied by a guitar.

I'll see you by the waters. The dark and lonely waters.

Suddenly, just like in Karl-Johan's painting when you look at it in daylight, Simon's body is gone, and all that remains in the former quarry is the dark and lonely waters.

'You know what you have to do,' Håkan whispers.

She hears a noise behind her and turns around. The crunch of gravel beneath narrow tyres, followed by the sound of a bicycle bell.

She wakes up slowly. The room is in semi-darkness, and she is almost immediately aware that she is not alone. Someone is dozing in an armchair in the corner, and for a second her heart believes that it is Håkan. Then her eyes grow accustomed to the gloom and her brain takes over. The person in the chair is Lisa Savic. Her left arm is in a sling across her chest.

Anna reaches for the handle dangling above her and uses it to pull herself up into a sitting position. The movement makes the bed creak and pulls at the tubes. One of the machines to which she is evidently linked makes a discreet beeping sound, which disturbs Lisa.

'You're awake,' she says, getting to her feet.

'Agn . . .' Her vocal cords aren't co-operating, so she clears her throat and tries again. 'W . . . where is Agnes?'

Lisa comes over to the bed and takes Anna's hand in hers, just as Håkan did in the dream.

'She's in intensive care.'

Anna's heart starts racing. She pulls her hand away, tries to get out of bed. Another machine beeps in protest.

'Help me, I have to go to her,' she says, tugging at the side rail and looking for a way to lower it. Lisa joins in, finds the catch, and Anna manages to swing her legs around. The room sways, her eyelids feel heavy.

'I'm not sure you should be . . .' Lisa says anxiously.

The door opens and a nurse comes in. 'Now, what's going on here?' She places a hand on Anna's shoulder. 'How are you feeling, Anna?'

'I h . . . h . . . have to get up. My d . . . daughter. Intensive . . .'

The nurse pats her gently. Her expression is kind.

'Wait a minute, I'll fetch a wheelchair.'

Agnes looks so small, lying there in the hospital bed. Her hair is spread across the pillow, a white dressing covers her forehead, and an oxygen mask covers most of the rest of her face.

Her eyes are closed, her hands neither warm nor cold.

'We're keeping her sedated until at least tomorrow afternoon,' the female doctor says, then goes on to explain something about concussion, lack of oxygen and water in the lungs. Anna does her best to listen, but somehow the words just don't stick. All she can see is Agnes in a bed that is identical to the one Håkan died in, all she wants to do is get out of her wheelchair and grab her daughter. Take her home.

It wasn't your fault, Håkan says. *You do know that, don't you?*

She doesn't answer him. Instead, she leans forward and rests her head on Agnes's arm. Presses as close as she can, inhales the smell of her, just as she did when Agnes was a little girl and had had a nightmare.

'I'm here, sweetheart,' she murmurs. 'Mummy's here. Everything's going to be all right.'

She hears the doctor and the nurse shut the door behind them. She stays exactly where she is, drifting between sleep and wakefulness. She gets the feeling they are not alone in the room. Håkan is standing beside her, with one hand on her shoulder, the other on Agnes's.

When she wakes up she is back in her own bed, with only a faint memory of the doctor persuading her to rest for a while. There is a large bouquet of flowers on the bedside table; it must have been delivered while she was asleep. She thinks she can see Call-me's signature on the card.

All of her strength is gone. Her muscles are aching as if she's done ten strenuous gym sessions one after the other, and she has to ask the nurse to open the pot of yoghurt on her breakfast tray. When she's finished eating another doctor comes in, reads through her notes and explains that Anna is suffering from exhaustion, she has swallowed some of the river water, and is badly bruised, but miraculously she hasn't suffered any more serious injuries, and can therefore go home as soon as she feels better.

After the doctor has left, Anna goes over the course of events. The brakes stopped working, the car skidded on a sharp bend. It left the road, rolled over and landed in the river. The doctor was too professional to say so, but clearly things could have ended very badly. If they'd hit a thick tree trunk, or if the car had finished up on its roof in the river, then none of them would have survived. The thought is beyond chilling.

A faint knock on the door makes her glance up. Jens Friberg walks in, his uniform pristine as always.

'How are you?' he says, looking worried.

'I feel as if someone drove a steamroller over me.'

'And your daughter?'

'Concussion. They're keeping her sedated until this afternoon.'

He gives a brief nod, refrains from saying how terrible it must be, which earns him another bonus point.

'Do you remember what happened?' he says, talking out his notebook. So, he's here in an official capacity, not as a friend. She deletes the bonus point she's just awarded him, and knocks off a couple more out of sheer pettiness.

'The brakes failed. I went into a big pothole on one of the logging tracks a couple of hours earlier, and I thought there was a funny smell just before we got into the car to drive down to Nedanås. I'm assuming the brake pipe must have been punctured, and the brake fluid had leaked out.'

Jens writes down what she is saying, but she notices that he is frowning.

'What?'

'Didn't a warning light come on?'

'No, not until the brakes failed, then the whole instrument panel lit up.'

'OK.' He makes another note, then sits in silence for a few seconds before moving on to his final question.

'Can you think of anyone who had a reason to want to harm you?'

After Jens has left, she asks if she can have a shower. She stands under the stream of hot water for a long time, trying to digest what he was hinting at.

Their car was parked by the barrier for just over an hour – plenty of time for someone with the right tools and knowledge to sabotage the brakes. In which case, who is in the frame? Lisa told Bruno and Marie where they were going, plus they talked to Alex Morell and Caia Bianca. That means at least four people had both motive and opportunity.

When she emerges from the shower, a nurse has laid out her clothes. They are clean and dry, yet she thinks the smell of the river still lingers. However, they are a significant improvement on the hospital gown, so she gets dressed and goes into Lisa's room, which is next door.

Lisa is holding the remote control in her uninjured hand and is zapping idly between TV channels. She looks very pleased to see Anna.

'Hi – I put my head around your door a while ago, but you were asleep. How are you? How's Agnes?'

Anna tells her what the doctor said, and adds that she's on her way up to see Agnes now. She wants to be there when they wake her. 'And how are you?'

'A broken collarbone and several cracked ribs – otherwise I'm fine.'

They both fall silent. Anna feels she has to say something about what happened in the water.

'I really wanted to help you, Lisa, but I had my hands full with Agnes. She was unconscious and . . .'

She makes an apologetic gesture, but Lisa waves it away.

'I understand completely – you had no choice. And you managed to undo my seatbelt in the car. If you hadn't done that, I wouldn't be sitting here. You have nothing to apologise for, Anna. Go and be with Agnes. If it's OK with you, I'll come and see you later.'

'Of course.' Anna smiles. She is growing increasingly fond of Lisa.

Out in the corridor she almost canons into Bengt Andersson. He is carrying a large, beautifully wrapped bouquet of flowers in one hand, and when he sees her his face lights up – at least two notches too much.

'Anna, how wonderful to see you on your feet! We were all so worried!'

He hands over the flowers and she mumbles her thanks. Wonders who he means by 'all'.

'Do you have time for a little chat in private?' he goes on, lowering his voice.

She glances at her watch. She'd prefer to go and sit with Agnes, but she has a few minutes to spare, plus she's interested in what he has to say. She leads the way into her room and pops the flowers into a vase on the shelf while he settles down in the armchair.

'Such a terrible thing, that car accident. I've spoken to intensive care. Göransson, the senior consultant, and I know each other from Rotary.'

'I see,' she says tersely. She almost asks whether membership of that particular club overrides the requirement for confidentiality, but he pre-empts her by holding up his hands defensively.

'He didn't give me any details, of course. I just wanted to be sure that Agnes was receiving the best possible care, and I can tell you that she's in the very best hands.'

'Good.'

His smile broadens. 'As you know, I'm the chairman of the board at Glarea. That business of the jumper – Rydell or whatever his name was . . .'

He waves a nonchalant hand to show that he barely remembers Joe Rylander's name or anything else about him. He is obviously lying. 'A sad business, both for Glarea and Nedanås.'

353

'Not to mention Rylander's family,' Anna says acidly.

'Of course, of course. But I believe he didn't have any close relatives. He didn't pay any maintenance for his children, and his eldest daughter barely knew him – isn't that correct?'

'He meant something to someone.'

'Sorry?'

'Rylander. He meant something to someone. Everyone does.'

Andersson shrugs, as if he has no real interest in what she's saying. 'Anyway, you've been investigating the matter for almost two weeks, and as I understand it there's nothing to suggest that we're looking at anything other than a tragic suicide.'

She doesn't contradict him, she merely registers the fact that Andersson is extremely well-informed for someone who pretended not to recall Rylander's name less than a minute ago.

'It's your case, of course, and it wouldn't be right for a layman like me to try and influence it in any way.' He holds up his hands again.

But, Anna thinks. There's definitely a *but* on the way.

'But I'm just wondering – with the greatest respect – whether it would be possible to bring this unfortunate episode to an end before it attracts unwanted attention. Many of us – both inside and outside the local community – would really appreciate that.' His smile is ingratiating and over the top in equal parts. 'We've worked hard to establish the good name of Nedanås, and I'm proud to say that we've had great success. As you know we should have a long-distance rail link next year, which will bring more businesses, more opportunities. People are moving into the area instead of moving away, and property prices are rising. Good schools and a low crime rate are key factors, and this business with . . .' he pauses, pretends to search for the name, 'Rylander risks giving us a bad reputation, which would be very unwelcome. You must forgive me if I'm a little crass, but to let a person like him destroy what so many others have built up over the years feels unreasonable to say the least.'

He clearly expects Anna to say something, but she chooses to keep quiet.

'I know that you and Henry Morell have fallen out, Anna,' he goes on, his voice softening. 'Personally, I think that's very sad. You're a very well-thought-of police officer, in spite of that story in the papers, and we really want to keep you here in Nedanås.'

He is still smiling, but there is a sharpness in his expression.

'But for that to happen, you need loyal friends. People who speak highly of you, people you can work with.'

She tries to remain calm, to ignore the underlying yet very clear threat in what he's just said.

'Marie, Bruno, Alex and Carina assaulted Simon Vidje on the night he died,' she says icily. 'Joe Rylander tried to blackmail them. Has Morell told you that as well?'

Andersson's smile fades. 'I did hear something along those lines.'

'In that case, I'm sure you understand why I can't simply abandon the investigation.' She looks him in the eye, holds his gaze for a few seconds. He has the same hard lines around his eyes and nose as his daughter.

'Can't or won't?'

'Does it matter?'

They stare at each other in silence.

'Right,' Andersson says, getting to his feet. 'I won't take up any more of your time, Anna.' He holds out his hand and she shakes it reluctantly. 'I'm sure you'd prefer to be with Agnes, and I have a few calls to make.'

When he's gone, Anna walks over to the window, which overlooks the hospital's main entrance. A familiar dark blue Volvo is parked in the space designated for ambulances. As Bengt Andersson emerges, the car door opens and Henry Morell gets out. He and Andersson have a brief but animated discussion, then they both turn and look up at her window. In spite of the distance, she's pretty sure both men are smiling.

Agnes is still in a deep sleep. Anna sits with her for a while, holding her hand, stroking her cheek, doing her best not to cry. After half an hour the doctor arrives – the same one Anna spoke to during the night.

'I've consulted with my colleagues and everything's looking good, so we're going to take Agnes off the sedative now. That means she should begin to wake up in about half an hour.'

'That's great.' Anna looks at her watch. 'Could I possibly borrow a phone?'

Her mobile is at the bottom of the river along with the car, so she has to call directory enquiries to get her solicitor's number. He answers almost immediately, even though it's Sunday. She's calling because of something that occurred to her after seeing Bengt Andersson and Henry Morell in conversation.

'Anna, good to hear from you. I tried you a few minutes ago but your phone is switched off.'

She doesn't have the energy to explain what's happened, and simply waits for him to get to the point.

'One of Santesson's team has just been in touch. Apparently, they've found DNA on the buttons of the infusion pump – the smallest of traces, but they think they'll have a match-ready profile over the next week or so.'

'Right,' she says, feeling the tiny amount of energy she'd scraped together simply draining away. No doubt that was why Andersson and Morell were smiling. 'And why are they telling us this?'

'Tactics, I imagine. There might not be enough DNA to produce a profile, in which case Santesson wants to have a back-up plan. His offer of a lesser charge in return for a full confession remains on the table until the end of the day. Think it over and call me back by six at the latest if you want me to take it further, OK?'

She ends the call, rests her elbows on her knees and puts her head in her hands. *Not this too. Not now.*

She is sitting with Agnes again. Holding her hand. The oxygen mask has been removed, which makes her look a lot less sick. It's almost as if she's sleeping. Exactly thirty minutes have passed since the doctor switched off the infusion pump delivering the sedative and wheeled it out of the room. Ironically, it is identical to the pump Santesson is holding above her head like the sword of Damocles.

Agnes's eyelids flutter. Her hand squeezes Anna's. Anna squeezes back and forgets everything else. Agnes's lips twitch, then she slowly opens her eyes. She seems to be having difficulty in focusing.

'Agnes? Agnes, sweetheart, can you hear me?'

Nothing.

She thinks about the water, about all those minutes when Agnes was deprived of oxygen. About what that might have done to her wonderful, fragile brain.

'Agnes . . .' Her voice breaks.

Agnes closes her eyes, as if she's gone back to sleep. Anna turns to the doctor, who has just come in.

'I'll examine her,' the doctor says quietly. 'It can take a while for—'

'Mum.'

Anna turns. Her daughter's eyes are open, her gaze clear.

'I'm thirsty.'

And suddenly the floodgates open.

Once the doctor has established that Agnes is doing well, under the circumstances, mother and daughter sit together quietly while Anna tries to gather her courage. The main lights are off and the blinds half-closed, leaving the room in a soft semi-darkness.

'I need to tell you something,' she says. 'Something I should have told you a long time ago. About your dad.'

Agnes straightens her shoulders.

'About the real reason why we moved here,' Anna goes on.

She takes a deep breath and begins. Slowly, almost without stammering at all, she goes through the whole story, in spite of the fact that it's the hardest thing she's ever done. She starts with how she and Håkan met at the police academy, explains why they split up, and finally she tells Agnes how he died. She includes every painful detail, leaves nothing out, even though tears are pouring down her cheeks.

Afterwards she sits on Agnes's bed with her daughter's head resting on her lap. Strokes her forehead until she falls asleep, just like she did when Agnes was a child.

My darling little girl, she thinks.

Our darling little girl.

She hears Håkan come into the room. Senses a shadowy presence over by the wall. No longer trapped in her head, but free.

You did the right thing, my love, he whispers. His tone is warm, yet sad. She knows exactly why. This is the real reason why she has waited so long to talk to Agnes. He comes and stands right beside her.

'Do you have to go?' she says. Or maybe she thinks it. 'Can't you stay – for just a while longer?'

He doesn't reply, he merely gives her a melancholy smile. Should she ask him again? Explain that both she and Agnes still need him? But she knows there's no point.

Time to go, he says softly, caressing her cheek. *Goodbye, my darling Anna. Everything's going to be fine.*

They go through the sequence together, just like the last time.

Three, three, seven, five, nine, two.

Select.

Then, with a faint sigh of relief, he is gone.

56

Autumn 2017

After Agnes has been moved to a general ward, Anna reluctantly decides to go home to Tabor. She needs something to eat and a change of clothes, and she has an even more important task to deal with: Milo. Agnes asked about the dog, and idiotically she allowed her Mummy-reflex to kick in, and said that he was just fine. A white lie. Coming out of an induced coma after a serious car accident, then finding out the truth about her father's death is more than any sixteen-year-old should have to deal with in one day.

The last time Anna saw Milo, he was in the back seat with Agnes. She's pretty sure the dog was knocked unconscious, and ended up at the bottom of the river with the car. The vehicle isn't due to be recovered until later in the week, so all she can do until then is hope that Milo somehow got out and made his way home to Tabor – six miles or so – but she isn't optimistic.

She goes back to her room to fetch her jacket, which is still damp, pays the two hundred kronor for her emergency treatment, then checks on Lisa before she leaves. Lisa is delighted to hear the news about Agnes.

'They're keeping me in overnight,' she says. 'Is it OK if I go and see Agnes tomorrow morning?'

'Of course!'

'By the way, what happened to her little dog?'

Anna forces a smile. 'I'm hoping he's OK, against all the odds. I'm heading home to look for him now.'

She is intending to call a cab in reception, but there's one already waiting at the entrance to the emergency department. Her body is still slow, her muscles are aching and her movements are stiff. As she reaches the taxi she notices a familiar truck with Polish number plates pulling into the drop-off zone. Two men jump out, and she recognises them immediately. They're two of the Poles from Änglaberga who helped her and Agnes move into Tabor. One has a large, bloodstained bandage around his lower leg. He leans against the other man for support as he limps slowly towards the door. The truck remains where it is. Anna recognises the driver too. He nods as she approaches, and winds down his window.

'What happened?' she asks.

'Accident.'

'Where?'

'In forest.' The driver looks as if he'd like to say more, but at that moment his uninjured colleague reappears and yells something in Polish that makes him start the engine.

'Sorry,' he says apologetically, closing the window.

The journey home takes forty-five minutes, and Anna has to direct the driver for the last section. As they pass the bend where she lost control of the car, she shuts her eyes. She doesn't want to see the police tape or how close to death they actually were.

Tabor is dark and silent when she arrives. Only the outside light is on, and she leans forward to see if there's a little white figure waiting on the top step. Nothing. She feels an increasingly heavy weight on her chest.

When the cab has gone she switches on all the lights in the house before going back outside.

'Milo!' she shouts. 'Miiii-looo!'

All she can hear is the wind soughing in the treetops.

She leaves the front door open in case he turns up. She picks up the cordless phone and after a couple of attempts remembers the pin code so that she can check the voicemail messages on her mobile.

First there's one from her solicitor, which she deletes, then one that surprises her.

'Hi, it's Alex ... Morell.' He sounds unsure of himself. 'I just wanted to check how you were. I've been thinking about what you said. About the boy I was, and the man I became. I don't know when my life stopped, but I'm intending to reclaim it. Whatever it takes ...'

He seems to forget what he was going to say, or else he simply changes his mind, because the call ends abruptly.

She moves on to the third message and immediately recognises the commissioner's rasping voice. He begins by saying he was sorry to hear about the accident, and that he's pleased and relieved to learn that they're all OK, but she knows exactly what he wants. The weight on her chest increases.

'... decided to transfer you to a new post here in Malmö in my office, where your unique skills will find a more appropriate outlet. Better career prospects, higher salary ...'

He makes it sound like a promotion, a step up. He even stresses the fact that he has absolute confidence in her, and ends by saying that the most important thing right now is for her to take plenty of time to recover from the accident and focus on her family. Anna has no doubt about what's happened; all she has to do is compare the times. The commissioner's message was left less than two hours after her meeting with Bengt Andersson. The car accident was the straw that broke the camel's back and made the commissioner give in to the pressure from Andersson and Morell's friends in high places, presumably with the scrawny little governor at the forefront.

An hour or so pushing papers around in order to magic up a suitable post for her, then she gets the sack. Because that's what's happened, in spite of the commissioner's assurances to the contrary. The men have won, and she's been kicked out. She is finding it difficult to breathe. The air in the kitchen feels thick, her lungs are far too small.

She goes outside and sits on the step. Takes several deep breaths, inhaling the cold evening air.

Still no Milo. Tomorrow she's going to have to tell Agnes that the dog her father gave her, the last link they have to Håkan, is probably dead. Suddenly she bursts into tears, with no warning. She and Agnes wept together earlier, but this is something completely different. She wraps her arms around her knees and rests her head on them, sobs so hard that she can hardly breathe. She wishes that Håkan was still inside her head, that he would say something reassuring, tell her that everything is somehow going to be all right. Tell her she'll be able to get through this setback. But Håkan has left her and Agnes, and he will never come back. Just like Milo.

She cries for several minutes, until she begins to feel a little better. Something cold touches her hand. She wipes her eyes and looks up.

It's Milo, his head on one side, looking as if he's pleased to see her, but isn't quite prepared to admit it. She grabs his collar, pulls the stupid dog close and hugs him as tightly as she can. Milo doesn't protest, and after a few seconds he begins to lick her cheeks.

She hears footsteps on the gravel. Mats Andersson is slowly making his way across the yard.

'So, you're back,' he says, glancing towards the kitchen.

'Only me. Agnes will be staying in hospital for a few days.'

'Oh.' His mouth turns down in disappointment. 'How is she?'

'Pretty good, under the circumstances.'

Mats nods. 'Aunt Elisabet told me about the accident, so I drove down. The police had put up that blue-and-white tape all over the place. While I was standing there, he came running.' The big man points to Milo, who is still sitting on her lap. 'He was cold and wet and hungry, so I took him home to Änglaberga, gave him a bath and fed him.'

'Thank you so much. Agnes will be delighted. I was . . .' She pauses, clears her throat. 'We were afraid he'd ended up at the bottom of the river with the car.'

Mats shakes his head. 'Not this little guy. He's way too tough for that.'

'Would you like to come in?' she says. 'Not that I have anything to offer you.'

He shakes his head again. 'No, I need to get home – I have things to do.' He leans forward, rubs Milo between the ears with an enormous hand, then turns away. Milo whimpers, wriggles free and runs after him.

'Mats, wait!' Anna gets to her feet and beckons him. 'Would you like to visit Agnes in hospital tomorrow?'

His face lights up beneath the shaggy beard. 'Can I?'

She nods, makes a decision. 'Actually, could I ask you to take Milo with you? It's probably not in accordance with the hospital regulations, but it would make all the difference to her.'

Mats's smile widens. 'No problem. I'll tuck him underneath my coat.'

He winks, opens his jacket to show her what he means.

'Excellent. Visiting is from nine o'clock. She's on ward nineteen, room four.'

Mats nods contentedly; he almost looks happy. Anna feels better too, as if the little dog and the big man have given her fresh strength.

'Thanks again, Mats,' she says, holding out her hand.

He shakes it slowly in a paw twice the size of hers. He still looks happy, but she notices him glancing up at the window of the chapel.

'By the way, you don't need to feel guilty about not telling Elisabet what you saw at the quarry, Mats. Marie had already told her.'

He is clearly taken aback; it's as if he doesn't really understand what she means.

'Your aunt already knew about the fight,' she clarifies. 'Marie told her just after your mother died. That's why Elisabet isn't angry with her.'

Mats smiles uncertainly.

'So, the fact that you didn't say anything doesn't matter at all,' Anna concludes.

He nods, and his face brightens again.

'I don't suppose you remember anything else about what happened after the fight?' Anna adds. Old habits die hard.

'No. I headed for home when the rain started.'

'How did you get home?' She is thinking about Simon's bike.

'Moped,' he says, quashing her hope that she might have solved that particular mystery. 'It was pouring down, I had trouble finding it in the darkness.'

'On the way home I met a car on a bend and came off, like I said. I've still got the scar.' He pats his leg. 'People drive like lunatics on the ridge, as you might have noticed.'

He scratches the back of his neck. There is relief in his smile now, as if he's beginning to realise the significance of what she's just said.

'Thank you for telling me about Marie. It's been on my mind for a long time, but I didn't dare say anything.'

'We're the ones who need to thank you, Mats. You saved Milo – you're the hero of the hour!'

His smile broadens and he nods in farewell, turns away and heads back into the forest with Milo skipping around his feet.

'Stupid dog,' Anna mutters. She is smiling too.

57

Autumn 2017

She starts the day by calling the insurance company and sorting out the practical details surrounding the car accident. Then she takes a cab to a car rental company on the outskirts of Helsingborg, hires a car and drives to the hospital. When she walks into Agnes's room, she is met by an unexpected sight.

Agnes is sitting up in bed with an excited Milo in her arms. He is busy licking every tiny bit of skin he can reach. Mats is standing by the wall looking very happy to be there. On the table beside him there is a bouquet of flowers that must have cost a fortune. It is not until she sees the other two people in the room that the picture makes sense. Elisabet Vidje is sitting in the visitor's chair, with Bror Klein standing next to her.

'Hi, Mum!' Agnes says in a cheerful voice that Anna hasn't heard for years. It immediately disperses all those gloomy thoughts about the commissioner, her job, and other irrelevant details. 'Look at the lovely flowers Aunt Elisabet and Klein brought me!'

Agnes seems to be enjoying being the centre of attention, and Anna doesn't begrudge her a second of it.

'Beautiful, darling.' She bends down to kiss her daughter, expecting Milo to growl as he always does in similar situations, but the dog simply looks up at her with his head on one side. He even wags his tail.

Anna turns to Klein and is about to thank him when Lisa Savic arrives. Her left arm is still in a sling, but she looks much brighter.

'Hi, Lisa!' Agnes says, clearly delighted to have even more visitors.

'Hi! Gosh, so many people!' Lisa says, smiling and nodding at Elisabet. Her expression grows serious when she looks at Klein. 'You were the one who rescued me from the river.'

Klein gives the faintest of nods. Lisa comes into the room, wraps her uninjured arm around his neck and hugs him tightly. Klein's stony face barely moves, but it is possible to detect a slight twitch at one corner of his mouth, and a brief flash of something in his eyes. It is over in a second, and he has rearranged his features long before Lisa lets go of him.

'Me too,' Anna says. 'If it hadn't been for you, we wouldn't be sitting here now.'

Klein gives a brief nod, then purses his lips in almost exactly the same way as Elisabet does.

'I was on my way down from the village,' he says. 'I saw the skid marks on the road and the cloud of dust among the trees – I knew something had happened. Anyone would have done the same.'

'You're far too modest,' Elisabet says, patting his arm. 'Enjoy the praise – you've earned it!'

Klein looks uncomfortable, and a faint flush colours his cheeks. Anna wonders whether it's down to the gesture or the situation in general. Are Klein and Elisabet really involved in a secret relationship? She's becoming more and more convinced that this could be the case.

'You must be his wife.' Lisa holds out her hand to Elisabet.

The handshake is a little awkward. 'No, Klein and I are just old friends. Or maybe I should say lifelong companions. Two people sharing one fate . . .' She pats Klein's arm again as Anna continues to observe them. Is this nothing more than a game?

'You look familiar,' Elisabet goes on in her usual direct way. 'But your accent isn't local.'

Lisa shakes her head. 'No, I'm only visiting.'

'Oh well, there you go – my memory isn't what it used to be. How's your arm?'

'Broken collarbone, but it could have been much worse.'

Only now does Anna notice how tired Elisabet looks. Her face is even paler than the last time they met, and the skin is so transparent that the veins are visible in places. Technically she is still angry with Elisabet, but right now she's finding it difficult to summon up those emotions.

'I won't disturb you any longer,' Lisa adds. 'If it's OK with you, Agnes, I'll come back later.'

Agnes nods. Lisa looks at Klein once more. 'Thanks again,' she says before leaving the room.

Oddly enough, the crowded room feels slightly empty when Lisa has gone, so Anna makes an effort to get some small talk going. She thanks Elisabet for her concern and for the beautiful flowers, which as expected provokes pursed lips and a dismissive wave. Agnes picks up on the atmosphere and talks to Mats about how soft Milo's coat is, asks what dog shampoo he used. The conversation fills the vacuum for a little while. Klein remains silent as usual.

After a while Elisabet laboriously gets to her feet and signals to Anna to follow her into the corridor. Klein moves to join them, but is immediately waved away.

'I really am sorry for how things ended between us last time,' Elisabet says as soon as they are alone. 'Klein and I have talked, and I now realise that I came across as . . .' she searches for the right word, 'cold. That wasn't my intention, and I hope you can accept my apology. You've been a great help to us, Anna, and we're very grateful.'

Anna doesn't respond immediately, and Elisabet looks uneasy. 'The fact is . . .' she goes on after a few seconds of silence, 'Klein and I are going to visit Karl-Johan in a while. His nursing home is less than fifteen minutes by car from here. I'd be very pleased if you'd like to come with us.'

Anna is sitting in the back seat of Klein's well-maintained old pickup truck. Mats has offered to stay with Agnes, and with both him and Milo there, she couldn't see any reason to turn down the trip. She has been curious about Karl-Jo ever since she was a little girl, and she also wants to take the opportunity to study Klein and Elisabet together.

Like most men over seventy, Klein drives a little too slowly. Neither he nor Elisabet say anything, and even though Anna usually has nothing against silence, eventually she feels compelled to break it.

'I met some of the Poles outside the emergency department at the hospital yesterday. Apparently, one of them had had an accident in the forest.'

Klein and Elisabet exchange a glance, and at first, he seems unwilling to comment.

'It wasn't an accident,' he says after quite a while. 'Pawel trod on one of Mats's traps. Mats knows he's not allowed to set gin traps, but he's got it into his head that he's going to catch a wolf. He won't listen to—'

Elisabet gently taps his leg, which makes him shut up. The gesture is so intimate that Anna can't help raising her eyebrows.

'We're here,' Elisabet says. 'You can park over there.'

The nursing home is surrounded by tall trees and green lawns. A nurse shows them into a visitors' room, her voice softening when she talks about Karl-Johan. Huge picture windows look out over the park, where two gardeners in yellow jackets are raking up leaves. Progress is slow; the park is so big and there are so many leaves that the task seems overwhelming.

Karl-Johan Vidje is sitting in an armchair with a blanket over his knees, facing the two men. Anna and Klein hang back while Elisabet goes over and kisses him on the cheek. He gives a start, then takes her arm as if he's glad to see her. Elisabet exchanges a few words with him, then beckons Anna to join them.

'This is Anna Vesper – I told you about her. She and her daughter have moved into Tabor. Anna has been a great help to us.'

Karl-Johan is well over seventy, but his hair is still blond rather than white, and he has surprisingly few wrinkles. His expression is kind, his smile warm. He is wearing a pair of close-fitting dark glasses.

'Anna,' he says, shaking her hand in a way that makes Anna think he's repeating her name silently to himself.

'We had one of your lithographs at home when I was growing up,' she says. 'I liked it very much.'

Karl-Johan nods, but something in his face tells her that he probably doesn't understand who she is or what she's doing there. She carries on talking anyway, telling him about the lithograph and where her father bought it. Karl-Johan keeps on nodding. In spite of the glasses and the dementia, there is something appealing not just in his face and smile, but in the energy surrounding him. She thinks about the photographs she saw at Änglaberga and in Klein's lodge, how attractive yet vulnerable he was. She can easily imagine why Elisabet fell head over heels in love with him. He may be blind and incapacitated, but Karl-Johan still makes an impression on the people he meets, and Anna is no exception. Would Elisabet really have cheated on him with Klein? Or is it just that the two of them have found support in each other? She chooses to believe that is the case, and reproaches herself for speculating about rumour and village gossip that has nothing to do with her. Whether she likes it or not, the Vidje family have got under her skin, and this visit merely confirms that.

She finishes talking about the lithograph, and doesn't quite know what else to say.

'Anna,' Karl-Johan says again. 'Anna.'

'We're living at Tabor,' she adds. 'In your old studio.'

His smile doesn't alter.

'I found your old sl ...' she swallows the stammer, takes a moment, 'slide in one of the outhouses.'

Karl-Johan's face lights up. 'Sl ... slide,' he says, tripping up over the word in exactly the same place as she did, which makes her like him even more.

'We used to use it. Simon and me, through the hole in the wall.' He nods, smiling warmly. 'My little boy.'

A sudden lump in her throat makes Anna swallow hard. She is lost for words, but Elisabet comes to her rescue.

'Anna and her daughter have settled in really well at Tabor. It's lovely, isn't it, Anna?'

'Lovely,' she replies, trying to sound cheerful, but it's hard. All she can think about is the photograph of Karl-Johan and Simon. How happy they both looked. *My little boy . . .*

She swallows again.

'Tabor,' Karl-Johan says, his smile more introverted now, as if his failing brain has conjured up an image only he can see. However, within seconds his expression changes and he looks anxious.

'The deer,' he says, shuffling uncomfortably in his armchair. 'The deer that died. It wasn't my fault. It wasn't my fault.'

He turns his head from side to side, as if his blind eyes see things in the room that are upsetting him. He grabs hold of Anna's wrist and pulls her close.

'It wasn't my fault. It wasn't my fault.'

Anna doesn't know what to do. His grip is tight, and she can't free herself without making a scene. He continues to repeat the words, louder and louder. There is despair in his voice, and his face is contorted in pain.

'It wasn't my fault. It wasn't my fault!'

Elisabet tries to talk to him, but he's not listening. He draws Anna even closer, his fingers digging into her wrist.

'It wasn't my fault,' he gasps right next to her face. She can see tears seeping beneath the frame of his glasses and trickling down his cheeks.

'I . . . I . . .' She still has no idea what to say or do. Karl-Johan shows no sign of letting go, he just keeps on repeating those same words as the tears flow.

Klein appears from nowhere and loosens Karl-Johan's grip, then almost pushes Anna away before bending down and whispering something in the older man's ear. She catches a glimpse of Klein's face. The stony mask is gone, replaced by the same tense expression she saw when they first met, up in the chapel.

She can't hear what Klein says, but whatever it is, it calms Karl-Johan. Klein pulls up a chair and sits down. Takes Karl-Johan's hand as he continues to whisper to him. Anna stays where she is, but all she can hear are sounds with no discernible syllables. It's as if Klein is humming rather than talking.

'Come away,' Elisabet says gently, taking her arm.

'I'm so sorry,' Anna begins as soon as they're out of earshot, but Elisabet dismisses her apology.

'It's nothing to do with you,' she says wearily. 'Karl-Johan's thoughts have a life of their own, and it seems as if today isn't a good day. Klein knows how to handle him. We'll leave them in peace for a while, then we'll go back to the hospital.'

When they emerge from the nursing home later on, the wind is rustling the treetops ominously. The sky above the sound is the colour of lead, and it has started to rain.

'There's a storm coming,' Klein says. The stony expression is back, with no trace of what just happened. 'The forecast is for a storm tonight.'

58

Autumn 2017

Klein pulls up in the hospital car park and apologises for the fact that they're not coming in; Elisabet needs to rest.

'Just one question,' Anna says as she's about to get out. She's had time to think, and she wants the matter cleared up. 'Simon's bike, the one he used to cycle to the quarry – what make was it?'

'An orange Crescent,' Klein mumbles. 'With drop handlebars.'

'Did you get it back afterwards?'

Klein and Elisabet exchange a glance.

'No,' Elisabet says. 'Not as far as I remember, anyway, but there was so much going on that I can't be sure. Is it important?'

Anna shrugs. 'I don't know. The bike isn't mentioned in the police report either; I just wanted to check whether you knew where it had gone.'

One of the stricter nurses has discovered Milo in Agnes's room, so it is decided that Mats will keep him for a few more days. He clearly thinks this is a brilliant idea, but Anna hates the idea of going home to an empty house.

Lisa calls in a while later. She has been discharged, and tentatively asks if she can have a lift back to Nedanås.

'Are you going home?' Agnes asks.

'Tomorrow – I just need to rebook my train ticket. I hope I can stay at the hotel for another night; I was supposed to check out yesterday.'

'Why don't you stay at our place?' Agnes suggests. 'My room's empty, and Mum doesn't like being alone.'

'What do you think, Lisa?' Anna says.

'That would be great – if you're sure it's no trouble.'

After lunch Agnes feels tired, and it's time to leave. Lisa gives her a goodbye hug, and promises to get in touch later in the week.

On the way home they stop off at the shopping centre outside the village, and Anna buys herself a phone like the one she got Agnes recently. With the help of the sales assistant she manages to transfer her old numbers to the new phone. During the rest of the drive they talk about Simon Vidje. Lisa has worked out who Klein and Elisabet are, and wants to know more about the visit to Karl-Johan.

When they reach Nedanås Anna drops Lisa off at the hotel, then continues to the police station. The storm over the sound hasn't yet made landfall, but the wind is stronger now. The smell from Glarea is noticeable; presumably they're burning as much as they can before they have to close down.

Her pass card still works, so she doesn't have to go through reception to reach her office. She unlocks the bottom drawer and takes out all the documentation relating to the Simon Vidje case, the garage fire at Änglaberga, and Joe Rylander's death. She photocopies everything, then places the originals in a neat pile on her desk. She folds the copies and puts them in her pocket. She's about to leave when she notices a fat envelope in her pigeonhole.

Anna Vesper, Police, Nedanås, it says on the outside in spidery handwriting. She slips it into her pocket as well.

At the bottom of the stairs she almost cannons into Jens Friberg. She swears silently to herself; he was the one person she'd hoped to avoid.

'Oh, hi,' he says. He is clearly embarrassed and doesn't know where to look.

'I'm guessing you've already heard?' Anna says.

He nods.

'And the commissioner has asked you to take over?'

No reply, which is the same as yes. A dull rumble makes the floor vibrate, but these days she barely reacts to the blasting.

'So, you got what you wanted in the end,' she says acidly. 'Your dream job.'

Jens shakes his head. 'I turned it down.'

'What? But why?'

'We're moving.' He says 'we', without elaborating who he means. Under different circumstances she would have been interested.

'Where to?'

Jens shrugs. 'Somewhere where the police work is less . . . complicated. I've applied for a couple of other posts, so we'll see what happens. Anyway, I wanted to thank you for trusting me. Involving me in the investigation in spite of our . . . rocky start. I've learned a lot from working with you.'

There is a slightly awkward silence. This whole conversation has taken Anna by surprise, and she doesn't know what to say. Jens reddens, tries to hide it by looking at his diver's watch.

'I've enjoyed working with you too, Jens,' she says, extending her hand. 'Good luck.'

'Same to you, boss.'

He holds onto her hand for a little longer than necessary, then gives her what could easily be a sympathetic smile.

She picks up Lisa from the hotel and helps her to load her case into the boot of the hire car. On the way home to Tabor she decides to forget her duty of confidentiality, and shares Alex Morell's account of what happened on the night Simon died. Lisa listens carefully, and asks a couple of questions.

'But he's sure that neither my mum nor my dad was there when the trouble started?'

'According to Alex, it was their departure that kicked everything off. The anger they felt towards Joe was directed at Simon instead.'

'So, you could say that it was all partly down to my dad . . . I mean, Joe. What he did to Carina was the catalyst.'

'Maybe, but what I gathered from Alex was that the other four had been getting increasingly annoyed with Simon all evening. Plus, they'd been smoking weed, some of them for the first time, and they'd drunk a considerable amount of alcohol, so there were several factors at work. A series of unfortunate circumstances, you could say.'

They pass the hairpin bend where they came off the road only forty-eight hours ago, and both fall silent.

'What a terrible story,' Lisa says eventually. 'Five people who were close friends, who really liked one another, get into a fight on that one evening. One evening out of all those years, and everything is destroyed. How do you recover from something like that? From being involved in someone's death? Someone you loved?'

The question is rhetorical, but because of her own experience, Anna feels compelled to answer.

'You don't.'

She parks the car and carries Lisa's case into Agnes's room. Her body is still tender, and even though the case isn't heavy, she notices that the small amount of exertion takes its toll.

She shows Lisa around the ground floor, then they go up to the chapel. Anna takes her time on the steep staircase, leaning against the shiny bannister where the impressions left by Karl-Johan's fingers can still be seen. Lisa spends ages admiring the view. The sky is dark grey now, and the treetops down below are swaying violently in the wind, shedding the last of their leaves.

'So, this is the famous painting?' Lisa crosses the room and stands in front of the mural. 'I can't see a body in the water.'

Anna goes over to the lamp that Agnes rigged up. She switches it on, wishing that Agnes was here to do it herself. Just as before, the light makes Simon's body appear. Lisa inhales sharply. Anna lingers for a moment, then decides to leave Lisa in peace while she makes a start on dinner. As she turns away she notices something on the floor, not far from the left-hand corner. There are black lines on the white floorboards. It looks as if they've been made by a thick rubber sole. She can't remember having seen them before – but surely she must have done?

After dinner she settles Lisa and her broken collarbone in front of the TV, takes out the photocopies she made earlier and spreads them across the kitchen table. One last look, then she's going to let it go. At least that's what she tries to tell herself.

She reads through the documents once more, tries to match them with Alex Morell's account. Just as before, she finds no discrepancies. Joe tries it on with Carina, there's a row, Simon defends Tanya and Joe, Tanya and Joe leave. Alex, Bruno, Marie and Carina turn on Simon. Five people who really liked each other, just as Lisa said.

We always have the worst quarrels with the ones we love.

She read that somewhere just after her divorce. At the time she thought it was just about romantic love, but now she's older and wiser she realises that the assertion can be applied to all kinds of love – between friends, siblings, parents and children.

She slits open the envelope that was in her pigeonhole. It contains a bundle of letters secured with a brown rubber band. They are all addressed to Joakim Rylander, and she remembers the voicemail message from Rylander's stepfather a week or so ago. Technically, the letters belong to Lisa now, but she decides to take a look at them anyway.

Rylander's mail consists mainly of bills, reminders from the probation service, and a couple of notifications from the police, along with direct advertising from credit card companies who don't seem too fussy about who they offer their money to. One envelope catches her attention. It's from a company in the USA called Regeneration. Inside there is a form made up of various boxes, plus a letter which she quickly skims through. It is written in English.

Dear Mr Rylander.

The samples you supplied indicate with a 99.99% degree of certainty that the two individuals concerned are not related to each other.

Anna tries to make sense of what she's just read. It seems that Joe Rylander sent material to the USA for DNA comparison. And there was no match.

She looks for the date on the form. Finds a box marked 'Sample Date', and an idea begins to take shape.

'Lisa!' she calls out. 'Do you remember when your father came to see you?'

'Twentieth of September, I think. Why?'

Anna looks at the box. The sample was received on 25 September. Her heart begins to beat faster.

'You don't remember if anything was missing after his visit?'

'No.'

'Something you couldn't find later on? Something that struck you as a bit odd?'

'Nooo,' Lisa says again, sounding a little more hesitant this time. 'Actually . . . now you come to mention it, there was something I never found an explanation for.'

'Go on.'

'My toothbrush went missing.'

The penny drops inside Anna's head.

'When were you born, Lisa?'

'Twenty-fourth of April 1991 – why?'

Anna does a quick calculation on her fingers. Less than eight months after the incident in the quarry. Eight months – that's why no one made the connection. Not until twenty-seven years later, when Joe Rylander receives a letter from Elisabet Vidje and puts two and two together. At last, she understands what actually happened that night.

'You were premature, weren't you?' she says.

There is a brief silence, then Lisa appears in the doorway. Lisa, whose name is not a coincidence. Lisa, which is short for Elisabet.

'How did you know that?' Lisa asks, frowning. 'How did you know I was premature?'

'Because Joe Rylander isn't your father,' Anna says slowly. 'It's Simon Vidje.'

59

Autumn 2017

Anna doesn't know why she didn't see the connection earlier. Lisa is blonde like Simon, and works with music. Plus, she has an aura that makes people take to her right away, just like Karl-Johan. Then there's Simon's cassette tape, which Tanya kept for all those years.

Both Caia Bianca and Elisabet said they thought Lisa looked familiar, and still Anna didn't react, which really annoys her.

Lisa hasn't said anything for several minutes. Her face is ashen, and Anna can almost see her thought process. She fetches a glass of water, and Lisa drinks it straight down. The colour slowly returns to her cheeks.

'We don't know for sure that Joe tested himself against me, do we?' she says.

'No, but it's highly likely. Who else would it have been?'

'What I mean is, how can we be absolutely certain that Simon is my father?'

'We'll have to do a new test, comparing your DNA to a close relative of Simon's – so we'll have to talk to Elisabet Vidje and explain that she's probably your grandmother.'

Lisa puts down her glass with a bang.

'I know it sounds weird, but is there any chance we could do that this evening? I have to go home first thing tomorrow, and I'd really like to be there when you tell her.' She sounds agitated, but resolute.

Anna raises her eyebrows and looks out of the window. It's dark now, the rain is hammering against the glass, and the wind is making the rafters creak.

'It might be better to wait,' she says.

'Why?' Lisa gets to her feet. 'If we've decided to talk to Elisabet, then we might as well do it now. It's not that late.'

Anna considers blaming the weather. The sensible thing would be to wait, think about what all this means, but a part of her is just as eager as Lisa to share what they've discovered. After all that's happened, to be able to give the tragedy of Simon Vidje if not a happy ending, then at least a happier ending. Plus, she has to admit that it's only right for Lisa to be there when Elisabet is told.

'OK. I'll get the car keys.'

The wind is roaring through the treetops as they run to the car. The windscreen is covered in dead leaves. Anna sets off, driving slowly along the dark forest track. Neither of them speaks; the atmosphere inside the car is tense and expectant at the same time.

They've almost reached the avenue leading to Änglaberga when they see blue flashing lights. They meet an ambulance just by Klein's lodge, and Anna moves to the side to let it pass. The driver is alone in the cab, and seems to be in a hurry. Anna and Lisa look at each other.

'Should we turn back?' Lisa wonders anxiously.

'Let's go and find out what's happened,' Anna says.

All the lights in the house are on, and the front door is ajar. Anna knocks and goes in. The place feels deserted. They hear a sound from the room where she and Elisabet sat the other day.

'Hello – is anyone there?'

One of the heavy armchairs is lying on its side. On the floor there is discarded packaging she recognises – the kind paramedics leave behind when they're in a rush.

Marie Sordi gets up from another armchair when they walk in. She is pale, her lips pressed together in a thin line.

'What's happened?' Anna asks. 'We met an ambulance by the lodge.'

Marie tries to compose herself.

'It's Aunt Elisabet,' she says quietly. 'I found her on the floor.'

'Is she alive?'

'Yes, but it doesn't look good. Klein went in the ambulance with her. I'm going to follow them as soon as I've ...' Marie gestures towards the mess on the floor, then tries to lift the armchair. Anna helps her. She's only known Elisabet for a few weeks, and they've had their differences, but the news has upset her. Lisa looks shocked too.

'What are you doing here anyway?' Marie asks once the chair is upright. 'It's gone eight o'clock.'

'We thought we'd call in and see Elisabet,' Anna says, turning her head to try and signal to Lisa not to give anything away, but Lisa has gone over to the fireplace and is looking at the photographs on the mantelpiece.

'I'm guessing this must be Simon?' She picks up the baby photo of Simon and his father.

'Yes.' Marie straightens up, adjusts her glasses.

'We're alike,' Lisa murmurs.

'Sorry?'

Lisa turns with the photo in her hand, realises what she's said. 'They're alike,' she says quickly. 'Simon and his dad.'

After a second or two, Marie nods.

'I have to go. Anna, could you possibly pick those up while I turn off the lights, then I'll lock up?' She gestures towards the packaging on the floor.

'Of course.' Anna drops to her knees as Marie closes the door behind her.

'What if we don't get to tell her?' Lisa says. 'What if Elisabet dies without knowing I'm her grandchild?'

Anna has already had the same thought. It would be terrible if Elisabet Vidje has waited twenty-seven years for some kind of justice, then dies just before the whole story takes a fresh twist.

'We'll just have to keep our fingers crossed that she recovers,' she says, getting up and going over to the wastepaper basket. There is a small picture of a lynx above the desk, painted by Karl-Jo. The animal is alive, unlike the poor creature in Mats's basement. She sees the stuffed lynx in her mind's eye, the pain etched on its face, the trap that has bitten through its flesh, all the way to the bone. She thinks about the poor Pole who has apparently suffered the same fate, and she suddenly remembers something. In all the confusion after the car accident, she has almost forgotten the recently bandaged wound on Joe Rylander's leg. An injury like that could easily have been caused by a gin trap.

She turns to the phone with the extra-large buttons and the sticky labels on the desk. She picks up the receiver and presses 3 for Mats. It rings out four times before he answers.

'Hello?'

'It's Anna Vesper. I want to ask you about your gin traps.'

Silence. 'I'll get rid of them. It's not my fault that Pawel can't read warning notices in Swedish.'

'That's not why I'm calling.' She realises how irritated she sounds, and modifies her tone. 'Where have you set traps?'

Silence again, as if Mats is trying to work out what she wants him to say. 'In the forest up here,' he says. 'Not far from where I caught that badger the other week, when you and Agnes were there. But I've put up notices.'

'Anywhere else?'

Another silence.

'You can't tell anybody. She'll be furious if she finds out.'

'Who? Where else have you set your traps?'

Mats sighs loudly. 'In Vargadalen.'

'Vargadalen? Behind Kotorp?'

She can almost hear the last pieces of the puzzle falling into place in her brain. Suddenly she understands how everything fits together.

'It's called Norrblicka,' Marie says from the doorway. 'Not Kotorp. Put the phone down please, Anna.'

Her voice is icy. In her hand is a black pistol.

60

Autumn 2017

A nna and Lisa are sitting in armchairs, while Marie is standing in the middle of the room in front of them.

'This belonged to my grandfather,' Marie says, weighing the gun in her hand. 'He got it from a German deserter during the war. Aunt Elisabet kept it in her safe, but before you get any ideas, I know that Klein tested it once a year to make sure it was still working, just in case . . .' She makes a little circle in the air with the barrel. 'And now is the time for "just in case", wouldn't you say?'

Lisa hasn't said a word for the last few minutes, but she seems to have recovered from the shock – partly, at least. 'Why . . .? What . . .?' She turns to Anna.

'Änglaberga,' Anna says slowly. 'This isn't about Simon's death, it's about Änglaberga. That was why Joe Rylander died, wasn't it?'

Marie gives a crooked smile.

'Marie's father, Bengt, and the local gravel company, Glarea, need new resources to replace the open cast mine down in the village,' Anna goes on. 'Marie's place has no land left, but there's plenty at Änglaberga. Rocks, gravel, stone that will last a lifetime, securing job opportunities, growth and property prices. And of course it will provide the seller with enough money to finish her dream project.'

Marie's smile grows a little wider.

'What they say about you is true, Anna – you really are good. So, tell me, what other conclusions have you reached?' She draws another little circle with the gun.

Anna thinks about the phone in her pocket, whether she should try to reach it. She moves a fraction to make it easier.

'You've worked hard for many years to build your relationship with Elisabet Vidje. The fact that you told her about the events leading up to Simon's death wasn't a way of easing your conscience, but a calculated risk to regain her trust. You hoped that she would eventually forgive you. Her niece, the only one who jumped into the water to try and save Simon, the only one who took responsibility.'

She pauses, cautiously slides her right hand closer to her pocket.

'But then Joe Rylander shows up. He uses Simon's song at the homecoming party to see what happens, and when his tactic succeeds beyond all expectation, Joe is convinced that the four of you have something to hide. He starts snooping around, determined to find out more – presumably here at Änglaberga, then after the party, when he thinks Bruno is still held by the police, at Kotorp.'

Marie raises her eyebrows – and the gun.

'I mean Norrblicka,' Anna says, slipping her hand into her pocket. She can feel the phone against her fingertips. She has to keep talking. 'But, unfortunately, Joe stands on a gin trap that has been set to catch a different kind of predator, and has to call for help.'

She's not at all sure about this part of the story, but she can't stop now. She pushes her hand a little deeper.

'So, you find him there, Marie. You help to free him, then take him back to your home. You even bandage his leg. At some point you work out who he is, and why he's snooping around.'

She looks to Marie for confirmation, but the woman's expression doesn't change.

'Unluckily for Joe, he can't keep his mouth shut. He doesn't know anything about Simon Vidje's death, but he's on the trail of another secret.' She turns to Lisa. 'He's realised that Simon is probably your father, which means there's a new heir to Änglaberga. Someone who, whatever it says in Elisabet's will, has the right to at least half of the estate.'

She can almost feel the front of her phone now. If she'd had one with buttons, it would have been fine; she could easily have called the emergency number. With a smartphone it's not that simple.

'So, Joe demands money to keep quiet about you,' she says to Lisa. 'But he picks the wrong person to blackmail. Marie has put everything she has into the family's building project, and is up to her ears in debt. She can't afford to pay Joe, but to let him reveal what he knows would cost her even more, and all those years of hard work and sacrifice would be wasted.'

'So, you killed him?' Lisa says to Marie. She sounds horrified, as if she still hasn't grasped the seriousness of the situation.

Anna searches for the button that will bring her phone to life.

'Joe was an idiot,' Marie says, unexpectedly. 'Now and twenty-seven years ago. He was the kind of man who wound people up just for the sake of it. Made things difficult both for himself and others, just because he could. But to answer your question – he actually killed himself. Anna is right about most things. I came across Joe when I was out walking the dogs early Sunday morning. He was lying in a hollow over in Vargadalen, whimpering like an injured animal. I helped him out of the trap, brought him to one of our outbuildings and bandaged his leg. When he started to feel better he got mouthy, started talking about Lisa, demanded money to keep quiet. So, I locked him in to give me time to think – but he managed to escape.'

She shrugs.

'It was pouring with rain, and he didn't know his way around up here. Plus, he was hurt. The dogs soon picked up his scent, and as we approached the viewpoint, I sent them after him. Joe ran for his life, in spite of his leg. I don't think he even saw the edge in the rain and the darkness. And so . . .' Marie lets out a descending whistle, 'bye bye, Joe!'

She smiles again, straightens her shoulders. She seems very happy to share her story. Anna has been holding her thumb on the start button for long enough to wake up her phone, or at least she hopes so. All she has to do now is suss out how to make a call without looking at the screen.

'Ideally we would have liked to get rid of the body,' Marie goes on. 'I shouldn't think anyone would have missed him if he'd simply disappeared, but as he had the poor taste to land inside the perimeter fence at Glarea, several metres off the ground in a tree, we couldn't get to him. So, we tracked down his car and moved it closer to the viewpoint to make his death look like suicide. We'd already taken care of his phone – which reminds me!'

She waves the gun, and her voice hardens.

'Take out your phones – nice and slowly.'

'I haven't got one,' Lisa says. 'It was damaged in the car accident.'

Marie turns to Anna, and sees that her hand is in her pocket.

'Could the ex-chief of police kindly take out her phone and throw it into that corner?'

Anna reluctantly does as she's told. Her phone skitters across the floor and lands next to the wastepaper basket.

'The car accident,' Lisa says. 'Was that down to you too?'

Marie stares at her, then nods.

'I realised who you were when we saw you at the viewpoint, and I couldn't take the risk that Joe had told you who your real father was. You said you were on your way to the quarry, so all we had to do was follow you. The brake pipe was already bent from the pothole earlier on; it didn't take much to snap it.'

Marie falls silent, listens. They hear the front door open, then footsteps approaching. Anna realises that Marie has used the word 'we' more than once, which means she's not alone; she has a helper. The footsteps echo through the hallway, and suddenly she is convinced that Alex Morell is on his way to join them. Alex, who has invested everything he has into the project at Kotorp, seeing it as his last chance to regain at least part of what he has lost. She thinks back to the message he left on her phone. 'I don't know when my life stopped, but I'm intending to reclaim it. Whatever it takes . . .'

She can picture Alex's tall, bulky body in the driving seat of the Saab as Marie tells him where to move the car to, pictures him lying underneath her car tampering with the brake pipe. She feels dizzy, sick. The door handle is pushed down.

The door opens and Bruno Sordi is standing there.

His face is white. He looks at Lisa, then Anna, and finally at his wife, holding the gun.

'Oh no,' he says with a sigh. 'Now what do we do, darling?'

'I've had some time to think about that,' Marie replies. 'How about another tragic fire, this time with a fatal outcome?'

Bruno sighs again, then nods.

'I guess we don't have a choice.'

61

Autumn 2017

Bruno has brought the Sordi family SUV and parked it next to Anna's car at the front of the house. The two German Shepherds are in the back, and don't jump out until Marie gives them the command.

'In you get,' she orders Anna. 'Back against the seat, make room for her.'

Anna does as she's told. Lisa sits between her legs with her head resting on Anna's chest. She feels the young woman trembling, hears her gasp with pain as she is forced to draw up her injured arm.

'Stay calm,' Anna whispers in her ear.

She finds it hard to follow her own advice when both dogs jump in. They are clearly not pleased at having to share the cramped space.

'The boys won't touch you as long as you keep still,' Marie says as she slams the door shut. The biggest dog lets out a low growl.

Anna closes her eyes. 'Stay calm,' she whispers again, as much for her own benefit as for Lisa's.

Marie starts the engine and sets off along the avenue. The closest dog has decided to lie down, pressing against Anna. She can feel its breath on her leg. It's almost completely dark outside. The rain is hammering on the roof, and the wind tugs at the car from time to time, causing it to veer across the road. Anna raises her head in an attempt to orientate herself, but one of the dogs immediately growls.

Lisa whimpers quietly, her heart beating in time with Anna's. Marie turns left onto a familiar dirt track. She is driving slowly, and after a while another vehicle catches up with them – Bruno, in Anna's hire car.

Bruno and Marie park outside Tabor and unlock the front door with the key they've taken out of her jacket pocket. They don't bother guarding the two women, because there is no need. As soon as either of them moves or speaks, the dogs start growling. Their jaws are at the same height as Anna and Lisa's faces, so close that they can feel their breath.

After a while the windows steam up, and they can't see what Bruno and Marie are doing. Lisa has slumped down, and barely reacts when Anna gently presses her left knee against her side.

'Don't give up,' she whispers. 'We'll get through this. Everything's going to be OK.'

The door opens and the dogs raise their heads.

'Out.' The animals instantly obey Marie's command and sit down at her feet, their eyes fixed on Anna and Lisa.

Anna looks over Marie's shoulder and sees that Bruno has spread a tarpaulin in the boot of her car. He is in the process of transferring two large bales of hay into the porch. Marie follows her gaze.

'I believe it's possible to find evidence of accelerants and petrol after a fire?' she says. 'I've seen it on TV.'

Anna chooses not to respond. Marie is right, of course. Petrol and other accelerants leave chemical traces. Hay, however, is organic material, and will leave very little behind.

'OK, let's get this over with.' She waves the gun, but Lisa doesn't react. 'Move, or I'll ask the boys to help.'

Anna gives Lisa a gentle push, and they clamber laboriously out of the car. The drive was short, but their bodies are stiff, and Lisa is clearly in pain.

Marie waves the gun again. 'Up to the chapel.'

Anna considers her options. She is fairly close to Marie and might be able to grab the gun, but one look at the dogs tells her that they would immediately attack. The thought of being bitten is almost worse than the prospect of being shot.

'Hurry up!'

Lisa has already set off towards the house, and Anna catches her up. Bruno has piled the bales of hay on top of each other just inside the door. He presses himself against the wall to let them pass.

'You don't have to do this, Bruno,' Anna says. 'Rylander's death was an accident, but this is murder in cold blood. Marie is c... c... crazy...'

'Shut the fuck up!' Something hard strikes her on the back of her head, making her jaws clamp together. She stumbles forward, but manages to stop herself from falling. She spins around to defend herself against the next onslaught.

Marie is pointing the gun straight at her, baring her teeth. Her eyes are black. For a second Anna is convinced that Marie is going to shoot her in the face. Bruno's horrified expression indicates that he thinks the same thing.

'Marie,' he says quietly. No response. Her knuckles on the hand gripping the gun whiten. A part of Anna wants to close her eyes, block out the shot and the pain, but she forces herself to keep them open. The dogs growl threateningly, baring their teeth in the same way as their mistress.

'You have no fucking idea,' Marie hisses at her. 'No idea what it means to be the one who always has to hold everything together. Carry all the expectations, all the responsibility. Every single thing...' She raises the gun a fraction, her forefinger squeezing the trigger.

'Darling,' Bruno says, a little louder this time. 'This isn't what we decided. We need to stick to the plan, don't we?'

Marie remains motionless for a few seconds, then slowly lowers the gun. A vestige of sanity returns to her face.

'Never say that again,' she hisses at Anna. 'Never!'

Anna nods.

'Would you please go upstairs,' Bruno says. His tone is so polite that it's almost funny.

When they reach the chapel, Marie gestures towards the painting.

'Go and sit in the corner.'

'Do you really think this is going to work?' Anna ventures. 'Do you seriously think that the police will believe a fire started for no reason?'

The ghost of a smile passes across Marie's face. 'I'm not a police officer, but I'm pretty sure the investigation will show that the foreign tradesmen Aunt Elisabet employed didn't follow Swedish standards when they did the wiring. A short circuit caused by the storm leads to a fire with tragic consequences.' The insanity is back. 'Not least because I'm very close to the person who will be leading the inquiry.'

Anna realises that her mouth has dropped open.

'Oh, didn't you know?' Marie adds scornfully. 'The commissioner has asked Uncle Henry to step in until they find a replacement for you. Jens Friberg turned out to be almost as much of a disappointment as you, so Henry will be in charge. And you already know what he thinks of Aunt Elisabet and her Polish tradesmen, who are putting his beloved Alexander out of business.'

Another wave of the gun.

'OK,' she says. 'For obvious reasons, I'm not going to tie you up. Even Uncle Henry would find it hard to ignore that kind of evidence. As I'm sure you know, there are only two ways out. It's up to you whether you choose to jump out of the window or die of smoke inhalation.'

Marie backs away, accompanied by the dogs, and disappears down the stairs. A second later they hear a thud, a rustling sound, then the front door closes. Anna leaps to her feet and runs to the top of the stairs. The two bales of hay are already burning, the flames half a metre high and spreading fast. Thick black smoke is rapidly finding its way up to the chapel. There is no chance of escaping by that route, and even if there were, Marie, Bruno and the dogs would be waiting for them.

Anna races down the other staircase, the one leading to the main door. She remembers the sturdy iron bar on the outside, but it's worth a try. The door doesn't move.

'Anna!' Lisa shouts. She hurries back to the chapel. The flames have already taken hold of the stairs, the bannister and the walls, licking up the dry wood with terrifying speed. The smoke makes her cough. She runs over to the window, grabs one of Agnes's camera bags and slams it against the glass as hard as she can. The hole she makes is the size of a football. She keeps on bashing, shards of glass and splinters of wood from the frames whirl around her, and the wind and rain come rushing in. She takes several deep breaths; the fire behind her is eagerly sucking up the oxygen. She pushes her head out through the hole and looks along the side of the building, desperately searching for something to help her climb or cling to, but there is nothing, not even guttering, just a steep roof and shiny tiles, as slippery as ice from the pouring rain. She avoids looking down.

'Anna!'

She turns and a wave of heat hits her full in the face. The fire has reached the top of the stairs, and a long orange pillar is climbing one wall – tall enough to lick the beams on the ceiling. The roar of the flames is mixed with the crackling of old wood, which is burning faster and faster. The acrid smoke sears her eyes and nose.

She sticks her head outside again, inhales the fresh, cold air and tries to work out how far off the ground they are. Joe Rylander's broken body immediately appears in her mind's eye. The drop is greater than the one at Glarea – seventy, eighty metres, maybe more, and definitely too much for anyone to survive if they jumped.

When she turns again, it is difficult to see because of all the smoke. She coughs and edges towards the corner where Lisa is sitting. Within seconds she has to drop to her knees. The smoke is thicker now; it's hard to breathe. Tears are pouring from her eyes, and she can only just make out Lisa by the wall. She crawls along, feeling her way across the floor. The heat is intensifying all the time.

'Anna ...' Lisa's voice is right beside her. They wrap their arms around each other and press their bodies up against the wood panelling. The stained-glass windows begin to explode because of the heat, and Anna is out of ideas. All they can do is huddle in the corner and wait for the inevitable end. Her head is heavy, she pictures Agnes. Agnes, who will be an orphan at the age of sixteen.

The whole building is creaking now; the fire has spread to the roof. Anna squeezes her eyes tight shut, blinking away the tears, coughing uncontrollably. Suddenly she feels a movement against her shoulder. The panel on her right shudders, then disappears outwards. At first, she thinks the place is beginning to collapse, but she can't understand why it's started at the furthest point from the seat of the fire. Fresh air comes pouring in, dispersing the smoke around them so that it becomes easier to see and to breathe. A hole has opened up in the wall, a hole so perfectly symmetrical that there must have been a well-hidden trapdoor. A trapdoor made to give access to a slide. She senses a movement, and a big head appears. It is Mats Andersson.

Without a word he grabs her arm and pulls her towards him. The movement is so rapid and forceful that she doesn't have time to react before she is out through the hole, hanging over Mats's shoulder. Her eyes are still streaming, but she can just make out an old iron ladder propped against the side of the house. At the foot of the ladder is a little white shape with its hackles raised, tail up. Mats drops her on the ground right next to Milo, but the dog barely gives her a glance. His attention is on the corner nearest the yard, and a faint gurgling is coming from his throat. The icy rain soon brings her round; she coughs and points to the upper floor to let Mats know that someone else is still inside, but he is already halfway up the ladder. He reaches inside, and in no time Lisa's apparently lifeless body is draped over his shoulder. Anna gets to her feet, rubs the rain and soot from her face and helps Mats to lay Lisa down. Her face is stained with tears and soot and her eyes are closed, but within seconds her eyelids flicker and she starts coughing. Above them the flames break through the roof, hissing angrily as they meet the pouring rain.

'H . . . how?' she asks Mats. She can't possibly form a sentence.

'I saw that you'd called me from Aunt Elisabet's phone, so I went up to the house. You were in the courtyard, and Marie was holding Grandfather's gun. She and Bruno put the two of you in the back of the car with the dogs, even though you don't like dogs. I heard her talking about Tabor. And a fire.' He points to the hole at the top of the ladder. 'I've got in that way at night a few times to look at the wall painting.'

The big man looks embarrassed despite the seriousness of the situation, and Anna understands why. He's the one she's heard up in the chapel at night. He's come in without permission and crept around up there, but this is hardly the moment to get angry with him.

Milo growls again, louder this time. Anna listens carefully; she can just make out voices through the roar of the fire. Marie and Bruno are still in the courtyard, which means the danger is far from over.

'We have to get away from here,' she says, helping Lisa to her feet. 'Can you run?'

Lisa nods, looking surprisingly determined.

'This way,' Mats says, loping off towards the forest. Anna takes Lisa's right hand to help her along.

They stumble between the trees, tripping over roots and uneven ground with increasing frequency as they leave behind the glow of the blaze. Anna is about to ask Mats to slow down because she and Lisa can't keep up with him and Milo when there is a loud shout from Tabor.

'Damn,' Mats mutters. 'They've seen the ladder – I should have taken it down. Hurry up – Marie will set the dogs on us, and they won't obey me.'

He speeds up, and Anna does her best to stay with him. However, Mats is used to the forest, plus she has to help Lisa. After about fifty metres Anna crashes headlong, unable to save herself. There is mud in her mouth, and she has scraped her forehead on something hard and sharp.

'Are you OK?' Lisa says. Anna gets to her feet and nods.

'We have to keep going.'

Mats and Milo have disappeared, and suddenly there is a cacophony of barking behind them. She turns and sees the beams of two torches among the trees. This time Lisa takes her hand, and they set off again.

Their eyes are becoming used to the darkness, and Anna recognises the little brook that she and Agnes once followed. It feels as if several years have passed since then, but in fact the incident with the badger was only a couple of weeks ago.

The barking is getting closer, and she can picture the two big German Shepherds racing along, catching them up metre by metre. She tries to run faster, but her body is sore and she has inhaled a considerable amount of smoke. The taste of blood is in her mouth, and she is beginning to panic. The dogs can't be much more than a hundred metres away now. The track is steep, and she can feel the lactic acid burning her thighs.

'Wait!'

Lisa slows down and Anna drags her over the top of the incline before allowing her to stop. Down on the left she can just make out a hollow, and on one of the nearby trees there is something that doesn't fit in with the environment at all. She takes a couple of steps forward and sees that it's a square sign. The handwriting is large, rounded and slightly childish.

DANGER! TRAPS!

It must have been Mats who put it up. She thinks for a fraction of a second, then tears down the sign and tosses it aside.

'Come on – we have to keep going!' She knows that Mats was hoping a wolf would be attracted by the protective terrain and had therefore set his horrible traps down at the bottom of the hollow. Wolf or dog, it doesn't really matter; all she has to do is lure the animals to the right place.

Lisa has taken off her sling and seems to have regained some of her energy – or maybe Anna's energy has run out, because now Lisa is the one pulling her along.

Her legs are getting heavier, the taste of blood is making her nauseous. Her lungs feel as if they're about to explode. Lisa is doing her best, but they are still slowing down. The barking is no more than fifty metres away now, and the torchlight flickers between the tree trunks.

'I can't go any further,' Anna gasps. 'You go on – straight ahead!' She waves her arm in the general direction of Änglaberga, suppressing a fresh wave of sickness.

'No!'

Anna frees her hand from Lisa's, then bends over and throws up. 'Go, Lisa! I'll delay them.'

She looks around for a weapon and finds a branch. It would be better if it were longer and thicker, but it will have to do. The hollow is between her and their pursuers, and with a bit of luck she should be able to send the dogs down into it.

Lisa hasn't moved.

'Go!' Anna says. 'I'll be fine.'

She has just enough oxygen left to manage those four syllables. Her heart is pounding, the contents of her stomach are halfway up her throat. She turns her back on Lisa, holds the branch in front of her like a spear.

'Go, Lisa!'

The torches are getting closer. She hears the rustle of leaves as Lisa begins to run, then she sees a black, four-legged silhouette among the trees in front of her, with another ten metres behind.

Too far to the left, she thinks as she realises that the dogs have gone around the hollow instead of down into it. The first dog has spotted her, and speeds up.

She pushes the hair off her forehead, wipes away dirt and water. Grips the branch with both hands again. Her heartbeat is thundering against her eardrums, the wind is howling through the treetops. The dog is coming straight at her. Ten metres, five.

She sees open jaws, ears pricked, a body gathering itself to attack. She raises the branch, tenses her whole body, ready for the pain.

She hears something between a roar and a bark from the left, and a white projectile comes flying through the trees. It strikes the

German Shepherd in mid-leap with such force that the big dog is knocked over. The roar grows louder before being interrupted by the sound of jaws clamping together. It's Milo. The little terrier has sunk his teeth into the back of the German Shepherd's neck, and the two of them tumble down the slope into the hollow. The bigger dog is yelping, doing is best to twist around and get at Milo, but Milo has no intention of letting go.

The second German Shepherd arrives, but has no interest in her. Instead, it plunges down the slope to help its friend.

'Milo!' she screams, but it's too late. The bigger dog attacks, and the air is filled with a horrible mixture of growling and roars of pain and anger.

She doesn't even think, she simply hurls herself into the hollow, using the branch to beat the nearest German Shepherd while kicking the other so hard that she feels the impact all the way up to her clenched teeth.

The animal whimpers and staggers away, and for a second, she thinks she's won, but the dog she hit with the branch has simply spun around, and before she can react it has sunk its teeth into her left thigh.

Strangely enough, she feels no pain. Maybe she's so full of adrenaline that the message can't get through. She even has time to study the dog's face, the black eyes, the upper jaw. She is surprised at her icy calm as she slams the end of the branch right between its eyes. The dog lets go and backs away a metre or so. Its teeth are still bared, but it doesn't seem to feel like making a fresh attack. She is aware of a movement by her right leg. Milo has got to his feet. He is a mess, one ear is hanging off and his white fur is bloodstained, but his hackles are still up. The dog she kicked comes into her field of vision from the right. He is limping, and one ear is damaged just like Milo's. It is showing its teeth and growling, but it doesn't look as if it wants to continue the fight either. Anna stabs the branch in the direction of the nearest dog, which makes pain shoot through her leg. She gasps, but at least the dog immediately backs away. She does the same to the first dog and this time Milo joins in. The result is the same. The two German Shepherds look at each other as if they're not quite sure what to do. The expressions on their faces and the damaged ear makes them look kind of pathetic rather than vicious.

'You see – that's what happens when you fuck around with the Vesper family!' she says, without really knowing why. Milo steps forward and barks, just to drive the point home.

Anna turns and looks up the slope. They don't have much time. The pain from the bite is definitely breaking through the adrenaline rush. The beam of a torch suddenly sweeps across the far side of the hollow and past the dogs before blinding her.

'Good dogs!' Marie shouts. 'Attack!'

Both German Shepherds react immediately. Anna can hear them growling, but the light makes it difficult to see them. She shades her eyes, which helps a little.

'Attack!' Marie yells again as she runs down the slope at the other end of the hollow. The wobbling beam makes it easier to locate the threat. The dogs are approaching; Milo barks again, but to no avail this time.

Anna sees Marie running towards her with the gun in one hand and the torch in the other. For a second the beam catches the other woman's face; she looks both triumphant and excited. There is a second beam behind her, which must be Bruno's torch.

We're fucked, Anna thinks. Her body is about to give up.

Marie is still running, with the gun pointing straight at her. The light of the torch is reflected in the raindrops in the air, creating tiny flashes.

'Att—' Marie yells just as something moves among the wet leaves at her feet. One of Mats's wolf traps clamps its serrated jaws around her leg with a horrible clang, transforming the command into a piercing scream.

Marie's body maintains its forward trajectory. The chain attached to the trap looks like a black snake, rearing up from the leaves. When it reaches its full extent, it pulls her over with a sudden jerk. She is still holding the gun and the torch, and cannot save herself.

A millisecond before her face hits the ground, Marie sees what is waiting for her. Her eyes open wide, the scream changes tone and is cut off abruptly as a second trap closes on her neck.

The gun flies through the air but the torch drops by her side, illuminating the horrific scene being played out just metres away from Anna. Marie's eyes are still open, her arms and legs are twitching, and a faint gurgling is coming from what is left of her windpipe.

'Marie!' Bruno hurtles through the hollow to his wife's side. 'Marie! No, no!'

He drops to his knees and tries to pull apart the metal teeth, but without success. Blood stains the leaves, diluted by the rain pouring down on Bruno as he continues to repeat his wife's name, until she stops moving and he lets out a protracted howl of despair.

The German Shepherds limp over to Marie's lifeless body and sit down on either side of her. After a few seconds first one, then the other joins in with Bruno's howl.

Anna staggers over to the spot where the gun landed. She picks it up, brushes off the leaves and points it at Bruno.

'It's over,' she says.

62

Autumn 2017

Anna is standing in the doorway of Elisabet Vidje's hospital room. The upper part of the bed is elevated so that the old woman can sit up. A nasal cannula is supplying her with oxygen, and along with her hospital gown and the rest of the equipment, it makes her look weak and frail. However, she is anything but weak.

'You have your father's eyes. I noticed that the first time we met,' Elisabet says to Lisa, who is sitting on the edge of the bed. She strokes the young woman's cheek. 'Your grandfather's too, actually.'

Anna can't quite hold back the tears. She looks over at the window, meets Bror Klein's gaze for a second. His eyes are suspiciously shiny, and his mouth is turned up in something resembling a smile. They both look away in embarrassment, as if neither wants to show their emotions to the other. She feels her phone buzz in her pocket and goes out into the corridor to answer.

It's Jens Friberg.

'I just wanted you to know that we've got most things sorted. Bruno has confessed to everything, and there are no more question marks. Bengt Andersson has organised some flashy lawyer for him, but that's not going to bring Marie back.'

'What about Tabor?'

'The fire service managed to save the ground floor and the external walls. The rain obviously caused some damage, but it won't be too long before it's habitable again.'

'OK.'

She pictures the shabby dressing gown, the photo albums, the box containing Agnes's baby things. The only physical remnants of the life she, Håkan and Agnes shared together.

'Are you all right?' He sounds genuinely worried.

Anna thinks about Agnes. About Lisa Savic and Elisabet Vidje. A few days ago, the loss of their home and possessions would have floored her. It would have been a blow from which she might never have recovered. But now . . .

'It's only stuff,' she says, and means it.

'So, what happens now?' Jens wonders.

'I don't actually know. Agnes is being discharged tomorrow. We're staying in a hotel for a few days, then we'll see. What about you?'

'I don't actually know either. There are a few loose ends to tie up here, so I'll hang on for a while. Fortunately, I've had a crash course in detective work over the past week or so, with an excellent teacher.'

Anna thinks he might be smiling. 'Keep in touch – let me know how it goes.'

'Will do.'

'Take care of yourself, Jens.'

'You too, Anna.'

She leaves the Vidje family in peace for a while and goes downstairs to buy a drink. The stitches in her thigh are pulling, forcing her to move slowly. The newspaper placards are screaming out the details surrounding what they are calling the Nedanås murder. No doubt the headlines are upsetting Bengt Andersson almost as much as the loss of his daughter, she thinks acidly. She buys a Coca-Cola and drinks it in the twilight outside the main entrance. It has stopped raining, but the wind has turned colder. After a little while she shivers, and goes back in.

Elisabet is resting. Bror Klein is dozing in the visitor's chair. His stony face is gaunt and there are shadows beneath his eyes; for the first time since they met, he looks his age.

'The old fool hasn't slept for days,' Elisabet says quietly. 'And he refuses to go home, even though he needs his medication.'

'I can pick it up if you like,' Anna offers. 'I'm going up to Änglaberga to collect Milo from Mats anyway. I promised Agnes I'd try to smuggle him in later – the night staff aren't as strict.'

She also wants to check on Mats. He saved her life, and Lisa's, and she'd like to make sure he's OK.

'Excellent!' Elisabet sounds surprisingly friendly. 'The keys are in his coat pocket.' She points to Klein's oilskin, which is hanging behind the door. 'His pills are in the bathroom cabinet.'

Anna almost says she already knows that, but manages to bite her tongue at the last minute. She's convinced now: Elisabet and Klein are in a relationship, and have been for many years. But that's their business; it's nothing to do with her or anyone else.

'If you have time, maybe you could pick up a few photo albums from the drawing room at Änglaberga too? I'd like to show Lisa some pictures of her father when she comes back. The key is on Klein's key ring.'

'No problem.'

Anna turns into the avenue leading to Änglaberga. Jens has provided her with an unmarked police car, because her hire car is being examined by forensics. Where should she go first? The main house, Klein's lodge, or to see Mats? She decides on the lodge.

The place is in darkness; the only light is provided by an outside lamp on the gable. There are at least ten keys on the ring, and it takes her a while to find the right one. The rooms inside somehow feel even more impersonal, even sadder in the evening, especially now no one is here.

She collects the bottle of pills and takes the opportunity to have another quick look at the bedroom. Nothing has changed – the same neatly made bed, the same book, the same photograph.

Her phone buzzes. This time it's her solicitor.

'Santesson just called me. The DNA match has come through,' he says.

'OK . . .' Her heart beats a little faster.

'It's Håkan's DNA. But you already knew that, didn't you, Anna?'

She doesn't answer.

'Santesson claims that given Håkan's condition, it would have been impossible for him to learn how the pump worked, plus he shouldn't have been able to reach the buttons.' He pauses, waits for her to speak. She says nothing. 'He believes that someone must have helped him.'

Still, she doesn't speak.

'Someone told Håkan which buttons to press, and moved the pump within reach. However, since assisted suicide is not a crime, Santesson will not be devoting any more resources to this matter. The case is closed.'

She feels the relief flood her body, and hears her solicitor take a deep breath. There is a silence as his professional persona fights with ordinary human curiosity.

'Did you do it, Anna? Did you help Håkan to take his own life?'

She ends the call without a word, and discovers that she is standing by the locked door of Klein's cellar. She ought to leave now; Klein's private life is none of her concern. But just as in the case of her solicitor a few seconds ago, curiosity wins the battle.

The lock and the door are old and sturdy, and it's easy to find the matching key. The staircase behind the door is in darkness, and she gropes for the light switch. The worn carpet suggests that the stairs are used frequently. At the bottom is an open door leading to a laundry room, with another locked door opposite. This one is newer, and made of steel.

Anna picks out the right key and unlocks the door. The room beyond doesn't have that 'cellar' smell of cold and dampness; it's much more pleasant. When she turns on the light, she sees that the walls are lined with custom-made bookshelves. There are thick rugs on the floor, and two wing-backed armchairs in one corner, each with its own reading lamp. She can imagine Klein and Elisabet sitting there reading, but is surprised that they've chosen such a tucked-away spot when the whole of Änglaberga is just a stone's throw away. Were they really so afraid of being found out?

The shelves at the far end of the room contain only books, but the three closest to her are crowded with photographs. The first contains only pictures of Simon. Simon as a baby, Simon as a blond, tousle-haired little boy, his first day at school, carrying a backpack that is far too big for him. In the photos that follow he almost always has an instrument in his hand – guitar, violin, trumpet. Then there are pictures from what must have been the studio above the garage, and finally Simon leaning against a beautiful red sports car, with his student cap on his head and a garland of flowers around his neck. She assumes this is Karl-Johan's summer car, the charred remains of which are still in one of the outbuildings at Tabor.

Photos of the Vidje family are displayed on the next shelf. There are the picnic snaps she's already seen, pictures on the beach, pictures from Karl-Johan's studio at Tabor with little Simon spattered in paint, or sitting on the blue slide. Pictures of Simon and Elisabet, side by side at the piano. Then another picture of Simon in his student cap by the summer car, but this time flanked by his parents. The wind is blowing Karl-Johan's blond hair, and even though Elisabet's expression is more severe than her husband's, it's clear how proud they are of their son.

The third shelf is a collection of pictures showing Elisabet and Karl-Jo together, starting with their wedding photo, but there are plenty of others taken at about the same time. Klein isn't in a single one, which strengthens her suspicion that he is the photographer. The last few are black and white: Karl-Jo, aged about twenty-five, perched on the back of a park bench, leaning forward. He is looking straight into the camera, and his gaze is so intense that its power can still be felt. Anna takes a step back. There is something so sad about this whole display. A rainy night, one false step on a slippery rock, and the love and happiness that shines from almost every photograph is gone, replaced by a dark tragedy.

She notices a record player just like the one her grandfather had. There is an LP on the turntable. It isn't dusty, which must mean that Klein plays it often. She reads the label: Edith Piaf – *Les Feuilles Mortes*.

At the far end of the room there is a small door. Above it hangs a portrait of a young man. It isn't his usual style, but it is obviously Karl-Johan's work. The subject is lying on his stomach on a bed. His upper body is bare, and it is just possible to make out the edge of a sheet. A patio door is ajar behind him; something about the door and the light outside tell her that the portrait wasn't painted in Sweden, but somewhere in Southern Europe – maybe France.

The man's face is half-turned towards the observer. His fringe flops down over his forehead, he is wearing a wry, happy smile, and it takes her a few seconds to realise that she has seen that smile before. She moves closer, but there is no doubt. The young man in the painting is Bror Klein.

She stands there for a little while, trying to work out what this means. The portrait is intimate, a private moment between two people, not meant to be shared with anyone else.

Cautiously she opens the door below, revealing a cubby hole with a guitar and a tape recorder on a shelf. There is something else in the far corner, where the light barely reaches. The frame is bent and the front fork is broken, but she knows exactly what she is looking at: an orange Crescent with drop handlebars.

Simon's bike.

63

Autumn 2017

Anna stands in front of the door trying to make sense of what she is looking at. She fights the urge to touch the objects inside, and leaves the door open as she sinks into one of the armchairs. What does all this mean?

Why does Bror Klein have Simon's things hidden away in his cellar? For twenty-seven years, it has been assumed that these items had either gone missing, or been destroyed in the fire. And why is there a portrait by Karl-Jo of a young Klein lying half-naked in a bed? She leans back in the chair. From here she has a good view of all the photographs – three whole lives. Four, in fact. Hidden away from the eyes of the world, just like the guitar, the tape recorder and the bicycle. She suddenly notices a well-thumbed leather folder on the seat of the other armchair. It contains only a single sheet of paper, a letter of some kind, written in pencil in a beautiful, ornate script. Words have been rubbed out and altered time and time again, which makes her think of the mural at Tabor.

> *Dear Elisabet,* the letter begins. *I have done something terrible, something unforgivable.*
> *But I did it out of love.*

As Anna reads on, she feels the room begin to spin slowly. All at once she understands how everything hangs together: the photographs, the armchairs, the objects in the cubby hole. And things she has seen and heard over the past few weeks acquire a new and more unpleasant meaning.

The rain.

'On the way home I met a car on a bend. People drive like lunatics on the ridge.'

The bicycle.

'Karl-Johan has always been a sensitive soul.'

The deer.

'It wasn't my fault. It wasn't my fault.'

The summer car.

'My little boy . . .'

The fire.

'I have done something terrible . . .'

She reads through the whole letter again, making a huge effort to keep her hands steady.

As you know, dear Elisabet, I was born different. You were the only one who understood me. I could confide in you about anything – my weaknesses, my imperfection. And thanks to you I found love, the love I'd thought was impossible.

Just like you, I loved Karl-Johan with all my heart. You could have hated me, but you didn't. Instead, you showed me understanding, yet again. For that I am eternally grateful.

We were all Simon's parents. When he was thirteen, he asked us straight out, do you remember? Karl-Johan explained that the three of us loved one another, in different ways. Simon couldn't tell anyone, because not everyone would understand. But Simon understood. He was a wonderful boy.

In the summer of 1990, I realised that something wasn't right. Karl-Johan stopped reading, and it took a while for me to work out that he was having problems with his sight. When I confronted him, he was furious. He denied the whole thing, made me promise not to say a word to you. Karl-Johan had always been a loving person, but now he became dismissive and withdrawn. He locked himself in his studio, and emerged only to go out in his summer car. He drove fast along the narrow roads. Revved the engine, took risks, almost as if he wanted something to happen to him.

One evening at the end of the summer, he hammered on my door in a panic in the middle of the night. He said he'd hit a deer over by the quarry, and it might still be alive. He asked me to drive out there and take a look.

As soon as I saw the bent frame of the bicycle, I knew what Karl-Johan had actually hit.

So I sat there in the rain with Simon's head resting on my knee, stroking his cheek. Told him how much I loved him, how much we all loved him.

And then I did what had to be done. I carried Simon back to the quarry and laid him to rest in the water.

That was the hardest thing I'd ever had to do, but I did it out of love. Love for Karl-Johan, for Simon and for you. Love for what we'd had, which was now lost forever.

Then I drove Karl-Johan home and put him to bed. Assured him that it had been a deer, and that it hadn't suffered. I hid the summer car in the garage, but realised almost immediately that it wouldn't be possible to get it repaired without arousing suspicion. So the following night I burned down the garage, the car and the studio, but I kept Simon's favourite guitar, and the tape recorder with his beautiful voice on it. And his bicycle. I just couldn't bring myself to get rid of it.

I'm only a human being. A human being who was prepared to do anything for love.

I had hoped that I would never need to burden you with my secret, but the minute I met Anna Vesper, I knew this day would come.

This, my beloved Elisabet, is my confession.

This is what I did.

My deed of autumn.

64

Autumn 2017

For the second time that evening, Anna is standing in the doorway of Elisabet's hospital room. Milo is sitting by her feet, looking at the three people who are there. Lisa is back, perched on the side of the bed as Elisabet flicks through the photo albums Anna has just handed over.

'Look, this is your father when he'd just been given his first guitar,' Elisabet says to her granddaughter. 'He's so happy! Karl-Johan bought it for him in Copenhagen – you were there too, weren't you, Bror?'

Klein, who is standing at the foot of the bed, smiles. Behind the smile, the handsome young man in the portrait is visible for a fraction of a second.

'Thanks for picking up the albums, Anna,' Elisabet goes on. Her voice and expression are warm and friendly. 'Did you manage to find Bror's pills?'

'I did.' She turns to Klein. 'I put them in your coat pocket along with your keys.'

'Thanks,' he mumbles. The smile stiffens.

Elisabet points out one picture after another to a delighted Lisa, but Klein is no longer fully engaged. He seems to be watching Anna, waiting for her to do or say something.

'Bror and I are immensely grateful for everything you've done for us, Anna,' Elisabet says.

Anna nods, unsure of how to respond. Klein's intense gaze is burning into her, and she is finding it difficult to keep the mask in place.

'One last question before you go.' Elisabet sits up a little straighter.

'Of course.'

'The quarry.'

'Yes?'

'What do you think actually happened that night, Anna?'

A part of her has been waiting for this question. Not long ago she promised Elisabet that she would find out the truth about Simon. Now she has done just that; she knows every tiny, terrible, tragic detail. So, how much should she share? She glances at Klein.

Twenty-seven years ago he made a decision; he couldn't possibly have foreseen the consequences. Would things have been different if he'd told the truth back then?

Simon would still have been dead, his friends would still have been tormented by the way they'd treated him. Maybe they would have felt worse. After all, it was their fault that Simon left the quarry and got on his bike, upset, angry and humiliated, and set off in the rain and the dark.

Elisabet would have been spared almost thirty years of bitterness, but would she really have preferred the truth? And Simon's father, who couldn't even bear the thought of killing an animal, would have been forced to face the fact that he'd killed his own son. Maybe Karl-Johan suspected something? Was that why Simon's body lay in the water in the mural, yet from certain angles it wasn't there, depending on how you looked. Depending on what you wanted to see?

From a purely legal point of view, it is too late anyway. Any crime that has been committed is well beyond the statute of limitations, and no one can be brought to account at this stage. Not in court, at least.

Regardless of what happens now, Simon Vidje's death is a tragedy that will continue to haunt the community when the horrific details are revealed.

ANDERS DE LA MOTTE

That is what Bror Klein's letter is about. The letter that is actually a speech.

Her suspicions are confirmed when Klein straightens his shoulders, licks his lips and clears his throat. Neither Elisabet nor Lisa have noticed anything yet. Elisabet's question still hangs in the air.

Klein takes a deep breath, opens his mouth. Boundless sorrow is etched on his face. His lips form the first syllable in his confession.

'It was an accident,' Anna says loudly, not taking her eyes off the old man. 'Everything indicates that Simon's death was a tragic accident.'

Elisabet nods slowly and sadly, then turns back to Lisa and the photo album. Their voices blend into a quiet murmur as Klein and Anna stare at each other. He looks confused, shocked. Then he slowly regains control of his facial muscles, realigns them one by one until the stony expression is restored. Then he goes over to the head of the bed and gently places one hand on Elisabet's shoulder, the other on Lisa's.

Anna is about to leave when she sees that he is looking in her direction. His lips move. She doesn't hear a sound, but she is sure of the words they are forming.

Thank you.

Anna makes her way laboriously along the corridor, with Milo limping beside her.

'We're not exactly on top form, are we?' she says to the little dog. Milo puts out his tongue in a comical way and tilts his head, with its bandaged ear, on one side as if to say that at least he looks better than she does.

'Stupid dog. Shall we go and find Agnes?'

The rain and wind whip up a few of the remaining dead leaves against the windows. No longer razor blades slicing into her, but fragile scraps of paper in shades of brown and rusty red, rattling against the glass before they disappear.

One last dance before winter, that's what Håkan would have said.

She misses him. She always will, and yet she feels unexpectedly carefree. It's as if something inside her has eased, been blown away by the autumn wind exactly like those last few leaves, allowing a new feeling to take its place.

'Everything is going to be all right,' she murmurs to herself as she opens the door of Agnes's room and sees her daughter's face light up.

Everything is going to be all right.

Author's Note

Nedanås and the small community of Mörkaby are, like Reftinge in *End of Summer*, fictional places. They are, however, inspired by the areas where I grew up in north-western Skåne, mainly Bjuv, Åstorp and Svalöv, situated on or near the beautiful slopes of Söderåsen ridge.

The disused quarry actually exists, and like its literary relative, is not marked on the map. Nevertheless, generations of summer swimmers know where it is, just as we are aware that the dark water is so deep that even in the middle of high summer it is never warmer than twenty degrees.

Keep reading for an extract of

Rites of Spring

Sunday Times Crime Book of the Month

As new life blooms, old secrets stir . . .

Skåne, 1986: On the night of Walpurgis, the eve of May Day, where bonfires are lit to ward off evil spirits and preparations are made to celebrate the renewal of spring, a sixteen-year-old girl is ritualistically murdered in the woods beside a castle. Her stepbrother is convicted of the terrible deed and shortly after, the entire family vanishes without a trace.

Spring, 2019: Dr Thea Lind moves into the castle. After making a strange discovery in an ancient oak tree on the grounds, her fascination with the old tragedy deepens. As she uncovers more and more similarities between her own troubled past and the murdered girl, she begins to believe that the real truth of the killing was never uncovered.

What if the spring of 1986 claimed more than one victim?

Available now

Prologue

19 May 1986

As soon as Little Stefan drove onto the marsh, he began to think about the dead girl. It was impossible not to. The game of Chinese whispers that had started on the morning of May the first had already travelled around the area several times. Filled his head with horrific images from which there was no escape.

Her lifeless body on the sacrificial stone in the centre of the stone circle. Her white dress, her hair loose around her head. Her hands folded over her chest, two antlers clasped in her stiff fingers. Her once beautiful face covered by a bloodstained handkerchief, as if whoever had taken her life had been unable to look her in the eye afterwards.

Most Tornaby residents were already absolutely certain that they knew who'd killed her, that the whole thing was a dreadful but simple story. A family tragedy. However, there were those who quietly maintained that something else entirely had happened during Walpurgis Night. That maybe it was the Green Man himself who had claimed his spring sacrifice.

It had been a long time since Little Stefan had believed in ghost stories, but he couldn't help shuddering. The marshy forest closed in around the dirt track, scraping at the paintwork with long, green fingers. This was the part of the castle estate he disliked most of all. The dampness, the smell of decay. The sodden ground that at one moment felt solid, at the next sucked your boots so deep into the mud that it was a real struggle to escape without help. *The marsh belongs to the Green Man*, his grandfather used to say. *People ought to stay away.* At least the superstitious old misery guts had been partly right.

The track led deep into the marsh, to Svartgården, where the girl had lived. Only a month or so ago he'd given her a lift to the bus stop. She'd sat right next to him in the front seat of the pick-up. She hadn't said much; she'd seemed lost in her own thoughts. He'd stolen glances at her from time to time, watching her face, her movements, and out of nowhere he'd been overwhelmed by a feeling he couldn't explain.

He was married, he had two young daughters, a house, a car, a good job. Things he usually valued, but at that moment, sitting beside that beautiful girl, they had felt like a burden. His whole life was already mapped out, one long, predictable journey without an ounce of the tempting, forbidden pleasures that emanated from her. He could smell it on her – sweet and sharp like newly opened lilac blossom. A perfume that evoked yearning. Desire.

At one point when she looked away, he'd almost reached out to touch her, as if that would enable him to access everything he didn't have. He'd stopped himself at the last second, but the sense of loss had lingered for several days.

He had to concentrate in order to avoid the deepest potholes the further on he drove. Lasse Svart was supposed to maintain the track, according to his lease, but needless to say he didn't bother. For years Lasse Svart had relied on the fact that the count would never be able to find another tenant; nobody was interested in a dozen or so acres of sodden forest, so he more or less did what he liked out at Svartgården. His own little kingdom, far away from laws, rules, and curious eyes.

But that was before Walpurgis Night. Before Lasse's sixteen-year-old daughter was found dead on the sacrifi cial stone, the ground all around ploughed up by hooves.

During Walpurgis Night the veil between life and death is at its thinnest. Things are on the move, nature is hungry and the Green Man rides through the forest.

Little Stefan suppressed another shudder.

The forest opened out as he reached the muddy yard surrounding Svartgården. Three dilapidated buildings huddled in the gloom beneath the trees, as if they were trying to hide. Rusty agricultural tools and machinery lay among the nettles.

He'd been here many times before, usually with Erik Nyberg, the castle administrator, and they'd always been met by a pack of yapping terriers before he'd even switched off the engine. Today there wasn't a dog in sight. The place was quiet; even the birds weren't making much noise on this spring morning. A strange, oppressive silence filled the air.

Little Stefan remained standing by his truck for a minute or so as he tucked a plug of tobacco beneath his top lip and waited for Lasse or one of his women to poke their head out of the door and ask what the fuck he wanted, but nothing happened. Lasse's red pick-up was nowhere to be seen, nor was the battered old Ford the women usually drove. He glanced at his watch: seven thirty. Who went out at this early hour?

He caught a movement out of the corner of his eye. A small dog was peering around the corner of the smithy; it was little more than a puppy.

'Hello! Come on then,' Little Stefan said, without really knowing why. The dog took a couple of cautious steps, keeping its belly low, tail tucked between its legs. Then it suddenly stopped and stiffened, as if it had heard something.

Little Stefan turned his head, but the house was still in darkness. When he looked back, the dog was gone.

He set off up the concrete steps leading to the front door; halfway up he realised it was ajar. He paused, unsure of what to do. On the wall next to the door he saw a half-metre-tall figure woven from fresh green branches. His grandfather had made one every spring and hung it on the front door.

So that the Green Man will ride on through the night. So that he won't stop at our house.

'Hello? Anyone home?'

The words bounced off the walls and came back like a distorted echo, as if it were someone else's voice. Someone who was watching him from the darkness. Imitating him, mocking him.

Little Stefan looked at the creepy fi gure again, and for a second he was ready to run back down the steps, jump in his truck and get out of there. Tell Erik Nyberg that no one had been home, and reading the water meter would have to wait. However, he was a grown man with a job to do, not some little kid who was scared of ghosts.

He knocked on the door frame.

'Hello?' he shouted again. 'Anyone home? It's Little Stefan, from the castle.'

No response.

The silence from inside the house was making him increasingly uncomfortable. His shirt was sticking to his back. He took a deep breath and knocked once more, harder this time. Pushed the door open and stepped into the porch. There was a weird smell, a stale odour that reminded him of animals – but what was it?

'Hello?'

He checked out the kitchen. The table was littered with dirty plates, glasses and cutlery for three people. Several fl ies were buzzing around among the remains of the food. One of the chairs had been knocked over. Through a doorway on the other side of the porch he could just see a neatly made bed.

'Hello!' This time he yelled up the stairs.

Still nothing. He was feeling very uneasy now, but he pulled himself together and made his way up the creaking wooden staircase.

The upper fl oor was in darkness. On the left was a bedroom with a double bed, also neatly made. The door on the right was closed. It took him a few seconds to realise that it wasn't simply a uniform green, but was covered in a carefully painted pattern of leaves. Almost a work of art, in fact.

Elita's Room, someone had written in attractive, ornate lettering at eye level.

So this was her room. This was where she had lived her life.

Elita Svart. The spring sacrifice.

Little Stefan reached for the handle; his heartbeat seemed to be reverberating throughout the house. He was on the point of doing something forbidden, stepping into a world to which he was not permitted access. An uninvited guest, an intruder.

Then he saw another message on the door. Small, distorted words that almost blended in with the artwork, but became clearer as his eyes grew used to the darkness.

Nature is hungry and the Green Man is riding through the forests.

At the same time he spotted something else. Hidden among the leaves there was a large, terrifying male face.

The realisation was sudden, and chilled his blood. He didn't know where it had come from or why, but the sensation was so strong that it made the hairs on the back of his neck stand on end. Something had happened in this house. Something evil that had made Lasse Svart and his women leap to their feet in the middle of their supper, run out to their cars and drive away in the night. Something connected to a dead sixteen-year-old girl on a cold stone, and a ghostly rider galloping through the forest.

Little Stefan let go of the door handle and took the stairs in three strides. Hurtled out through the porch, down the steps and into his truck.

He started the engine and set off with a screech of tyres. He didn't even glance in the rear-view mirror until he was absolutely certain that Svartgården had disappeared, deep among the trees.

End of Summer

You can always go home, but you can never go back . . .

Summer, 1983: Four-year-old Billy chases a rabbit in the fields behind his house. But when his mother goes to call him in, Billy has disappeared. Never to be seen again.

Today: Veronica is a bereavement counsellor. She's never fully come to terms with her mother's suicide after her brother Billy's disappearance. When a young man joins her group, he looks familiar and when he talks about the trauma of his friend's disappearance in 1983, Veronica feels a flicker of hope. Could Billy still be alive after all this time? Needing to know the truth, Veronica goes home – to the place where her life started to fall apart.

But is she prepared for the answers that wait for her there?

Available now

Dead of Winter

The nights are closing in . . . and so is the truth

Winter, 1987: Laura is excited to spend Christmas as usual with her beloved aunt Hedda and her friends. But her festive mood soon turns sour as she finds both old faces and new are keeping secrets from her. When a fire claims the life of her best friend, the scars of that night will remain with Laura for the rest of her life.

Today: With her aunt's death, Laura inherits the cabin village Hedda used to manage and is forced to return to the town she hasn't set foot in since the tragedy. Laura's presence stirs up repressed emotions in the small community and it isn't long before a series of arson attacks cast suspicion on her. Though Laura is desperate to leave, she learns her aunt discovered something about that fateful night not long before she died.

But someone wants the past to stay buried . . .

Available now